DEADLY COMPANIONS

"All right, boys," I called. "You've had your fun, now it's time to clear out. You're on private property—"

"Like hell!" Ives's understrapper shouted. "We know the dimensions of your claim. Ain't nothin in the law says we can't stake alongside—"

"You boys are inside our six hundred and forty, and I advise you to clear out before someone gets hurt."

From someplace amongst them a rifle cracked, the slug whizzing past not three inches from my head to slap into a rock and go whining away. "Get under cover and let them have it," I growled."

MULE MAN

Squatting down, having motioned Harry out of the way, with my hands I brushed back enough of the loose sandy soil to see that the cadaver had been planted face down, to make out the dried blood and powder marks on his shirt. "Shot in the back close up. With a pistol. Turn him over."

Harry's sweat-shiny face was a picture of horror. Shaking like a leaf, he drew back in repugnance. "For Chrissake," I said, "He's not goin' to bite you!"

I caught hold of the hair, jerked the head up enough for him to see it was Joe, then let it fall back, "Cover him up."

Other *Leisure Books* by Nelson Nye:
CALIBAN'S COLT

Double Westerns:
PISTOLS FOR HIRE/TOUGH COMPANY
THE TEXAS GUN/GRINGO
WILD HORSE SHORTY/BLOOD OF KINGS
COME A SMOKIN'/HORSES, WOMEN AND GUNS
THIEF RIVER/THE SEVEN SIX-GUNNERS
**TREASURE TRAIL FROM TUCSON/THE FEUD
    AT SLEEPY CAT**
CARTRIDGE CASE LAW/THE OVERLANDERS
TRIGGER TALK/THE WOLF THAT RODE
SHOTGUN LAW/HELLBOUND FOR BALLARAT
GUN QUICK/THE DESERT DESPERADOES
GUNSLICK MOUNTAIN/ONCE IN THE SADDLE
IRON HAND/THE NO-GUN FIGHTER
**GUNS OF HORSE PRAIRIE/
    WILDCATS OF TONTO BASIN**
GUNSHOT TRAIL/TEXAS TORNADO

Triple Westerns:
**DESERT OF THE DAMNED/HIDEOUT
MOUNTAIN/ROGUE'S RENDEZVOUS**

**GUNFIGHTER BRAND/BREED OF THE
CHAPARRAL/THE KID FROM LINCOLN
COUNTY**

NELSON NYE

DEADLY COMPANIONS/ MULE MAN

LEISURE BOOKS　　🅱　　NEW YORK CITY

A LEISURE BOOK®

May 1996

Published by special arrangement with Golden West
Literary Agency.

Dorchester Publishing Co., Inc.
276 Fifth Avenue
New York, NY 10001

If you purchased this book without a cover you should be aware
that this book is stolen property. It was reported as "unsold and
destroyed" to the publisher and neither the author nor the publisher
has received any payment for this "stripped book."

DEADLY COMPANIONS Copyright © 1987 by Nelson Nye

MULE MAN Copyright © 1988 by Nelson Nye

All rights reserved. No part of this book may be reproduced or
transmitted in any form or by any electronic or mechanical means,
including photocopying, recording or by any information storage
and retrieval system, without the written permission of the Publisher,
except where permitted by law.

The name "Leisure Books" and the stylized "L" with design are
trademarks of Dorchester Publishing Co., Inc.

Printed in the United States of America.

DEADLY COMPANIONS

For RUTHIE
on our 50th Anniversary,
and for John Douglas Gilchriese
who helped us through some of the stickiest bits.

Chapter One

The Lady Is Hiring

Someone said she was hiring and would likely be at the
hotel until noon, that her name was Wendy Eldridge, last of
an old territorial family principally known for being high in
the instep. Two strikes against her right off the bat.

This was Tucson, not a great while after the turn of the
century. Her spread was off in that overgrazed country south
of the Mission. Her iron, I was told by a loquacious barkeep,
was Broken Arrow, which she slapped on whichever critters
were too slow to get away. I didn't much care for what I'd
heard so far.

Few top hands liked to work for a woman. I didn't myself. But I'd found out back in Santa Ana country a man
could be a top hand and be shunned simultaneous. A waddy's rep, like an evening shadow, could stretch a far piece
ahead of him, and two seasons of riding grubline had me

pretty well convinced I wasn't ever going to make it in Texas.

This was a jumping-off place if ever I'd seen one. Something around twenty thousand, hot, dusty, and as far past the bloom as I was my own self, a cowtown long on sand and chili eaters.

Didn't seem like to me this Eldridge female would need a big stick to beat off the applicants. I was not a heap anxious to be signed on by any petticoat spread, much less a hardscrabble one that, from what I'd heard, was probably on its last legs. Still I wasn't getting any younger and, having Texas in mind, was just about ripe to take any job I could latch onto.

Having taken a look at myself in that back bar mirror, I was no more impressed than she was like to be. Beard-stubbled cheeks, gaunt as a church mouse in brush-clawed duds and run-over boots. Perfect picture of a saddle tramp. I'd be lucky, I reckoned, if she'd even so much as talk to me.

I got on my dun horse and jogged over to the hotel hitch-rack, still of two minds about wasting the time. An old family, they'd said, run-down like my boots. Well, the worst she could do was tell me to get lost. So I finally got down, tossed my reins across the tie rail, and climbed the plank steps.

I rapped on the door I'd been told was hers. A husky voice bade me enter. I thought straight off to read scorn in her stare, but she said cool enough, "Name?"

"Hardigan."

That stare went over me from top to bottom, and if she'd missed anything it sure wasn't evident. "Got a handle to that?"

"Mostly I'm known as Hard Luck Hardigan."

"With a chip on your shoulder."

I clapped on my hat and started for the door. I was reaching for the knob when she said cold and arrogant, "Sit down and take the weight off your boots."

My glance turned uncertain. "Any point to this?"

"Could be. I'm not hiring ranch hands. I've something else in mind." I saw that gray stare swiveling across my shell belt, coming up unreadably to rummage my face. "You any good with that pistol?"

"Sure—quick as a wink," I told her derisively. "That what you're hirin'?"

"I'd consider it a bonus, though it's not what I'm actually after. What I'm hunting is loyalty—a man I can depend on."

"Ain't that kind of old-fashioned? I mean loyalty ain't a commodity you can go out and buy. If you can dig up the price you can get any number of grab-an'-shoot killers. Being I'm not in that category, I'll not take up any more of your time." I smiled at her sourly and picked up my hat.

"Get back in that chair," she snapped with her chin up. "Don't try to tell me what I want or don't want."

"Well, pardon me all to hell, ma'am." For the first time I considered her fully, an erect imperious shape in a man's shirt and Levis, with a strong-featured face below sorrel hair pulled back in a knot. In her twenties, I judged. I saw that condescending stare sweep from my run-over boots to the ratty old Stetson dangling from my hand.

"On Broken Arrow," she said, "*I* do the telling, and don't you forget it."

With hot cheeks I said, "Look—we're both wasting breath. You've got no use for a confirmed down-an'-outer who's too long in the tooth to set up as a pistolero."

She was tall for a woman, almost tall as I am, with a

well-scrubbed look that made no pretense of being other
than it was, plain as a gotcher's knife and just about as
compassionate. Her silence and that scrutiny began to get
under my skin. "So I'll be takin' myself off," I said, and
got determinedly up.

I got up, yet didn't go. For there was something about
her that compelled a second look. I couldn't figure what it
could be, but it was there like her breeding that showed in
every line. I thought for a second to find her amused, but a
closer look made me reckon I'd imagined it.

"I'll make you a proposition," she said, ignoring my
rudeness. "I've got this ranch and whatever cattle still carry
my brand. I've a cook and no crew. I'm so close to being
broke I couldn't possibly pay you. So I'll put up the ranch
and cattle and cut you in for a full half-interest in what I've
got and in whatever with your help I can manage to lay
hands on." Her lip curled again beneath the rasp of that
stare. "Take it or leave it."

Chapter Two

Suddenly a Partner

I felt an increase in the tension I had sensed in her before. The watching stare in that expressionless face looked hard as granite. She considered me, I bitterly thought, fully as low in the human scale as in past times she'd regarded her father's cowhands. Like something yanked out of a dung heap. A necessary adjunct to whatever she had in mind, a thing to be used so long as it served, used and thrown out when she'd got what she wanted.

I could feel the heat surging up past my collar, a fury she roused with her stinking arrogance and the cool assumption I would jump at her offer. I was minded, by God, to walk out of this, till the remembrance of two years on the grubline intruded to stir a mite of caution into the churn of my temper.

She said with the contempt that had been bred into her,

"You don't care much for me, do you?"

I put a lock on my feelings. "What we think of each other isn't under discussion. You've got something in mind that calls for a man with guts and few scruples. A kid could see that. Because nothing better's at hand and you figure I'm worn down enough for your purpose, you're offering me half of whatever I can get you. That cover your proposal?"

She laughed. "Just about," and that merciless gray stare swept over me again. "You're being given the half interest to make sure you've a stake you can't afford to walk out on."

We swapped hard looks through half a dozen heartbeats. "Well," she said with unconcealed impatience, "are you taking me up on it?"

"Not my habit to buy pigs in a poke. What are you after?"

"You'll not learn that until I have your acceptance."

"You'd take my word?" I looked at her, astonished.

"Yes—of course." She showed again that curl of the lip. "That overweening pride in your conception of yourself would certainly hold you to it."

I was minded to hit her. I was being played like a fish securely hooked. And she was too damned right! Both of us knew it. "All right," I grumbled. "I'll go along with it."

Nothing changed in her face. "There's a lawyer down the hall. We'll step into his office and have him draw up the papers—"

"What papers?"

"The details of our partnership. It's as much in your interest as it is in mine."

*   *   *

12

In this fashion, and in mutual distrust, I became Wendy Eldridge's partner.

When we got back to her room I said, "Now that we're tied to each other all legal, let's have it. What's the source of our hoped-for prosperity?"

"A lost mine. A ledge of gold that's incredibly rich."

Her laugh rang out at the expression on my face. "Oh, it's there, all right. An Apache showed it to my father almost forty years ago. I've never been there myself, but I've seen the samples father sold the bank—"

"If that much is for real, how the hell did this mine get lost?"

"An Apache who was indebted to my father showed him the ledge after he promised to keep the secret and promised he'd show the ledge to no one else. Once a year he was to hack out what he could transport himself and make sure the ledge was concealed before leaving. My father," she said with that curl of the lip, "was an inveterate gambler. After some ten years and a long run of bad luck he took ore out twice in one month to liquidate mortgages he'd put on the ranch. Broken Arrow became a going concern; Cyrus Eldridge became a man of considerable influence, both in public affairs and in the Territorial legislature.

"Then his gambling reduced him to borrowing again. His bad luck continued. In addition to the plasters he'd put on the ranch, he became deeply indebted to one of his cronies, who had also picked up his notes from the bank. To cut a long story short, he agreed to show this man the hidden ledge, and did so. The next time my father went out with two pack horses and supplies for ten days he never returned. Two weeks later he was found with his skull crushed."

She gave this explanation without sign of either horror or

remorse. I said, "What was the name of the man he took to the ledge?"

"It doesn't matter. The man was killed, as my father had been, some twenty days later."

"Who holds the notes on Broken Arrow now?" I asked. "And what is your total indebtedness in round figures?"

"Around a hundred thousand dollars."

"Is the bank holding the notes?"

"Some twenty thousand dollars' worth. The others are held by three different men whom you'll meet in due course."

"And how do you expect to pay off these notes?"

"With the ledge, of course." She smiled at me thinly.

"Do you know where it is? Do you think you can find it?"

"I know it's someplace inside a thirty-mile circle. A stream runs past it within a few hundred yards. I thought perhaps we might fix up a map. Cut the map up and—"

"Trade off the pieces for what you owe?"

"Something like that." Her gray eyes watched me turning it over, coolly weighing the depth of my reaction. "Does it put an unbearable strain on your principles?"

"Why would they be fools enough to trade a sure thing for a probable illusion?"

Her lip curled again. "They won't think of it that way. This ledge is almost legendary—I'd be surprised to learn there's even one person around here who has not heard of it. The men we'll be dealing with have actually handled choice samples my father passed round as earnest for his borrowings." The sardonic laugh in those startling gray eyes openly mocked my disquiet. "They'll go for it all right."

A premonitory chill raised the hairs on my spine. "Let me get this straight. You're proposing to fix up a fake map to this ledge, cut it up, and sell—"

"Not entirely a fake. They already have some idea where it's at. I'll put in enough landmarks they'll recognize to make sure their greed will take care of the rest." She twisted her lips in that arrogant smile. "We're not selling them anything, just offering them a trade they can't pass up."

"And what," I said angrily, "are you figuring to do when they discover they've been tricked?"

"We'll cross that bridge when we come to it. First off, they'll not believe they've been tricked." She twisted her neck to look up into my face. "I know these cheap bastards, and if they *do* get suspicious I'm counting on you to—"

"For Chrissake, Wendy! You know damn well they'll be suspicious!"

Her mouth made a flat, hard line. "That's where you will start earning your share in this. You've been around, you'll do what you have to. And they'll know by the look of you why you're my partner—they'll think a long time before they open hostilities, believe me."

Eyeing her hotly, I could believe one thing with no doubts whatever. This scheming skirt had maneuvered me into a first-class trap! A bind I'd most likely have to shoot my way out of. I felt like the fool she obviously thought me. "Who are these men? Put names to them, damn you!"

"Well," she said, her eyes laughing at me, "there's Benjamin Swink, who's in a lot of things. There's Rabas, the sheepman. And my neighbor and cowman, Nicholas Ives, whose range borders mine. He's been trying for years to marry it." Her stare slewed abruptly away and she said, "Any suspicions that are raised will come out of Rabas—he wouldn't trust his own mother." Her glance came back in a kind of contemplative look. "But he will think a good while before he tangles with you."

15

I could tell her what she could do with her partnership. I could ride out of this now and she'd have no way to stop me. But I had to believe she had already thought of this and made up her mind I'd not do it, that the rags of my pride wouldn't let me.

Arrogant, coldblooded bitch! Now I could see what I'd let myself in for, that whether I liked it or not I was stuck with it. Someway, somehow, she had learned about me and the Jonah rep that past troubles had saddled me with. She must have primed that barkeep to head me her way. I was just what she'd been waiting for, a raggedyass gunslinger down on his luck.

I took a hold on myself. "What's the next move you've set up?"

"A little get-together with those three to lay out my proposition and make them acquainted with my partner." She smiled at me real pleasant. "Ives thinks he's backed me into a corner where my only out is to marry him. I'm really going to enjoy this, Hardigan."

"You've got that map all drawn and ready?"

"Of course. This isn't a stunt I just thought up yesterday."

"When's this get-together going to take place?"

"I'm inviting them, each one separately, to have dinner with me out at the Broken Arrow at five o'clock sharp."

"Aren't you cutting it rather fine? Might be they'll have plans of their own—"

"They'll be there, all right," she said with that arrogant confidence. "They won't let anything stand in the way."

Her old man, I thought, must have spoiled her rotten. Her eyes glinted with amusement as they watched my face. "Let's get out there. Salaratus—my cook—will need a little time to get things ready."

* * *

The ranch house at Broken Arrow was a low, rambling structure built in the Spanish fashion around a central patio. Red tiled roofs and whitewashed walls. The whole look of the place, corrals and all, showed the passage of time and lack of upkeep, yet was still impressive with its bell tower and strings of chili peppers hung out to dry.

"Look around," Wendy said, "while I freshen up and get Salaratus started."

The livingroom, as expected, had a scatter of worn but expensive Navajo rugs, six fat leather-covered chairs, low Mexican mesquite tables covered like drumheads with painted hides, and Indian ashtrays. Shabby, but still conveying a feeling of wealth. Steer horns and stuffed animal heads on the walls. Narrow windows barred with wrought iron to keep out the undesirables.

She presently joined me in a low-necked dress of some pale blue cloth pulled in at the waist with a sash of bright red. Her earrings were oxblood coral, and a strand of the same swung about her neck and down across breasts I found it hard to keep my eyes off of. She made, as intended, a frankly seductive picture. She said with that mocking curl of red lips, "They'll be a lot more impressed than you are. Ives won't be able to keep his stare off me."

She looked at a tall clock ticking away in a corner. "One hour to go."

I said to her, scowling, "When did you find time to invite them?"

"Oh"—she smiled—"I took care of that yesterday."

"You didn't even know me yesterday."

"Call it a hunch." She laughed at the disgusted look on my face. "Someone told me a saddle tramp might be headed this way—"

"Which is just what they'll take me for, a down-and-out saddle bum."

"Not a chance. First door on your right is the room you'll be using. I've laid out a razor, clean towels, and a washcloth. You can go and spruce up if it will make you feel more human."

At the door I paused. "How much land have you got with this place?"

"About forty thousand acres, half of it overgrazed. It would feed a good many cows if we could kill off the vermin that's been stealing me blind."

"Do you have any idea who's back of this rustling?"

"Probably Swink and my so-devoted neighbor, Nicky Ives."

"How's the water situation?"

"Hadn't you better go scrape your face?"

Chapter Three

A Surprise Party

Scrape is what I sure as hell did, nicking my chin in three different places, being in no mood to be handling a straight-edge. That damned designing female could powerful easy get me killed!

The bank I wasn't worried about, but the other three holding her notes were likely to take up a lot of my sleeping time. They'd be sure enough headed for some real sod-pawing when this sorrel-haired dolly flung me into their teeth. Only way she could hold them in line was to paint me as an exterminating sonofabitch, another Tom What-shisname; and I could see plain as hell this was what she was up to.

Sure I could handle a hogleg. But that didn't make me any kind of a gunslinger. Back there in Texas some three years ago I'd made one horrible mistake; I'd been set up and, trying to bull out of it, had killed a half-growed kid. No warrants were out; where it happened it had been known for exactly what it was, an unavoidable mistake. But what with one thing and another, the word had got round that Hardigan was strictly bad news. Nobody had wanted me within ten miles of them.

I knew damned well I ought to get out of here, and by the shortest route.

But she had figured me right, had sensed the chip on my shoulder and played her cards according. She had no more scruples than a goddamn snake.

I came back into the sala trying to pull myself together. She looked like butter wouldn't melt in her mouth, sitting there prim as some hidalgo's daughter, knees together, hands folded in her lap, that chestnut sorrel hair hung out like a halo on the top of her head. "Feeling better?" she asked, all mock concern.

"Haven't you worried somebody might latch onto that ledge ahead of you?"

"Not really," she smiled. "A good many numbskulls have taken a whirl at it. Those Apaches are experts at hiding things. Swink and Nicky have been the most persistent, and a lot of good it's done them. That's pretty rough country."

"How come nobody's homesteaded that area? Seems a logical—"

"Not if you've seen it. It's all cut up with draws and gulches, and most people figure it's too close to the Reservation for comfort."

"It's not *on* the Reservation?" I asked, surprised.

"No. Near as I can guess it's about four hundred yards west of the Reservation boundary, which is probably the reason those Apaches have been content to keep it hidden. Those murders have tended to discourage lone hunters from getting too close.'' She looked toward the window. ''Sounds like one of our guests is about to arrive.''

Dropping into a chair I watched her move toward the door, admiring in spite of myself that long-legged stride, the swing of her body, and easy assurance. She had more guts than you could hang on a fencepost.

I watched him come in with a jingle and scrape of big rowelled spurs. He wasn't far off from being an albino, with that white ropelike hair and unpigmented skin. He made a gaunt, high shape against the outside light. He shot a disparaging look in my direction. ''Who's this? What's he doing here?''

''Ben,'' she said, ''I'd like you to meet my partner, Phil Hardigan from Texas.'' She paused to enjoy the look on his face. ''Phil, shake hands with Benjamin Swink.''

I didn't put out a hand and neither did he. ''What's that name again?''

''Hardigan,'' I said. He stood there stiffly, finally gave a gruff laugh as his glance, the color of bullets, shifted to Wendy Eldridge. ''I hope you know what you're doin'. Seems a far piece to go for what some of us right here would have been glad to provide.''

''Not really,'' she declared, and gave him a look at that irritating smile. ''You see, there's nobody hereabouts with his kind of reputation.''

More hoof sound outside. A heavy fist banged the door, and Wendy moved lithely across to pull it open. ''Hi, Nicky—so glad you were able to be with us.'' If the newcomer was surprised to find others in the room, he managed to conceal it with a nod to Swink as Wendy led him forward to make my acquaintance. ''Nicky, I'm sure you'll be glad to meet my new partner, Phil Hardigan. And this, Phil,'' she said, grinning, ''is my neighbor, Nicholas Ives. Nick's ranch, the NI Connected, adjoins ours on the north.''

Ives's face was a study as he reached out absentmindedly to shake my hand, while his narrowing stare, sharp with suspicion, fastened on Wendy. "You're pulling my leg.''

"Not at all. I had to do something, the way things have been going, so I've taken a partner, hoping to breathe new life into this place." She broadened her smile. "Wish me happy.''

His cold eye fixed me in a dark and moody stare. "Hard Luck Hardigan. The man who shot that kid.'' He had a brawler's shoulders and the weight and build of a successful cowman, and the face to go with it. Long, full lips and a heavy nose below eyes that were inspecting me with a thin and taciturn interest while Swink looked on with a malicious amusement.

And that was how we were when Rabas came through the shoved-open door. Short and stocky and smelling of sheep, he pulled up with an oath, staring unpleasantly about, furiously angry as his mean little eyes took in the assembled company. He was ugly as gar soup and, in an explosion of temper, demanded to be told what the hell was going on.

Swink, nastily grinning, hastened to explain. "Our Wendy's givin' a little party, it looks like, to celebrate the arrival of Hard Luck Hardigan, her new Texas partner.''

"Partner!'' Rabas yelped. "What's she want with a partner for Chrissake? Place won't hardly support her an' that dough wrangler—''

"I'll tell you," Wendy said in her most arrogant tone, "I figured it was time I got in someone to kill off a few rustlers before I went to the poorhouse. And, since I'd no cash to pay him with, I've made him a full partner. We signed the papers this morning.''

In the gritty quiet that fell over the room it was plain to

be seen that none of them liked it. And that was when Salaratus yelled from the kitchen, "Come an' get it 'fore I throw it to the hawgs—I mean the four-legged ones."

It was about the most comfortless meal I ever sat down to.

No one but Wendy had anything to say. Angry looks were passed around freely and it seemed any moment the place would go up in smoke. Looking around with bright eyes, she said in the manner of providing a real treat, "When we've finished in here we'll adjourn to the sala and hear some discussion about the lost Yuma mine."

When all of us were seated in the fat leather chairs, at least three of us visibly smoldering, Wendy announced casually from the corner by the clock, "Several of you gentlemen hold notes against this ranch. In my hand I have what purports to be a map to the lost Yuma mine—let me finish, if you please. I'm willing to cut it up and trade off the pieces for those notes. Do I have any takers?"

Greed glimmered in Ben Swink's stare. Ives, the cowman, said, "How many pieces?" And Rabas growled, "Not till I have a look at that map!"

"You'll just have to take it on trust." Wendy smiled. "You're all aware that my father visited that mine several times and brought back gold, which Ben and Nicky both saw and handled. Ben, who was the bank's assayer, pronounced it incredibly rich. I believe, Ben, you said it would run at least ten thousand dollars to the ton."

Swink nodded. "A very conservative estimate."

"With all due respect for your integrity," Ives said, poker-faced, "I'm afraid, my dear, no one's going to trade in their notes for a piece of a map they haven't examined. Is it in your father's hand?"

"I don't think so. Perhaps it was drawn by the Apache who first showed him the ledge. All I can say is that it was among my father's papers."

"And why are you only now bringing it to light?" Ives asked in a tone of disbelief.

And Rabas sneered, "If you're so sure it's authentic how does it happen in your situation you haven't put it to use yourself?"

Wendy smiled. "I've been saving it for a rainy day."

Nicholas Ives smiled nastily.

"If you doubted its existence," Wendy said to Rabas, "why have you spent so much time hunting it?"

"I don't doubt the existence of that ledge. It's this story and that bit of much-handled paper I don't want any part of. You must think we're a pack of fools," he jeered. "I can lease all that roundabout land from the state and not pay a quarter of what those notes are worth."

Ives, looking thoughtful, said, "Why haven't you?"

"Because," Wendy said, grinning, "he's afraid it wouldn't include the ledge, and for any other purpose his lease would be worthless. His sheep would starve to death in that country."

Swink said, "Why don't the four of us form a pool—a syndicate—put together an outfit and, if we find it, split whatever we take out four ways. That, seems to me, would be the sensible course."

"It may seem sensible to you," Wendy said, "but I've got the map and a partner who's entitled to as much or more than any of you. You're not going to find it without the map, and you don't get the map until I have those notes."

"If I cancel your notes," Ives said with no more expression on his face than a stove lid, "how much of that map will I be entitled to?"

"If you return my notes and the others won't—"

"Hold on," Swink growled, "I've not said I wouldn't!"

"Are you going to?"

"I don't know . . . I might at that," Swink muttered, intently studying Ives's expressionless face. "The idea has one serious drawback." He looked at Wendy. "You owe differing amounts to each of us, don't you?"

"Yes."

"The largest amount, I presume, is to Ives. When you cut up the map he gets the biggest slice?"

My brash partner nodded. "I can't think of any fairer way."

"Are you damn fools," Rabas squawked, "goin' to fall for this swindle?"

"Since you're obviously determined to be dissatisfied anyway, suppose I buy you out?" I said.

"Who gave you leave to shoot off your mouth?" Rabas shouted, red-necked and furious.

"Them papers I signed this morning made me half owner of this outfit *and* of the map," I pointed out.

I got some pretty hard looks. So I thought *what the hell* and tucked in some more. "You want to argue about it, maybe we should step outside where the bullets won't scar up the furniture."

Swink looked uncomfortable. You couldn't tell how Ives was taking this, but Rabas's skun-back lips and livid face suggested he was on the brink of an explosion. Then of a sudden, though still in the clutch of his furious temper, he seemed to be short of breath and his mouth worked like a fish out of water.

I said, "There's nothing in the terms of Wendy's loan that forbids its being paid off if she decides that's what she wants to do."

Since it had not occurred to any of them that *I* could possibly pay off her notes, this shoved them into a fine sweat of thinking.

Ives, with the biggest lien at stake and a full-grown desire to annex Broken Arrow, cleared his throat and suggested we drop it for now and get together again over an eight o'clock breakfast. Swink wasn't sure if his stomach could take it. Rabas clapped on his hat and slammed the door back of him. "All right," Wendy said. "Let's go Dutch and eat at the hotel."

Chapter Four

The Torn Treasure Map

So far as Broken Arrow was concerned, the night produced nothing of interest.

Wendy remained unchanged in her determination to trade off that worthless map for her indebtedness. She gave in that I had a right to see it and, looking amused, presented it to me. Worn and grubby, it had the appearance of having been considerably handled, folded, and refolded a great many times. If she had, indeed, concocted it herself, she'd done a first-rate job of making it seem to be older than she was. So authentic it looked that, eyeing her skeptically, I suggested perhaps it had been drawn by the man her father had taken to the ledge. All this effort got out of her was a laugh.

It didn't look like to me it was the key to anything. "It

wouldn't have done them much good if you'd given them a look at it.''

"Wouldn't have done me any good either. Letting them see it would have diminished their interest, for, as you've discovered, there's no X on it, nothing to show where the ledge has been hidden.''

"If they agree to a trade,'' I said, frowning at her, "they'll damn soon discover they've bought a pig in a poke.''

"I think you're wrong about that. If they don't compare notes—and I'm sure they won't—it's going to work to our benefit because each of them will be sure one of the others has the piece that shows where the ledge is.'' A grin got away from her. "That's just human nature.''

We rode into town and left our mounts at the hotel's tie rail. It still lacked a good ten minutes of the time agreed on, but their horses were anchored alongside ours and they were all in the dining room—even Rabas, still simmering.

Swink, the assayer, said hello with a somewhat uncertain smile. Nicholas Ives managed a nod and Rabas scowled. Breakfast was eaten without conversation. Swink, as we got up from the table, asked if Wendy had fetched the map and she said yes. I said, then, "Did you bring those notes?''

"You bet.'' He grinned, and the other pair looked half minded to hit him.

"We better have a private room,'' Ives said, and arranged it.

It lacked considerable of being as large as the Broken Arrow sala, but we fitted ourselves into it, sitting in cane-bottomed straightback chairs. Ives took the floor.

"We've talked it over,'' he said gruffly, "and since Wendy hasn't kept the interest paid on any of those notes, we've come to the conclusion we'll be a lot better off if we simply foreclose.''

That must have hit Wendy like a hoof in the gut. She turned red and then white and then looked like she'd choke. I said casually, ''I hope you fellers have all got insurance and have your wills all properly attested.'' I scrinched up my eyes like I was peering through smoke. ''Man never knows when he'll be called to his Maker.''

''Now see here,'' Ives blustered, ''if you think you can sit there and maneuver me with threats—''

''Threats, Mr. Ives? I've never had to threaten anyone in my life.''

All puffed up with his righteous indignation, Ives snarled, ''I'll get a court order—''

''Be a waste of time and money,'' I told him. ''Be reasonable, Ives. You take that course and you'll never in this world be around to see it served.''

An apoplectic flush came into Ives's cheeks. He jumped to his feet, wild-eyed and spluttering, waving his arms at his goggling confederates. ''You heard him!'' he yelped. ''I call on you—''

''Not me,'' Rabas said.

''Me either,'' declared Ben Swink, the assayer. ''You'll not drag me into any court action.''

Wendy got up, looking considerably disgusted. ''Come on,'' she said to me. ''I know five or six persons who'll be only too happy to put up cash money for a piece of that map,'' and she started for the door.

''Hold on—'' Swink cried. ''I came prepared to negotiate.''

Wendy paused. ''How much do I owe you?'' she finally asked.

''Ten thousand dollars.''

"You sure you want to trade?"

"Absolutely!"

"All right," she said as though reluctant. "You go down to the desk and get a pair of scissors, and when you come back I'll cut the map into tenths."

Swink hustled out of the room, and he had scarcely got through the door before Rabas piped up to say he wanted the same deal. "The map," Wendy said, "is an oblong. It has four separate folds. When Ben comes back with the scissors I'll cut straight across these folds. It is ten thousand I owe you, too, isn't it?"

Rabas, gritting his teeth, nodded.

"And how about you, Nicky?"

"Hell with you!" Ives said, glowering, and stomped from the room.

"Where's Nick?" Swink asked, coming back with the scissors.

"Gone off in a huff," Rabas told him. And, to Wendy, "Since there's only the pair of us involved in this deal, don't you think it would be fairer to cut it in fourths?"

"Yes, I suppose it would," Wendy graciously acknowledged. "Why don't you do the actual cutting, Mr. Rabas? Then you and Mr. Swink can each pick up one of the sections. Mr. Hardigan and I will take the two that are left, *after*—" she smiled—"you've handed over my notes."

They exchanged nervous glances but eventually produced the notes, which Wendy, after a careful reading, tore into tiny fragments and thrust into a pocket.

"Now," she said, "before we go any further, is it still your desire that the four of us should form a syndicate?"

Rabas rubbed his nose. "I dunno," he said with his eyes swiveling round.

"I believe," Swink said, "it would be to our mutual interest. I feel sure there's enough in that ledge to—even split four ways—put each of us in clover. What's your notion, Rabas?''

Again Rabas tugged at his nose. ''Seems like a pretty hefty gamble any way you look at it.''

''Sure. It's a gamble. But we're already in for ten thousand apiece—you and me anyhow. If there's hanky-panky mixed up in this—''

''Somebody's like to get killed,'' Rabas growled.

Swink looked shocked. ''Come on,'' he smiled, ''I've known Wendy since she ran around in pigtails. Knew her father, too.''

''All right. I'll go along,'' Rabas said, ''but I still think we've been a couple of suckers,'' and he glowered at Wendy when she handed him the scissors.

''Kind of late to back out now,'' Swink said.

''Who'll pay for the supplies,'' Rabas asked, ''an' the packstring?''

Wendy said, ''I'll furnish the packstring if you two will foot the bill for supplies. And if more is needed we can all chip in.''

And on that understanding it was settled. Rabas picked up the scissors and cut the folded map into four equal slices. ''Who gets first pick?''

''Let's flip a coin,'' Swink said, and handed me a penny. ''You call, Rabas.''

I flipped the coin. Rabas called heads and lost.

Swink took one of the two middle sections. Rabas clutched the other, leaving Wendy and me with the two outer cuts. While the suckers were busy looking over their selections I fished out a stump of pencil and, just for the hell of it, drew an X on mine. Wendy, watching, looked at me derisively.

31

It amazed me what a difference in outlook had swept over me since becoming part owner of this gone-to-seed Broken Arrow. Despite the possible target she'd made of me, I was beginning to feel more like my old self.

"Well," Wendy said in that take-charge voice, "let's get down to business. I've agreed to furnish the packstring—you two have agreed to take care of the supplies. That includes food. What else do we need to put this deal on the road?"

I said, "What do you figure Ives will do now?"

Wendy shrugged with a complete indifference that showed all too plainly she couldn't care less. Rabas said, "I want to know what's in the cards once that ledge is discovered. Do we split four ways or do we work for the finder?"

Wendy's look showed what she thought of him, and of the rest of us for that matter. But she said with that arrogant edge of contempt, "We split equally, of course."

Swink and Rabas appeared a little less anxious once this decision was put into words. "I don't think," I said, "we can leave Ives out of this. I don't believe he intends to ignore us."

"No," Rabas said. "That hombre's too used to bein' cock of the walk."

"I don't see what he can do," Swink muttered, eyeing me uneasily.

Rabas swore. "He can dog our steps every inch of the way!"

"Then we'd better find some help," I said, and Rabas nodded. "He's got a tough crew. If we find that ledge he's goin' to try to grab it away from us—I've had dealings with him before."

Wendy said, like she was Moses laying down the law,

"He's just one man against the four of us—"

"Don't you believe it," Rabas growled belligerently. "That puffed-up pelican has no more scruples than you'd find in a starvin' wolf!"

Chapter Five

The Syndicate Prepares

Wendy said skeptically, "If Ives is the sort you make him out to be, I'm surprised he hasn't run you out of the country."

"Don't think he hasn't tried. I've plumb lost count of the times we've tangled—that whoppyjawed bastard has cost me a fortune! Things he's done has forced me to hire at considerable expense more damn uglies than I can honestly afford."

"That," I said, "brings on the next question. Are you willing to loan our venture three or four of these hombres? We've got to have some kind of a crew and your uglies sound like just what we need."

Rabas stood frowning awhile, turning this over.

"If it's the expense that's bothering you, I expect," I said, "the rest of us would be willing to contribute—"

"It ain't that so much as what might happen to my sheep." He chewed awhile on his lip, but finally nodded. "Okay. I'll furnish three men."

Wendy, looking down her nose at him, said contentiously to me, "Don't you think you're being pretty reckless putting that much dependence on this fellow's trustworthiness?"

Rabas's face turned white in the clutch of his temper. "It's your kind, missy, that brings on revolutions!"

I had a hard job holding back a grin but said, hoping to ease the furious stares being exchanged, "I'm sure we can depend on Rabas's experienced judgment. He's a survivor—"

"He was a two-bit rustler till he took to growing sheep!"

"Now look," I said, "we're all in this together. Unless we're all willing to pull in the same direction, we may as well quit right now. Those who are against having Rabas's men brought into this venture kindly stick up a hand."

The only hand that went up was Wendy's.

"I guess you're overruled," I said, and looked at Swink. "How soon can you and Rabas have things ready for us to take to the road?"

After swapping views and figuring, they decided we could be ready to take off in about five days; and for the sake of keeping our departure as private as possible, suggested assembling for the takeoff somewhere in the vicinity of Mammoth, which was a good piece north of town.

During the following days of readying for the big try, Wendy and I had a number of conversations, mostly having to do with various aspects of the venture. Several times she brought up her distrust of Rabas. On one occasion I said, exasperated, "For the love of Pete, Wendy, we've got to work with the man! If you don't quit antagonizing him we might as well forget the whole thing. I wouldn't trust your friend Ives any farther than I could throw him. He's not going to take this lying down—we *need* Rabas, and we need whatever bully boys he's willin' to let us have.''

She didn't like being crossed any more than Ives, but she needed me too and finally shut up about him.

On another occasion I asked if she had any range leased from the Apaches. It put her chin in the air. ''Some,'' she admitted, eyeing me like something the cat had dragged in. ''What's that got to do with this?''

''I don't honestly know. But if things should get sticky and you've any money owing, they might decide to take it away from you, including whatever cattle are on it.''

''They wouldn't dare!'' she said, and left me smothering a curse.

She wasn't interested in my selection of horses for the packstring and gave me a free hand. I figured a round dozen with the necessary equipment ought to be about right and I conferred with Salaratus on the best way of getting them up to Mommoth with the least speculation on the part of outsiders.

''It'll be a much tougher trip, but if you go through—or where you can, skirt—the Tucson Mountains west of here, you hadn't ought to meet up with anyone. But you'll have to keep your eyes peeled.''

''Has she said anything to you about maybe going with us?''

The man shook his head. So the next time Wendy condescended to have a confab, I mentioned the advisability of having a cook along. ''Looks like we'll have six in our outfit, and it's a cinch none of the principals will care to waste his time wrestling pots and pans.''

She said, frowning, ''I suppose not. Just the same I don't

like to leave the ranch with nobody on it. Oh,'' she said, probably considering the kind of meals we were likely to get from Swink or Rabas, ''go ahead and include him.''

That afternoon Nicholas Ives paid us a visit. She took him into the sala and gave him a drink and spent about an hour with him, while I, uninvited, spent my time with the horses. She came out to the corrals after seeing him off.

I looked at her brightly. ''Have a nice visit?''

''Not especially. He wanted to know when we figured to leave, and I said that hadn't been decided on. He asked how many we figured to have in our party, and I told him that hadn't yet been settled. Then he said the whole thing would be a waste of time and I told him time meant nothing to me and that our horses could do with the exercise.''

''I'm surprised he didn't suggest being included.''

''Oh, he did,'' she said with a grin. ''I told him he'd have to see you about that, and he got red in the face and called me a fool. I told him I thought it was time he went home.''

Just as we started back to the house, Salaratus stuck his head out the door to yell we had company. Wendy and I exchanged puzzled glances and went into the house.

Standing nervous in the sala was a pigeon-breasted woman in a print dress that was getting too small for her and a wide-brimmed hat tricked out in fake cherries. She had a tired face and faded blue eyes that regarded Wendy with considerable suspicion.

''Why, Mrs. Swink,'' Wendy said, ''how nice of you to call. Won't you sit down?''

''No, I won't.'' Mrs. Swink said belligerently, ''Where's my husband? What have you done with him?''

''How would I know where he is?'' Wendy asked. ''Last time I saw Ben was in town three days ago.''

" 'Ben' is it? I wonder you don't call him Benny like the rest of his women!"

"I can assure you, Mrs. Swink," cried Wendy, white-cheeked and trembling with anger, "I am *not* one of his women!" She pulled up her chin to say icily, "I think you had better leave."

"The nerve of that woman!" Wendy said, furious. "To come here with her innuendos and suggest I'd be carrying on with the likes of Ben Swink! The very idea! That skirt chaser—why, he's no better than a clerk!"

I could hear Mrs. Swink rumbling off in her buggy. I said, to change the subject, "Have you thought what you'll do if we find that ledge?"

She didn't bother to answer, just threw up her head and strode out of the room.

A few minutes later the sound of hoofbeats rang out and through the window I saw her taking off like a twister.

The next morning after breakfast she called me into her office.

She said, "Perhaps Nicky Ives was right. . . . I wonder if we ought to go on with this thing?"

"What we should have done," I told her, "was home-stead that area—"

"Six hundred and forty acres!"

"As many six-forties as it would take to make sure the ledge—"

"Six-forty is all you can file on." She said in her top-loftiest manner, "Can you picture me squatting out there in that desolation of dust and heat and cactus and gila monsters and sidewinders—"

"You wouldn't have to. Others can be hired to prove up. It's being done all the time. Moguls like your father and

Ives never got all that range by *buying* it.''

She gave me another of her condescending looks. "In relation to that ledge, what's the point of it? The mineral rights, in Arizona, don't go with the land.''

"Rabas thinks—''

"What's that trash got to think with?''

"I suppose in your view I'm trash, too—''

"Not *you*, Hardigan. It was your old-world manners—that endearing charm that persuaded me to make you a partner. I'm going to show you something. Take a look at this!'' she said with a grin, and tossed me a hand-sized chunk of rock.

White quartz it was, and cram-jammed full of shiny stringers of gold. "This come from that ledge?''

Her eyes were sparkling in that frame of red hair. "It's the kind my father sold to the bank.''

"How much to you reckon this chunk to be worth?''

She laughed to hear the excitement in my voice. "About six hundred dollars.''

"And you've been sitting on this stuff all this while? Why the hell didn't you trade it off for your notes?''

"It's the only piece I've got, that's why.''

I could understand now why such a passel of people had been hunting that ledge. "I don't know much about gold,'' I admitted, "but I expect this must be about on a par with what came out of that Lost Dutchman mine.''

She nodded. "Just about.''

We looked at each other through a long thoughtful silence. Finally I said, "We're powerful short of ready cash if I read you right. Why don't you take this in to the bank?''

"I'm afraid they'd apply it against what I've borrowed. But if you took it in—you being a stranger—they might give you cash. As you've said, we could use it.''

Nelson Nye

* * *

So that's how I came to be in Tucson that morning.

"I'd like to trade this for cash," I told the goggle-eyed teller, handing Wendy's quartz to him under the grill.

"Yes, sir—just a moment," he said when he got back his breath, and went off with it through a door marked *private*.

Coming back empty-handed some five minutes later he said, "That'll be six hundred fifty-eight dollars and twenty-seven cents," and, counting it out, shoved it under the grill.

First person I saw as I came down the steps was Rabas, who went wheeling away with a jerk of the head. Following him off to one side I said, "What's on your mind?"

He tugged at his nose, giving me the once-over. "You reckon we've a Chinaman's chance of findin' that ledge? I've got a lot ridin' on this."

"We'll find it," I said. "I'm going to trust you, Rabas, and you better trust me. No telling what we'll be up against. If you're sure of those three hardcases of yours you can tell them what we're up to and promise them a share of whatever we find. And you've my guarantee they'll get it."

He gave me a weighing look and nodded.

"Who do you think's been making off with Wendy's cattle?"

"'Fraid I'm not in a position to say, but I can damn sure tell you it ain't been me! Look, I'll send them hands over this evenin'. You can put 'em up overnight and get off to an early start—like about three o'clock, which'll get you past the Mission before anyone's stirrin'. Okay?"

"Okay," I said and left him.

I was just making ready to climb into the saddle when neighbor Ives hailed me.

"Like a word with you."

40

I said, "I usually charge for a consultation," and showed him a smile.

Ives was in no mood for pleasantries. "You honestly aiming to make a hunt for that ledge?"

"That's right. Maybe you could pop over to our place occasionally and sort of keep a neighborly eye on things."

"I guess not. Just what are you up to, Hardigan?"

"Call me Phil," I said, ignoring his unpleasant looks. "Being neighbors and all, it doesn't make much sense to be standing on ceremony."

"I wouldn't care to be in your boots if those Apaches get wind of your cockeyed intentions."

"Look," I said bluntly, "if you're hunting for trouble you've come to the right place."

With the bark of a laugh he jounced his spurs up the steps and went into the bank.

Chapter Six

A Nosy Observer

Rabas's three hands spent the night in the bunkhouse and we got off with the twelve pack horses, heading north, scarcely fifteen minutes past the time agreed on. With Salaratus in the lead, we passed the Mission through a dark that was thick enough to clatter if you hit it.

Our course led for several miles along the Santa Cruz river, which was currently dry, though Wendy said that whenever a cloudburst descended on Mexican Nogales, this wash would be running bank to tank, that right along here she'd seen it thirty-eight feet deep.

From what Salaratus had earlier told me we were in for a long day. "Mammoth's higher, and from there on through them roundabout hills it'll git rougher than a cob. Down here in the valley the biggest problem's keeping out of sight."

A sparse scatter of lights to the right of us, Wendy said, was Tucson; and right after she spoke Rabas came riding out of the starlighted murk to fall in beside me, and a train whistle throbbed its long wail somewhere off in the distance. "Freight on its way to Phoenix," muttered Salaratus. "Be there 'fore we can git to Mammoth. I've fixed us some sandwiches. We'll eat 'em come noon while we're restin' the caballos."

We nooned in the shade of some paloverdes. We were by this time well away from the river, so we had to let the horses drink out of our hats from water poured out of our canvas sacks.

The country hadn't changed much, fairly level and sandy with a lot of pear and cholla interspersed with the grey thorny wands of wolf's candle and now and again a towering saguaro.

About an hour after we had got underway, an olive-skinned hombre on a piebald mare came loping out of an arroyo and began to slog along with us, much to Wendy's disgust. He wore a black patch across his left eye, and the other, snake bright, examined us with interest. Very free with his grins, he was, and quite impervious to the hard looks he attracted.

"My name's Mungo," he mentioned. "You guys headed for Phoenix? Reckon you won't mind if I join you—gets powerful lonesome ridin' solo."

"We ain't goin' to Phoenix," Rabas told him. "Nor feelin' the need of company. Savvy? Better take off while you're able."

Mungo said, "A real sociable outfit," while his snake-bright good eye roved over us like he was storing up faces. But when Rabas's three uglies started drifting his way with their hard-nosed looks and their spread-fingered hands he

43

must have had second thoughts. He buttoned his lip with a shrug and rode off.

"Smelled like a packin' plant before the pure-food laws," Salaratus snorted.

"You ever see him before?" I asked Wendy.

She shook her head.

Rabas said, "Think I've seen that galoot someplace, but he ain't one of Ives's bunch, without he's just been hired." He rode awhile silent, tugging at his nose. "He's goin' to remember them horses with the empty pack saddles. I got a strong hunch we'll be seein' him again, an' probably where we least want to."

"Had an old army glass bulgin' his pocket," one of Rabas's men said.

I nodded. "Maybe we better head east for a spell till we can put some high ground behind us—"

"He could still foller our tracks," Rabas mentioned. "No problem at all with this many horses."

I thought of some very choice oaths I could exercise had Wendy not been riding beside me. Wendy said, "All we need now is for Ives and his bunch to come pushing their horses like a four-alarm fire."

So we didn't change direction but kept straight on. "What are we going to do?" Wendy asked.

One of Rabas's boys said, "We could probably take that horse away from him—"

"And leave him afoot," Wendy cried delightedly.

Another one said, "We could shoot the horse and waste less time."

Third man said, "Why not shoot Mungo?"

"No, I don't think so," Rabas answered. "Might look a little drastic."

I said, "We'll post him a warning saying if he values his

health to get lost in a hurry, then wait behind the first high ground. If he stays on our track we'll shoot the horse.''

So Rabas dropped back to leave Mungo our thought, which he wrote out and left on a stick. Back of a butte we all pulled up to wait. Ten minutes later we heard oncoming hoof sound, and Rabas, down on one knee, put his rifle to shoulder. One shot, and Mungo's horse dropped as though he'd been poleaxed. With Rabas remounted we pushed on. After this demonstration I hoped Wendy's distrust of the sheepman might not be quite as virulent.

We came up with Mammoth about an hour short of dusk with no sign of Swink. "If he's here," Rabas said, "he'll be in a honkytonk—he's got the idea he's God's gift to women."

So we cooled our heels at the south edge of town for the next twenty minutes. "You want to eat here?" I asked Wendy.

She shook her head. "We'll camp east of town. Salaratus can feed us out of the supplies. If Swink hasn't forgotten to purchase them."

Somewhat unsteady on his feet, Swink hove in sight under the guiding arm of Rabas, who assured us the supplies had been purchased and were stacked on the loading dock back of the mercantile. Rabas let go of Swink and, beckoning his three uglies, took off with the packstring and fetched them back loaded. It was Rabas who suggested we forgo supper and push right on.

"I don't see any sense in it," Wendy objected. When Rabas explained that our supplies had occasioned considerable loose talk, she looked at him nastily. "We'll camp east of town. Let 'em talk their damned heads off!"

Rabas's notion, I thought, was a heap more prudent, but

as already proved, anyone the least interested in us or our provisions could easily track our twenty shod horses. It might have been even worse had we outfitted in Tucson. Among other irritating notions galloping around through my thinking was the question of when Nick Ives would decide to show his hand. That he'd every intention of doing so was as certain as God and little green apples.

We went into camp about three miles east of town. Swink and Rabas had bought a tent for Wendy and an extra large tarp to fling over our supplies. Salaratus, while Rabas and Company were unloading the packstring, gathered up a couple buckets of dried cowflops and with a few sticks of greasewood built up his fire.

Rabas, once we'd finished our meal, posted guards. The rest of us hit the sack.

After an uneventful night and a breakfast of biscuits and speckled Mexican beans we broke camp, loaded the packstring, and set off on the second leg of our journey.

I was riding beside Wendy when Swink came up at a trot to ask when we figured to get into the vicinity of our coveted goal. Wendy, with a disparaging glance, said she'd no idea. I guessed this was the truth but I could see Swink reckoned he was getting a brushoff, and it was plain he didn't like it. His glance swiveled to me. "Shouldn't we be putting that map together again?"

"To what purpose?" Wendy asked with her stare frosting over.

"So we can all see whereabouts is that ledge," Swink said, bridling. "That's what we're here for, ain't it?"

Wendy said with a laugh, "Show him your piece, Hardigan," and rode back to have a few words with our cook. I passed Swink my section of the map and saw him staring perplexedly at that spurious X.

"What seems to be the problem?"

Scowling, he pointed. "That ain't where the lost Yuma's at."

"How do you know?"

"Well, I don't know. But by all the signs and signal smokes it oughta be someplace up around here," and he stuck his finger farther north and a bit west of where I had drawn the phony X. "There's a lot of folks think it's in the Dripping Springs range. Some think it's on the San Carlos Reservation. Still others figure it's just a mite off the trail that runs from the Reservation to Globe. No one's ever suggested it's where that X is." He considered me through narrowed eyes.

"Matter of fact," I said, "when I picked up that piece there was no X on it; I just penciled it in for the hell of it."

Swink gave a gruff laugh. I could see he didn't believe me. I said, "From what I've heard it can't be over thirty miles from the junction of the Gila and San Pedro rivers."

He said with a flush crawling into his cheeks, "That's a big help. Take more years than I've got to cover that much ground! What are you an' that stuck-up dame trying to pull?" He rummaged my face with his angry stare. "Did you know her old man was a cashiered army officer, that he went for years by the name of 'Yuma,' lived with the Sioux before he got married, and was at one time thought to be Sittin' Bull?"

I could see he was too riled to be pulling my leg. "No, I didn't. But I'll tell you this in strictest confidence—Wendy figures that ledge is in a cave. Eldridge was a trader here at one time, wasn't he? Before, I mean, he went into growing big cows from little ones?"

"He traded mescal to the Apaches—that's how he got onto that mine in the first place. He'd gamble on anything

47

a feller could think of. Cards, women, even the length of a cow's tail! You can hear all kinds of yarns about him, at least half of them hot air, but from where I sit he was slicker than slobbers.''

"So how did you manage to get his note for ten thousand?''

Swink's lips cracked apart, his eyes bored into mine, and his mouth pinched into a white-rimmed slit while a flush sprang out of his hung-open collar. I could see the effort he made to clamp hold of his temper, and said to him quietly, "Sure you didn't fix that up after you learned he'd been killed?''

Chapter Seven

Into the Wilderness

What I'd said to Swink had only that moment crossed my mind. Now, in light of the man's reactions, a whole new avenue of thought was opening up. Suppose what I'd suggested were true? And what about Rabas, who had also produced a note for ten thousand?

Here were notions that could stand looking into. . . . But Wendy's reckless haste had closed that door when she tore up the notes. Those tiny fragments she had thrust in a pocket . . . be a jigsaw puzzle trying to patch them together. One thing, however, stood out sharp and clear. Having made that remark, I'd be a fool to let Ben Swink get behind me.

I wondered if Swink and Mungo were long acquainted.

"A penny for your thoughts," Wendy said, putting her mount alongside of mine.

"Just where are we headed for? The trail between San Carlos and Globe?"

"I thought you were unfamiliar with this region."

"Well, I am," I said, seeing the sharp way she eyed me. "Swink's just been filling me in on some of your father's exploits and the prevalent notions as to where that ledge is. He said a lot of people think it's in the Dripping Springs Range."

She wrinkled her nose disdainfully. "Ben Swink's a fool and an inveterate gossip! The Dripping Springs Range has been combed from one end to the other. The so-called Lost Yuma Mine has never been lost to the Indians—they know where it is, or enough of them do. It's not over four hundred yards from the Reservation boundary."

"So the question would seem to be which part of the boundary."

"You've put your finger on it." She flashed that secretive grin at me. "That's the crux of this whole situation."

"You haven't answered my question."

"No point in it," she said. "You'll know when we get there."

"Has the place you're making for been largely combed over?"

"They've all been combed over. I suppose Swink told you about my father living for a while at Fort Yuma, and about General Walker?"

"He didn't mention either."

"Over the years a lot of the rabble around these parts have believed the general knew where the mine was. One of the wild stories making the rounds has it that on the last trading expedition my father undertook, he invited the general to go along with him. This yarn hasn't more than an ounce of truth in it. It's been claimed that the final item traded on that jaunt was ten gallons of mescal. Well aware of the danger from drunken Apaches, my father and the general departed in a great deal of haste for the security of Tucson. On their way home they visited the fabulous mine, scraped off the loose dirt with tin plates, and broke off a large quantity of the 'sparkling quartz' with their hatchets— now what the hell were they doing with hatchets?'' Her eyes laughed at me. "The whole thing's ridiculous! You may as well hear the rest of it. The pair are said to have speedily filled their saddlebags, replaced earth and brush—thus hiding the ledge, and made 'a record' dash for home.

"This imaginative story went on further to list a number of well-known citizens to whom specimens of this loot were shown, and who could vouch for the truth of the ore's marvelous richness. And I quote, 'Some large chunks were so studded with bright gold that a pinhead could not touch the quartz between the beads of precious metal.'

"You've examined the best specimen my father ever brought home. Almost incredibly rich, yet it hardly fits that exaggerated description. Everything that's been said of this mine has been embellished in this same silly manner.

"Shortly after this episode is said to have taken place, General Walker became agent to the Papagos. Within the week, we are told, 'the whole country swarmed with the bloodthirsty demons.' A man named Page was killed at Cañon de Oro and there were 'many victims of Indian cruelty' close to the city limits of Tucson. You can read all this yourself in the back files of the *Citizen*. 'Terror reined everywhere,' '' she quoted with a laugh. "It's preposterous."

"It does sound a bit farfetched when put like that."

"There's no other way to put it. This particular version goes on to say my father was killed 'at noontime, while resting under a mesquite tree. He fell asleep, and his Papago vaqueros took clubs and beat out his brains.' "

Shaking my head, I thought that unless she had private information I wasn't aware of, we might as well call this hunt off right here. She told me then, "I'm pretty sure I can pinpoint the location within one mile, from things my father has said."

"Then why haven't you gone after it before this?"

"I didn't want to go into that region by myself, and I was afraid if I took anyone with me I'd be in even more danger. Then"—she smiled—"I thought when you came along, it might just be possible to relocate this bonanza."

I considered her skeptically. I'd already discovered she'd no qualms about fostering untruths. I said, "We could very well be stepping into really big trouble once our friends know where the mine's at."

"Yes. Well, that's your department, isn't it?"

After Salaratus had fixed a noon ration of sandwiches made from cold biscuits and refried beans, and these had been eaten and we were again on our way, I dropped back to where Salaratus rode just ahead of the packstring and Rabas's three uglies.

"Have you any idea where we're heading?"

Elevating his hat, our cook scratched his head. "If I'm not too far out in my figgerin', we're aimin' for that trail that runs between Globe and the Reservation." He pushed something around through his thinking, then said, "Expect we'll be hittin' it about midway between those two places."

"And when do you reckon we'll arrive?"

"If we keep on at this pace, we'll likely get there in about half an hour."

I wondered what sort of game she was up to now. "Any houses around there?"

"Not unless some squatter has put up a shack."

"Pretty desolate, is it?"

"Dunno's I'd say that. Kind of rough country. Lot of draws an' gulches, if my memory ain't slippin'. Ain't been over this way in a skunk's age."

"What are you figuring to dish up for supper?"

"If we stop at the springs, I thought maybe corned beef, cabbage, mashed spuds, and cornbread."

"Sounds mighty fine," I said, and loped on back to the front of the line where Wendy rode in solitary splendor, Swink and Rabas some three horse lengths behind.

"Do you recall when it was your father borrowed that money from Swink?"

"Not really. I never was able to keep up with his borrowings the last couple years before he was killed. He borrowed from anyone fool enough to let him. And mostly against our equity in Broken Arrow."

"You heard Ives's suggestion. Do you think he was serious?"

"You mean about foreclosing?" When I nodded, she said, "Yes, I expect he was, in a way. He's had his eye on our place for quite a while."

"It doesn't worry you?"

"Sure it worries me. It's why I decided to hunt for that mine."

We were getting into cut-up country now. A lot of rock, ravines, and gullies opening up all around. She said, "We'll be reaching the springs in about ten minutes and setting up our camp there."

I studied her for a couple of moments. "How close are we to the Reservation?"

"Roughly about four miles."

"You expecting any trouble from the Indians?"

"I don't anticipate any. After all, we're leasing range from them, but trouble with Apaches is always in the cards." She gave me one of her irritating grins. "Life is better for them at San Carlos than it ever was in Mexico— they've got turquoise and peridots and quite a bit of good graze. They're pretty good neighbors if you can keep the firewater away from them."

"Do you reckon your father was dabbling in that?"

"I wouldn't put it past him. The springs where we'll set up our base camp ought to be in sight when we round this next bend."

We rounded it. Her cheeks turned dark. A furious anger flashed in her stare. I looked ahead then and saw the horses.

The springs were preempted. Somebody else had got there ahead of us.

Chapter Eight

Company at the Springs

"Well, damn if it ain't the treasure hunters larruping up to make amends for their rudeness. Come right in—plenty of room for all," Ives cried with a flash of teeth.

With her haughtiest look, Wendy demanded, "What are you doing here?"

"Setting up housekeeping, by the look," Rabas told her.

"That's right—give the man a cigar," Ives said grinning. Like the wolf in Red Riding Hood, he informed Wendy unctuously, "It's something I should have done a long time ago if you hadn't distracted me. I'm homesteading this section. Give me another couple weeks and I'll have all my fences up—"

"You can't cut people off from that water!"

"Don't talk like a dude! You know better than that." Ives grinned at her happily. "Who's going to stop me? This water ought to fetch me a pretty fair income, and once I've put up a toll gate, I can double my money in no time at all.''

"There's a name," Wendy said, "for people like you."

"Come, come," Ives chuckled, "you'd have done it yourself if you'd had enough sense to pound sand down a rathole. You know, Wendy, you should have grabbed onto me while you had the chance. Makes me shudder when I think of the wasted years I spent courtin' you. That's life, I guess. Go ahead and water your stock—won't cost you a thing till I get that fence up.''

He laughed at the look on Wendy's face. "Best water in the world, these springs—leached through limestone. Ninety-nine percent pure.''

"You turd!" she cried, and would have spun her horse and ordered us away if I hadn't caught her arm and growled, "Use your head—don't listen to the bugger. These horses have got to have water. We'd better refill our waterbags, too.''

Ives's five tough hands showed jeering grins as we piled off our mounts and led them to water. It griped the hell out of Wendy to be in any way beholden to that tub of lard. It griped me likewise, but this was no time to be resorting to gunplay with Ives's outfit, all set like they was and just spoiling for a scrap.

"Much obliged," I said when we were ready to leave. "Some time, perhaps, we can return the favor.''

"Any time," Ives said expansively. "Always glad to see old friends—even some that ain't so old. If you find that ledge, let me know. Might be I'll make you an offer.''

To say Wendy was furious would be a rank understatement. She was all swelled up like a carbuncle, so I shoved off to talk with Rabas and give her time to simmer down.

While my horse was drinking, I took the trouble to look at some of the rocks in that water. They were, sure enough, limestone with tiny marine fossils embedded in them, and limestone often as not meant caves. It seemed to me somebody, sometime, and not too far back, had said something about a cave in connection with that mine.

I said to Rabas when I came up with him, "Do you think that Mungo hairpin has, maybe, a possible connection with Swink?"

Rabas tugged at his nose while giving this notion his fullest attention. "Gosh, I dunno. It's possible, I guess. What's in your mind?"

"He might figure to be more comfortable if I wasn't around any longer."

The sheepman seemed a little surprised, till I mentioned having suggested to Swink his ten-thousand-dollar note might have been cooked up in a back room someplace.

"Ah. . . ." Rabas nodded. "Could be. But Mungo . . . I dunno. Swink, I'd say, will be playin' a lone hand in a matter of this sort."

I went on to try another of my notions on Salaratus. "You ever hear of any caves at this end of the cactus?"

"Seems to me there *is* a cave back a piece from this trail somewhere." He peered at me like he was turning it over. "My memory ain't too hot any more. Seems it was closer to the Reservation—in that direction, anyway. Might make a good base camp if we could find it."

Dropping back again to Wendy, I said, "Let's cut away from this trail for a bit. I want to pass those springs again without Ives knowing."

"Any special reason?" Seemed kind of odd the way she was eyeing me.

"Cook thinks there might be a cave off closer to the Reservation that would make a good base camp since we can't use the springs.''

"We've got to have a place with water," she said, and gave me a hard stare. "What are you up to?"

"I think he's going to try and take over this mine if we're lucky enough to find it. If we find a cave and it's deep enough, we may find some water."

So we bypassed the springs and about two miles later returned to the trail, heading toward the Reservation. Beckoning the cook, I took the lead.

"It's about a mile or so yet, somewhere off to the right, where this track swings in close to the boundary," Salaratus said. About a half hour later he said, "Along about here, I reckon. Let's cut right a bit. You can't see it from the trail with all this brush grown up like it is."

"You ever been inside it?"

He shook his head. "I ain't what you'd call extra partial to caves. Them big ones, it's powerful easy to git lost in."

Abruptly he grabbed hold of my arm. "Over there— where you see all them rocks. Great place for snakes."

Wendy pushed up beside us, peering intently at the hillside ahead of us. "You know," she said, excited-like, "this might be it."

"You mean the lost Yuma?"

"Yes. I remember my father saying 'It's hell to get into— all that damn brush.' "

"There's certainly brush enough," I said, looking around. The chaparral ran halfway up the hill.

"Over there," Salaratus said, pointing. "That dark place there between them big boulders."

"We're leaving a track big enough for an elephant," I said, looking back over a shoulder."

"Some of this brush will spring up again," Wendy said. I didn't tell her that any halfway smart tracker could tell from the broken stuff which way we'd gone.

The three of us stopped in front of the two boulders. Now that the rocks weren't three feet in front of us, we could all see the passage where it went angling into the hill between the two largest of these boulders on a kind of down slant. "I sure hope," Salaratus said dourly, "This ain't no bear's home."

Wendy laughed. "There haven't been any bears in this region for years."

"This passage," I said, "looks wide enough for a horse. "Go back and get a lantern, Coosie, and tell those boys with the packstring to hold them right where they are till we've had a look around. And tell 'em to cut out the gab."

Salaratus got off his horse and went back through the brush.

"Won't be no mine in here," I told Wendy.

"How do you know?"

"According to the legends, when your old man was here with Walker they threw off the brush and 'scooped away the dirt with tin plates'—remember?"

"That don't mean anything," she said. "You can hear all kinds of stories—every time they're told the teller adds something extra."

Salaratus came back with a light, and, dismounting, we stepped cautiously between the two biggest rocks and passed warily through the opening into a black silence that seemed awesomely old. The ground leveled out as our light played across it, and the walls in there looked some forty feet apart. Straight ahead, however, we saw nothing but blackness. I said in a whisper, "Play that light on the floor. See if you can find any tracks."

The only tracks we could find appeared to have been made by coyotes and did not seem very fresh. No evidence of cooking fires.

Wendy said, "Let's see how far in this cave goes, Coosie."

Reluctantly, Salaratus moved warily forward. "Should of fetched a rope," he muttered. "Be a damn chancy thing if we git lost in his hole."

I could feel Wendy shiver. "We won't go that far," I told him. "Just a couple hundred feet, then we'll go fetch a rope and bring in the horses."

We went another hundred feet with the walls widening out, lost in the dark and nothing but darkness ahead of us. "It's a great cavern," Wendy whispered. "No telling how far it goes."

"Dry, too," I said, "but you'll notice the floor slopes down ahead of us. I think we're going to find water in here. We'll go back to the entrance and bring in the horses. We've got plenty of room and if we post a guard back there with a rifle we could hold off an army."

We brought in the horses and unloaded the supplies. I got another torch from the supplies and handed it to Rabas. "Take one of your boys and a couple of ropes and see how far this place goes."

After they'd gone off, I told his other two uglies to clear a ten-foot strip in front of the entrance. As they cut away the brush, I fetched it in and told Salaratus to start making us some supper. "And don't build no fire near the entrance. We don't want no smoke bringing Indians down on us."

I stood around thinking until Rabas's boys brought in the rest of the cut brush. "Take your rifle," I told one of them, "and go find yourself a seat just inside the entrance. I don't

60

want you shooting anyone till I've had a look at them.''

Rabas came back with the hand he'd taken with him. ''There's two big rooms in this place,'' he reported. ''At the end of the second one, which is quite a bit lower, the floor levels out again and there's a big pool fed by some underground river. Pool's about twenty foot across, and near as I could tell, no sign of a wall beyond it. Fair gives me the creeps, this place does. No tracks except what's been left by dogs or coyotes. Must be a vent someplace off beyond that pool—we could smell cook's fire but no sign of smoke.''

Swink came up and dropped a hand on my shoulder. ''You reckon that mine's in here somewhere?''

''I doubt it,'' I said, ''but we're sure going to look.''

Chapter Nine

Camping at the Cave

The money I'd got from the bank for that chunk of ore Wendy'd asked me to sell I had given to her, so after we'd eaten I suggested she send one of Rabas's boys in to Globe with enough cash to buy us a half-dozen carbide miner's lamps. She took the opportunity to remind me once more of the dangers and hazards I was placing both of us in by my foolhardy trust of that "trashy sheepman."

My own pet suspicions and worries tended to congregate more about the hefty person of Nicholas Ives, our cattleman neighbor who had seized the springs we'd intended to camp at. He fit the cattle baron mold about as well as any man I'd ever known; it was plainly beyond his concept to acknowledge anyone's rights but his own. The kind who meant to have his way come hell or high water. And, since with his hardnosed range roughers he'd taken over the springs, it was in my mind he'd not hold back from seizing the mine if we were fortunate enough to find it.

After I'd seen Rabas's man off to Globe, I sent his third ugly out through the dark to relieve the man who was guarding the entrance leading into the cave. I probably should have kept two men on watch, but with so many other notions crying for attention, I suppose this precaution simply didn't occur to me. I wasn't no more infallible than anybody else.

Rabas had put up the tent for Wendy and before we turned in I broached a couple of the things on my mind. "Is General Walker still above ground?"

She shook her head. "He passed on several years ago."

"What gave you the notion this lost ledge could be within four hundred yards of the Reservation boundary?"

She gave me one of her arrogant looks. "Must you question every single thing I say?"

"I don't," I said. "But if you really hope to latch onto that mine I'll need to know everything you can tell me, particularly anything that has to do with its location."

"I've no idea what put that into my head. It must have been something my father said. You have to remember that when all that took place I was hardly more than a child. I doubt if I was paying a great deal of attention."

"You also said," I reminded her, "you could pinpoint the location to within a mile. Do you reckon this cave is inside that mile?"

"Yes. I would imagine so."

"Then it must be pretty close to where we're standing right now. The Reservation boundary can't be—according to Salaratus—much more than four hundred yards from this cave."

"It *could* be right here."

"I suppose it could—we'll know more about that when we get those lamps."

She went into her tent and I went off to dig out my bed-roll.

It took me a good while to get to sleep. I was well aware of the risks of having Rabas and three of his hands in the bosom of our company. But it was Wendy who'd accepted Rabas in exchange for his note against Broken Arrow. I had persuaded him to fetch the three uglies, but we had to have some kind of crew, and she'd none of her own. Rabas was not my ideal of a partner, but it was Ives that put me into a lather of worries. Ives was big with both threat and influence, and we were about as vulnerable as a handful of ants on an elephant walk. Without Rabas and those three tough hands, we'd be a pushover; and I was afraid if push came to shove, we might be anyway.

I must have finally drifted off, because the next thing I knew I was sitting bolt upright with the echoes of a shot ringing loud in my ears.

I flung back the covers and, grabbing my six-shooter, leapt to my feet. In the confusion of sounds I couldn't be sure, but it seemed like to me that shot had come from the entrance where I'd posted that guard. It didn't take me but seconds in the grip of this caldron of blackness to get to the scene. Against the starlight outside I could see the crouched shape of Rabas's man in the entrance. The burnt-powder smell was strong all around me. I kept my voice down, despite my churning temper. "I gave orders there was to be no shooting without I was called."

"No time for that. He'd have been in here if I'd gone back to wake you. He'd been snoopin' around for the last ten minutes and me settin' here hearin' him. He wasn't twenty feet off and comin' right at me when I squeezed off that shot.''

I heard the rest of our bunch jostling around just behind me. "Did you hit him?" I said.

"Well, he sure as hell dropped.''

"I'll go look," Rabas said, pushing past me.

A dozen fresh worries took on substance to plague me. Then Rabas emerged from the shadow-filled brush and came soundlessly into the cleared space to say, "Dead as a doornail. We can be glad anyway it wasn't no Apache. It was one of Ives's boys, one of them at the springs.'' He beckoned his man. "You better lug him off an' get rid of him, Craig.''

Chapter Ten

Partner Trouble

After that there was no more sleep for any of us. I left Rabas and Swink on watch at the entrance, promising to send Rabas's third man to relieve the assayer, and spent a rough time wondering if that shot had reached Indian ears. I didn't reckon Ives's bunch at the springs would have heard it, but when that dead hombre failed to show up for breakfast, I knew damn well Ives would begin a search.

I thought some more, briefly, about Mungo, the outsider who'd attempted to join our party the first day out—the one we'd left horseless. An outsider, all right, but hardly a freelance. I put no stock in coincidence. He'd appeared because someone had made it worth his while, and it wouldn't have been Rabas, who already had three hands in our outfit. Had Mungo just happened along, how would he have known of our party? So, I thought, he must have been hired, and who more likely to hire him than Ben Swink?

When I went back to attend to my bedroll, there, right on top of it was a very short note on a small scrap of paper held down by a fist-sized stone. Without heading or signature it said starkly: RABAS'S BOYS ARE GOING TO PUT YOU AWAY.

I showed it to Wendy, who, without hesitation, said, "I told you not to trust that trash. Well, what are you going to do about it? You ought to get rid of them—you know that, don't you? Killing Ives's hand—"

"I don't blame the man—Craig, wasn't it?—for shooting. That galoot was heading straight for the entrance—what else could Craig have done? The man had a rifle and, given a chance, would have certainly used it. The fault is mine for not having put two men on the job."

She walked off, unconvinced.

About an hour later Rabas came back to where I sat on my blankets. "Craig's back," he said, "I left him on watch with Swink. He took that feller onto the Reservation, buried him in a wash, and turned the horse loose."

"All right," I said, and showed him the scrap of paper I'd inherited.

Rabas gave a short laugh. "Someone tryin' to make trouble. Have you shown that to Swink?"

"Not yet, but I will. Put your other man on watch with Craig at the entrance and tell Swink I want to see him."

When Swink showed up, I handed him the note. He took it over to cook's fire and read it. "Kind of underhanded, but I have to go along with the sentiment. Some of Wendy's work?"

Pretty cool, I thought. Sounds from the entrance sent me to learn what new aggravation had caught up with us. It was the fellow I'd sent to Globe for the lamps—Brady they called him. He'd come back with seven lamps; I didn't ask how he'd managed it in the middle of the night, but Wendy did, and Brady said with a chuckle, "Couple of Chinese fellers have opened a mercantile—a sort of general store—that never closes its doors."

I saw Rabas wiping the grin off his mouth, and cook sang out for us to come and get it, and we all filled our pans with sowbelly and beans. I told Brady to see that the horses got fed and watered, knowing Ives would pretty soon start wondering about his missing hand.

Apparently Wendy's thoughts were going down the same alley, for she said abruptly, "We'd better stay under cover for a while." I nodded, feeling sure he'd be onto our tracks before noon, for with this many horses he could hardly miss them. And that broken brush this side of the trail. There just wasn't any way we could keep Ives from finding us.

"Coosie," I said, "fix up four of those lamps. It's time this place got a thorough going-over."

A few minutes later Wendy, Swink, Rabas, and myself set out to explore the confines of our shelter.

We looked and we looked but found no mine. Beyond the pool in the second cavern we found another, and two more rooms, if you could call them that, beyond where the second cavern swung to the right. I knew that somewhere in the intense dark that stretched everywhere around us there had to be some kind of vent. We could feel the push of a breeze against our faces, and the smell of cook's fire was fairly strong even here.

On account of the echoes we didn't do much talking. After passing the second pool, our lamps couldn't find a wall in any direction until we presently came to the far end of these caverns. "How far underground do you think we are?'' Wendy asked in a stifled tone. I said that I reckoned maybe three hundred feet, but it was anyone's guess. ''We could move camp down here, and there'd be less likelihood of Ives or anyone else discovering us, at least for several days. A fire down here couldn't be seen from the entrance, and the smoke would be carried off in this breeze.

''Of course there'd be tracks, but we could brush those out near the entrance. Biggest drawback would be the long haul for the stick and brush Coosie'd need for his fire.''

Wendy said, ''We can't keep out of Ives's surveillance for long, no matter what we do, so why bother?'' Her eyes challenged mine. When I didn't dispute this she said, ''Even if he finds that fellow Craig shot, he can't prove we had anything to do with it.''

Swink hadn't said a word since breakfast, and he said nothing now, but I could tell from the tightened look of Rabas's face that he was thinking, like me, that Ives wasn't the kind to give a damn about proof.

We followed the left-hand wall back into the cavern where we had our camp. Rabas said, ''I'll go up and relieve those boys at the entrance.'' He woke Brady up and they went off through the dark, Rabas having left his lamp with Salaratus.

Wendy ducked into her tent, and I took off for another look at those pools, having some kind of notion I couldn't bring into focus.

The weird stillness of this underground place and the dark that was almost thick enough to cut bred strange fancies I found difficult to shake off. I didn't think these pools were fed by any river; I felt sure they were the result of hidden springs. If I got too fed up with the problems of this lost-ledge hunt, I reckoned I could like enough sell out my half of Broken Arrow and look for greener pastures, though I'd a hunch deep inside I'd probably never do it.

I found myself wondering if Wendy's distrust of Rabas had any real foundation. I'd been acquainted with other hombres like him in the past and knew that a man running sheep in cattle country had to have sharp wits, a lot of backbone, and not too many scruples. By my assessment Rabas fit this mold.

Had that note Swink traded in for his fourth share in this dubious venture been nothing more than a cooked-up forgery? Surely Wendy could recognize her own father's handwriting. His signature anyhow.

In a vague sort of fashion, I'd been thinking for some time that probably the best way to hide that ledge of white quartz was to build a house over it. But Salaratus had assured me he could not recall any houses or even shacks in this vicinity.

I kept remembering, too, that story of throwing off the brush and scooping away the dirt with tin plates. Which certainly didn't sound as though the ledge was very carefully hidden. Wendy had scoffed at this tinplate yarn and it suddenly occurred to me that maybe the ledge wasn't covered by dirt, that maybe it was under *water*. And the more I thought about this, the more I began to feel that it might well be, or why hadn't someone latched onto it?

I was approaching the first of the two pools now, the one at the far end of the second room of the cavern, and could see the dark glint of the water. If that ledge was out in the open it didn't seem as though throwing a few shovelfuls of dirt across the face of it would keep a good rain from exposing it.

These notions were beginning to excite me a little. I began to think I might be right and put a bit more hustle into my stride. I'd thought before that the lack of any but small

animal tracks was a sure indication this place had been un-
visited for a considerable while—centuries maybe. After
handling that sample I had sold to the bank, I couldn't really
believe this. Tracks could be brushed out.

I stepped to the edge of the pool to peer into it, dazzled
by the reflection of my lamp on the water. I was bending
forward, trying to see past this, when something smashed
down on the back of my head and I knew I was falling,
unable to catch myself.

Chapter Eleven

Some More Headaches

Blackness everywhere.

Not a pinprick of light came through the monstrous dark that held me in its velvet grip. Indistinguishable sounds crept vaguely about in this impenetrable night, but too far away to make any sense.

The next thing I noticed was the smell, very faint and pleasantly distant, like a field of flowers in a gentle breeze. And finally, when I got my eyes open, tiny flickers of light dimly glimpsed through the murk.

I lay carefully still, trying to think where I was, afraid to move lest the blinding pain overwhelm me again. I remembered the pain and closed my eyes with a shudder.

It seemed warmer now. The scent was still there like lilacs in bloom, and a hand lay softly against my forehead. I turned my head and opened my eyes, and the first thing I saw was Wendy's face hovering over me. And later—how much later I couldn't tell—I gradually realized I was still in the cavern and that the flickers of light were from the flames of cook's fire.

"Are you awake?"

Wendy's voice. I would have known it anywhere.

I cleared my throat to get the cobwebs out of it. "I think so." That sounded pretty feeble even to me. "How did I get here? Last I remember that pool was about to swallow me."

She considered me awhile, passed a hand across her jaw, and said, "I dragged you out."

"I'm obliged."

We studied each other for a longer interval. Indifferently she asked, "Did you see who hit you?"

"Is that what it was? I thought the roof came down on me."

"You must have had a concussion. When I got you out there was quite a knob on the back of your head."

"How long have I been lying here?" I tried to sit up and fell back in frustration, head pounding.

"Two days," Wendy said.

I must have stared at her incredulously. As the hammering lessened, things began to come back to me, and I cried, "What's happened?"

"Nothing."

"Ives hasn't found us?"

"Oh, he knows where we are."

"They found the entrance and haven't tried to come in?"

"We had some conversation. He told me his crew have taken over Broken Arrow, that he meant to foreclose if we didn't come out of here. When that failed to budge us he threatened to bring charges, and I told him to go right

73

ahead—if he thought he could make them stick.''

''And then?'' I said with what was probably a grimace but was intended to be a grin.

''And then,'' she said, grinning back at me, ''I told him to come ahead. He finally got back on his horse and rode off in a passion, leaving three of his hands to make sure we stayed put.''

''Good for you,'' I said with approval. ''Now how about some grub? My stomach feels like it's been yanked through a knothole.''

''I'll have Coosie make you some broth.''

I glared and tried again to get up, only to fall back on my blankets with a groan. ''Get up any time you've a mind to,'' she said and, with a laugh, went away from me.

She woke me up to spoon soup into me. I asked for a steak but she paid no attention. When her bowl was empty, she said that perhaps, if I behaved myself, tomorrow I might have something more substantial.

I must have slept again. The next time she fed me it was evening, and I could hear the gabble of voices around cook's fire. ''You trying to starve me to death?'' I growled at her.

''I'm tired of your whining.'' She set the bowl in the sand alongside of me. ''Sit up and feed yourself, you big lummox,'' and I discovered I could.

''What have you been doing?'' I asked.

''What is there to do in this black hole?''

''You might do some more looking. I believe that mine's in here.''

''We've done some more looking. We've searched this place from one end to the other.''

''Did you give any thought to that pool you pulled me out of?''

She looked at me blankly.

"I had an idea that ledge might be underwater."

"Is that what you were doing when the lights went out?"

"Did you examine that pool?"

She shook her head. "Seems kind of farfetched, but I'll give it a look in the morning."

"Tell Swink I want to speak with him when he gets through eating."

"I'm afraid that isn't possible—"

"Why not?"

"Swink's disappeared."

It was my turn to stare. "You mean you don't know where he is?"

"I told you, we've searched this place from one end to the other and haven't seen hide nor hair of him."

"Did you question the boys at the entrance?"

"Of course. They swear he never went out by that route. Nobody will admit having seen him since Brady and Craig carried you back from the pool."

I said in a temper, "There must be another way out of here!"

"Well, go ahead and find it. Rabas came to the same conclusion. But, despite all our hunting, we still haven't found the faintest sign of one."

Giving her back her bowl, I said, "Send him over here."

"How's the head?" Rabas asked.

"I guess it's still tied onto me. Looks like we've hit the bottom of the barrel. You reckon Ives's bunch will try to get in here?"

"Not likely. He must know as well as we do that charging into the dark from bright sunlight would just be asking to get slaughtered."

"Do you think it was Swink knocked me over the head?"

"I sure can't think who else it would be."

"What do you think of Ives's claiming to have grabbed Broken Arrow?"

"He probably has. It's about what I would have expected him to do. I doubt, however, if he's gone so far as to start foreclosure proceedings."

"Why not?"

"He's tough and cocksure, but there's a cautious streak in him. And there's your reputation. I expect he'd want to know which way the wind's going to blow before he risks driving you to retaliate."

I turned that over and looked awhile at it. "Can't be many hands left on his place right now . . . ," I said, thinking hard. "Might be we could take over his headquarters."

"Count me out." Rabas's laugh was gruff. "I've got sheep to think of, and with three of my uglies wastin' time in here . . ." He shrugged. "I can't afford it."

"Can you believe Ben Swink has actually found a way out of here?"

"Don't seem likely, but I've got to believe it. We've raked over these caverns with a fine-toothed comb."

I said, "We'd better homestead this place. If Ives can lay claim to those springs, I see nothing to stop us from latching onto these caverns and a good bit around them. If the both of us file, we can grab two adjoining sections."

"Pretty worthless for cattle, and not much good for sheep."

"It has a certain nuisance value. And if the mine's around here, that will probably lock it up."

Rabas's face wrinkled into a scowl, but he nodded. "All right. I'll go along, if you can figure some way of getting out without leavin' most of our blood on the cactus."

"We'll get out the way Swink did."

Rabas grinned. "Show me."

I nodded. "We'll look again tomorrow morning. How's the grub holding out?"

"I reckon it'll hold out another three days. Your partner thinks I shoved you into that pool." He chuckled.

I chuckled too. "Pretty near has to be either you or Swink."

"That's right. If Wendy done it, why pull you out?" That sardonic smile crossed his shaved-hog cheeks. "What profit could I get from a trick like that?"

"Same applies to Swink."

Rabas said, "I'm reasonably predictable. Swink is a goddam out-an'-out rat."

Chapter Twelve

Looking for Swink

There was a certain amount of logic in what Rabas said. Of the two, I would sooner trust Rabas any day in the week. Swink was shifty, though pretty cool in the clutch. I thought of that note I'd found on my bedroll and that a short time later I'd been dumped in that pool. Why would Rabas write a note that pointed straight at himself? Had Rabas done the writing, it would have pointed at Swink—or would it? I didn't think Rabas had that kind of mind.

"Wendy tell you we found that vent? In the roof of that farthest cavern. We lit some brush back there and watched where the smoke went. Straight up and into a sort of longish crack. Even if you could manage to get up there—and you couldn't without a ladder—that crack's too narrow for a man to squeeze through."

"If he's not still in here, we'll try in the morning to find how he got out."

"Let's not forget that feller Mungo," Rabas said. "I can't get it out of my head we'll see more of him."

Most of the boys were sitting round cook's fire. Salaratus had dug out his mouth harp and was playing "Red River Valley." Wendy, apparently, had turned in for the night. When Coosie, after tapping out his harmonica in the palm of his hand, swung into "The Strawberry Roan" it occurred to me I'd better bed down too.

Next morning, soon as breakfast was finished and Rabas had changed the guard at the entrance, the three of us—Wendy, the sheepman, and myself—set off to find out what had happened to Swink. At Rabas's suggestion we started with the last cavern, where he called my attention to the crack in the roof. No question of anyone using that for an exit.

We went round the walls slowly, giving much care to the prosecution of this search, at least one of us feeling our lives might depend on it. We tapped and pried at each likely spot. We intently examined the pool in this cavern. We could see the rough limestone bottom, with its center five foot at its deepest, and agreed there was no quartz ledge under that water. There were no man-made trapdoors in the floor.

We moved into the next room with no better luck.

"Maybe," Wendy said, "there never was any Swink—perhaps we just imagined him." And Rabas said if he could believe that, he would feel considerably easier in his mind.

"In what way?" Wendy asked without interest.

"Well," Rabas said, "with his bent for women, that little vinegarroon could get us into real trouble with the Indians."

He didn't need to elaborate; we could both see what he had in mind. Apaches weren't people to stamp and yell *boo* at.

We moved into the cavern where I'd tried out the pool. As we turned to look round, our lamps sent grotesque shadows aswirl in a horridly lifelike manner.

We peered into the pool. The water was clear; every inch of the bottom could be clearly seen. "No quartz ledge in there," Rabas grunted. "No Swink, either," Wendy pointed out, scornful.

We commenced our long hike around the walls. Clockwise, beginning where we'd entered from the room we'd just examined. We came to where it was joined to the first (or initial) cave and could see cook's fire glowing like a Cyclops's eye in the distance. "Well, that's half of it," Wendy said, disgusted. "Let's get over the other half and see what Coosie's dishing up for lunch."

"Either of you looked," I asked, "at that stretch back of the pool?"

"Of course we've looked at it," Wendy said, intolerant of what she took to be criticism. "It's not more than twenty feet from the water. We didn't go feel of it if that's what you mean."

There didn't, indeed, seem much use in going closer. We could see it plain enough, and that little tuft of rabbit brush, in the light of our carbide lamps. And both Rabas and I, practically simultaneously, cried, "Rabbit brush!" Rabas snarled, "How could rabbit brush grow in this place?" and we both ran toward it, Wendy at our heels.

I grabbed hold. It came away in my hand without roots, and back of it was the exit Swink had used to get out of here. A hole hardly two feet in width, level with the floor, its sides daubed with dried mud. To conceal the shine of quartz.

We had found the lost ledge.

80

Chapter Thirteen

Some Got Away

How long we stood, scarcely breathing, staring like fools at that bolt hole, is anybody's guess. We all started talking at once, and Rabas, perhaps quicker to grasp the implications than either Wendy or myself, dropped to his knees and went wriggling away out of sight.

I would have let Wendy go next. She wouldn't have it that way, and with a frantic impatience motioned me on. The squeeze of that hole was of short duration; almost immediately the fault widened out both horizontally and vertically. We were soon standing erect beside Rabas, staring astoundedly at the glistening beauty of that gold-filled quartz in the light of our lamps.

"We'd better see where this passage goes," Rabas muttered, nervously peering into the black gut ahead of us. He set off, us right behind him. It soon bent to the left, and we found ourselves climbing a thirty-degree slope, the passage widening to perhaps six feet, angling toward the right again, and swiftly narrowing to a brush-clogged exit.

None of us at the moment cared to push through that brush into the windy open. Crouched there like cave dwellers out of a distant past, we deliberated what should be next on our agenda. We couldn't fetch horses through this passage and couldn't leave these caverns the way we'd entered without risking a shoot-out with the hombres Ives had left to keep us bottled.

"We ought," Rabas said, "to get into town and file homestead claims to this area right away—"

"But ownership of land," Wendy cried, "has nothing to do with the mineral rights, and it's the mine we want to patent."

"Dead right," Rabas nodded. "Two of us ought to go, but it's a pretty good hike from here to Globe, and more than twice as far to Tucson."

"You and Rabas," I said to Wendy, "better light out for Globe and stake our claim to this ledge and file for homesteads. You can get the measurements from maps in the County Recorder's office. Looks like quite a walk, but maybe you can latch onto a couple horses on the way."

"You go," Wendy said, "I'd just as lief stay here." I recalled her antipathy to Rabas and guessed that was the main reason she wanted me to go in her place.

Likely Rabas had come to the same conclusion. "All right," he said, eyeing me, "Let's get out of here."

Emerging from the shoulder-high brush that obscured this exit, we found no sign that anyone was around keeping tabs on it. I said, "We'll make better time on the trail. How far away is the Reservation? I don't see any fence."

"No," he said, "only part of it's fenced. I don't think the boundary's much farther off at this point than where we entered those caverns—between four and five hundred yards I'd say. Mebbe, if we do our hiking on the Reservation side of this trail, we might chance on some Indian who'd sell us a pair of ponies."

"Worth trying." I nodded, and luck was with us.

We hadn't gone half a mile when we met up with a pair of mounted Apaches. "Let me do the talking," Rabas said. "I savvy enough of their lingo to make myself understood anyway." He told them what we wanted.

They looked at each other, then back at us. The older one appeared dubious, but the younger said, "How much you give?"

"Fifty dollars apiece."

"You throw in gun?"

"No gun," Rabas said. "Fifty dollars each. Take it or leave it."

The two Apaches drew off and went into a huddle. The younger one finally said, "We take," and keeping hold of the reins, slid off his horse. Rabas pulled out a roll and peeled off fifty dollars, handed it over in exchange for the reins, and looked up at the other Apache. The fellow seemed to have a hard time making up his mind, but greed presently won, and he reluctantly dismounted. Rabas peeled off another fifty and passed it to him.

"Where you go?" the younger one asked.

"Globe," Rabas said, looking askance at the moth-eaten blanket which the Indian used in place of a saddle. The other horse wore a beat-up old army McClellan, great for a horse but hell on a man. Rabas said to me, "You take the saddle. I'll make out with this blanket." We bade them goodbye and cut back to the trail.

"These nags," Rabas grumbled, "ain't worth no more than ten bucks apiece, but they're better than walkin', though I expect I'll be itchin' till I can git under water."

"We better give Ives's springs a pretty wide miss," I said, recalling the cattleman's temper.

"Yeah," Rabas nodded. "If he finds we got out of there, he'll be fit to be tied." With a scowl reshaping the lower half of his face, he said, peering ahead, "We better get off this trail before we run into the hands he left watchin' our hidey hole."

I'd forgot about them. We swung back onto Reservation land again and went deep into it until the springs were behind us.

Back on the trail, Rabas said, "Let's see if we can get a mite of hustle from these critters," and kicked his mount into a lope. The one under me preferred a bone-racking trot, so Rabas had to pull his down to keep pace with me. "I'm right glad," he grinned, "you wanted the saddle."

"You paid for them. Reckon you had a right to take your pick. Any of them fleas got to work on you yet?"

We weren't but a couple of miles from Globe when Rabas looked back and swore. Something in his tone pulled my head around. There was a dust boiling up about a mile behind us. We kicked our ponies into a run. "Ives?" I yelled.

"Apaches," Rabas answered. "Them two probably claim we stole these critters!"

This was a complication I didn't care for at all. Some of that bunch were sure to have rifles. "Start yellin'," Rabas shouted. "It's the only thing Injun horses understand!"

Between beating the ponies' ribs with the heels of our boots and yelling our heads off, we managed to make it into Globe ahead of our pursuers, but only just about. They levered a few scattered shots in our direction, all but one of

which went wild. That lone exception must have caught my
horse someplace in the back end. His rump went up, and
his head went down, and I went flying like a bat out of
Carlsbad.

"You can git up now," Rabas called. "If you don't want
that mob running over you."

I looked up to see half the town of Globe, drawn by the
shooting and armed with everything from scythes to buffalo
guns, straggling toward me. A twist of my head in regard
for the horse found him all spraddled out, too dead to skin.

Swearing, I got onto my feet. Scooped up my hat.

And looked for the dust cloud.

It was going the other way.

We found the county recorder's office and, with Rabas
the Pathfinder taking the lead like he was running this show,
marched up to the ledger-littered counter where two big-
hatted jaspers were bent over a map. I nudged the sheepman.
"How's them for apples?"

His look went over the pair, sharpening into grim focus
on Swink.

At the same time, Swink caught sight of me and froze in
a half turn, twisted cheeks going a fishbelly white. He
clutched at the counter like his knees had gone wobbly. We
could see his mouth work, but nothing came out.

"Benjamin Swink, I presume," Rabas drawled, soft and
silky.

I thought the assayer was going to faint in his tracks as
his clutch jumped from counter to the arm of his companion.
The companion wheeled and showed Mungo's black-
patched face. "Just hold it right there," I said, hand on gun
butt.

"Tough luck," Mungo said through his teeth. "We've already filed."

"What's going on?" a frightened clerk cried, hurrying up to the counter.

Rabas's stare bored into him. "What's this pair of claim-jumpers filed on?"

The clerks' look jumped from Rabas to Swink. The lump in his throat went up and down convulsively. "Wh-wh-why—"

"Just show us the entry," I said grimly. "Everybody else stay right where you're at."

"I—I'll have to go look it up," the clerk gasped.

"Don't bother," I said and, stepping up to the counter, spun the ledger around. MINING CLAIMS it said on the cover. I thumbed through the pages to the final entry. And there it was, sure enough. The Golden Grab, Swink and Mungo, owners.

Chapter Fourteen

Swink and Mungo, Proprietors

"It has just changed hands," I informed the clerk, dropping a cartwheel on the counter, "for one dollar and other valuable considerations. Get that look off your mug and make out a quitclaim in favor of Eldridge, Hardigan, and Rabas."

Swink looked pretty well cowed, but not Mungo. "This is barefaced robbery," he snarled at the clerk, "and I call on you—"

"It might be your last call if you don't button your lip," I told him. And to the clerk I said, "This pair have concocted a nice little swindle, which you have abetted. If you don't want to find yourself hauled into court in one of the biggest scandals of this century, you had better stir your stumps and do as I told you."

With a last, flurried look the clerk hustled about his legitimate business and, in no time at all, having filled in the particulars, shoved it in front of Swink and Mungo for their signatures.

Swink, like the rat he was, bared his teeth but signed his name. Mungo took a little more persuasion. I said, "We can write *deceased* under your name, buster, if that's what you're hankering for."

"You ain't heard the last of this," he promised as he grabbed up the pen and scribbled his name with a splutter.

Ignoring him, I said to the clerk, "I want to see this transfer recorded in your book," and tossed a couple more cartwheels onto the counter.

Swink slunk out of there. Mungo stormed after him, glowering like a catamount. Rabas said to me, "When we leave this place, you better keep your eyes skinned. One of them bastards is likely to put a hole in you."

"I don't think so. Not out there on the street, anyway." I picked up and folded the quitclaim deed and thrust it into my pocket. "Come on. Let's give him a chance."

Rabas slanched me a look I didn't try to decipher. I pushed through the door and stepped into the street. "Which way's the livery? I've got to have another horse."

The sheepman picked up the reins of his Indian pony, reached down to scratch himself, and led the way without comment. Striding along beside him, I said reflectively, "Them buggers sure put an apt name on our mine."

Rabas barked a short laugh. "It come within an ace of not bein' ours, partner."

"As the old saying has it, 'All's well that ends well.' "

"Yeah," Rabas said. And I reckoned he was thinking, like me, that it was a far piece from ended.

At the livery, I looked at several forty-dollar horses and was about to pick a pretty fair-looking sorrel, when the proprietor said, "Not much of a horse for a man of your caliber. I've got a real fine stepper in the barn. You want to give him the once-over?"

"Why not?"

So we followed him into the barn and watched him lead out a big grulla with zebra marks on his knees and a red dorsal stripe. Good legs, long underline, short back, and good head. "This here," the man said, "is a horse that'll take you to hell an' back."

"That's a place I'm trying to miss. How much?"

He looked me over again. "For you . . . one fifty."

"Okay. Charge him to Broken Arrow."

"Um . . . not this one, mister. This one's cash on the barrelhead."

"Just wrap up that sorrel and throw in the gear."

"You're a hard man to please."

I worked up a grin. "You got that right."

"How about one twenty, an' I'll saddle and bridle him."

"I haven't got that much on me."

"Damn," the man said. "Mebbe your friend here . . . ?"

"Nope."

"Take him for a hundred, and I'll be losin' my shirt."

"'Fraid not. Saddle up that sorrel—"

Rabas said, "I'll give you a hundred for him."

The stableman gave him a dubious glance. Rabas dug out his roll and peeled off two fifties. "Put something on him I can git my feet into, and you've got a deal."

The fellow looked again at me. I shook my head, and the man reluctantly reached for Rabas's hundred. With the two bills in his pocket the man reached down a surcingle.

"Chrissake," Rabas grumbled. "Do I look like a rodeo hand?"

"Well . . . I got an old postage stamp you can have for another twenty."

"Let's see it."

The man fetched out an old beat-up racing saddle, and, grimacing, Rabas forked over the twenty.

We went back to the corrals, and the livery keeper led out the sorrel I had asked for. No comparison to the grulla, but he looked sturdy enough and he walked all right. "How much to throw in a saddle and bridle?"

"Another thirty." he said with a look that showed how much in his opinion my stock had slipped.

I dug out the seventy dollars and we saddled up.

When we were back on the street I looked again at the grulla. "Looks a real goer."

"Guess he'll do," Rabas said with his customary flair for reticence.

"What are you figuring to do about that pony you gave fifty bucks for and left in front of the livery?"

"He can have him."

"You know," I said, "we ought to have demanded bills of sale for this pair. Those Apaches should've taught us a lesson." I eyed Rabas's grulla again. "You got any cravin' to be hanged for a horse thief?"

"Ah, to hell with it," Rabas muttered, and we took off on the trail to the caverns.

The sun was inching toward dusk when he said, "Better cut over to the right a bit here, unless you're figuring to pay Ives a visit."

I wasn't, so we did. Then I recollected the three Ives hands that had been left on our doorstep. "You want to leave your new horse outside our back door?"

"No," he growled, looking hard at me and nodding. "I'd plumb forgot them three rannies. You reckon they'll clear out if we tell 'em to get the hell off our property?''

"More like to shoot first and talk later, I'd imagine. What do you want to do?''

"I sure don't want to get this horse shot.''

"All right," I said. "We better tie these sprinters in the brush someplace and see if we can get the drop on those jaspers.''

We got off and anchored our mounts, and set off on foot for the cavern's entrance. Night wasn't far off now. We skinned back our ears for sounds from Ives's men. And didn't hear a thing. "Funny," Rabas muttered.

"Maybe they've sacked out.''

"Drunk, more like. They wouldn't all three of them sack out.''

We moved on warily, guns in hand, still not hearing anything to get our blood up. We could see the entrance now beyond the broken brush. "You reckon he's called 'em off?" Rabas scowled.

"Give a signal to your boys.''

Rabas gave a nighthawk call. Another call came back. "We're coming in," I said, raising my voice.

"Come ahead," Brady called.

"Where's Ives's hands?" Rabas growled.

"Ain't they out there?''

Rabas took the lid off his can of private cusswords. "You stay here," I said. "I'll go get the horses.''

When I came back with them, Rabas was waiting in front of the entrance. "Somethin' funny about this. They've gone sure as hell," he said.

Chapter Fifteen

Defending the Golden Grab

Rabas and I got Wendy off to ourselves before we joined the others around Coosie's supper fire. I could see how excited she was to learn we three were now the owners of record of the renamed lost Yuma mine.

"The Golden Grab," she said thoughtfully after the initial flush of elation, "isn't a bad name when you consider its history. But changing the name won't disguise the ore from any who've seen the chunks my father brought out, even if Swink and Mungo don't talk." She stared at me. "Have you given any thought to what's sure to happen?"

Rabas said, "You mean more people out combing the country?"

"Yes. And if those two talk, and I'm afraid they're bound to, we're going to have to contend with a full-blown stampede."

I had spent considerable energy thinking, wondering, and guessing without turning up any happy solutions. But I had discovered what I felt to be a number of urgent musts. I said, "Salaratus and Rabas's three hands had better be given shares in this bonanza, or they're like to be hatching some pretty dangerous notions. If there's one single thing we three can't afford, it's a mutiny."

Right off the bat, Wendy's back went up. "Why," she cried indignantly, "should we divide with a bunch of hired hands? You must have bats in your belfry, Hardigan!"

"We've got enough enemies now," I said. "I said. "In addition to Swink and that hardcased Mungo, there's Ives to be reckoned with and, quite possibly, Apaches. To me that's ample reason not to antagonize four more, who, so to speak, are in a position to cut our throats."

"Hardigan's right," Rabas said with conviction.

Wendy, up on her high horse, glared. "My father would never—"

"Your father, Wendy, got himself killed."

She had on a divided skirt and blouse. The skirt was of leaf green corduroy, and the blouse was a print—blue cornflowers on a yellow ground. With her head thrown back and green eyes flashing, she made an arresting picture.

"Use your head, girl," I said, having no time for beating around any bushes. "We'll probably—almost certainly, have to manage some way to barricade this place. To do that, we'll need willing workers, persons who have a real stake in the outcome. Think! This morning we were no better off than they were. Now we're owners of an incredibly rich ledge. How can we afford not to give them a share in it?"

"He's right," Rabas said.

That was like pouring oil on a conflagration. Wendy's

chin shot out, her eyes turned furious, but before she let go of the words bottled in her, she must have seen the look on my face because she bit down on her lip and finally let out some of her rage in a sigh.

"How much?" she demanded, the words dropping into the silence like icicles.

Rabas looked at me. I said, "We came on this hunt with a firm understanding that whatever we found would be divided in fourths. Now that Swink's out of this, his share could be divided between our four hands. We three would lose no more than was already agreed on, and the people we will have to depend on will have a real incentive—"

"Incentive for what?"

"To stick with us instead of helping destroy us."

As her father's daughter, brought up as she was, she found it hard to see justice in anything that diminished her own inclinations. We contained our impatience and gave what I'd said sufficient time to sink in. She still didn't like it but presently said with at least some effort to tone down her resentment, "Very well."

"It's my belief—I nodded—"that we should tell them right now."

None of them said much when I announced the decision which made them part owners of The Golden Grab. Their faces went through a gamut of expressions, but on the whole it seemed evident we had bought, if not loyalty, at least the incentive I had felt they must have, to bind us all in a common self-interest.

I said, "It seems Ives has pulled off the three hired guns he had keeping cases outside. Why, we don't know, but I believe we can expect them back very shortly. Meantime, we've got to barricade the way out past that ledge—we're too greatly outnumbered to keep an eye on more than one place at a time. Among the supplies we fetched in here are quite a number of canvas oresacks. Swink got out of here by an exit he discovered leading out of the second cavern, beyond the pool.

"It's my notion we should fill enough sacks with sand to block that exit just back of the brush that, from outside, conceals it. Later, if desirable, we can fill some of the other bags with ore from the ledge to strengthen this defense. I suggest two of you should take care of this while the other two help Rabas and me to widen the passage that leads to this exit. I further propose we get busy on these projects right away."

Craig, one of Rabas's three hands, spoke up to inquire who'd be watching the original entrance. I said, "Miss Eldridge has graciously offered to do this," and was pleasantly surprised when she raised no objections.

Brady and Crag offered to work on the wall and went off to get picks and shovels, while Salaratus and the other ugly departed to get sacks and another shovel to aid in the filling. Rabas picked up three rifles and followed me into the second cavern, where we waited for the picks and shovels by the entrance to the escape hatch.

Soon as the two with the hardware appeared, we put them to work making this hole wide and tall enough to accommodate a horse, having in mind a later possible need. Rabas asked if anyone had thought to feed and water our transport. Craig said he and the third Rabas hand had taken care of that while we were talking to "the madam."

The two hands got to work with a will, while Rabas and myself shoveled the debris out of the way. In half an hour they'd enlarged the opening to a height and width that satisfied all of us. We then got to work widening the gut to an even greater dimension, digging into the ledge some six or seven feet, all this accomplished with no alarms from where Wendy was keeping her vigil.

Rabas and I stacked the larger chunks of ore against the opposite wall, to be picked up by the bag fillers, who already were carrying filled sacks to the exit and building a wall that shut out any vestige of daylight. Rabas had thought shoulder-high would be sufficient and would allow for returning the fire of anyone outside who might be trying to get in. Lead plums coming in from outside, I reminded him, could make this gut untenable with ricochets flying all over the place. So we walled up the exit. "If they try tearing it down, one gun in the cavern-end shouldn't have much trouble driving them off."

"Unless," Rabas said, "they should ignite a few sticks of dynamite."

This sobering thought was a dire possibility I hadn't considered.

By first light we had the place about as safe as we could make it, with the exit blocked by a solid wall. And back of that another good foot of stacked ore from the ledge. As we all tramped off to join Wendy for breakfast, our four helpers indulged in an enthusiastic gabble about the unusual high quality of the ore they'd been handling.

She had not been idle and produced pans of refried beans, two biscuits each, and a gallon of scalding java.

While we were eating, Rabas suggested putting at least one guard on the entrance again. "We don't want to be surprised if Ives's boys come back or those Apaches decide to pay us a visit."

"What do you suppose Ives is up to?" Wendy asked.

"Whatever it is won't be to our advantage," Rabas said.

"I'm more worried right now about them red devils than I am about Ives—and we don't want to forget Swink and that hard-nosed Mungo."

"How deep do you reckon that ledge goes down?" Brady asked.

Rabas shrugged.

"Your guess," I grumbled, "would probably come nearer the mark than mine."

"You know," Rabas said, "I've been thinkin'. There's damn little law around these parts. We're pretty vulnerable here. Special if word gits out—and I reckon it's bound to— about our filing this claim. The location's on tap in that ledger in the Globe recorder's office. Anyone could go in there and have himself a look, and from that it wouldn't be no time at all before a swarm of gold-hungry galoots is camped right on our doorstep. And here's another notion we better consider—suppose Swink and Mungo team up with Ives? And suppose after that, Ives brings his whole crowd down on us?"

Wendy chewed on her lip. "Do you think he'd dare?"

"If he could see a good enough profit, Nick Ives would dare anything, and that Mungo could turn wilder than a hydrophoby skunk."

We didn't have to wait long to get a foretaste of what that trip to the recorder's office was like to put into motion. Before we got into our blankets that night, Craig, coming off his stint of guard duty at the entrance, said grimly that a couple dozen hombres loaded down with picks and shovels were setting up housekeeping just this side of the Reservation trail.

Though we'd halfway been expecting something like this, the fact of its happening shook up all of us. In a babble of concerned exclamations, every last one of us took off for a look.

They were there all right. Tents were going up. Men were pacing off dimensions as a preliminary to staking claims, amid a gabble of voices. "I was afraid of this," Wendy said, and the slap of her glance against my face said plainer than words that she held me accountable. "Well, what are you going to do?" she demanded.

I took a hitch on my temper. "What do you expect me to do?"

"Get them out of there!"

"I'll sleep on it," I answered. "Chasing off thirty jaspers who figure on becoming overnight millionaires is going to require a heap of thinking."

She gave me the sort of look most men wouldn't take without it came from a wedded wife. But, managing by considerable effort to keep my mouth shut, I strode off to my bedroll and turned in for the night.

It was plain—at least to me—that stamping a boot at those clowns wasn't like to get us anyplace. We were going to have to come up with something pretty drastic, and on that thought I finally got to sleep.

By morning the stampede had doubled in size and no sign of a let-up.

Rabas said, after we'd finished eating, "How do you want to handle this?" and, before I could answer, Wendy cried, "I don't care how you do it, just get that rabble out of here!"

"Worst thing we could do," I said, "is kill somebody. I'll go talk to them."

Wendy's lip curled. "A fat lot of good that'll do. I hope I haven't misjudged you, Hardigan!"

With heat surging into my face, I beckoned Brady and

Rabas and went striding off to the entrance. I couldn't see but one of Ives's crew in that mob but reckoned one rotten apple would be more than plenty. While I was looking them over, Craig joined us with a pair of rifles under each arm.

"All right, boys," I called, raising my voice. "You've had your fun, now it's time to clear out. You're on private property—"

"Like hell!" Ives's understrapper shouted. "We know the dimensions of your claim. Ain't nothin' in the law says we can't stake alongside—"

"You boys are inside our six hundred and forty, and I advise you to clear out before someone gets hurt."

That got some attention. That whole bunch quit whatever they'd been doing to put angry eyes on me. Ives's man yelled, "Havin' a homestead claim to this land's got nothing to do with it! A mineral claim—"

"A mineral claim," I cut him off, "won't keep you from getting shot."

From someplace amongst them a rifle cracked, the slug whizzing past not three inches from my head to slap into a rock and go whining away. "Get under cover and let them have it," I growled, "but no killing." I grabbed one of Craig's rifles and knocked a leg out from under Ives's rep. He let out a shout and went down in his tracks. Before the rest of that bunch shook loose of the shock, all four of us were safely under cover.

Six or seven of the stampeders flung themselves into saddles and spurred off out of range. A dozen others opened fire, and ricocheting slugs filled the air with shrill whines.

"We've got to scare the hell out of them," I muttered, and knocked another man sprawling. We winged five more in as many seconds, and while a few kept shooting back at us, most of that bunch out there ran for their horses and took off like the heel flies were after them. When two more of them dropped, one of those left commenced waving a white rag. "You win," he cried. "Gives us time to put those boys on their horses and we'll clear out."

Fifteen minutes later there wasn't a stampeder in sight.

I told Craig, "Go set fire to those tents."

"What about them picks and shovels?" Rabas asked.

"Break up the shovels and fetch the pick handles back."

When I went back inside, I said to Wendy, "Somebody better hightail it for Globe and take out homestead papers to cover these caverns."

She said, "What good will that do?"

"At least it will keep someone else from doing it. I'll send Rabas."

"No," she said, "someone might put a slug into him. I'll go myself. I doubt they'll want to be accused of shooting a woman. I'll fetch back a burlap sack full of groceries."

"I'd better send someone with you, or go myself."

"You're needed here. And I don't want anyone with me. I'll be safer alone."

I wasn't sure about that, but arguing with Wendy looked about as useful as talking to stone.

After she had departed, I went out and helped Rabas collect the picks left behind and get the handles out of them; these, I reckoned, would be first-rate for keeping Coosie's fire going—there must have been close to four dozen, though neither of us bothered to count. We took the shovels along also and told Salaratus to use these first. "An' what'll I do with the shovel part?" he asked.

"Pile them up somewhere out of your way."

By this time the tents were nothing but ashes, including most of the things left inside them. Craig said, "We'll probably have a new crop on hand by morning."

Rabas shook his head. "Word'll git around, and with at least a dozen of those galoots with holes in either their legs or arms it don't seem a heap likely too many others will be wanting to risk it. We could put up a *Private Property* sign, but with the kind of cover we've got and no cover for them, it'll take a pretty brash fool to try that again. We'd better pull up the stakes those buggers put out—more wood for Coosie."

It was late evening, almost supper time, before Wendy returned.

"How'd it go?"

This got me one of her high and mighty looks. "A lot of talk going round. And," she said with an edge to her voice, "that sheriff gave me a lecture on people's rights. Said he'd had a good many complaints."

"A wonder he didn't arrest you," Craig said.

"I thought he was leading up to it. I said if he did, our bunch would come in and wreck the town. So he backed off but said if he got any more complaints he reckoned he'd have to do something about it—he didn't specify what."

"Did you file for a homestead?" I asked her.

She nodded, and I said. "Let's have the measurements and I'll get it staked."

Rabas said, "Where's the grub you were going to pick up?"

"I got the grub," she said, looking ready to bite nails, "and about three miles out of town four of Ives's hands waylaid me and took it away from me. They talked pretty rough about what they'd do to the next one of us unlucky enough to fall into their hands. I recognized one of them, that fellow they call Moriarty."

"Never mind," I said, patting her shoulder. "You did

101

first-rate—a whole heap better than any of us could have done.''

''I don't think I'd have been stopped if you'd been along,'' she said, sounding vengeful.

''Yes, well . . .''

''If he'd been along,'' Rabas said, ''I expect they'd have killed him.''

''Yeah,'' Brady said. ''That Moriarty's meaner than gar soup sprinkled with tadpoles.''

Chapter Sixteen

Encounter at Globe

These were dire things to think of.

I said, trying to find reassurance, "We're pretty well fixed to hold off anything except a determined mass attack. Or dynamite," I reluctantly added.

"Well, there's one more thing we could do," Rabas nodded. "We could build up two foot of sandbags about forty feet this side of the entrance to give us some protection if it comes to a shoot-out. And we could rig a couple trip wires about ten feet inside the opening. If we had any wire, which we haven't."

"We got plenty of rope," Brady said, "and if we string it back of the bend where light from outside won't show it up, we could sure play hell with any horsebackers tryin' to git in here."

"Good thought." Rabas nodded. "Take care of it, Brady.

And Craig and Arbuckle can be filling more sacks to build a redoubt we can shoot from behind."

"And soon as that's done, I want it manned by two men with rifles. And the rest of us, except Miss Eldridge," I said, "can be hacking some more ore out of that ledge. Fix up the carbide lamps, Coosie."

"You bet," Salaratus said, "and I'll help dig."

So Rabas and me went back to the ledge with a lamp apiece and started hacking. When Coosie joined us, we began to see progress. "Too bad we don't have a wheelbarrow," Rabas said, "to get this stuff out from underfoot. We got any more empty sacks back there?"

"Not over a dozen," Salaratus said. "But we could pile some of it back of this barricade where we put those big chunks."

It occurred to me if we had to bust out of here in a hurry, a lot of loose rock would be no advantage, but we'd troubles enough without hunting for more. "How's the grub holding out?"

"We've still got some canned stuff, but that's about all," Coosie answered. "If you want, I'm willin' to light out fer Globe. . . ."

"Be some risk," Rabas said, gloomily adding, "We might not be here long enough to bother."

"I'll go," I said.

As I went after my horse, it came to me that at one time or another I'd done some pretty foolish things, but this probably topped the lot.

I encountered no difficulties getting to Globe and walked my new sorrel around to the loading dock in back of the mercantile. Being short of cash, I had brought along a chunk of ore about the size of a turkey's egg, which I had inside my shirt. I just chanced to glance through the window on my way to the front door, and lucky I did, for there, leaning a hip against the counter back of his toothbrush mustache and black patch, was Mungo. Which was enough to send me back to my horse.

As I snatched up the reins and was reaching for the horn, the back door flung open, and Swink, gun in hand, bulged into the blaze of the lowering sun. That glare full in his eyes was all that saved me. In the second it took him to get me in focus, I put a slug alongside his head and he went out of sight behind the slammed door.

I went into the saddle with one leaping jump as a gun beat up the echoes behind me. No need to look—it had to be Mungo. I looked anyway just as the sorrel took me round the far corner. Something like a hot poker rapped me back of the shoulder, and only by grabbing onto his mane was I able to stay with my hard-running horse. But I had seen all I wanted—a pair of Ives's gunslingers firing from the window.

My whole shoulder felt numb, but I clamped my teeth on the unwanted knowledge that I had to get away from this town in a hurry. I sent the horse between buildings, hunting protection, and larruped him onto the Reservation trail, knowing I'd soon have the whole pack behind me.

With the sorrel stretched into his best pounding gallop, I kept telling myself all I really had to do was just hang on. I wasn't sure that I could, with the pain knifing through me; but knew if I didn't this would be my last run.

When I heard them behind me, I sent the game sorrel slamming through brush with the slap of lead plums snapping twigs all around and the screech of a ricochet shuddering past me. I reckon I prayed—for the horse, not for me. Without the sorrel there would be no tomorrow.

I hadn't much hope I could shake them off, but they wouldn't be knowing about my brush with Apaches, so the deeper I could get into Indian lands the less likely they'd be to continue the chase. This, at least, was what was brightest in mind.

I could feel the stickiness of blood on my back. What I yearned for most was some kind of distraction, and I think in those moments I'd have welcomed Apaches.

Ironically enough, no yelling redskins appeared; the brush thinned out and we were hurtling across the spine of a ridge with dust ballooning back of us. I flung the heaving sorrel down a slope at right angles in a desperate bid to get back on the trail.

Chapter Seventeen

A Desperate Trip

We must have reached it ahead of them—I couldn't be sure with things getting hazy, but it seemed like we must be well past the springs.

It came into my head—with a crew large as Ives had— that some of his hands might be back at the caverns and I'd better slow down before I ran full tilt into them.

With terrible effort, I got my head turned around for a stare at the backtrail. All I saw was a blur of dying sun splotched with shadows and a dark-like river fog thickening up to close around me.

I seemed to be losing all sense of direction. The horse, still heaving, had dropped to a walk. Things were black, getting blacker; I tried to tighten my grip, sensing that all too soon I'd likely pitch from the saddle.

Abruptly, dimly, a sound of voices came through the fog,

and I felt hands take hold of me, and I seemed to float down a long spiral into a softness that was wholly black.

I imagined I would float in this dark silence forever. I thought that if this was death, I must have crossed the divide, but it wasn't so bad as I had guessed it would be. I didn't hurt anymore. I don't reckon I felt anything except perhaps a serene kind of lethargy.

Next thing I noticed was a rough sort of thing digging into my cheek, and someway I got my eyes jerked open and found it was a fold in the blanket under my head. This appeared so odd that I sent my glance rummaging round and discovered what looked to be the glimmer of a fire off to the left of me someplace. That seemed queer too.

I don't know how much later it was that I heard the crunch of boots getting louder, apparently coming nearer, and I shifted onto my back. The bootsteps stopped. "How do you feel?" a casual voice asked indifferently.

The voice seemed familiar, but I couldn't see anyone until I realized my eyes were shut and jerked them open. It was lighter now in a flickery sort of way and I reckoned someone had thrown fresh wood on the fire. And I saw Wendy bending over me. I said, "Are you here, too?"

"Of course I'm here—don't you know where you are?" And then, back of her, I saw Rabas; things began to come back and it came to me I must be in one of the caverns. And then abruptly I remembered being chased out of Globe. I tried to get up and fell back with a groan.

"Take it easy," Rabas growled. "Rome wasn't built in a day," he said gruffly.

"How long have I been here?"

"You been damn lucky," Rabas grumbled.

"How long?" I demanded ungratefully.

Wendy was eyeing me with considerable disdain. "Three days and four nights."

I reckoned that explained the way my gut was behaving. They had me naked from the waist up. To take care of the bandaging, probably. But I'd been studying my arm. Didn't look like the arm I remembered. Seemed thinner and the meat didn't cling to the bone like it used to. "No wonder I feel like the last rose of summer."

Wendy flushed. Rabas said, to give credit where due, "She's been spooning stuff into you—"

"Slop, I reckon."

Wendy cried, indignant, "You needn't act put upon— we've been living on rations ever since you left! Where are the groceries you went after?"

So I told them how it had been at Globe and why I'd got out of there in such a hustle. And Rabas said, "You should've taken the grulla."

"Lucky I didn't—he'd have made a great target."

And Wendy said, "Those damn hired hands!"

I expect I was easily riled right then, too ornery to put a hobble on my tongue. "I was a damn hired hand till you up and made me a partner."

Flushing, she said, "I wasn't poking at you—anyway, you're different."

"Trouble with you is you jump at conclusions. You latched onto me on account of my rep—you reckoned I'd gun you out of your troubles."

"What's wrong with that?" Wendy bridled.

"It's just like the way you lay into Rabas. No justification. I can generally manage to hit what I aim at but all I ever been was a cowhand. That's what you bought, not a gunslingin' killer."

She listened bitterly and when I got done she said, "I'll go collect Salaratus and get him started on supper."

When she had gone, Rabas said, "You hadn't ought to of spoke to her that way—she thinks a heap of you, Hardigan."

I gave a snort of disgust. "Never would have reckoned you had bats in your belfry. What you been doing while I've been laid up?"

"Just hackin' away at that ledge like the rest of them. Sometimes I think it goes halfway to Frisco. We've got a forty-foot passage out there beyond the water—cut a regular goddamn room from that gut."

"What have you done with the ore?"

"Dumped it into the pool. Best storage we could find."

"Working like peons—"

"Just protectin' my investment," Rabas grinned.

"You got any idea why Wendy's so down on you?"

"Don't you reckon you ought to get a little rest?"

"For Chrissake, Rabas, answer the question."

He eyed me queerly, let out a long breath. "Aside from the way her old man raised her, cow folks generally don't cotton to sheepmen."

"Sheepmen come in all shapes and sizes."

"Yeah. Well, her old man figured he was two or three cuts above the common herd. Must of been a powerful bad day for him havin' to come to the likes of me for enough spare cash to tide him over."

"He borrowed money from you?"

"That note against Broken Arrow. Guess you reckoned I'd forged it."

"Sorry. I'd forgot about that."

"Because a man raises sheep don't guarantee he's a

crook. More money in sheep than there is in cows—a sight more.'' He showed a grim smile. ''More work, too.''

''How well did you know Wendy's father?''

''Didn't know him at all. He come to me when his cow-crowd friends got tired of bailin' him out.''

''Seems he got into Ives pretty deep.''

''In them days Ives figured to marry it back.''

I said to him curiously, ''Must be costing you something, keeping three gunfighters here.''

Rabas dug up a smile. ''Well, yes an' no. Got me a bigger stake in this deal than I figured on. Hell, what are friends for?''

I said, ''I can't understand why we've not heard from Ives.''

''We'll hear from him, don't worry. I expect he wants to make sure of his edge.''

''Do you think he's foreclosed?''

''That takes a bit of time. If he's moved onto your spread, he probably figures he's put in the spadework, possession bein' something the law tips its hat to.''

Chapter Eighteen

A Little Visit

The next day they let me get up for a while. The shoulder felt a mite stiff, like a saddle that's been in the barn too long, and seemed addicted to twinges if moved without caution.

I was plumb bored with resting. And considerably worried about the shortage of grub. I mentioned this to Rabas. He said, "I could send them three uglies to Globe and like enough, nobody'd jump them. But I've got me a notion this could be what Ives is waitin' on."

I'd have been willing to chance this but they weren't my hands. I was anxious to have a look at what they'd accomplished while I'd been keeping that damn blanket warm, and mentioned this to Wendy after Rabas went off to join the workers on the ledge.

"Well, maybe tomorrow if you think you feel up to it," she conceded.

Not that it mattered, but I couldn't see how Rabas came by the notion that she had any more use for me than for one of his uglies. And maybe not as much now that I'd told her I was no pistolero.

"You been tending me all this while?" I asked.

"Off and on. Rabas helped."

That was a concession at any rate, giving the sheepman any credit at all. She was looking off toward the fire, a bundle of contradictions, I thought. "Must have burnt a heap of brush since we've been here."

She nodded. "They've cleaned out everything right up to the trail."

"Fine," I said. "Make it harder for anyone to surprise us."

"They'd be fools to attempt to get in here now."

"The world's full of fools," I reminded her. "Some might say *we* were fools barricading ourselves in this sort of place where we're cut off from food or anything else. Just a question of time, and we'll be starved out."

She said, sounding scornful, "Must you always look on the gloomiest side?"

"Well, I've had a lot of practice." I said, "If you'll fetch me my razor and a pan of water, I'll scrape off some of the hair I've been growing."

As she started away without bothering to answer, I called after her, "How's that horse I was riding?"

"He hasn't turned up his nose at the oats he's been getting. And that's something else we're about to get out of."

She came back with the water and razor and the small pocket mirror she'd brought along for herself. After I'd

113

shaved, I felt considerably more able to face up to our plight. We were in a bad bind but I could easily recall having been in worse.

It was my left shoulder that had taken the bullet and who-ever had worked on it—probably Rabas—had done a good job, for it was healing nicely. But whenever I lifted that arm I could feel something grate and was forcibly reminded that I was not recovered yet.

With her help, I managed to get into a shirt, but she'd seen me wince. For a second I thought to read concern in her glance, but it was gone so quick I might easily have imagined it. She said, "Tell me again what happened at Globe."

So I went over it once more. And she said, darkly thoughtful, "So it was one of Ives's hands that shot you. I hadn't realized that. Do you think Swink and Mungo are tied in with Ives?"

"Guess they could be. Or it might just be they saw a chance to get even for that roughneck that Craig shot."

Still looking thoughtful, she asked, "If you weren't a hired gun back in Texas how did you acquire such a repu-tation?"

I still couldn't imagine she was at all interested in me as a person but I told her about the bar brawl that had led to the death of that fifteen-year-old boy. "He hadn't anything to do with it," I said. "He rushed in from outside just as this bruiser came after me with a broken bottle. I was al-ready pretty banged up from the ruckus. The whole room knew he meant to finish me off. I was too beat up to take any more, so when he lunged for me with that goddam bottle I yanked out my gun, intending to let him have it. Just as I fired, this kid ducked in front of me and caught it. The town marshal was right behind him and saw the whole thing. He locked the bruiser up for starting the brawl and told me to clear out. The garbled story got around and inside two weeks the only truth left in it was my killing of that kid. After that nobody would hire me—they figured I spelt trouble. Prejudice, of course. Same kind of prejudice you feel against Rabas.''

I reckon I shouldn't have added that last. I saw the furious look she flung me, but before she could speak, Brady called out from the entrance, *''Hold it right there!''*

Wendy's startled look crossed mine and Craig came out of the shadows to say, ''They want to talk with an owner—''

''You're an owner,'' Wendy said.

''I think they want Hardigan.''

''Probably want to see if I'm still above ground—''

''And if you are, they'll finish you off!'' Wendy cried angrily. ''I'll talk to them, Craig.''

So we both went out there and in the glare of the sun saw five or six horsebackers just this side of the trail sitting their saddles like they'd just bought the place. The one with the toothbrush mustache hailed our arrival with a grin. It was Mungo, of course, and in top form.

''You're lookin' at Ives's new foreman, sport, and this is my sidekick, Mr. Benjamin Swink, who used to be an assayer of other folks' ore but is figurin' right soon to be assayin' his own. Seems like somebody's jumped his claim, so I said we'd come along and straighten things out.''

''Very obliging of you, Mungo. And just how did you reckon to do that?'' I asked.

''If the jumpers ain't got no better sense . . . by sheer weight of numbers,'' Mungo informed us. He tossed a bright look at Swink from his good eye. ''Do I have that right, Benny?''

Swink licked his lips and said, "You sure have."

"Very interesting." I nodded. "The latchstring's off—come right in whenever it suits you."

We eyed each other awhile. Mungo chuckled. "You're lookin' right chipper, and brash as ever. I'll remind you, sport, this ain't the only way into those caverns, and I don't reckon them peons you've got workin' for you are goin' to be anxious to get themselves slaughtered."

"Matter of fact," I said, "we're all owners here. You better get some more help."

"We got plenty of that," Mungo answered. "No problem at all. It's just that we don't like to see innocent lives get cut off in their prime. Now you boys, an' the lady, come out empty-handed and you're free to go any place you've a mind to." He showed his teeth in a nasty smile. "Otherwise . . . well, you know the old sayin' about dead men tellin' no tales, I reckon."

"I know a lot of old sayings," I told him, casual. "But the plain truth of the matter, Mungo, is you haven't a Chinaman's chance of taking over this ledge."

"Matter of opinion," he came back with a chuckle. "We got this place sealed up, sport. No way you can git out of there without we're agreeable. And we can always blast you out. Think it over while you're starving."

Wheeling his horse, he took off down the trail, the rest of his outfit strung out behind him.

"Well," Wendy said, "where do we go from here?"

"We don't go nowhere. We just sit pat." I looked at her grimly. "Only way they'll risk using dynamite is if no other way will budge us."

"You know," Craig said, "now that bunch has rode off would be a first-rate chance to git grub from Globe."

" 'Fraid not," I told him. "They've probably planned it this way, hoping we'd think so. Anyone trying to make Globe will get shot." I looked at Wendy. "How big a crew has Ives got, all told?"

"At least twenty," Wendy said in a worried tone. "He always keeps a big crew—makes him feel important, and he can well afford it."

"See what I mean?" I said to Craig. "He's sure to have three or four hanging out at Globe and others scattered along the way, Apache style, waiting to bushwhack whoever tries to get through."

Wendy and I went back inside. "I'm going to habla with Rabas." I struck off for the ledge, feeling less confident than I hope I sounded. Honestly, I couldn't see any way out of this if Mungo and Ives had the patience to wait.

"They won't wait," Rabas said when I found him. "Before you're a day older they'll be trying somethin' else. I know Ives from long experience. He likes the edge, but he's short on patience. I'm surprised he hasn't stormed this place already." He spat on his hands and grabbed up his pick. "Set down and rest while I help these boys get out some more ore."

We got through the day and, on mighty short rations, another night. Next morning, bright and early, Rabas said to me, "I've got a sneakin' hunch we'd be wise to have us a look at the country outside that blocked ledge exit. I don't want to unblock it. You got any ideas?"

"Take a couple horses and ride out for a look."

"My thought exactly. I'll git Brady—"

"No," I said. "I'll go with you myself."

"You reckon you're up to it?" Rabas said, concerned.

"Sure. I'm tough as whangstring."

Rabas saddled his big grulla and I took the sorrel, and with no more ado we rode into the open, my first jaunt outside since I'd come back from Globe. Every once in awhile a nerve grated in my sore shoulder, but it was nothing I couldn't put up with.

Sun was turning the eastern sky faintly pink, forecasting its imminent climb above the crags. Birds were chirping off in the brush and back inside the cavern some horses let out a whinny. "Hate to see us go off without 'em, I reckon," Rabas mentioned. "Keep your rifle handy."

This last was compatible with thoughts I was thinking. I was not surprised we'd been allowed to come out, even though we'd discovered no sign of surveillance. Ives's watchers, if any, probably wanted us far enough into the windy open to give them a good chance to cut us off.

"You know how far off that ledge entrance is?"

"Not much over a quarter of a mile. I took a look awhile back. You'll remember, I expect, there's a mort of brush thereabouts." He said, as though picturing it in his mind, "But not close up. I had the uglies clear about forty foot next to the exit."

We were taking it easy, walking our mounts. They were getting thinned down like the rest of us. With a wary eye peeled to scan the roundabout brush, I was startled when Rabas, reaching out, caught hold of my arm. The urgency of it jerked my head around. He gestured with his chin. "Over there."

What looked like a huddle of discarded clothes lay in a heap not ten feet from the entrance to the ledge.

Chapter Nineteen

The Body Out Back

"Well," Rabas said, "this is one piece of deviltry I hadn't been expectin'."

"You know who it is?"

"Let's find out."

We urged our reluctant horses, rolling their eyes and nervously snorting, half a rope's length nearer. They didn't like it no better than we did.

Rabas got down, pushed the fellow over with his boot and said, "Uh-huh—Swink. Bushwhacked," he added. "Shot in the back from mebbe two foot away."

"Why do you suppose they'd kill one of their own?"

Rabas gave a short laugh. "They'll lay it onto us. Killed, so to speak, right on our back doorstep." He stood awhile thinking. "They'll be fetchin' some law out here. Question is—do we move him or don't we?"

"If he's not here when they come, they'll say we dragged him off, tried to hide him. . . ."

"And if they can't find him," Rabas said, "they've got no case."

"If they bring dogs they'll find him."

"I doubt there's a bloodhound nearer than Tucson. And anyway they'd have to have a piece of his clothing, a boot or something that's got his smell on it." He looked at me quizzically. "You're the boss."

"Well, damn it, I don't want to be."

"Me, either. But the longer we stick around, the more likely we'll be tagged with this frame. If you don't want to move him, there's another thing you might do. Pick up his pistol and put four shots into one of them sandbags. Then drop it beside him. But we can't claim self-defense with that bullet in his back."

I swore. Gritting my teeth, I said, "We'll move him."

Rabas removed the six-shooter from Swink's holster and put four shots into a pair of the sandbags that were about breast high. He tossed down the pistol. Then, scowling, snatched it up and shoved it into Swink's holster. "Be dumb to leave it layin' there. Catch hold of my reins—I'll see if I can get him onto my horse."

The big grulla sidled round but Rabas presently got the body draped across his saddle, tied it down, and climbed up behind me. "Let's get the hell back where we belong."

"Thought we were going to bury him someplace."

"You bet," Rabas said. "I don't know no better place than in them caverns. Let's git outa here."

We caused plenty of excitement and some consternation when, ten minutes later, we rode through our front entrance. We both got off just inside and led both horses over the trip ropes and around our little barricade of sand-filled sacks.

"Are you out of your minds?" Wendy cried, looking with horror at Swink's limp body.

"We're going to bury him deep in that farthest cavern. We'll tell you about it later. Right now three of you boys grab picks and shovels and come along on the double," I said as Rabas led the grulla off into the dark. "Better bring along three or four lamps," I added, "so we can see what we're doing."

Half an hour later we had Swink's body seven feet under the dirt we'd dug out, packed down firm and with the top nicely leveled, flush with the cavern's floor. On top of it we piled up ten sacks of ore.

Then we all went back to cook's fire for a good-sized helping of refried beans, washed down with a couple cups each of Coosie's oft-diluted java. This was when we told Wendy and the others about finding him.

We hadn't long to wait.

About ten o'clock we heard approaching hoofbeats and Craig up at the entrance yelled, "Company comin'!"

Rabas and I followed Wendy up there to learn the worst.

Five of Ives's crew, plus black-patched Mungo and a sheriff's deputy, sat their saddles in our brush-cleared dooryard some twenty feet this side of the trail. "You're riding in pretty poor company, Sheriff," Wendy remarked in her scornfulest voice.

"It's been reported," he said, "that someone called Hardigan shot and killed Ben Swink last night. What do you know about this? And where's Hardigan? I've a warrant for his arrest."

Mungo said, "That's Hardigan standin' alongside her, with Rabas."

"Who reported this cock-and-bull story?" Wendy wanted to know.

"It was reported by Mr. Ives's foreman, Mungo, and sworn to by these boys with me. I call on you, Hardigan, to—"

"Just a minute," I said, stepping away from Wendy. "I think perhaps you're barking up the wrong tree. Last time I saw Swink was day before yesterday when he showed up here with this same bunch of hardcases you've got with you now, demanding we turn over to them the lost Yuma mine Miss Eldridge's father—"

"The truth," Mungo said, "is that these people are trespassin' on land belonging to Mr. Ives under the Homestead—"

Wendy gave a scornful laugh. "All who believe that can stand on their heads. Mungo's nothing but a trigger-happy gunslinger Ives has hired to get us off this mineral claim—"

"Which belonged to Swink, as the Globe records—"

"Those records," Wendy said, cutting him off, "will show that he voluntarily gave up that claim in favor of myself and partners."

I was watching the deputy, who couldn't have been much more than twenty and who now appeared considerably bewildered. "So, as I was saying when that gun-fighting foreman of Ives interrupted me, there are two ways of getting into these caverns. This right here is the main one, the one we use all the time—or did before this bunch you've got with you decided to bottle us up in here. The other entrance is by way of Eldridge's old Yuma gold mine. . . ."

"Yes," Mungo cut in. "That's where it happened. We were all over there tryin' to reason with these claim-jumpers. That ranny, Hardigan, had us under their rifles and told us to clear out. As we were turning to leave, he fired and poor old Benny fell out of the saddle."

"And what," Wendy asked, "makes you think Hardigan shot him?"

"The rest of your peons had gone off. Hardigan, at this point, was the only one there."

Rabas said, "He wasn't there. He was layin' on a blanket in this cavern right behind where we're standing now."

"Where he'd been," Wendy cried, "for the last four days after one of those gunfighters you've got in your posse shot him in Globe and then chased him all the way back here!"

Mungo yelled, "That's a barefaced lie! He was with your crew at the ledge entrance yesterday—we all saw him, heard him tell us to clear out under threat of those rifles, and then, when we were fixin' to do it, he shot poor Benny in the back!"

"Where's the body?" I asked. "What did you do? Leave your poor friend lying there?"

"He's there. How could we get him with your guns on us?"

He was talking, of course, as he'd been throughout, strictly for the deputy's benefit. I said to that bamboozled young fool, "Isn't it a bit unusual to get out a warrant simply on the words of a man who only showed up in this country less than a week ago?"

By now the deputy didn't know up from down, and looked it. "Have you examined the alleged body?" Wendy asked.

"No, ma'am. We . . . uh . . . hadn't got that far."

"I would have thought," she said with curled lip, "that would have been the first order of business."

When he started stuttering and spluttering she asked, "Do you know who I am?"

"Sure."

"Where is this man you accuse Hardigan—my partner—of killing?"

The deputy looked at Mungo, who said, "As mentioned before, the last we saw of him he was spraddled out in front of that other entrance to this place." He looked back at Wendy with a nasty sneer. "I suppose by now you've dragged him—"

"You crummy gunfighter," Wendy said, "we're not giving up Hardigan for you to kill along with this deputy on the way back to Globe." And, to the deputy, "Let me see that warrant."

He dug it out of his coat, passed it over. Wendy gave it one look and tore it up. "A pack of lies—"

"But these men," the boy cried, "have all sworn they saw Hardigan gun Swink down in cold blood!"

"That kind of riffraff would swear to anything. Show me the body."

"The sheriff is not going to like this—"

"I don't like it, either," Wendy snapped. "I think I'll ride in and have a talk with the sheriff and get this preposterous situation straightened out. Something else he should know is how these two-bit killers Ives has got on his payroll have bottled us up here intending to starve us into—"

The deputy threw up his hands. "I'm going to pick up the body, ma'am, and take it back to Globe and let the sheriff sort it out."

"That's just what you should do," Wendy approved.

Mungo, looking furious, swore. He snarled, glaring at the deputy, "You got no more backbone than a goddamn piece of paper!" He slammed back onto his horse. "I'll have a few things to say to the sheriff myself!"

*   *   *

"What do you suppose they'll do now?" Wendy asked me after the posse had taken themselves off.

"That deputy will go after the body. When he can't find a body, he'll go back to Globe and make his report."

"I'm afraid we haven't heard the last of this," Rabas growled. "Ives ain't goin' to give up that easy."

I said, "It looks like we're dealing with a political sheriff. If Ives and Mungo can't produce a body, I think he'll wash his hands of the whole thing. With an election coming on he'll try to keep his nose clean."

"Short of oats and short of grub, where's this going to leave us?" Salaratus wanted to know. "Without we get some of both, an' pronto, we sure can't hold out more'n another couple days."

"Tell you what," Rabas said out of the general gloom, "I'll take Brady and a couple pack horses, mosey over to my camp, and see if we can't pick up enough to tide us over. I don't reckon we'll be bothered—they'll probably figure we've pulled out."

I said, "Not when they spot you coming back with supplies."

Rabas laughed. "We'll cross that bridge when we come to it."

Chapter Twenty

Some Countermeasures

With the two pack horses, Rabas and Brady set off within the hour. I wanted them to take a few ore samples with them to use in place of money, but Rabas shook his head. "Can't afford to have my herders gettin' gold fever."

So we wished them good luck and settled down to wait. Salaratus and Arbuckle went back to work on the ledge. Craig elected to play guard at the entrance. Wendy and I sat around nursing our thoughts. "Suppose," she said, "the sheriff comes back with a search warrant?"

"I don't think he'll be doing that yet awhile. If Ives puts enough pressure on him, he might make a hit-or-miss hunt for the body, but I doubt if he'll work very hard at it."

She looked a bit dubious. "Well, I guess you know this class of people better than I do. You've been around them, know how they'll react. To me they're just riffraff, an alien breed."

For once I had the sense to keep my mouth shut. I reckoned her old man had shaped her attitude and nothing I could say was going to change it now. Now that Mungo's try at framing me with Swink's killing had sort of fizzled out for the moment, I wasn't too worried—wasn't, anyway, as uneasy as I had been when we discovered his body.

But I wasn't discounting how this was like to strike Ives. He would be hellbent to hatch up something else, but, as Rabas was fond of remarking, I could cross that bridge when I came to it. I didn't, right then, see what else he could do short of an all-out attack on these caverns. And I thought he would be too cagey to risk that.

What I tried to do while we sat around was figure some way of creating a distraction that would keep his bunch away from here. Like cutting his fences, maybe setting some of his buildings afire. The way he'd got himself extended, there couldn't be much of a guard at his headquarters.

More I thought of this notion, the better I liked it. At the least, I figured, it would relieve some of the pressure his deviltries was piling on us. But now with Rabas and Brady gone off to his sheep camp, we'd be pretty short-handed here if I slipped off too.

I told Wendy of this notion, and, instead of the veto I confidently expected, she appeared to be all for it. "That's a great idea," she declared, "and now would be just the time to do it while most of his hired guns are up there at Globe trying to prod the sheriff."

"That's a far piece, though," I said, eyeing her intently. "Sure you'll be safe here while three of us are gone?"

"I doubt they'll be back until they've wrung a favorable

decision from the high sheriff. He's a prize procrastinator. I'll be all right.''

So, still not quite easy in my mind, I saddled up the sorrel and, picking up a pair of wire cutters, set off.

Ives's spread—the northern boundary, at any rate—was just below the Reservation. To cut down the time I would have to be away, I took the trail for as far as it went, then cut across the lower part of the land the federal government had given the Apaches. There was some risk in this, but placed against the saving in time, I reckoned it was negligible. Most of the families lived farther north. And I expected, in the event I ran into a confrontation, to be able to talk my way out of it.

It was a fine afternoon with fluffy white clouds sailing across the blue like three-masters in convoy. I felt pretty good after wriggling out of Mungo's frame-up without being lugged off to jail—not that I'd ever expected to get there. To get rid of me once and for all, they'd have had nothing to do but finish me off as they had the assayer, claiming I'd tried to escape and had killed the deputy in the attempt. I couldn't doubt they were up to it. They were about as ranicky a bunch of conscienceless villains as I'd seen in a good while.

I reckoned that sooner or later I'd have to do something about Mungo. There was no quit in him.

By the time I got off the Reservation the sun was just about down, sending mile-long shadows across the juniper-studded range. It was cooler, too, with a wind coming up off the desert, and on account of the grit I had to pull up my wipe across nose and mouth. Even this little maneuver was not entirely risk-free; anyone seeing me might take me for a bandit and let go with the fireworks without bothering to do any talking.

When night closed around me, I felt considerably better. I had stopped several times to give the sorrel a breather. It must have been close on to seven when I came to Ives's wire. What I hoped to do was strictly illegal but we had to strike back—and soon, or see ourselves washed out of the picture, and that fat hog in possession of our bonanza.

This fence, like many of the cattle-baron stunts Ives got away with, was likewise illegal, having but four strands where the law demanded five. The only hesitation I had in cutting it came from trying to make sure I wasn't caught in the backlash; barbed wire can really tear a man up if he gets careless.

The wire parted with a *zing* as I jumped back to avoid it. One cut, three to go. The ends whizzed safely away in the second cut, and again in the third, whipping past the two nearest posts like the 4:45 out of Tucson. I looked again to my footing and safely made the final cut. And got back on my horse.

I surely ought, I thought, to open up more holes in Ives's fence, though even in this starlit dark I purely hated to spare the time. After thinking through the pros and the cons, I decided to put off more cuts till I was on my way out.

This whole thing was built on impulse and launched by Wendy's manifested delight—the vindictiveness of a woman who hadn't enough savvy to get out of the rain. This thought didn't occur to me until much later; right then I pressed on in my hunt for Ives's buildings, the location of which I should have learned before engaging in such a hare-brained exploit.

So I wasted two hours in this nervous search before coming onto them, lightless and stark in the shine of the stars.

From the rise we had paused on, peering through branches in a huddle of squat cedars, I conned the place for another ten minutes without any sound but our breathing, seeing no motion, no sign of activity. At last, satisfied, I kneed my flax-maned sorrel toward them.

I had never been particularly aggressive by nature but even a rat will bare its teeth if cornered, and I'd been shown all too clearly that this hog and his conniving foreman meant to separate us from this bonanza we'd filed on; meant, if they could manage, to bury me without compunction.

I felt around to be sure I'd plenty of matches and, seeing that the late-rising moon was about to show its face, told myself I could have done without it. I rode warily closer, seeing nothing to alarm me, and approached the back porch.

I sat there a few moments before getting out of the saddle, finding it hard to believe they'd left no one on guard. The only thing I could hear was the occasional snap and creak of cooling timbers as this old ranch headquarters settled on its foundations and, in the far-off distance, the yammering of a coyote.

I stepped down off the horse and up onto the warped, sun-bleached planks of the porch. I couldn't think why I should feel so nervous. Pushing open the door, I stepped into the kitchen, feeling my way in the dark past what appeared to be an office. I moved on into the house's main room, about the size of the sala at Broken Arrow. No curtains on the windows, no papers or magazines cluttering the table.

I edged back to the office, found a ledger on the desk, and ripped out a couple handfuls of pages. These I crumpled and, going back to the livingroom, thrust under a sofa and ignited with a match snapped to light on a thumbnail. I went back to the kitchen, moving faster now, anxious to get out of there before leaping flames should sound the alarm. In a corner by the pump-handled sink I found a coal-oil can that, by the heft, was half-full. I splashed some around in the office, went back to the livingroom dripping a little trail and flung out the rest of it. Tossed down a handful of lighted matches and was wheeling to make for the nearest window when the front door was thrown open and Ives's outraged voice yelled, *"Watch the windows!"*

He fired from the hip as I flung myself out of the brightening room. I heard the thump of slugs splintering the doorframe, wheeled past the office and into the kitchen. As I slammed through the door a hunched-over shape stepped around my horse and flame spat wickedly from the gun in his hand. Twice I fired and saw him go down as I sprang for the saddle. The sorrel was moving at his fastest gait when my feet found the stirrups.

Stretched out along his neck like an Indian, I rode through a hail of too-hurried shots, streaking for that huddle of cedars as Ives emptied his pistol, cursing like a drunken squaw.

Looking back, I'd no trouble making him out against the leap of flames bursting out of his house. I grabbed my rifle out of its scabbard, minded to knock him hellbent and crooked, but something restrained me; I just couldn't bring myself to do it—that damn soft streak, I reckoned, passed on from my mother.

Plainly apparent the house couldn't be saved, I knew Ives would be after me hellity-larrup with whatever hands might still be at headquarters. I wasted no regrets on the man I had shot but single-mindedly set out to put all the distance possible between myself and those towering flames back of me.

For ten minutes at least I kept the sorrel running full-out before I found enough sense to ease him into a lope. We had a long way to go and nothing but shanks' mare to go on if I ran this horse plumb into the ground or broke his leg in a gopher hole.

And it was just about then that another thought jolted me. We, in hatching this deal, hadn't given a thought to the possibility of Ives being at home. How had this happened? I recalled Wendy's enthusiasm, her malicious delight in the idea of burning Ives out, and shuddered.

Had this crazy girl deliberately set me up?

But that made no sense; she'd no more way of knowing if he was at home or away than I had, and it had, after all, been my own idea. But other things, past things, crowded into my thinking, and I recalled the lures she'd thrown out to Swink and Rabas with those cut-up pieces of worthless map.

She had conned them deliberate to cancel a debt of twenty thousand dollars. She'd conned me, too, with that offer of a partnership, a half interest in a run-down ranch that was mortgaged to the hilt, binding me to her because she thought me a down-and-out gunslinger, a man who'd be glad to kill for her benefit. And as I remembered these things, I recalled in scorn the ease with which she had steered us to those caverns, to the ledge whose location she'd claimed not to know.

But she *had* stood up for me in the matter of Swink's death, even though I'd told her I was no pistolero. She'd taken care of me after I'd been shot. When I'd proposed sharing the mine with people she regarded as no more than trash she'd agreed; reluctantly, I reminded myself, and only after I'd made her see the danger of turning our crew into vindictive rebels.

132

But there were other things that kept cropping up that helped me to think I'd been played for a sucker. I didn't want to think so—no one does. And she seemed to have been making some effort of late to act halfway human, to really treat me as a partner. . . .

All the better to dupe me, I told myself bitterly.

Yet I couldn't quite believe in such duplicity from her. Vain and arrogant she certainly was, opinionated, sometimes insufferable. Still, in some way I couldn't manage to put my finger on, with her sorrel hair and freckles she'd got under my skin. And I kept remembering how she'd sometimes looked when she thought I wasn't noticing.

Call me a fool—I guess I was, but it was obviously possible Ives had returned to the ranch of his own accord. For all I knew he may have been there all along, puttering around in one of the outbuildings. And, try as I did, I couldn't see how she could have managed to warn him even had she wanted to.

I did my best to put it out of my mind as I rode through the light and dark patches of open and brush with the moon, by now, sailing high overhead. Once more I heard the far yammer of a coyote and though I cast frequent looks at my backtrail, I could find no dust boiling up behind.

I guessed Ives had his hands full fighting that lovely fire I had started; I took a pleased satisfaction in the thought of his fury. In fact, except for my nagging suspicion of Wendy, I was feeling pretty good with myself when I came to his fence and stopped to give the sorrel a breather and consider whether to follow the wires to the gap I'd put in it or make a new hole right there where I was.

I expected it would infuriate him more if I cut a new hole, so I got down off the horse and, approaching the fence, fished around for my cutters, finally to realize I no longer had them.

While I stood, scowling, wondering which way to go to find the opening I'd made, the decision was taken out of my hands by the distant drumming of hard-running horses. Something inside me turned cold and crawled, for they were coming my way—no doubt about it!

Chapter Twenty-one

A Barbwire Trap

Seemed like this newest chase went on forever, but it probably wasn't over half an hour before my over-worked sorrel began to show very evident signs of distress. The fresher horses behind us began to close what was now, I judged, a mile-long gap.

I could see them vaguely, strung out along that uncut stretch of wire, and realized the hole I'd cut—far from saving me—was away back in the other direction. Then, to make matters worse after this grueling pace, I saw too late the pursuit wasn't on my side of the fence. Those were Apaches who were raising that dust!

So now I turned south again, away from those lethal strands of barbed wire and the racketing yells of the thwarted Indians, only to find, as we swooped through a gully, another dust boiling from the ridge ahead.

I was finished and knew it. Short of killing my horse, there was nothing to do but pull up and wait. While I sat the heaving sorrel, grimly waiting, it came into my head what Ives had shouted coming through that door—*"Watch the windows!"* A trick intended to send me flying straight into the gun of that lout he'd positioned out by the back porch.

That I hadn't been killed right then and there had been no fault of Ives's.

There were only three of them dropping down off that ridge, Ives and two hands, all showing a keen satisfaction. As they came up and sat looking me over, Ives said in his heartiest manner, "Imagine meeting you here! Get shucked of those weapons, boy, and do it real careful."

Perhaps, if I'd been the gunslinger he thought me, I could have shot my way out of this, but I was just a poor cowpoke who knew I'd done wrong. I was only astonished I wasn't dead already.

I tossed down my six-shooter and passed him my rifle.

His beefy, red-cheeked face with the heavy nose and pig-gish little eyes considered me with undiluted pleasure. "You'll sing a different tune from here on out. Get down and lead that horse up the ridge. Start walkin'!"

I understood, deep inside, I wasn't going to get out of this. I'd been too big a bother. That I hadn't been shot full of holes already proved only that he had some worse fate in store for me.

Leading the sorrel, I trudged up the ridge and spent the next hour walking with the three of them riding comfortably behind. He wanted me, I guessed, to have ample time to regret having fallen into his hands.

I could hardly have been in a much worse fix had I been taken by the Apaches.

Whenever his rage began to surge up again, he'd send one of his hands along to bash my bad shoulder with the butt of a rifle. By the time his headquarters hove into sight in the gray light of another day, I could scarcely put one foot before the other. Not even the look of that ruined house with but one blackened wall and a chimney left standing was able to lessen my misery.

They herded me over to one of the outbuildings, an eight-by-ten shack with no windows. It had a heavy plank door with wrought-iron hinges and a big, shiny padlock hanging from the hasp. "Get that door open and shove him in," Ives ordered, "and don't be too gentle with the sonofabitch."

A rifle butt in the small of my back sent me reeling across the packed-dirt floor to fall spraddled out against the far wall. The door slammed shut, the big padlock clicked, and I was left scarcely more than half-conscious to listen to the receding crunch of their bootsteps.

When I began to take note of my surroundings, the sun must have been well up in the heavens, for the shack felt like the inside of an oven. I was sick and retched up what little I had in me and lay there gasping till I passed out again.

It must have been after noon when I came out of my hellish dreams to get onto an elbow and drearily stare at the gray walls of my prison. This shack was built stout and, with no windows, should have been black as the farthest reach of those caverns, but wasn't because the roof had a hole for a stovepipe. There was neither stove nor pipe so I could see to look around, had there been anything but four walls to look at. I was the only thing in there and that hole was at least three feet out of reach when I finally got myself off the floor.

The hours dragged by. With my back against a wall, legs stretched out limp in front of me, I'd more than enough time to consider my predicament. I was alive and filled with aches and pains and presently discovered a long splotch of dried blood on the front of my shirt where their fun with that rifle butt had reopened my wound. To tell the truth, I was pretty near ready to wish I'd been killed outright.

There was absolutely nothing in this place but me. No way at all for me to get myself out. And no way of guessing what fate Ives had planned for me. That, I reckoned, was part of my punishment, the leisure to imagine all manner of atrocious endings being kept in store for me.

Wendy, of course, knew where I'd set off for, but I found little cheer in remembering that. Nor did I reckon Ives had gone, or sent, for the sheriff. I was damn well sure he wasn't done with me yet!

I tried to get some sleep, mainly as a means of passing the time, but the best I could do was a little sporadic dozing, which may have helped my aches but did little to refresh me.

I wondered if Rabas had got back from his sheep camp or ranch or wherever he had gone, but couldn't believe that he had. By now, had I not been caught, I should have been back to the caverns, but I couldn't think Wendy would be worried enough to send someone hunting me. Nor believe, if she had, their luck would be any better than my own. Ives, I thought, would be ready and hoping for something like that. He had to figure I'd be missed.

I still had a few matches but decided if I could manage to set the place afire they'd sit out there watching and never lift a finger. Also, it was possible there was nobody here but me and the chickens. If they had any chickens.

I got up and limped around hoping to find a loose board or something I could use to get out, but there were no loose boards. This shack they had put me in was built completely of planks; none of them would budge by even the slightest fraction.

Every now and again I'd look up at that stovepipe hole and wish to hell there was some way I could reach it, but there wasn't.

I got to wondering then if Ives had in mind some sort of trade having to do with our mine. It didn't seem too likely, knowing Wendy as he did. I thought it even less likely she'd agree to trade anything for me. Why should she?

Chapter Twenty-two

Kicking the Dust

The light from the storepipe hole disappeared, so I knew it was night. I sat there a good while staring at where the light had been and, all of a sudden, still in a kind of hopeless stupor with my shoulder hurting like an ulcerated tooth, I got to wondering if there was a chance I could dig myself out.

A search of my pockets found nothing to dig with. Fingers were useless. The ground was too hard, too well packed down. But hope dies hard.

I tried lying down, stretched out on my back, figuring to see what I could do with my boot heels. First few tries they just skidded over the surface. Then one of them caught and ploughed a shallow furrow. I kept trying with the other and presently had two furrows. Mere scratches, really, but vaguely encouraging, though it looked at best an all-night job. And the worst of it was—even if I could get it deep enough—to get myself out under that door, I'd have to dig a good foot on the other side of it.

But I kept doggedly on, hoping not to be interrupted. A nerve-racking business, tedious and tiring, and the muscles in my calves kept threatening to knot up so that I had to keep stopping to give them a rest.

Time the hole was six inches deep, I was wringing-wet despite the cold that came with the night. A scatter of thoughts kept pace with my feet, none of them productive of anything but despair and futility. Still I kept on.

One of the notions that kept recurring was the possibility of trading my share in the mine for my freedom. I thought Ives might go for that, but I also reckoned my partners would consider such a deal a rank betrayal. Which from their point of view it certainly would be, Ives being one to exploit every weakness. Give him a toehold and his greed wouldn't rest till he'd gobbled the whole thing up for himself.

Another thing I'd thought much about during the intolerable heat of the day was the complete lack of the bustle and stir of two-legged activity. No sounds outside, except from birds and insects and the occasional faint whinny of a horse—mine presumably. Though there may have been others in one of the corrals. Not once had I heard a human voice. Through the night as I labored in feverish haste, I mightily regretted not having started my dig straightaway. I had a feeling of racing against time in this effort, for what would this drudgery avail me if that devil came back before I was finished. . . .

The night must have been at least half-gone when presently I had my hole a foot deep and had scooped the loose dirt away from the door. To tackle the ground beyond the door I anchored my back in the burrow I'd made to provide enough leverage to break ground beyond it. I'd feared the outside part of my dig would prove insurmountable; actually it was easier than what I'd already dug. The false dawn was grayly embracing the yard when at last I reckoned to get myself out of there.

I was already squirming beneath that damned door when hoof sound seized me by the throat, the rhythmic thump of a walking horse.

In the ghostly quiet of that early hour, it seemed to be approaching from someplace behind me—in the way of a cat with a mesmerized mouse. Stumbling out of my burrow, I breathlessly staggered to the shack's nearest corner, but the hoof sound seemed to have got lost or stopped, and into this vacuum burst a rash of whinnying from Ives's corrals.

The new horse, throwing up his head to answer this clamorous welcome, made just enough motion to catch my eye before the rider stopped it with a compelling hand. Rooted beside my erstwhile prison, I waited in a kind of awful paralysis for men to come spilling out of the bunkhouse, but no one came. I peered in vain for shapes behind that shadowy horseman who was again edging nearer, between me and the nickering, rifle in hand.

Then with a suffocating leap of the heart I recognized Wendy, and throwing caution to the winds, I cried out her name and stumbled into the open, to stand there in the grip of a relief I could hardly credit.

"What are you doing here?" she demanded testily. "Why didn't you come back? What the hell's going on?"

Same old Wendy, I thought, staring back at her.

Rifle ready to spit at the first sign of danger, she moved her horse closer, sat peering down at me with the strangest of looks from concerned gray eyes. "What have they done to you—and your *shoulder*?" she cried, her stare filled with horror.

"Yes. Well, they bashed it a few times with a rifle butt, shoved me into that shack and locked it. Been trying to get out ever since yesterday morning—just made it when I heard your horse. I think we better get out of here," I said, sounding urgent.

"I doubt they'll be back real soon. I slipped in through that gap you cut in the fence. Quite a few of Ives's steers went through, by the look—I expect he'll have his hands full trying to get them back." She continued, still seeming concerned, "Do you think you can walk as far as the corral?"

"Right now I reckon I could hoof it to Tucson," I said with justified exaggeration. "Here, let me catch hold of your stirrup. Any talking we do can keep for later."

She was considering me dubiously. "You don't look good . . ."

"Come one," I growled. "Never mind my looks." And, a moment later, "I've had enough of this place!"

Chapter Twenty-three

Building Barricades

It was late afternoon when we got back to the caverns and I have to admit I was feeling pretty puny. A heap of the zip had been shaken out of me even though—apparently out of consideration for my condition—she'd kept the horses pulled down to a walk once we'd got away from Ives's spread. I ached like a man in the grip of pneumonia.

On the way back she managed to get from me some of the more frothy highlights of my experience as a guest of the NI Connected. She'd appeared indignant and outraged at the treatment accorded me and called Ives an unmitigated bastard.

I asked about Rabas and she said he'd returned and fetched back enough of the necessities in the way of groceries to tide us over for perhaps another week. I asked about his sheep and she said he had lost some. She seemed unaccountably shy of a sudden and made very little talk during the rest of the journey.

Brady, keeping watch at the entrance, welcomed us back. Wendy said, in passing, that I'd cut a big hole in Ives's fence and gutted his ranch house. Craig took our horses and Salaratus helped me over to the fire.

I was famished and, despite Wendy's mother-hen warnings, tied into Salaratus's grub with real enthusiasm; a meal, I thought, truly fit for a king. When we'd finished everything in sight, the boys wanted to hear of my adventures, and so once more I skimped through them and then limped off to the pool to soak some of the misery out of my bones.

When eventually I got back to my blankets and Rabas helped me to get as comfortable as possible, he told me what he'd found at the sheep camp. "Pretty sickening," he said. Some of Ives's tough hands had raided it, shot two herders, and put twelve hundred sheep over a forty-foot cliff. "Far as that camp's concerned, they just about wiped it out," he said grimly.

"Can you stand such a loss?"

"Expect I'll have to. I've got three other flocks not so handy for his crew to hassle." He sat awhile in a kind of studying silence, then asked abruptly if I thought those redskins had really been after me.

"I did at the time, but I think now they were just making sure I stayed off their land. No arrows sailed past—nobody shot at me. I think they were just trying to hand me a scare. I wonder how Ives is making out with them over the cattle that got out through his fence."

"If he gets back one in ten he'll be lucky. They *could* impound the whole lot. Do him good if they did. While he's dickerin'," Rabas said, "he might try to nudge them into comin' after us account of that ledge we've latched onto.

Until now it's never been properly located. For years it was known as the old Yuma mine, but Wendy's old man had no more title to it than the Apaches. In a good many ways it was like the Lost Dutchman. Quite a passel of folks knew about it, but nobody seemed to be able to find it, though plenty of them hunted. I did some huntin' myself. It was the Indians, though, that had it in the first place."

"And you think Ives might try to stir them up?"

"I expect a deal of hot air and a couple gallons of rotgut might prod some of the younger bucks into takin' a whack at us. It's a possibility we oughta keep firm in mind."

"Would they try, do you think, to get in here?"

"Might, if they git liquored up enough." He looked pretty grim, I thought, as he said this.

"Have we got anybody on guard at the ledge?"

"Don't know." Rabas shrugged. "I've had other things fillin' my head."

"In the morning, maybe we better take one of your uglies and have us a look at it."

He nodded and went off to find his blankets. And shortly afterward Wendy came over and sank down beside me with her back against the cavern wall. She said she was beat and seemed to study me awhile with those gray searching eyes as though never before had she taken a good look at me. She said in a kind of considering way, "When you didn't come back I thought you'd been shot. . . . I had the weirdest feeling." We sat in silence awhile. She seemed to be turning it over like a dog with a bone.

I said, "I thought of you, too," and we looked at each other sort of nervous like; and to get away from my own thoughts I said brusquely, "That note Ives held against Broken Arrow . . . do you reckon that got burnt up with the house?"

Considering me slanchways, she allowed she didn't suppose so. "We couldn't be so fortunate. Mostly, I believe, he keeps all his paper assets at the bank."

"Have you ever had a look at that note?"

"He's got several. He has a small one of mine and three or four from my father. Those I haven't looked at. Are you suggesting they might be forgeries?"

"I had a notion they might be."

We sat and thought about that, and she presently sighed. "I guess they're genuine enough. In his later years my father had a reckless habit of passing out notes to anyone foolish enough to let him have cash."

I watched her, astonished. As recent as a few days ago it wouldn't have occurred to her to sit and talk with me like this, almost as though I was no longer one of the hired hands she was used to ordering around. She had made me a partner but, I was sure, had never thought of me as such. On the surface, to all outward seeming, she appeared as coolly composed as she'd been accustomed to being since she'd herded me into that lawyer's office to put our partnership into a legally binding form. Yet, now, I seemed to sense a warmer feeling, a closer relationship I found hard to understand.

Beneath that sorrel crown, behind that spatter of freckles and the searching gray eyes going over my face, she seemed a different woman, strangely shy, a far more likable person. "I would like for us to be friends, Phil. . . ." She put a hand on my arm. "Do you suppose we could?"

I was amazed, couldn't hardly believe this was Wendy Eldridge speaking. But the hand on my arm, the earnest look in those eyes, the flushed cheeks beneath, hustled me into saying, "But of course we can—of course! There's nothing I'd like better."

* * *

Later, as I was striving mightily to get to sleep, I was abashed, appalled to remember such a thought coming out of me with such fervent assurance. I reckoned I ought to be bored for the simples. I'd been carried away in the spell of an illusion. How could a woman, spoiled and cossetted as she had been, give a damn about friendship with the likes of me? Something important to her had to be behind this, another of her tricks, another means of compelling me into something she knew could not otherwise be managed.

Yes, that was it. I had only to wait to see it unfolded. Her coming after me this morning at Ives's place—it was all of a pattern. There was something she wanted . . . something desperate, outrageous.

Next morning, with clouds piling up beyond the mountains and a cold wind whipping in off the desert, I had other things to think about. After we'd eaten, with a fresh charge of carbide moistening in our lamps, Rabas, Brady, and I set off for the ledge. Quite a fairly large room had been chopped out of what originally had been Swink's escape route after bashing me at the pool. We took a good hard look at the barrier of sandbags we'd erected from the floor pretty near to the ceiling in the hope of keeping out unwanted persons. Two and, lower down, three layers deep, it looked substantial enough to stop bullets. "But," I said, "we should have made a few holes for rifles. As it is right now, we've no way of stopping outsiders from tearing it down."

Both of them nodded. Rabas said, "Only way I can see of fixing it now is to take down the top half of this inside layer to about chest height, set in a few of those short lengths of pipe Swink insisted on buying, and build up the wall again over them."

"Swink bought some pipe?"

"Yep. Don't ask me why—I tried to argue him out of it.

Five lengths, I think. Each of them about sixteen inches long, with an inside diameter of maybe three inches. Said they were something to do with his assaying.''

I said, "Sixteen inches will just about go through two thicknesses of these sand-filled ore sacks. Let's get to work."

We hadn't been long at it when Brady said, "I thought we made this barrier two-sacks thick?"

"That's right."

Brady, who'd been lifting off the sacks and handing them down to Rabas and me, said, "Up here, anyhow, there ain't but one."

Half an hour later we were able to see that this was so. "Keep working," I said. "We'll send Craig back to help you. I think Rabas and I better go take a look at the outside of this barrier."

I was all for getting myself into a saddle but Rabas said, "It ain't all that far. We can hoof it, and if we find what I suspect, we can get back inside by climbing over the barrier."

He was right. Sometime fairly recent, and probably at night, some bright soul had slit every sack in that outside layer down to about belt height. Needless to say, most of the sand had run out of these. "Someone's been figurin' to come in by this route," Rabas said, eying me darkly with his mean slatelike glance narrowed down into slits. "Won't have to think twice to guess who it is."

"No," I said. "Either Mungo or Ives or one of their understrappers."

"Point is," Brady drawled, "how do we counter it?"

Rabas tugged at his nose like he was doing some hard figuring. "Not much chance of riding onto his place again . . ."

I shook my head. "Best thing we can do is fix up some means of giving them a hot welcome in case they return. If I was a bit smarter we could fix up a few mines."

A grin came over Brady's tough-hombre face. "I can do that. Used to be powder monkey at one of the big copper mines."

I considered this a spell, not much liking it, but we were fighting for our lives against an unscrupulous range hog who wouldn't think twice about eliminating anyone who got in his way. So I gave him the nod. "Dig into our equipment and take what you need. Guess we got plenty of blasting material."

Brady went off and sent Salaratus back to take his place. I remembered I'd been going to send Craig but had forgotten in the excitement of what had happened to our barrier. Just as well, I reckoned. Someone had to be on watch at our front entrance. I hated the way this had all the makings of turning into a killing feud. But it looked like violence was in the cards anyway. We certainly had a right to defend our property against such pirates.

By the time we had the barricade fixed to our satisfaction, with some of those higher sacks hauled down and used to strengthen the lower part, we were hungry enough to eat a dead coyote. I made the suggestion we keep someone on the watch here night and day. "In shifts." Rabas nodded and we tramped back to the front cavern, where Wendy had pitched in to provide us with supper.

Brady rode in just before we got finished, turned over his horse to Arbuckle, and said with a grin plainly weighted with malice, "Next batch of uglies that come meanderin' around that ledge are like to get a quick trip to glory."

I told Wendy what we'd decided on. She looked kind of subdued but put up no argument.

Chapter Twenty-four

The Sheriff Stops By

Though we kept a guard on watch at both entrances, the night passed without interruption. A rare and much exclaimed-over treat, provided courtesy of Rabas, was a breakfast of bacon and eggs that all enjoyed. To round it out, Coosie had brewed a fresh pot of coffee instead of leaching the water through last week's grounds.

When there was nothing left to eat, I got me a freshly charged lamp, picked up a rifle, and went off to relieve the man at the ledge. Thanks to those short pieces of pipe, we could see the cleared ground beyond the barrier now—enough of it, anyway, to open a field of fire. "A quiet night," Arbuckle told me before he departed to take care of the horses.

I set down my lamp on a big chunk of quartz and had a look through our peepholes. A bright sunny day with blue skies above and nothing alarming in sight down below. Someone had cut down the close-up brush that had formerly concealed the ledge entrance. Which was all to the good the way things stood now. Especially if Ives managed to stir up the Indians. I got to wondering what it must be like to be a man of red skin in a country under the dominance of pale-faces and didn't reckon I'd much care for it.

In the clarity of great need, I addressed myself to the business in hand. Mungo, I thought, was the man to watch out for. Ives, personally, though a top-drawer bastard, was not in the long run as dangerous as Mungo, who, aside from his life, had little to lose. Both were opportunists, both were driven by their ambitions and hatreds, but Ives, the cattle baron, would obviously be the more cautious of the two. Ives's rages might thrust him into reckless behavior. Mungo was reckless by nature and—like a good many gunfight-ers—in any direct confrontation considered himself unbeat-able.

A gloomy prospect any way you eyed it.

Wrapped up in this thinking, I heard steps approaching and a moment later Wendy fetched her sorrel hair and freck-les into my sight. Yesterday, after my soak in the pool, she'd insisted on having a look at my shoulder and I recalled the dismay with which she'd eyed it. Rebandaged, I'd told her it felt a lot better, but the truth was it gave me a good deal of pain.

"Oh, Phil," she cried, "what are we going to do? I'm just about ready to climb out of my skin."

"I expect I'd probably better post the outside of this bar-rier with a sign warning people away from here, and right away. If you'll stay here a few minutes, I'll get it attended to."

"Yes," she agreed, and I went off to dig through our

store of equipment. Cutting the largest side off a corrugated box, I found a suitable piece of charcoal and printed: GOLDEN GRAB MINE. *Trespassers are hereby warned there is extreme danger of explosives. Stay well away from here. Phil Hardigan, Mgr.*

I told Brady to fix it prominently on the sandbag barrier at the ledge entrance.

Going back through the caverns, I rejoined Wendy. "That ought to do it. At any rate, they're warned," I said after explaining what I'd done. And recalled of a sudden that we had no papers, no bills of sale, for the pair of horses we'd bought from that liverykeeper at Globe, but I saw no point in worrying Wendy by mentioning it.

"Did you have any particular reason," she asked, "for coming to Arizona?"

"No. I just couldn't see any future for me in Texas after two years riding the grubline. Guess I kind of hankered for new pastures. I wasn't run out of there, just fed up with it." I said, with my glance touching her look again, "Don't know if that makes any sense to you."

"But it does. I'm well acquainted with that sort of notion. Doing the same old things, seeing the same old faces day after day. Boxed in with debts and no relief in sight. It was in this kind of trap that I devised the scheme of selling pieces of that worthless map. Knowing it to be without value, I didn't suppose I would find anybody sufficiently gullible. Then I hit on the notion of a trade."

I gave her a nod. "On paper, at least, you gained twenty thousand, so you were that much better off. And at least," I said, "you must have had some idea of where your father's mine was."

That fetched me a sharp look. "But I didn't, not really. It was just that I seemed to remember from things my father let drop that it had to be somewhere close to the Reservation. Within a few hundred yards. We were lucky to stumble onto these caverns.''

Yes, I thought. And if Swink, trying to get loose of us, hadn't found a way out of that farthest cavern after hitting me over the head by the pool, we might never have come onto Yuma's lost ledge.

''I've been wondering what you will do afterward if we ever get clear of this trouble with Ives,'' she said.

I'd been wondering myself.

''Would you,'' she asked, ''consider staying on here, taking charge of this property, helping me build up the old Broken Arrow?'' She must have read the hesitancy in my expression. ''Please, Phil—at least think about it. I've no real business experience, no aptitude for it.''

Seemed like she really meant what she was saying; I could read the earnestness in her look. I had thought first off she was up to her tricks again, but now I wasn't sure. While I was trying to make up my mind, Craig joined us to say with a kind of odd look, ''Sheriff's out front. Says he wants a word with you.''

''Stay here,'' I told Craig, ''and don't let anyone cross that mine field.''

''More trouble,'' Wendy said, half running to keep up with me.

''We'll know when we get there, I reckon'' was all the answer I could think up to give her. Then, seeing that new concern in her look, I said lightly, ''Probably wants to swear me in as a deputy.''

On the way to the front entrance I borrowed Coosie's six-shooter, dropped it into my open-topped holster, seeing the frightened look Wendy gave me. "Don't worry," I said, "I don't aim to shoot him."

When I came out into the sunshine where the sheriff still sat on his big bay gelding, a picture of importance like most politicians, he assumed a genial air and pulled off his white Stetson when Wendy came up beside me. "Howdy, ma'am—you're looking real chipper. Understand you've sold the Broken Arrow."

Wendy fired up and then said with white cheeks, "I haven't sold anything. If Ives told you he bought it, he's lying. He's moved onto the place without my permission."

"Them's harsh words, Miz Wendy. I can't believe Mr. Ives would do a thing like that—"

"Then you don't know him as well as I do!"

"He tells me"—the sheriff smiled imperturbably—"he holds a seventy-thousand-dollar note against your daddy's old ranch, that you haven't kept up the interest, and that he'll have to foreclose."

"I've never seen any such note," she said with her chin up. "All I have is his word for it, and his word's about as reliable as a three-dollar bill." She gave him one of her most arrogant looks. "If you had any backbone you'd move him off my ranch."

"Now, now," he said, darkly flushing, "that's no way to talk to the law. He showed me the note so I have to believe it. He also claims Mr. Hardigan here set fire to his house—"

"Did he tell you what some of his crew did to Mr. Hardigan?"

A flash of surprise briefly showed as he turned his stare on me. "Do you have a complaint?"

I shook my head. "Any complaints I may have had in the past are wiped out. But you can tell him for me that if

I have any new ones they will be taken care of. Personally.''

The sheriff clucked like an old mother hen. Then his look toughened up. ''The liverykeeper at Globe tells me you have a pair of his horses you haven't yet paid for and that he'd appreciate payment at your early convenience.''

I said, ''I'll keep it in mind.''

''Anything else?'' Wendy said, looking furious.

''Well, yes. As a matter of fact I've had a complaint from the Indian Agent who accuses you of trespassing and—''

''Looks like we've been keeping you pretty busy, Sheriff. Have any of these complainers sworn out a warrant for my arrest?''

He considered me thoughtfully. ''Well, no . . . not yet. But I'll tell you frankly, Hardigan, I'm not about to stand for any range wars in my bailiwick.''

''I think you better speak to Ives on that subject.''

He picked up his reins with a final hard look and was turning his horse right back where he came from when Wendy said, ''Just a minute, Sheriff. As you've doubtless heard, we're doing some mining here, all legal and above-board, and we're about ready to move some ore to the Tucson bank. Or the bank at Globe. I think we're entitled to an official escort. What day would best suit you?''

The sheriff's stare jumped around. He looked considerably flustered. ''I . . . er . . . I'll have to have a look at my calendar, ma'am. None of the mines around Globe have applied for an escort.''

''They probably haven't been hassled as we have. Perhaps Mr. Ives hasn't got around to them yet,'' Wendy said disagreeably. ''Or perhaps he's only interested in high-grade *gold* ore.''

The sheriff hung onto his temper with a visible effort. He scrinched up his mouth and said, ''I'll have to look up the law on that. Right now I'm pretty short-handed, ma'am. I certainly can't furnish you with an escort outside my baili-wick."

"I think Globe's in your bailiwick."

"Yes, indeed. Well, I'll look up the law and let you know. Probably be a few days." He put his hat back on and made ready to leave.

"If you can spare the time to run errands for Nicholas Ives," Wendy said, "I expect you can manage to escort my ore to the Globe bank or smelter."

I guess it cost him something, but he managed to ride off without another word.

Chapter Twenty-five

Wendy Goes for the Marshal

Next morning, soon as breakfast was out of the way, Wendy called a meeting of shareowners to find out where we stood and what, if anything, could be done about it. "What's the next step we can look forward to?"

"A warrant for my arrest," I reckoned.

Rabas nodded. "Yes," he said, "that's fairly certain. A nuisance thing. What they're up to is to get you in the slammer where a lynch mob can finish you off. And I don't imagine your request for an escort will be given a second thought."

It was my turn to nod. "They're pretty obviously working up to a raid on this place."

"What about an appeal to the governor?" Arbuckle asked.

Brady said, "What about calling in the U.S. marshal?"

"Nearest marshal's office is Tucson—too far to go," Rabas muttered. "Whatever we need is needed right now."

"We came the long way around gettin' here," Craig said. "We could save fifty miles cuttin' across lots."

Rabas tugged at his nose. "I suppose we could probably hold off a raid till a marshal's deputy gets here, if you want to go that route. But where will we be if our mineral claim's dumped out of the records book? Have you thought about that? Seems a sure-fire move on Ives's part."

"What we've got to do," I said, "is hand them a good scare."

"That's the ticket," Rabas said with some show of enthusiasm. "I've had considerable experience of Ives and his didoes. He don't want no setbacks. I think what we most need right now is for Hardigan, Craig, Brady, Arbuckle, and myself to take a fast trip into Globe. We need to make sure our claim's still on file in that ledger. Then we ought to pay a visit to that lying liverykeeper."

"And we better make sure that conniving sheriff goes with us," I said. "And if our claim's been deleted from the records, we ought to swear out a warrant to take that clerk into custody for tampering with the records and conspiring with Ives. And it's my opinion we should go right away before any more of Ives's deviltry gets afoot."

"Yes," Rabas agreed. "Before you get lugged off to jail, that's for sure. If we could get a big enough jump on that hog, we might be lucky enough to settle this ruckus before it gits to be an all-out shootin' war."

Wendy looked at me. "It's certainly worth trying," I said. I kind of regretted now having suggested putting out those mines. If Ives's bunch rode into them it would stop them all right, but the repercussions . . . "Damn it," I said, "we've got to put enough pressure on him to make him think twice before he goes too far to pull back.'' I told Coosie, ''While we're gone I want you to make up another sign about explosives and put it in plain sight outside this front entrance.''

Most of the funny business on the part of Ives's henchmen had been concentrated outside the ledge entrance—Swink's escape, Swink's murder, those cut-open sandbags. But we'd no guarantee Ives was about to stop there. Having focused our attention on the back door, so to speak, logically his next move might well be directed elsewhere.

''Let's get movin','' Rabas said. The meeting broke up and we went off for our horses. But as we neared out main entrance I dropped back to say to Wendy—sort of yanking a page from the sheriff's act, ''You're looking powerful nice this morning, partner,'' and she peered at me, startled.

''Feeding me sugar, are you? What are you up to?''

But she seemed pleased, I thought. ''That notion about calling in a U.S. marshal is a good idea—we need someone with authority to consider our side of this rumpus. If you could hold down the fort for just this morning, you might write a note and have Coosie take it to Tucson. What do you think?''

''A good idea, but I've got a better. Leave Coosie here, and instead of a note, I'll go myself. That will put more punch in it.''

''Good girl!'' I said, and we left it at that. ''Take care of yourself and steer clear of Apaches.''

Catching up with the others, I passed along Wendy's notion, and all agreed she was a heap more likely to get some action than sending Salaratus in with a note.

We rode into Globe a little short of nine and while the others sat their mounts in front of his office, I went in to prod the sheriff and try to get him off his fat behind.

As expected, the great man was comfortably wedged into his swivel, booted feet on desk and a cigar in his mouth. He did not show any excess of enthusiasm when his glance came up and encountered my face. He did not say anything, either.

I had no time to waste beating around any bushes and came straight to the point. "We've ridden in," I said, "to make sure our claim is still on record, and I'm requesting you to accompany us and make a bona fide examination."

He eyed me a while without much favor; with a scowl he snatched up his hat and levered himself off his comfortable perch. "Okay. Let's get at it." When we got outside and he saw the tough-faced outfit I had brought for a backup, his scowl grew downright angry. Rabas got off his proud new horse and came along with us. In the Recorder's office we went straight to the counter, where the sheriff spun round the big ledger, looking like someone had stamped on his corn. "Hmph!" he growled. "When did you file this claim?"

I told him. He said, "No record of it here." Rabas shoved him aside and, after looking himself, beckoned me nearer and tapped the book with a stubby finger. I looked and said grimly, "Take a glance at the page numbers—the one with our claim has been cut from this book, sheriff."

The clerk started edging away from the counter but nervously stopped when he found Rabas's eyes boring into him. I told the sheriff, "I'm swearing out a complaint for that man's arrest. I want him taken into custody for malfeasance in office, tampering with the records, and conspiring with Ives to do us out of our mine."

The sheriff, snatching his three chins off his chest and turning a ruddy shade of purple, glowered at the quailing clerk as though minded to tear him limb from limb. He couldn't seem to get enough spit to talk with, but his action spoke loud enough for everyone. He caught the clerk by the front of his shirt, hauled him over the counter, and quite ungently shoved him toward the door.

"Wait—wait!" the man cried. "Ives made me do it! That page ain't destroyed. . . . I've—"

"Why, you mealy-mouthed whippersnapper!" the sheriff snarled, and gave him a bash that sent him sprawling.

When the fellow, cowering, picked himself up and said, "I thought that's what you'd want me to do." I looked for the sheriff to have an apoplexy, but he finally got himself in hand and, with us ready to render assistance, marched the culprit off to the jail.

When the man was locked up I told the sheriff, "We might have another lodger for you. We'd like for you to come along to the livery and show us the man who said we'd two of his horses still unpaid for."

Sheriff said angrily, "He probably made a mistake. . . ."

"Right," Rabas nodded. "We'd like you to be on tap when he admits it." So we all fell in line and tramped over to the livery. The proprietor saw us coming and eagerly called, "So you caught them, Sheriff. That's damn good work."

I said, "You'll not be so cheered up about it in a couple of minutes. Arrest this rascal, Sheriff. I demand he be taken into custody and charged with slander and an obvious attempt to cheat unsuspecting customers."

"Did you sell these galoots two horses?"

Under the sheriff's furious stare the liverykeeper nodded. "Did they pay you for them or didn't they?" was the sheriff's next question. The man said he guessed, now he thought of it, we had. "Did you write out a bill of sale?"

"I . . . I don't believe I did."

"I'm goin' to press this thing," Rabas said. "A plain premedicated case of slander. I want him locked up till the case can be heard."

"But . . . but who's goin' to take care of my horses an' the boarders that's in here?"

"I'll have one of my deputies look after it. Come along."

We saw him safely stowed in the cell next to the records clerk. "Who'll we go after now?" Rabas asked, and I said, "I think we better visit the mercantile; it was from one of their windows, you'll remember, that I got shot. Might be some more of Ives's crowd hanging out there. Come on, Sheriff. You needn't be so timid—we're not going to let them clobber you."

"Be a good time," Brady said, "to lay in some more grub," and the other uglies signified their willingness to go along with that notion. We got on our horses for this jaunt.

The sheriff said, "You won't be needing me."

"Since we're not mind readers and can't know that," I told him, "you better come with us and see that no ambushes are being laid up for us."

Chapter Twenty-six

Into the Lion's Den

At the mercantile, we found two of Ives's hard-faced pistoleers with their butts on the counter, legs swinging, while they munched on crackers lifted out of the barrel. The sheriff hailed them gruffly. "Can't Ives find no better work for you to do?"

"Yes, sir, Sheriff. If you'll just step outside for a jiffy we'll git right at it."

I hadn't missed the way they eyed me and Rabas. "I expect," I said, "you better take them in, Sheriff. What that jasper just said sounds to me like a threat to disturb the peace. Otherwise, I'm going to have to deal with them myself. I doubt if you'll want any blood spilled in here."

The sheriff took a quick look at me and at Rabas with a fist already on his iron, swallowed a couple of times uncomfortably, and told Ives's hands, "Lay them guns on the counter, boys, and head for my office.''

"Doubt if your office will hold them, Sheriff. You're going to feel a lot safer with that pair in jail.''

Biggest one snarled, "Ives ain't goin' to like this—''

"I didn't much like it either," I said, "when one of you vinegarroons slapped that chunk of lead through my shoulder—''

The smaller rogue yelled, "I never did!''

"Take 'em in, Sheriff. I'll swear out a warrant against that biggest one.''

Rabas, darkly eyeing the littlest lout, said, "That's Pete Moriarty—I ain't forgot that hangdog face. I'm swearin' out a warrant agin' *him*! He's one of Ives's gunnies that helped put twelve hundred head of my sheep over a cliff last week. Hangin's too good for him!—like to see him get life. Left one of my herders dead, they did, and another bad hurt.''

All the time we were there the gray-cheeked storekeeper never opened his trap.

Following the sheriff and his prisoners back to the jail, we saw them locked up and, going on to his office, filled out the complaints. Then we picked up our crew and headed for home, feeling reasonably satisfied with this morning's work. It would certainly give Ives something to think about, and it wouldn't hurt that sheriff to know we could show a few teeth if we had to. We probably should have bought some more groceries. . . .

Salaratus met us at the entrance with a rifle but reported no alarms.

Wendy wasn't back yet, nor had we expected she would be; Tucson was too far south from our mine to reach and get back in a single day without, of course, you had a relay of horses. We had the horses, and they could have done with some exercise, but moving loose horses was no job for a woman.

Mashed spuds, tinned peas, corned beef, and cornbread, Coosie said, was the menu for this evening. Craig and Brady told him to get at it and took his place just inside the entrance just to make sure doubly certain we weren't handed some kind of a surprise. Ives, we figured, would be considerably chafed when he heard of the morning's happenings at Globe. "And he'll be hearin' quick enough," Rabas grumbled. "Sheriff'll see to that, you can bet."

Arbuckle unfurled his bedroll and took forty winks while we waited for Coosie to yell, "Come an' git it!"

While we were putting away this elegant feed, Rabas brought up the possibility of Ives sicking Mrs. Swink onto us. Brady said, "How?"

"Well," Rabas said through a mouthful, "Swink was one of the original partners—"

"But he tried to kill Hardigan," Craig objected.

"What's that got to do with it? She probably never knew he had anything to do with us. But all Ives would need to do would be to hint that her husband had shares in a gold mine, point her in our direction, and she'd be after us hammer and tongs."

Brady chewed awhile, then scowlingly grumbled, "She's no right to a share. He skipped out before we even knew the mine was here. Be less for the rest of us if she gets into this. . . ."

"Does she have any right to be in on this ledge? Let's take a vote—"

"Wendy ain't here," I objected.

Arbuckle said, "We got a quorum."

"So all those," Rabas said, "in favor of resurrecting Swink as a partner, stick up a hand."

No hands went up. "Wait a minute," I said. "Maybe we could sic her onto Ives—must have been one of his rannies that killed Swink. Shot in the back, too!"

Rabas nodded. "Had to be murder. Mebbe we could get her to go to the sheriff and demand Ives's arrest—he had to be mixed into it someway."

"All right," I said, "but she's back in Tucson."

"Ives could have her fetched up here."

"Okay. If she shows up, we'll try it," I said. And Arbuckle said, "Let's just forget her. We got enough troubles."

"Maybe," Craig said, "after this mornin', Ives will pull in his horns."

"As a wish, that's a corker," Rabas commented. "He's in this too deep to back out now—besides, it ain't in his nature."

Brady said, "I've heard he keeps a room in the hotel at Globe. Maybe there'd be somethin' there we could use . . ."

Might be, I thought, though I couldn't think it too likely.

"Well," Arbuckle grunted, "I better get back to my horse chores—we ort to take turns at this feedin' and waterin'."

All his friends nodded but nobody offered.

First thing I thought of when I woke next morning was Brady's notion of Ives keeping a room at the hotel in Globe. It kept nagging at me like an opportunity wasted. I told myself I'd be a fool to go back there, that there'd be nothing in it of any worth to us. But all through breakfast it kept buzzing my mind like a fly in a bottle. After throwing our weight around in that town yesterday, to be seen there today shouldn't be too risky. Unless, of course, those two uglies of Ives's were back on the street. And that they were, I reckoned, was a pretty fair assumption.

I could send one of the others. But my old man had brought me up on all the old saws, like if you wanted a thing done right you'd best do it yourself. I wished to hell Brady'd kept his damn mouth shut.

After awhile I took Rabas aside, mentioned what I had in mind. He looked me over with a jaundiced stare. "Somehow it never struck me," he said, "your first name was Daniel." He looked at me some more. "Guess I better go with you. A pair of guns ought to be some better than one."

I pushed it around then shook my head. "I'll be all right."

Ten minutes later I was on my way.

Globe didn't look the sleepy town it had yesterday. I'd forgot today was a Saturday. Evidently it was also payday for the mines. Spring wagons and buckboards clogged the main drag and there were horses and kids all over the place. It crossed my mind that Rabas may have been right, that sticking my head in a lion's den could well be an apt description.

But now that I was here, I felt I owed it to myself to at least have a look. I considered, very briefly, inviting the sheriff to go along but lost no time dropping that from my thinking.

Having never been near the hotel before, there seemed pretty good odds the clerk wouldn't have any reason to know me. There were people in the lobby—cowmen, mine bosses, a few ladies even. I stepped up to the desk. "Mr. Ives in town?"

Without looking up from his handful of papers, "Upstairs," the clerk said. "Room two twenty-four."

I went up the stairs like I belonged in the place. And it was just my luck that as I went down the hall a door opened on my right, and there was Ives, staring, startled, not three feet away from me.

"Morning, Ives—the very man I was coming to see. If you can spare me a couple of minutes—"

Ives snarled, "Get out of my way!"

"Believe you'd do well to listen to me, Ives. We've fixed that mine and both entrances to polish off anyone foolish enough to try and bust in there. I'm giving you fair warning. Try jumping that claim, and you are sure going to have a lot of loose arms and legs to pick up when the dust blows away."

I could see in his eyes the violence churning inside him as he started for me, both arms swinging, face twisted into a murderous look. I backed toward the stairs, less than ten feet behind me. Ives lunged. I ducked, came up, and slammed my fist against the hinge of his jaw.

Ives was spun half around by the force of impact, lost his balance, made a grab for the wall, and tumbled down the stairs in a tangle of limbs and a series of thumps that must have been heard all over the building.

I flashed a quick look around, remembered he hadn't thought to lock his door. Three long strides put me into the room. I shut the door with the greatest of care, knowing if Ives still had hold of his wits he'd have people after me in no time at all; have them watching outside, pounding up the stairs, flinging open every door on this floor that wasn't locked. Catching up the room's one straight chair, I wedged it under the knob and took another look around.

There wasn't much to see. A bed, a chest of drawers, a club chair upholstered in green leather, a chamber mug under the bed, and the straight chair I'd shoved under the doorknob. I could hear a babble of voices below. The room's single window overlooked the street. I went through the chest of drawers in a hurry and found not a thing of interest. I could hear feet pounding up the stairs. Only a fool would try to leave by that window, and, I reckoned disgusted, I fit that category.

Through a mumble of voice sounds, I heard doors flung open and angry protests. I had to do some quick thinking. Could I get out of this room without being seen? Very doubtful, I thought. Those who knew this for Ives's room would probably ignore it, but would there be among those heavy-footed sounds from the hall one searcher who was not on Ives's payroll and, therefore, ignorant of which room was Ives's?

Very gently I removed the chair I'd braced against the knob. I looked for the hinges and positioned myself where the door, when opened, would shield me from view, hopefully. But not really counting on any such luck.

Some of those booted feet outside seemed to be on their way down the stairs, when, abruptly, I saw the knob turn. I caught the door before it banged into me, held it a moment, and slammed it into whoever had been about to enter.

He must have thought he'd been hit with a bat. I heard him fall, stepped over him, my gun in hand; then having a better thought, passed Ives's room, tried the next three doors, entered the third when I saw women's duds laid out across the bed.

I shoved the gun in my holster, snatched up a dress, pulled it over my head, fastened the buttons, pulled up my pantlegs, and put on the picture hat and elbow-length gloves which had lain beside it, leaving my own hat behind. I heard another door open and booted steps in the hall. As they passed this room, I eased the door open and fell in behind the two men moving down the stairs filled with gab and indignation. As they stepped into the lobby, less crowded now, somebody called, "Did they bust into your room, Farley?"

Not waiting for the answer, I crossed the lobby and went down the verandah steps to the street, expecting with every step to be challenged and discovered. Two doors away, just this side of the courthouse, I could see my horse switching flies at the tie rail.

I'd bent the wide brim of the hat to put at least some shade on my face but reckoned I made a rather odd-looking female in this calico dress—too tight in all the wrong places and with scuffed cowhand boots shuffling along underneath it.

With less than a hundred yards between me and my flax-maned sorrel, I fell in behind a pair of Cornish miners bound in the same direction and reckoned I had it made, until the sheriff stepped out of the courthouse.

I could feel the thump of my heart mighty plain when he threw the butt of his cigar into the street and came striding toward me, with Ives moving out of the door behind him.

Chapter Twenty-seven

Mungo's Message

Ives had my hat in his hand, and I could hear the angry snarl of his voice as he caught up with the law, still rumbling a storm of protests. I could see, even from here where I huddled behind the two Cornish miners, the apoplectic look of his face. Anyone could tell he was furious.

I couldn't think what was the best thing to do. To dash for my horse would be a dead giveaway, riveting their attention—the last thing I wanted with this dress preventing me from reaching my gun. But to remain as I was, walking back of those Cousin Jacks, would bring me abreast of them in no time at all. I was caught like a mouse with the cat's paw reaching. With only seconds to go, I could see what my foolishness was like to wind up in.

And then they came even with us, even and passing with Ives still exhorting, giving the sheriff his most thundering

172

abuse. I could hardly believe it, felt sure I was dreaming, the pair of them scarcely two feet away and going straight on like I wasn't even there!

My knees was so weak I could hardly stay upright. Seemed like for sure I was going to heave up my breakfast with my head-turning horse softly blowing his welcome, and me clinging to the horn like a sinner in judgment, that cracked old saddle the only hope of salvation.

I was a mile out of town before I tore off that dress, still figuring I was bound to wake up any moment.

It was just past noon when I arrived at the caverns, and a more appreciated sight I seldom had seen. I'd forgot I still had that damn hat on my head, and normally I'd have been in for some ribbing, but I could sense right away in the looks of this crew the situation here was a far piece from normal.

"What is it?" I said, and Rabas handed me a folded slip of paper.

I took it in at a glance, then read it again in cold, crawling horror: *I've shot your marshal. I have Wendy Eldridge. If you want her back in mint condition leave* QUITCLAIM FOR THAT LEDGE *on right-hand gatepost at Broken Arrow inside 12 hours.*

There was no signature, but it almost had to be Mungo. Ives was in Globe.

With that paper in my hand, I stood there like I'd been struck dumb. Everything round me began to spin as though caught up in the grip of a twister. It was Rabas's fist clamped to my arm, shaking me, that finally pulled me out of this quagmire. "What are we goin' to do?" he muttered.

"We'll do what he said to do . . . up to a point. When'd you get this?"

"Not over ten minutes ago. Some galoot on a crowbait set out there an' howled till I went out and got handed it." Rabas's eyes searched my face. "We ain't got much time if we're goin' after her."

"Brady! Go help Arbuckle saddle four horses, including that grulla, and don't stop to pick any daisies."

With that narrowed stare still searching my face, Rabas said, "Count me in—"

"You're stayin' here," I told him. "This could be another of their tricks. We can't take any chances. I'll take Brady. Rest of you stay here and keep your eyes skinned."

Rabas said, angry, "You tryin' to get yourself killed?" He spat out his chaw. "Ives must have half his crew at Broken Arrow."

"I don't think so. What I'm trying is to keep half a jump ahead of that sidewinder. Now go find me a pencil so I can write up a quitclaim—"

"You outa your head?" Craig demanded.

"We will damn soon find out." Someone handed me a pencil, and I wrote the quitclaim on the back of Mungo's note. Rabas's glance brightened a little. "That's the ticket—he'll play hell puttin' that on file. But I still think you're crazy ridin' over there alone."

Brady came up to us leading four frisky horses. I said, "Now here's how we'll work it," handing Brady Mungo's paper. "Brady'll ride up alone to the Broken Arrow gate and anchor this with a rock to the top of that right-hand post. Then he'll take off as though heading for home and come onto the ranch from another direction, keeping out of sight till he's needed. I'll be out there someplace, watching that gatepost. When Mungo comes after that quitclaim, I'll nail him."

"And," Rabas growled, "the rest of that outfit will salivate you sure!"

"That's a chance I'll have to take. I don't think, including Mungo, there'll be more than three of Ives's crew there. I think he'll be bunching them to hit these caverns."

"You don't think he's in on this?"

"I think he'll be expecting to find this place deserted."

While the rest of them were still grumbling, I climbed onto the grulla and took off at a lope, Brady right back of me.

Staked out where I could see but not be noticed as the dusk thickened up on its way to becoming full dark, I lay—rifle in hand—with my sights on that gatepost, hoping that Brady could get into a position where he could be of some use. I was sure he'd been watched and seen leaving that paper and then, apparently, riding off toward the caverns. Mungo, I didn't reckon, would come after that paper till he had enough dark to make a poor target. Probably, with two horses apiece, we had got here sooner than expected.

We had tied our horses back in the brush some quarter of a mile from where I lay waiting. I didn't think they could be seen by Mungo or any hands he might have scouting our arrival. We had been mighty careful moving up on this place. Brady had been carrying a white rag on a stick when he rode up to the gatepost.

I had plenty of time in the quiet of the evening to wonder some more if this wasn't a trick to draw at least most of us away from the caverns, thus improving Ives's chances of grabbing our mine. I had time enough, too, to cogitate about that trip to Globe, knowing as well as I'd ever known anything that there'd been no excuse for the risk I'd been taking. I could imagine what Wendy would think of such a caper. And this, I supposed, coming here like a fish swimming after the bait, could be thought about as rattlebrained. If they weren't holding her hostage and this *was* just a trick, I guessed I'd be kicking myself all the way back.

At least it seemed I'd been right in reckoning most of the crew he'd moved onto this ranch had been pulled out. No sign of any presence had I seen up to now. No coming and going, no faintest sound of voices. No movement at all except a breeze through the trees.

It was now full dark, so dark I couldn't see the gatepost and knew I'd have to get nearer. I was just about to move, when the flare of a match let me see it again and a shape reaching up to feel along the top of it. I should have fired straightaway, but that soft streak I had wouldn't let me. "Mungo!" I yelled, and flame spat from his hip before I squeezed off a shot. I jacked another into the breech and fired again, and he was down, thrashing around like a headless snake as I ran forward clawing the pistol out of my holster. I wasn't ten feet away when he fired again, and the snarl of that bullet passed so close I thought to feel it. I shot twice more, once to either side of the muzzle flash and stayed in a crouch till I was sure he was done for.

I grabbed the paper out of his hand and started for the house with the pistol shoved in my waistband and rifle at the ready. The paper I stuffed inside my shirt and moved even slower as the porch loomed in front of me. Only sound to be heard was the chirping of crickets.

Chapter Twenty-eight

Fight at Broken Arrow

The adobe Broken Arrow ranchhouse seemed empty, but I was in no rush right then to make sure.

There were three steps to that porch, and I was on the warped planks when the first shot slammed past, and I was down on them, rolling, when the second kicked splinters into my cheek. I let go of the rifle, hearing its clatter, as a shape came erect at the porch's far corner.

I yanked up the pistol and let him have it, driving him backward to go down in a heap as I flung myself at the open door.

Two slugs screamed past, and a third bit the frame; someone back of an overturned table rose up with a cry and fell forward across it, as Brady, crouched over a smoking six-shooter, came through another door to ask, "You all right?"

"I guess so—is that all of them?"

"I ain't heard no others.

"Where's Wendy?"

"Tied up in the sala—marshal, too."

He followed me in there carrying the lamp, and the first thing I saw beneath the hair and freckles and the gag across her mouth was Wendy's great, staring eyes fixed upon me. I went straight over to the chair she was tied in, feeling weak as a gopher in the relief flooding through me. "Wendy . . . ," I said, and several times while getting the ropes off her I had to stop lest I cut her, my hands were shaking so. Brady didn't take half as long freeing the marshal.

We helped them get the circulation started, especially for Wendy's marshal who had a punctured wing, courtesy of the late Mungo. His name, he said, was Witter, and Wendy had taken care of his wound before they'd been tied up. If someone could fix up a sling for the arm, he reckoned he'd be ready to ride straightaway if someone could fix him up with a horse. And just to keep the record straight he was a *deputy* U.S. marshal, he said.

I wasn't much interested in him at the moment, all my thoughts being occupied by Wendy, whose jaws were still too cramped from the gag they'd put on her to have a heap to say in the way of conversation. Perhaps, I thought, it was just a woman's natural shyness. I felt a bit flustered myself, fussing over her.

The marshal's deputy wanted to know how we'd happened to find out they were prisoners, and where, so I passed him the paper that had set things in motion, and he clucked over that. Brady said he'd go fetch the horses, and Witter asked what had happened to Mungo. I gave him the rundown and he called after Brady to bring the body up to the house.

"I take it," he said, "these bushwhackers worked for this Ives Miz Eldridge was telling me about." I nodded.

"He must have a deal of influence around these parts to think he could get away with—"

"He's got the sheriff in his pocket," I said, and recounted that business of our mineral claim being cut from the record book and the story of the chiseling liverykeeper. "And last week after some of his crew had moved onto Wendy's ranch, some more of his crew ran twelve hundred of Rabas's sheep over a cliff, killed one herder, and wounded another."

The deputy shook his head. "Seems pretty high-handed, I have to admit. And I suppose you have proof for all of these notions?"

"We can prove what happened to those sheep, I expect. Rabas recognized one of Ives's crew—fellow called Moriarty. . . ."

"And that assayer—Swink, was it?—that you found shot in the back outside your ledge entrance. What proof do you have to connect Ives with it?"

"All I can say is that the sheriff, under pressure from Ives, has been trying to lay that murder onto us."

We heard hoof sound. I took a cautious squint from the window and, seeing it was Brady, went out to help him get Mungo into the house. Far as I was concerned, the buzzards and coyotes could have had him and welcome.

I went out and fed what horses were in the day corral and left the bars down so they could forage for themselves. I was feeling a mite impatient about the time we were wasting when every minute's delay in getting back to the caverns might be a life-or-death business for the partners we had left there.

Wendy had fixed up a sling for the deputy's arm. "Someone," he said, "will have to come back and bury these

179

people. Ought to do it right now, but I can see you're itching to get back to your mine. Well, I'm ready.''

It took us almost twice as long to make the trip back as it had to get down there. Wendy thought fast travel would be too rough on Witter's punctured wing; told me she felt responsible for it since it was she who had fetched him into this scrape. I tried to tell her wounds went with his job, but it was just like talking at the side of a wall.

It was broad daylight when we got to the caverns, and I saw no sign that they had been under siege. Craig hailed our arrival and led off our horses, and Wendy introduced Witter to our shareowners. And they all had to be told what had happened at Broken Arrow. And the deputy sent Arbuckle off to plant the cadavers we'd left behind. Nothing, Rabas said, had happened at this end. Just the same old sixes and sevens. They'd dug a little more ore, he said, brightening, and perked up considerable when Witter told him there was at least a possibility he'd eventually be compensated for the sheep Ives's bunch had run over the cliff.

Salaratus cooked us up some grub, and after we'd eaten, the deputy said he'd like a look at the ledge. He wanted to inspect that wall we'd put up and hear about the booby traps Brady had put down outside it. And, what with more gab and all, these things took up a couple of hours. Nobody mentioned our burying Swink.

We had hardly got back to Coosie's fire when Craig called from the front entrance that the sheriff was sitting his horse outside with a warrant for my arrest. Wendy told Witter he could now see for himself what kind of law we had around here, and still wearing his sling, he went along with us to hear what the sheriff had on his mind.

Sitting his horse with his three double chins and the importance of his office draped around him like a toga, the sheriff demanded, like he was Moses addressing the wayward Israelites, "What's the idea of all this guff about explosives?" He pinned me with a pretty rough look.

"That's not guff," I told him. "Considering the way your friend Ives has been behaving, it's only natural we'd want to protect our investment. We've put out a few booby traps that won't bother anyone, so long as they stay off our property."

"Well, you go dig 'em up—such things are out of place in a peaceful community."

"Just a minute," Witter said. "Are you denying these folks the right to protect private property?"

"Who are you? Some kind of smart-ass lawyer?"

"I think you should know that under federal mining law a man has a legitimate right to protect his property against hoodlums, claim-jumpers, and invasion of privacy."

"In this county *I'm* the law," the sheriff said with his chins up and eyes some colder than a dead frog's legs. "I've a warrant here for Hardigan's arrest—"

"On what charge?" I cut in.

"You're being charged with the back-shooting murder of Benjamin Swink!"

Witter said, "I think we'd better have a look at your evidence—"

"That'll all come out at the trial."

Rabas's short laugh was filled with contempt. "What he means is a trial by lynch mob."

"You keep your yap outa this!"

"I believe," Witter mentioned, "you can safely leave this man in my care if I guarantee to produce him for the preliminary hearing."

"They'll have him strung up before ever they git around

181

to any hearing.'' Rabas eyed Witter grimly. ''That's the whole point of this arrest. This carpetbaggin' cuckoo hasn't even looked into the loss of my sheep!''

''Let's just take one thing at a time,'' Witter said with his look swinging back to the sheriff. ''I think,'' he said mildly, ''Hardigan will acknowledge the arrest if you remand him to my custody until the preliminary—''

''I don't know you from Adam!'' the sheriff cried angrily.

''Let me introduce myself,'' said Witter, smiling. ''I'm Archie Witter, deputy U.S. marshal out of Tucson. And here are my credentials.''

The sheriff, visibly trying to get hold of himself, waved them away.

''I take it,'' Witter said, ''you have the cadaver?''

Looking mad enough to kick a dog, the sheriff wheeled his horse and, without another word, departed.

Chapter Twenty-nine

The Sheriff Searches

"That was a very nice touch," I told Witter. "I don't think we'll hear any more on that subject."

He slanched me a kind of odd sort of look and said, "Miz Eldridge tells me you've been working this ledge pretty steady here lately and have quite a bit of ore stacked up to go to the bank in Tucson."

"Yes, we've got quite a bit. In addition, I mean, to what you saw in that wall we put up. We intended to sack it and take it in by wagon. But until we can use the sacks you've seen in that barricade, we've no way of moving it. We can't empty the sand from those sacks until it's safe to pull down the barricades. And even then, as she's probably told you, we would hesitate to move anything that valuable without an escort, and the sheriff isn't interested in discussing an escort. Claims he's shorthanded."

"Looks as though you folks are in a bind. What do you aim to do?"

"Guess we can't do anything but try and sit it out," I said, "until this feud with Ives is resolved."

"Let me think about this," Witter said. "Meanwhile let's get some idea of how much ore you'll be wanting to move."

So Wendy and I went back to the ledge with him, then on to the pool we were using for storage. "And there are ten more sacks," I told him, "in that last cavern—filled sacks, I mean."

"You'll need two ore wagons or burlap sacks and a string of mules. Considering the kind of ground you'll negotiate, I expect you'll be happier with mules. Between twenty and thirty, I'd say offhand."

Wendy looked exasperated. "Where are we to get that many mules?"

"How many horses do you have?" Witter asked.

"A dozen that are used to packing—say twenty in all."

"With a dozen pack horses, I think you could get by with ten stout mules. You should be able to pick those up in Globe."

"We don't have enough cash money to buy ten mules," Wendy protested. "And if we use ore to buy mules, we'll probably start a stampede." She looked at him doubtfully. "Even if you agreed to go with us, there'd be only eight persons to stand off whatever Nick Ives can scrape up to throw at us. I think we'd fare no better than the Mexican smugglers Curly Bill's outfit wiped out in Skeleton Canyon."

Witter said, "I can't believe Ives would be so reckless."

"That's because you only know him by hearsay," Wendy said with her most obstinate look. "We'd be safer right here. There are too many places for ambush between here and

184

Tucson—*you* should know!" she said angrily.

"The most sensible course is to take the ore to Globe. There's a whistle stop—Miami—not two miles from the heart of town. There's a smelter there—"

"I don't think," Wendy said, looking stubborn again, "you quite realize what we're up against here. Globe is a stamping ground for Nick and his crew. He's just about got that town in his pocket."

"I'm sure you're exaggerating." Witter smiled. "There are quite a few mines in and around Globe, and I would think their owners would have at least as much say in that community as Ives, who's a cowman and ranching clean at the other end of the county."

I said, "Let's have your best thought on the subject."

"Well," Witter said, "Miz Eldridge is right in thinking you folks would be safer right here in these caverns—you're pretty well dug in, but this isn't getting your ore to market. While I'm here, Ives would be the brashest kind of fool to make a try at taking over these caverns. But he can wait longer than you can. And I've got other commitments."

It made sense to me, but I couldn't think Wendy gave a damn about logic. "Go on," I said. "Just how would this work?"

"You can't keep that ore bottled up here forever, it's no good to you here. To realize its potential, it's got to be in circulation—that is, its worth has. My advice—and I don't say you should take it—is go to the bank at Globe and open an account with a couple sacks of this ore in the name of Eldridge, Hardigan & Company, look around for mules, find out what they will cost, and pay with a cashier's check from the bank in that amount. I'll go with you and be introduced as a deputy U.S. marshal. This will give you some standing and perhaps help to counteract some of the sheriff's steam."

"When do you suggest putting this into motion?"

"First thing in the morning."

It was plain to me that Wendy was far from enthusiastic. Two weeks ago any such solution to the bind we were in would have been denounced in her most arrogant terms. And I could see, myself, the weakness and dangers of trusting our wealth to this sort of transport, strung out as it would be for probably half a mile through country so compatible to ambush. Ives, I thought, would love such a chance. But that was the crux of it; that was what Witter wanted, a situation where Ives would be enticed into irrevocably showing his hand—an indiscretion he could not wriggle out of. An act of piracy no court could put aside.

"And what of our ore?" Wendy cried furiously. "And all the blood that would be spilled?"

Witter said blandly, "You can't make an omelet without breaking eggs. If you want this ruckus with Ives to be resolved, the plan just suggested will answer the purpose. Of course there'll be risk. There's at least as much risk to remaining in these caverns. If your opponents become sufficiently impatient, a few sticks of dynamite could seal your fate."

His glance swung to me. "I can telegraph Tucson for a couple more men; this would raise your strength and provide the independent witnesses needed to put Mr. Ives where you think he belongs."

Our conference was adjourned when a call from the entrance informed all and sundry the sheriff was outside with two deputies and a search warrant. By his look, it seemed to me that Witter had been at least halfway expecting this. Rabas said to me under his breath, "One will git you five he's hunting for Swink." And Brady whispered, "With that deputy here he won't be taking you up for murder without he's got a corpse.''

''You think it over,'' Witter was saying to Wendy. ''If you want to get this business out of your hair once and for all, the way I've suggested should get the job done. If he attacks that mule train, he'll hit it with everything he's got, and he'll be there in person to make sure none of us are left to tell the tale.''

''Yes,'' Wendy said. ''That's what I'm afraid of.''

Witter could see I didn't like the prospect of the sheriff and two helpers snooping around inside our caverns. ''Cheer up,'' he murmured, ''the quality of your find will be public knowledge the moment you approach either a bank or a smelter.''

''And the moment he gets back to Globe all the interested parties will know precisely how prepared we are—''

''I'd say that's all to the good,'' Witter nodded. ''When you start buying mules they'll have something else to think about.''

The sheriff and his deputies poked around through the caverns with the torches they had brought for pretty near two hours. They rode off at last without uncovering Swink's body but bulging with the sort of information sure to set tongues wagging.

Arbuckle returned from his burying chores at Broken Arrow, and supper that night more than did justice to Salaratus's chuck-wagon skills.

Bright and early next morning Wendy, Witter, and myself set off for the bank at Globe with four sample sacks of ore. Very little conversation enlivened our journey; with so much riding on the success of this expedition, we were all, I suppose, too taken up with our thoughts.

Leaving our mounts in front of the bank, we followed Wendy in and asked to see whoever was in charge. This turned out to be the president, who eyed our sacks with considerable interest. Witter, introducing us, casually mentioned his status as a deputy U.S. marshal, and we got down to business.

Wendy informed him that we wished to open a commercial account in the name of Eldridge, Hardigan & Company, owners of the lost Yuma mine, now rechristened The Golden Grab, and that our initial deposit was to be made with the samples in the sacks we'd placed alongside his desk.

Our reception, I thought, was rather on the cool side until he opened up one of the sacks, at which point his eyes bugged out above a dropped jaw. "Whew!" he exclaimed, trying to pull himself together. "Is the same grade of ore in all four sacks?"

"You'd better look for yourself," Witter told him. And he did, very thoroughly. He then considered us with a great deal more interest. "Of course you realize we'll have to get this assayed. But I believe we can safely open your account in the amount of twenty thousand dollars. If that is satisfactory?"

"I expect that's fair enough," Wendy answered with a touch of her old-time flavor.

She accepted the receipt he personally made out, said we'd come in to buy mules, and where did he think would be the best place to get them. This information he was glad to furnish, and after some very cordial handshakes, we set out for the place he had mentioned.

We were received with such gracious attention, I guessed someone from the bank had got here ahead of us. We selected, on Witter's whispered advice, fourteen mules and asked the price, which seemed steep but not unreasonable in a mining community. Wendy said we wanted them delivered, gave directions, and said we'd be back with a cashier's check to include packsaddles and stout cotton rope.

The man assured us he'd be happy to go get the check himself and wrote out an itemized bill of sale, which he handed to Wendy with many assurances of being privileged to serve us.

Time we were ready to start for home, I was finally beginning to feel like a mine owner.

Chapter Thirty

The Golden Mule Train

The mules arrived the next day, the same animals we'd picked out, and in good shape. Witter urged us to get packed and ready to go as soon as his two men from Tucson showed up. "I wired them right after we picked out the mules. They should be here tomorrow," he told Wendy, who still wasn't reconciled to the risky travel he had talked us into.

Nor were Rabas and I at all enthusiastic about dismantling the wall we had built across the ledge entrance. "Don't look so glum," Witter told us, pitching in as best he could to help empty the sacks we needed to transport the ore. "Everyone and his uncle will guess that after buying those mules we plan to move ore, that we'll be out in the open with a fabulous cargo. Whatever he intended, Ives won't give a second thought to it now—he'll be after the ore we put on those mules."

"We ought to leave the ore here and fill them sacks with rocks," Rabas said.

"It's a thought," the deputy admitted, "but it wouldn't solve your need for ready cash. Anyway, as far as a raid on this ledge is concerned, I don't think with those booby traps out there you need worry about anyone getting in here—"

Showing plain her disquiet, Wendy said, "There's nothing to stop them coming in from the front!"

Craig and Brady made it known they agreed with her, but Witter waved that away with a nonchalant grin. "Ives will be too busy trying to knock off that mule train."

"And if them mules take off across country in the midst of that racket," Arbuckle growled, "that ore will be scattered to hell and gone!"

"You sound like a bunch of old women," Witter said. "Call it off if you'd rather have Ives harassing you for the next three, four years."

So, with an occasional grumble, we began sacking the ore. It was hard, sweaty work and not to be accomplished in any handful of minutes. As sacks were filled, they were put in a pile in the second cavern, not far from where the mules were being held.

Night had fallen by the time we were finished, and I, for one, was plumb ready to eat. Coosie got out his harmonica after the pans were all piled in the washtub and played old range songs accompanied by Arbuckle on the Jew's harp. With both entrances guarded against a surprise, the rest of us sought our blankets, though nobody bothered to get undressed.

At first light we were up and tearing into Coosie's sausages and beans, washing them down with that damn scalding coffee. Witter's two men showed up about seven, hard-faced and taciturn, and within half an hour, pack saddles in place, we began the arduous job of loading. The mules were cranky, the pack horses frisky and full of high spirits.

"If we get away by noon, I'll be surprised," Wendy said, but Witter just laughed.

"We'll do better than that," he replied in good humor, and we did. By eleven o'clock we were on our way—ten riders strong and every one of us packing a rifle, pockets stuffed with cartridges.

In single file we made quite a caravan, strung out a good half mile, as inviting a target as Ives could ask for. Rabas was in the lead because he knew this country like the palm of his hand. Wendy, most important of the owners, since in earlier days this mine of ours had contributed to her old man's notoriety, could ride where she pleased, and right now it suited her to be alongside of me.

"You've knocked around some," she said of a sudden. "Ever considered traveling in double harness?"

"Who—*me*?" I chucked her a startled glance with the hairs straight up along the back of my neck. "Not since I got old enough to know up from down!"

"How long since you've enjoyed a good old-fashioned home-cooked meal? Nothing like it, they tell me. Of course," she added, peering straight ahead, "I've never tried my hand at cooking, but I expect I could learn if I put my mind to it.

"Cat got your tongue?" She quit trampling around through the tules then and looked straight at me. "It's your turn to say something."

"Yes, well . . ." I had a hard time finding spit enough to get the words out. "I'll get back to you," I finally managed, and spurred my sorrel up ahead to where I'd spotted Witter gabbing with Rabas. I purely needed a mite of time to get all that digested.

"This the best pace you figure—"

"Won't do," Witter said, "to run all the gumption out of these critters before it's needed. Rabas thinks Ives'll probably hit us about four miles from here, more than likely." He looked around at me. "You got a white handkerchief?"

I passed it over. He said, "I want Rabas to tie this round the muzzle of that buffalo gun. When he reckons that bunch is about ready to jump us, I want that Sharps straight up over his head where we can see it. That's the signal. Also, it just might confuse those bushwhackers at the same time it's alerting us. If he spots any of that crowd, or if some excited numbskull jumps out of cover, he's to incline the barrel in that direction. I'll pass this along as I ride back. Now if he juggles that barrel up and down it'll indicate we're right on top of those buggers.

"In that case I want all these critters—everything with four feet—bunched up where he's at. When you hear me yell, I want these mules and horses slammed right into an' over Ives's crowd—stampeded! Savvy?"

"Hell's fire," I said, "you'll be scattering that ore from hell to breakfast!"

"Never mind that—you can pick it up later. Important thing is to scare the livin' daylights out of them—I want Ives's outfit plumb demoralized. Pick off any that attempt to get clear. I aim to put that bunch—and especially Ives— behind bars, and if this works out, that's where most of them will be. Biters bit, and we'll win hands down and maybe never lose a man."

"And if it don't work?" Rabas said.

"If it don't you'll do whatever you have to, but I'd a

heap rather see them crippled than killed. A dead villain ain't half the example of a live one pounding little rocks out of big ones for the rest of his natural. Keep in mind it's Ives's intention to wipe out the lot of us."

Witter's bum arm was out of its sling, and I was encouraged to learn he was not as callous of the state of our health as I had figured him to be. Seemed like he knew his business all right, and I was wasting no time feeling sorry for Ives; but although Witter's ingenuity had put that bugger pretty near where we wanted him, it did cross my mind that Ives might be smarter than he was being given credit for. Then I recollected Wendy and set off to rejoin her.

The look I got out of those gray eyes was a little unsettling. She said, "Reckon you must have had a burr under your saddle."

"No," I said, "just figured we ought to know what Witter and Rabas were about to cook up," and told her the strategy Witter had decided on. "Country's getting rougher," I said, looking round. Then I met her stare squarely. "How long you been coddling this notion?"

"Popped into my head," she said with a grin, "when you came larruping to Broken Arrow after me."

I nodded, solemn-faced, recalling the way she had looked when I stepped into the sala to cut her loose. I didn't know what I wanted, and that's a fact, but I could see plain enough this was something that had to be handled with considerable more care than I knew how to give it. While I was squirming to find the right words she said, "I believe we could rub together at least as well as most. You don't cuss a lot, and from what I've seen you wouldn't smoke up the house. You look reasonably rugged, and you're not afraid of work." Her glance sharpened up. "How do you feel about it, Phil?"

That's where she had me, because I plain didn't know. I kind of wanted to put it off till I had more time to push it around, but it seemed like any weighing of values was a long way from being what she had in mind.

I said, not wanting her to feel like she'd demeaned herself, "I ain't never tried this, but it sounds good to me. I expect if it don't work out—"

"It will work," she declared in a reassuring tone, "if you'll meet me halfway and put up with my notions." And she managed a kind of tremulous smile below that sorrel hair and freckles. "Now what about this scheme of Witter's—do you see any chance we might come out on top?"

"I'd say it looks pretty good. If he's figured it right. Rabas has some reservations, but he don't like counting chickens before they're hatched. Still . . . Witter's pretty sharp or he wouldn't be in the job he's got. I'll allow we've a fifty-fifty chance anyways."

She caught hold of my arm. "Oh, I *hope* so, Phil! I'd hate to think after all we've been through—"

"Me, too," I said, and we left it at that.

We'd been walking the packstring, and we stayed in that pace, wanting to have them fresh as might be when Rabas hoisted the signal. There was a bunch of fluffy white clouds overhead and enough of a breeze coming down off the rimrocks that we didn't have to keep mopping the sweat off our faces. Like Rabas, I guessed, I was more worked up over the possibility of scattering that ore over half the county than I was about the prospect of tangling with Ives.

He was tough and unscrupulous and used to having his way, backed up as he was by as mean a crew of cutthroats as I had ever come across, but we had already proved he wasn't infallible. He had a tight grip on the county machinery but up till now anyway it hadn't functioned quite as slick as he'd had reason to expect. Another thing in our favor was the rage we'd got him into. It was bound to affect his judgment, and with so much impatience and frustration clawing at him, it might lead him into a rashness he'd be unable to wriggle out of. And this, I assumed, was the key to Witter's strategy.

Chapter Thirty-one

Every Man For Himself

We were into a series of gullies and hogbacks, not as rough on our animals as it was on our nerves. Mostly Rabas was steering clear of the gullies, keeping to high ground wherever possible. Even so, there were times when some part of our outfit was clean out of sight. And the wind was getting up, more fierce, more gusting, picking up grit along with the dust and, to make matters worse, blowing straight into the animals' faces.

Flanking the packstring like all of our outfit, both Wendy and myself at this point in time were positioned about midway of this procession, and it crossed my mind we were too strung out, and that unless this were swiftly corrected we might never get them bunched in time to implement Witter's strategy.

I yelled at Wendy, "I'm going back to try and hustle them

up! Watch for Rabas's signal and keep these dang critters movin'!''

They didn't like facing into that grit, and half the riders had wipes across their faces.

"Close up! You want to leave your bones out here? You're too far behind—watch for the signal an' close 'em up!''

They'd been told the plan and must have understood that everything depended on our being able to get the stock bunched in his immediate vicinity almost as soon as Rabas hoisted the signal. Way it seemed right now, we'd not have more than half of them available. There was far too much space between mules, each of them twenty to seventy feet apart. If this wasn't changed in a considerable hurry, the stampede Witter was counting on was like to become a rout unless Rabas waited for us—and how long *could* he wait?

Racing down to the end of the line, I whirled my horse toward Rabas again and tore into the mules with a rope's end. "Get 'em up there!" I shouted. "What are you damn fools thinkin' about? Close 'em up, you numbskulls!''

Peering through the dust in the midst of this confusion, I discovered we were bucking an especially sharp slope that, with these obstinate mules, was certain to defeat us if we couldn't prod them into a run mighty quick. Yelling, cursing them, lashing the bastards, the three of us—Craig, Arbuckle, and myself—slammed into them furiously, the wind, the slope, and the goddam grit all working against us. It was, literally, an uphill fight; but it wasn't until I glimpsed the white patch of that handkerchief above Rabas's head that I could see we weren't going to make it.

We had them running now at a lumbering gait but it wasn't enough—not nearly enough as I could desperately see. And it was just about then I heard the far crackling of rifle fire, and through the gray fog of swirling dust saw two of our boys torn out of their saddles and the bunched broncs about Rabas suddenly drop out of sight, Rabas with them.

"Never mind—" I yelled, "keep 'em moving! Keep 'em moving! Bat 'em across the ass with your rifles!"

It was plain if we didn't get these mules up there pronto this was like to turn out just as Ives had envisioned it. In this crazy confusion and rumble of hoof sound the crack-crack of rifles slammed viciously, foretelling the havoc that was still out of sight. And now a new worry hit me. I couldn't see Wendy anyplace, nor Witter.

We now had the mules pretty well extended with the crest of the rise scarcely twenty yards ahead. Should we hold them up or use this momentum to hurl them down into the maelstrom below?

A crucial decision, no two ways about it.

By stopping them here, pulling out of this fight, we might save the mules and the ore they were packing, and perhaps save ourselves at the expense of the friends we still couldn't see.

Conflicting emotions burst through my mind as the front-running mules tore onto the crest. It was unthinkable that we should abandon our partners; all three of us knew that and pushed the brutes harder, yelling like Apaches to hustle them faster, knowing by God we were going for broke!

Down that declivity we swept like a whirlwind into the raging inferno below. It was downright impossible to tell friend from foe in that smother of dust boiling round us, in that bedlam of yells and staccato of gunfire, screaming animals and ricocheting bullets.

There were no choices left; we all understood it was every man for himself.

I felt my horse lurch and flung myself clear through that

thunder of hoof sound. With all those years of chasing cows' tails I knew how to fall. Just the same, when I picked myself up with dust in my gullet, I didn't have enough breath left to curse with. I glimpsed Ives briefly, Moriarty alongside of him, and then they were gone; I was into a stumbling run, seeing in these last explosive moments Ives's crew, flustered in the onslaught of plummeting mules, mindlessly attempt to claw their way out of this holocaust.

I saw Witter once, still clamped to his saddle, teeth bared, hat gone, flame darting red from the muzzle of his rifle; saw one of Ives's crew suddenly throw up his hands and drop in his tracks.

When the haze presently lifted and the guns were all still, I caught sight of Wendy gingerly picking her way through that carnage of crumpled shapes, and my arms closed round her as she flung herself at me in a shuddering whimper.

It was finally over, all but counting the cost.

We had lost three of ours, old Rabas among them, Coosie, and one of the two men from Tucson. Two mules had been killed, five ore sacks ripped open, and gold lay in sparkling clumps in a shining cascade across the face of the slope.

Four of the bushwhackers showed motionless among the strewn shapes of dead and injured horses, which someone was going to have to shoot. Six other roughnecks who'd come through unscathed had been rounded up and stood sullenly watching a livid-faced Ives being shoved in among them, with both wrists cuffed behind his back. The rest of his crew had managed to get clear and were extremely unlikely to surface again.

That punctured shoulder was giving me fits, but no blood stained my shirt so I guessed eventually it would feel more or less normal. I was going to miss Rabas, no getting around it, and Coosie's harmonica wailing "The Yellow Rose of Texas," "The Buffalo Hunters," "Git Along Little Dogies," and the "Little Rosewood Casket."

As Witter and a couple of helpers herded the prisoners along toward the horses, Wendy said to me, "You know, I've been thinking. It's going to take awhile to get Broken Arrow back on its feet, but with money coming in from the mine, we can do it. Those corrals will need fixing. We'll have to buy some more cows and a couple of good bulls, and fix up the house—Phil! Are you listening?"

MULE MAN

For RUTHIE,
who suggested one of the
story's most scintillating moments.

Chapter One

For a footloose ex-Ranger who'd come out of that fight at the Hashknife with a bullet-made limp and some nightmare memories of Mossman's resolve to clean up this Territory, I guess you could say I had heard the owl hoot. Several wasted years had gone down the drain since Cap Mossman had turned in his badge and taken up ranching over in New Mexico and I had quit, too, to drift back to Half Step and a humdrum life of trading heirlooms for cash.

Broiling glare of the Arizona sun was scarce two hours from dropping back of the mountain when I rode into the plaza at Ajo.

The bad boys were beginning to ease back into this country, in spite of the Rangers, now that old Burt wasn't around to harass them. Once again gun sound was banging through the hills and dealing with tame Injuns made me think more than once of signing up for another hitch, bad leg and all. As one of Mossman's Rangers I'd come to spot the breed soon as I laid eyes on them and like an old fire horse I could feel the pull of remembered excitement.

I had taken in most everything in sight time I pulled up Gretchen by the hitchrail fronting the assayer's office. Ajo was mining with a capital M. Cow outfits were in town, a sure sign of payday. Wasn't no big crowd lallygaggin' in the plaza, but tied horses and buckboards was thicker than flies on a spill of sorghum. I'd been aiming to get back to Half Step and tell my old man I wasn't cut out to be no counter-jumper, that routine chores couldn't never make up for the kind of a life I'd known with Burt Mossman.

To tell the plain truth I was bored plumb silly.

Getting out Durham and papers while slanching around one more cautious look I twisted up a smoke and set fire to it, rummaging my mind what I had better do next. I could eat and push on or—willing to risk a bit—could spend the night here and slip away first thing in the morning. What I purely wanted was to get myself home.

I hauled my weight into the saddle, ignoring the dubious look Gretchen flung me. Off to the left about a whoop and a holler was a near bleached-out sign spelling LIVERY; and that's where we ambled, up a gut-narrow alley that presently fetched us to a barn's hoof-tracked ramp.

An old duffer reluctantly got up off his peach crate. "Yeah? By the week or the night?"

"Expect one night'll take care of our needs. Give this animal a good feed of oats. Rub her down—proper." I peered around. "All right if she swipes a drink from that trough?"

"What it's there fer. Two bits ever' time she lowers her head."

"Water must be a heap scarce in this community."

I could see he was fixing to get on his dignity. "Never

mind. She's worth it," I grumbled, and flipped him a cartwheel. "Where's the nearest grub for a two-legged specimen?"

"Buck, two doors down, can take care of your tape-
worm."

Racked by saddle cramp I took myself back to the alley
mouth, crushed the butt under a bootheel and stretched another long glance the full length of the square without latching onto anything to put my wind up. Place he'd touted said
BUSTED CROCK, a two-by-four hash house right next to the
stage office.

Getting out of my brush jacket, I slapped out the dust
against the nearest wall. My gimpy leg was giving me hell;
bullet holes don't cure up like an overnight cough . . . un-
fortunate. I didn't see anything showed a need to squat and
reach. Place would liven up before long without any prod-
ding. A few of those old varmints we hadn't shot and buried
might recollect my face; something I'd forever have to be
watching out for.

I mounted the porch and went on inside.

Five-six shapes held down stools at the counter. Only
table occupied was in a corner by the window. A woman
sat there over a half-finished meal. Preempting another halfway down the long room, I gave my order to the biscuit-
shooter and made a careful point of minding my own
business.

Carving up my steak, cramming my gut with frijoles, I
couldn't escape the scrutiny I was getting from that dame,
the feel of her probing my face, sorting out the rest of me.
I put up with it long as I could and then, shelling out some
silver, shoved back my chair and headed for the door.

Her heels tap-tapped behind me and I swung round on
the porch with a smothered oath.

She put a hand on my elbow. "I'm Fern Larrimore. Could I speak with you a minute?"

I gave her a scowl, not wanting any part of this. "I don't usually," she said, "approach strange men in this fashion."

"All right. Let's get away from this door."

We moved down onto the walk, her arm slipped through mine. Not like a hustler, more like she had it in mind I might try to get away. "Would you tell me your name?"

"Corrigan—Brice Corrigan." We stopped in front of the stage office. "What's the problem?"

"That's just it." She looked at me undecided and puzzled. "I don't really know. It's just a feeling I have. Would you be free to take a job?"

"What job?"

"A sort of watching brief. You see, my brother's an anthropologist—interprets fossils and relics. He has a couple of months' leave from the university to see what he can turn up about those old cliff dwellers, the faraway ancestors of today's Pueblo Indians. Specifically the Basketmakers—"

"I wouldn't know a Basketmaker if one jumped up and bit me."

A quick and brief grin streaked across the contours of that scrubbed-clean face. "You have the look of belonging. Jeff—my brother—has to have a guide, he knows nothing about this part of the country. He's out here to make a dig, nothing elaborate, a kind of probe is all, to see if there's anything here to be found. I'd like to hire you."

"I don't want to be hired. I'm trying to get home."

"Is your home around here?"

"No."

Her blue-green eyes kept trying to take me apart. A sigh came out of her. "Look—" she said, "I've an uneasy feeling we're going to need more help than my brother is counting on. . . .Whatever your business is, whatever your stipend, I'll double it.''

I stared at her, astonished, yanked my glance off her face to throw another look around. More horse sound, more jabber, more movement in the plaza, more people sifting around and about over the rough plank walks. No ore wagons in sight but plenty of ranch rigs, a lot more jaspers standing around by the tie rails. I eyed the look of her again. Younger than I'd reckoned. Not much more than twenty, well built but no beauty. "Why me?"

"Sometimes," she said, "you have to fight fire with fire."

She had a pretty sharp eye for a girl her age and a dude at that. She had me picked for a bravo, I could see that plain enough. "Figurin' to buy a . . ." I let it go, to say, disgusted, "This thing your brother's after. Some kind of loot, is it— buried plunder, that sort of thing?"

A rush of color came into her look, flushing some of the paleness out of her cheeks. A touch of resentment sharpened her voice. "Of course not! I've told you; he's an anthropology major, an assistant professor at a Chicago university. He's hunting for Indian artifacts, to learn whatever he can, to pin down the time these cliff dwellers arrived here from Asia and Siberia, the length of their stay and why they aren't still here. That sort of thing. This is very important. We want to know what their day-to-day life was like."

She said, more composed, "Jeff's got hold of a man called Harry Hatcher who grew up in this territory, knows all about it. Mr. Hatcher's going to show us the best places for a dig. He's told Jeff about some caves that have petroglyphs—he's been on digs before, understands what is needed. It's the men Hatcher's hired that makes me uneasy."

"This Hatcher, what do you know about him?"

"Only what Jeff learned from the bank—"

"Bank, eh? Bank vouch for him? Guarantee him, did they?"

"Not exactly. They say he's been a guide, takes out hunting parties. Took a party of archaeologists into the Tonto Basin—"

"And where is he proposing to take your brother?"

"Into the Chaco Canyon country."

"Pretty well into the back of beyond. Damn rough country, lady. No place to be draggin' a woman through—"

"Yes. That's what he said."

"But you aim to go anyhow."

"That's right. I've got a stake in this."

"Don't sound much like a woman's business. I wouldn't expect your brother would care to put you at risk. Let me get this straight. As I understand it, the reason you want to rope me in is because you don't like the kind of crew Hatcher's put together—"

"It's not so much the crew I dislike. It's this fellow Fletcher and another called Clampas. I don't like the looks of them."

"Have you told your brother?" I said. "What is it with you? Can't you talk to him?"

"I've told them both—him and Hatcher. Jeff only throws up his hands. 'Women's notions' he calls everything I point out. Hatcher says we have to understand this place where we're going is bleak, rough country, a maze of draws and ridges where anything could happen—wild and desolate. He thinks we might run into fugitives, renegades, even hostile Indians. He says we need me like Clampas and Fletcher as a kind of insurance. Jeff calls them 'rough diamonds.' He thinks it's all in my head."

"I don't think they'll want me along in that case."

Her chin came up. "Perhaps not, but I'm the one who is putting up the most of the money for this dig—my inheritance. Without my support there won't be any dig."

I looked her over again. I blew out my breath. "Lady," I said, "I've got to get home. I been away too long now."

She met my stare with a kind no man cares to get from a female. "Have I been wrong about you?"

Chapter Two

She had me there, no two ways about it.

Man could be a rightdown bastard, yet even the worst had to have some value of self to hang on to. Graveled me plenty to be pushed and shoved by the likes of this kid who had nothing I wanted and wasn't no better looking than the handful of others I'd left wailing in the past.

"Shit!" I said, and didn't care that she heard it. I felt meaner than gar soup thickened with tadpoles, too damned riled to keep a hitch on my lip. "Ain't it crossed your mind latchin' on to me could be jumpin' from the skillet straight into the fire?"

Just breath wasted. I said, "This brother of yours—where-at will I find him?"

She half turned, lifting an arm with the ghost of a smile. "Over there at the hotel. With Harry. You going to play this my way?"

I charged off through the clutter of horses and wagons,

too disgruntled to answer. She could think what she liked and to hell with her. I felt like a fool being choused around this way.

She wasn't two steps behind when I reached the far walk and stepped onto the hotel veranda, hating to think what damage this fine brother of hers could do pawing around in his greed for more facts. "Dudes!" I muttered, but this Larrimore filly with her mop of roan hair had a lot more to her than appeared on the surface.

I paused to say grimly, "Aside from this Hatcher, big brother, yourself and that pair you don't cotton to, how many others is roped into this deal? What's the size of your crew?"

"Well . . . let's see. Hatcher's picked up four men—"

"With me—if I go into this, that makes an all-over total of ten in this party?"

"Twelve, counting the Mexican handyman and cook."

I looked down at the dog sitting patient by her legs, a shaggy mixed breed of some sort, black and tan. "That dog goin' too?"

"Flossie? Certainly. I sometimes think she has more sense than my brother."

"This Hatcher, now. What do you think of him?"

"He's all right, I guess." She pushed hair off her cheek. "A little glib perhaps. Seems very knowledgeable, easy to get along with."

"Yeah. I bet. Who's assembling the supplies, the stuff you'll have to pack into that country?"

"Hatcher has that all taken care of. We're planning to leave first thing in the morning." Her glance swung up, openly curious. "Are we likely to meet the sort of riffraff Harry mentioned?"

"Can't tell what you'll meet up with these days. There's

riffraff anyplace. Far as Indians go there's actually no saying. Some of them's gettin' a mite touchy here of late. Come on, let's get at it."

I limped after her into the lobby. Stuffed animal heads decorated the walls. The floor held a scatter of Navajo rugs; club chairs were grouped about an oversize fireplace, and three paunchy gents in the garb of ranch owners had their heads together off in a far corner. Girl led the way toward worn leather chairs where two men leaning forward were engaged in what appeared to be an earnest conversation. They looked around as we approached. The one I reckoned to be Hatcher stood up fairly pleasant as Fern stopped in front of them.

"Jeff, I want you to meet Brice Corrigan, who'll be going our way. Brice, this is my brother, Jeff Larrimore. From Chicago."

Larrimore said, getting onto his feet somewhat surprised, "Glad to know you, Brice," and put out a hand, which I shook as a matter of simple courtesy. "Do you live around here?" he asked, curious, civil.

"Not too near, I'm afraid. My old man runs the trading post at Half Step."

His eyes changed a little but hung on to his smile. "That so? We're going north for a tour through the Basketmaker country, looking up the remains of what these Navajos call the Ancient Ones. University is sponsoring a kind of small dig."

"Big country." I nodded. "Rougher'n a cob."

"And this," Fern said brightly, "is Harry Hatcher, who will be in charge of the route and our crew."

"You been at Half Step long?" Hatcher inquired, shaking my paw.

"Born there."

"How are the natives around those parts? Any truth in the rumors I hear going around?"

"Could be. Some of them seem a mite restless lately. But I don't figure any trouble you run into can be charged up to natives. Renegades," I tucked in, "ain't confined to one color."

"True enough." He laughed. "Arizona's got their share all right. Did I understand Fern to say you're also heading north?"

"He's going with us," she put in without beating around any bushes. "I've hired him to round out our safari."

Through what had the makings of an awkward silence Harry Hatcher said with no loss of charm, "Glad to have you with us, Corrigan. Bigger the party the more likely we'll be to come through in one piece." Behind his bland mask he was giving the look of me a thorough going-over.

"You expectin' trouble?"

"Not at all," he assured us with a comforting smile. "Just one of them fellers feels it pays to be prepared."

Bobbing his head, Larrimore chipped in. "Harry's been around. I haven't turned up one person since I've been out here who knows as much as he does about the people we're trying to find—the Anasazi. All the Indians I've talked to just look at you and shrug. They don't know the first thing about those old cliff dwellers."

"Understandable." Hatcher nodded, confident smile enveloping Fern. "They have no written history, no way of bridging the gap of centuries. For all practical purposes the folks Jeff's interested in disappeared from this region about 1400 B.C., give or take a handful of fortnights," he said, much admiring his own wit, it seemed like. "I'm going to take him back where probably no other whites have ever been, right into the heart of that Basketmaker country."

He had the right line to take with young Larrimore. Fern's brother looked pleased as a cat with a fine plump bird by the tail. "Yes," he told me, "quite a bit of serious work has been done on the Pueblo peoples but they came later. First pueblo we know about has been dated no later than seven hundred and fifty, and that's after Christ. Practically modern compared with the aboriginal people I'm trying to get a line on.

"You see, what we need is more artifacts. We've a great need to understand more about primitive man. These Basketmakers come fairly close to being as near as we can get to early man in this country," he declared with conviction. "Near as we know now, they arrived here from what we call Siberia either during or immediately after the Ice Age."

Hatcher with his smile appeared to be in full agreement. "What we're trying to do here is a lot like hunting for the Missing Link, with apologies to Darwin. So little, truly, has been discovered you could practically"—he chuckled—"put the whole bundle in a teacup. Jeff hopes to embark on a voyage of discovery, wants to pioneer the forgotten world of the Anasazi and go straight back some twenty-five thousand years!"

Yep. You had to hand it to Harry. He'd come as near in tune with Larrimore as two peas out of the same pod. I thought to see right then at least a partial reason for the girl's disquiet. I wouldn't trust this Hatcher half as far as I could heave him. "Just what," I asked Larrimore, "are you hopin' to find?"

"If we can get onto the right location, I believe there's a possibility we can unearth some primitive tools and weapons, bones of prehistoric animals they've killed, artifacts used by them in everyday living—that sort of thing. The scientific community, the anthropologists and scholars, so far as these people are concerned, haven't managed to come up with the definitive answer.''

Hatcher said, ''We'd like to be able to pin down the source of whatever it was that drove these folks here from their former homelands. From wherever they came from, be it fire, floods, famine, pestilence, drought or whatever. An ambitious concept? Certainly. But Jeff feels strongly if he can come onto remains that haven't been tampered with—''

Larrimore cut in, fairly bubbling with excitement. ''Harry thinks he can put me onto some graves.''

''Where?''

''If I remember correct,'' Hatcher said persuasively, ''it's someplace in the vicinity of Chaco Canyon. Lot of cliff dwellings back in that cut-up country.''

''Cliff dwellings, sure,'' I said. ''I don't remember any graves. I went through there several months ago.''

Harry showed his smoothest smile. ''You didn't get back far enough. There's places back there no white man's ever seen—''

''And what do *you* expect to get out of all this?''

Hatcher laughed. ''Maybe I'd like a little piece of the credit when Jeff makes his big find. That's reasonable, ain't it?''

''You'll have it,'' Jeff said earnestly. ''This could be a big thing!'' He pulled in a gusty breath. ''The pots, pans and bones of man's culture. Going back pretty near to the beginning!''

I hadn't no doubt he was sold on it, but Hatcher to me didn't seem hardly the kind to give a whoop about credit. He had to be in this for something more substantial if I knew anything about the cut of his jib.

The dog sprawled at Fern's feet had the look of watching

Harry with a jaundiced eye, too. Larrimore, still flushed with enthusiasm, bit off the end and lit up a thin cigar he produced from a pocket of his silver-buttoned vest. "If we could get even one absolutely conclusive answer—"

"I think we've talked enough," Fern said. "This place is filling up. If you fellows expect to eat, you had better get a move on."

Harry nodded. "I guess we've got the subject pretty well covered. If you're goin' with us on this jaunt," he said in my direction, "be down at the corrals by five o'clock tomorrow morning to help us load. Jeff's counting on an early start."

That broke up the conference. The girl, the dog and young Larrimore moved away.

Thinking a drink would go pretty good right then, I was turning around to go hunt up one when Hatcher thrust out a hand. "Let me ask you somethin', Corrigan. How'd you manage to work yourself into this?" His eyes, bright and hard, locked into mine. "Where'd you meet up with that girl?"

He plainly didn't like the way I grinned. "You look like a saddle tramp—a damn grubline rider!"

"Reckon that was it," I said. "Miss Larrimore's got a heap of compassion. Offered me a job, she did. An' being chock full of pity myself, I signed on. Just as simple as that."

To keep an eye on Gretchen—make sure she wasn't tampered with—I talked myself into a deal with the livery keeper that got me the right to bed down in his hay-filled loft. I must've tossed and turned pretty near the whole night. Too many questions, too few answers, too many faces flitting through my head. I hadn't met the pair of hombres that had driven the girl into taking me on . . .

My thoughts jumped around to Burt Mossman. People claimed Arizona Rangers never looked back, but Burt was one who stuck to a trail like heelflies after a fresh-butchered calf. And I was mighty sure, too, Harry Hatcher hadn't missed my occasional limp. In this much time that leg should have cured itself. There was a heap of talk these days—and a heap of agitation, about this Territory getting to be a state.

A good few of the pictures flitting through my mind had to do with Fern Larrimore and this thing I had let her auger me into. Hell, a kid in three-cornered pants ought to've had more sense than let himself be prodded into this kind of trap!

No one had to tell me a ranny like Hatcher didn't give two snorts for Jeff Larrimore's Injun ancestors. Nor for Fern. No girl could compete with the kind of return that slick catamount was hunting! What he saw in this deal had to be real dinero, and scratch around as I would and damn sure did, I couldn't see big mazuma in old bones and pot shards.

I got down next morning to the corrals ahead of schedule, aiming to have me a plumb thorough look at what kind of a crew handsome Harry had picked up to make sure this deal went the way he intended. I saw with disgust there wasn't no answer there. Four of these five hombres was just ordinary cowhands of the twenty-five-dollar-a-month sort. The fifth, Turtle Jones, might be a cut above them, both in gumption and savvy, which to my way of thinking wasn't saying a whole heap. The other pair—the ones that had got Fern's wind up—was a different breed of cats, a breed I knew from the bootheels up.

Fletcher turned up first with a jingle and scrape of bigroweled spurs. His look showed the hardness long years had ground into him. Pale flaxen hair beneath a squaw man's hat and pale blue peepers above his sneering mouth. A short-barreled .44 was shoved into his waistband and he came striding through the crew like he owned the whole shebang. "What the bloody hell," he rasped at me, "d'you think you're doin' here?"

"Hadn't given it much thought. You the boss of this outfit?"

He stood like a coiled spring, tipped forward, hands working with his mouth pinched into a tight-rimmed slit. "That's Corrigan, Fletcher—new man we've signed on," Hatcher called. "Get off your high horse and help stow these packs."

"You hire him?"

"He was hired by Miss Larrimore and don't you forget it. Now quit pawing sod and get busy." Hatcher turned away to speak to a man who had just come into the corral where the pack string was being loaded with boxes and bulging gunnysacks. "Keep your eye on that fool. I want no trouble round here!" Then off Hatcher went, all smiles, to greet the Larrimores, who had just come up with their saddled mounts.

"Reckon you must be Clampas," I said to the man Harry'd spoken to. "Looks like we'll have a good day to get off on. I'm the new hand—Corrigan."

This Clampas—if that's who he was—would have had to stand twice to cast one shadow, so thin he was, so tall and gangling with that flat tough face above the wipe at his throat and the six-shooter slung at either hip. The gaunt cheeks twitched, amber eyes crawled over me like fingers and he flung away with a bridled impatience, never opening his mouth.

No wonder, I thought, the girl was uneasy. That pair was no kind to stamp your boot and yell *boo!* at.

I slanched a look round for Fletcher as Fern's black dog came sidling over to test the air at my legs. Reaching a hand down for sniffing, I heard Clampas demand of Hatcher in a grumbling growl, "How come that waddy ain't helpin' the boys load?" I didn't catch Harry's answer because just then Fern, stopping beside me, said, "Where's your mount?"

I cocked my head to where Gretchen stood on grounded reins. The girl's face showed a considerable astonishment. "You surely must be teasing. Nobody rides *mules*!"

"I been ridin' this one a heap of dry miles."

She stared, disbelieving. Even when I mentioned the mule and me went together and she couldn't have one without having the other, she couldn't seem to take it in. Gretchen waggled both ears in obvious approval and heaved up a sigh like a bunch of hailstones coming off a tin roof. Fern had to laugh.

I said, "Where's the cook?"

"Backed out." She looked provoked.

"Expect we'll manage to make do if we put our minds to it." I sent a look at the overhead. All along the horizon the gray blank of sky was taking on a pinkish tinge. We watched Fletcher and Clampas ride out of the corral. "You don't truly think"—it come out too solemn—"I'm whacked from the same bit of goods as that pair?"

She got into her saddle and sat looking down at me. You had to like the way she wrinkled up her nose. "Expect we'll just have to wait and see, won't we?"

I knew her eyes were laughing but reckoned to glimpse a suggestion of warmth that hadn't been there before. Bitterly damning the notion, I sent an irritable hand across new-shaven chin and told myself there was enough on my plate without indulging that sort of foolishness.

Fletcher and Clampas rode off into the brush, the crew with the pack string swinging in behind, followed by Hatcher and the Chicago professor, young Jeff got up like Montgomery Ward's version of what the well-dressed Western gentleman will be wearing this fall. "Don't you think he looks real nice?" Fern asked.

Eyeing the flat-topped hat, white shirt, red tie, that cowhide vest with double row of silver buttons, sand-colored whipcord pants stuffed into knee-high boots with huge-roweled shiny nickel-plated spurs, I could only wonder.

"Very nice," I told her. "Time to get crackin'." Then I climbed onto Gretchen.

We went along in this strung-out fashion for maybe half an hour without no more gab.

Then abruptly she said, "What sort of work were you doing before we ran across each other—I mean, were you working for one of these ranches?"

"I was headin' for home."

"And before that?"

"Oh . . . a little of this and some of that."

"You aren't very forthcoming, Corrigan."

"Ain't much I can say. Most of the time, like now, I been ridin' for a livin'."

Her glance was like a pair of hands digging into me. "Would you describe yourself," she persisted, "as—"

"Mostly I been what you might call fiddle-footed. Haven't stayed too long anyplace, I reckon."

"Tell me about your home. Was someone ill that you wanted to hurry back?"

"Reckon," I said, "they're healthy enough. I wasn't hurryin' particular, I just wanted to get there. Matter of fact I never knew my mother; goin' by what I've heard I guess she died pretty young. Old man's all right, never been sick a day in his life.''

"Doesn't he get pretty lonesome?''

"Not that I ever noticed. Runnin' that tradin' post don't leave much time for lonesome.''

"What does he sell?''

"Anything folks'll buy, I reckon: beads, food, flashy gewgaws, blankets—that kinda stuff.''

"Doesn't he sell whiskey?''

"Not to Indians he don't!''

"Well, you needn't take my head off about it.''

"They got a law against that. My old man wouldn't want to lose his license. Or any other privilege, come to that.''

I could feel her studying eyes going over me. "I have noticed,'' she said, "when you're not thinking about it you have a tendency to limp. An old hurt perhaps?''

"The leg got bit by a bullet.''

Expect it come to her goddam notice the conversation was definitely adjourned. She rode off after her brother, who rode alone up ahead of us.

Country was beginning to show its teeth a bit now, not yet what you'd call rough but increasingly cluttered with rocks and such barbed growth as mesquite, yucca, Spanish bayonet and wolf's candle. An occasional saguaro reared its spiny length some thirty or more feet into the rapidly heating air above this sandy floor. The sharp spikes of hedgehog with their curled-up crimson blooms were generously mixed among the prickly pear, cholla, fishhooks and barrel cactus. I'd been living with such for the past couple weeks and paid them scant heed other than to yank the blue wipe up across my nose in the hope of filtering out some of the dust.

After a couple hours of reasonable progress young Larrimore in his grit-covered finery dropped back to share some

223

chunks of his learning about things nearest to his heart, in especial the long-gone Anasazi, mainly Basketmakers of the earliest variety.

I said, "Let's hope you don't run into any chindis."

"What's that?" he questioned, twisting around to eye me, curious.

"Chindis," I told him, "are what Navajos call the spirits of the dead."

He gave that some study, considerable more than you might reckon it warranted. "But the Navajos aren't related to the cliff-dwelling Anasazi, nor to the people who built the early pueblos even. The Navajos showed up here a good while after the Basketmakers quit this region."

"If you're sure of that, tell me where they took off to."

This was evidently something he wasn't able to answer. It undoubtedly griped him but he brushed it aside. "I'll tell you something else," he earnestly declared. "Over the centuries both the Basketmakers and their near kin the Pueblos received and amalgamated continual additions to their cultural inventory. Such improvements eventually as stone axes and pottery, the hard cradleboard, permanent housing and that marvelous weapon the bow and arrow—none of these luxuries had come to this country with them. They even learned to domesticate wild turkeys."

"What about the horse?"

"They knew nothing of horses. The Spaniards didn't set foot in America until two or three hundred years after the last of Basketmakers had completely disappeared. The term *Anasazi* in the Navajo use of it means simply 'ancient enemies,' " he assured me, "but why those old Basketmakers should have been considered enemies is completely up in the air. The two cultures, far as we know, never even came close to any confrontation. Indeed, how could this have been possible when the Navajos' arrival found this region up for grabs?''

"Do you reckon," I said, "if I had gotten here sooner . . ."

Jeff laughed. "Anyway, according to the best current advice on the subject, somewhere about two thousand years ago this primitive and extremely simple people lived scattered in pretty small groups over much of this region. In appearance and culture they've been likened to the Australian aborigines—not that our present Indians bear much resemblance. It might surprise you to learn I've been told a man can step back seven hundred years and more just rounding a bend in some of those draws and canyons. Kind of grips you, doesn't it? These ancient long-abandoned ruins, I'm told, are mostly found in sandstone country, tucked away in caves and plastered overhangs.''

"I expect we can promise to show you a few. Don't know as you'll discover a great deal you'll want to cherish. Might even come up with one nobody's seen except for those usin' it. There's still a few hostiles runnin' loose and, hard though he tried, there are still a few scalawags Mossman an' company never got their hands on.''

He peered around sharply. "You honestly believe—?''

"Wouldn't surprise me a heap if we run into some pretty hard cases. Not red ones though. You won't find many Indians around those ruins—live ones, I mean. They don't consider such places healthy. Too much chance of scarin' up a chindi.''

"Spirits? You don't imagine they really *believe* in such foolishness?''

"You bet," I told him. "Never mind. You've got a forty-sixty chance of stumbling onto some ruin nobody yet has ever blundered into.''

225

Chapter Three

Having fixed my own grub times without count, I thought maybe offering my services as cook might take a little heat off my own situation so far as it applied to Hatcher and company. According about the middle of the afternoon I pushed a reluctant Gretchen into overtaking Fern where she rode with Jeff a broiling hundred yards ahead.

"How's the dust back there?" Jeff asked, swabbing a wipe across flushed cheeks.

"No worse than it is up here," I said. "What are you folks fixin' to do about a cook? I could patch up a meal if you can't do any better."

She kept whatever reaction she had under cover. "Turtle Jones has agreed to take over that department. Seems he spent last fall being roundup cook for Colonel Green's outfit."

"That's fine." I grinned. "Can't say I was ackshully lookin' forward to that sort of chore." After her brother rode

226

off to rejoin Hatcher up ahead I said to Fern, "How long does Hatcher figure it's like to take to put Jeff where he can start his hunt?"

"He says he don't want to push these horses. That it most likely will take us five or six days."

I looked off through the smudge of heat and dust where the pack string plodded up a shallow draw. A couple of the crew were hoisting canvas water bags to put a bit of damp on their whistles. "You ever think to ask Harry what he hopes to get out of this?"

"Get out of it? You've already asked; we both heard what he said. What could he think to get beyond the fee he and Jeff agreed on?" Her stare seemed puzzled. "It isn't Harry you've got to watch. Why, Jeff thinks Hatcher is the luckiest find he could possibly have made!"

"Just what's he payin' Harry, if you don't mind sayin'?"

She looked at me intently, halfway shrugged and presently mentioned Hatcher was to get one hundred and fifty dollars a week to furnish crew and transport, locate a suitable spot for the dig and fetch all Jeff found back where we'd started from. Pretty good pay I was bound to agree, but someway it left me less than satisfied. I glanced at the dog ambling alongside Fern's mount with her tongue lolling out but still going strong and taking pleasure in this romp.

"And who picks up the supplies, the grub and what-not?"

"Harry picked them up under Jeff's instructions; Jeff and I paid for them. Look—" she said, "I don't see the point to this. What are you getting at?"

"Nothin' wrong with the deal. It all hinges on Hatcher. If you can take him at face value, if you're satisfied the feller's no more than he claims to be, this trip could be duck soup." I touched Gretchen up with a spurless heel, Fern scrambling after us.

"I told you Jeff trusts him, sees nothing in Fletcher and Clampas to bother him."

"But you went out of your way to pull me into—"

"That's right," she said with no attempt to duck around it. "I'm afraid of those two. I don't like their looks, can't see why Harry, if it was simply a matter of running into something we hadn't allowed for, couldn't have found—"

"Yeah. You told me. He obviously picked them figurin' if we ran into gunplay they'd be tough enough to earn whatever he's payin' them. Same notion you was fondlin' when you came after me." I considered her disgustedly. "What if Harry can't control them? Were they known to him beforehand? An' what do you suppose'll happen if he can't? If he decides to pull out?"

"If you want to back out—"

"Get rid of that notion. I'm not backin' out. Just tryin' to make sure you understand where you're at in this business. That's a damn lonesome country Harry's takin' you into; you better go into it with both eyes open. Your brothers's a babe in the woods."

There was color in her cheeks, an angry sparkle in her glance. "You sound—"

"Never mind that. If Hatcher decides to pull out and leave you—"

"Leave us where?"

"In that wonderful place he's been talkin' about that no other paleface has ever set eyes on."

"We've got a contract with Harry. I don't see how he could pull out. The bank assured us—"

"If Hatcher's got other plans, that piece of paper won't stop him."

*   *   *

About an hour short of sundown Harry threw up a hand. Declared we'd gone far enough for the start of this journey and would make camp here where these mesquites and ironwoods would afford some protection should a wind come up and start belting through this sand.

It wasn't a bad place. Plenty of dead wood for the fires and a small creek gurgling over gray rocks between moss-covered banks. Ample room to set up the tents, one for Fern and the other fetched along as a cover for our supplies. He told Turtle Jones to get busy with the small fire and fixings, and the rest of the crew to get our stuff off the pack string. Fletcher he picked to take care of the horses and Clampas he posted atop a rock with a rifle. He seemed to know what he was doing.

I took Gretchen to the stream and let her have a small drink. I considered the scanty forage as I rubbed her down with a piece of gunnysacking, then limped over to the bags of grain we'd brought along for the horses and dumped a couple quarts of oats into a nosebag for her. I didn't bother with hobbles, knowing from long experience she wouldn't stray beyond reach of my call. They had the horses, likewise with nosebags, penned inside a hastily thrown up rope corral.

With no chuck wagon to work from you had to give Turtle Jones high marks for the potluck meal he put together this first night. As Jeff remarked in the midst of our eating, "That chef we stole from the Waldorf-Astoria has more than lived up to his great reputation," and handsome Harry cried, "Stand up, boy, and take a deserved bow!"

"Aw, shucks," Jones muttered with his cheeks firing up, "ever'thing come outa cans but them biscuits. If I kin ever git organized I'll try to do better."

Most everyone sat around the fire that first evening singing old range songs to Alfredo the handyman's accompaniment on his mouth harp. Fern left Jeff to come and flop down beside me with her mop of roan hair, eyes brighter than the stars, that splatter of freckles across her nose hardly showing and denim-clad legs tucked snugly under her.

"Mighty well-behaved dog," I said, eyeing Flossie where she crouched nearby with her behind reared up, face on paws, glance fixed on me intently.

Fern laughed. "I think she likes you. Look—she wants to play! She almost never barks, she puts all her thoughts in body language."

"How'd you come to give her that name?"

"She's named after a girl I went to school with. She wasn't even weaned when I got her, just a pitiful stray I picked up off the streets. We had to feed her from a bottle. When she got old enough to eat from a pan, she insisted on me holding it while she lay stretched out across my lap. When finally I refused any longer to accommodate her she used to sprawl on the floor beside her pan—it was nearly a year before she'd eat standing up. See! She knows we're talking about her."

The dog rolled over on her back, watching me upside down, waggling her paws. "I don't think she'll let you but that's what she does when she wants her stomach rubbed."

I reached out a hand. Quick as a wink the dog ducked out from under it. "She's shy." Fern laughed. "Come on, Flossie. Time to go to bed."

We all turned in fairly early that night, myself finding sleep hard to come by, too many wild thoughts chasing through my head like a herd of spooked horses. Coyotes yapped back and forth across the moonlit distance. Crickets chirped and nighthawks swooped and between unrestful periods of dozing I tried to keep a weather eye on Clampas and

Fletcher taking turn and turn about atop that twelve-foot flat-topped rock.

The night passed without untoward alarms or excursions. It was Jones beating a racket from his washtub with a ladle brought me out of my soogans while the only light in the solid dark came from the built-up breakfast fire. "Come an' git it!" he yelled.

By my figuring we had covered some thirty miles—perhaps a bit more than less—in that first day's travel toward an uncertain future. On this second day we did better. The horses' high spirits in the cool of that early morning and the exasperated shouts and cursing of the crew were not allowed to impede Hatcher's schedule and there was no lallygagging permitted on the trail.

During most of the morning Fern rode ahead with Harry and her brother and I'd had plenty of time to sort out my notions had I been able to put my mind to it. There was always the chance Jeff was right about Hatcher though I couldn't persuade myself that was likely. The man was too glib, too agreeable, too obliging in furthering Larrimore's views and aspirations.

About Fletcher and Clampas I had no doubts at all. Until Mossman's advent this state had been more than rife with their kind. Cut-and-run killers of every shade and description had all but taken over the towns; stages were stopped, often ransacked and burned, rustlers and horse thieves made ranchers' lives miserable. Claim jumping had become the biggest business you could find in the outback. Some of these rascals had become so slick that, as Burt Mossman had been heard to declare, it took one to know one.

Burt's boys, the Rangers he'd been picked to head and organize, could not afford to wear any mark of their calling.

Arizona was a gun-governed country and its Rangers looked just like anybody else. Tough and enduring, hard-nosed survivors on call night and day, loners by necessity.

The sun grew hotter as the day wore along; you dared not rest a hand on any piece of metal. An egg would have fried anyplace it was dropped, but we had no eggs and we ate in the saddle, ignoring the customary stop for noon. "We don't have to push these broncs," Hatcher said, "but on the other hand we don't want to waste a lot of time. Steady riding will eat up the miles and put us in the next camp with something still left in case it has to be called for." His quick stabbing glance brushed across sweat-streaked faces. "Keep your minds on your business and be damn careful with that water."

It occurred to me to wonder where Harry imagined he was bound for but I didn't figure it behooved me to put in my gab in the face of his authority. Unless he got on to himself before we squandered tomorrow, the schedule he'd laid out was going to come up mighty short. It crossed my mind Larrimore might like a look at Inscription House, a ruin so named for the seventeenth-century date chiseled onto it by some forgotten Spaniard. Jeff, I reckoned, wouldn't come within miles of it.

Hatcher was being only prudent in warning the crew to conserve their water. But I thought those very words showed the man lacked considerable of being near as smart as young Larrimore esteemed him. Nothing but sheer ignorance could get a man killed of thirst around here. This was Basketmaker country; as Jeff delighted in mentioning, they had lived in this region for hundreds of years and they certainly hadn't thrived without water.

Toward the shank of the afternoon Jeff dropped back for a powwow. Seemed a bit embarrassed about announcing what he'd come for. "Get it off your chest," I said. "You must've come back here for somethin'."

"Well . . . doesn't it look like to you Harry's going the long way around?"

"How so?"

"Hadn't we ought to be heading a lot more to the east than he's taking us?"

"Why not ask him if you feel strong enough about it? Ain't he the one you're payin' to get you there? He's the man you said was on back-slappin' terms with these environs."

"But you said," Jeff protested, "you'd recently come through the place we're supposed to be heading for."

"Some fellers say a heap more'n their prayers. Direction he's goin', there's all sorts of red cliffs—"

"But not the ones I'd figured to be finding." He looked a mite grim about the edges of his mouth. "I might be what you call a tenderfoot," he said pretty harsh, "but by cripes I haven't yet lost all my marbles! If you won't tell me, would you advise my sister?" He was some het up, no two ways about it.

Lifting one of those skinny cigars from his pocket, I bit off an end and fired up.

"Wouldn't want me to cramp Harry's style now, would you?"

He slammed me a long look and suddenly, spinning his mount, took off for the head of the line again.

Result of all this became immediately evident. A considerable commotion broke out up ahead. Dust churned as the whole file of horsebackers, pack string and all, stopped like they had run plumb into a brick wall. Angry voices sawed through the confusion. *"Where's that sonsabitchin' mule*

233

man!'' Hatcher shouted, and here he came with blood in his eye.

Pulling up so short his horse reared, snorting, right on top of me almost, his yell crashed out of a livid face. "What d'you think you're playing at, Corrigan! What'd you tell that goddam fool?"

"Seemed to think we'd got off our course, wanted me to confirm it." I smiled at him thinly. "Told him you was runnin' this outfit; if he had any beef he should take it to you."

The hot glare from those eyes showed him still a far piece from any kind of shape to be reasoned with. I thought it best to try anyhow. "Your contract," I said, "as I understand it, gives you authority to take this outfit in whatever direction you figure will best serve. So why not go on with it?"

"You trying to get me fired off this job?"

"*Can* he fire you?" I said to him soberly. "He's just one dude against the whole push of you. Wouldn't think he'd get much change out of that."

"Maybe not," Harry growled after rummaging through it. "Just the same, you keep your damn yap out of this," and he went pounding off in a great rise of dust.

No telling what he said to young Larrimore but evidently they managed to patch up their differences because not ten minutes later our whole line of travel bent off to the right.

Chapter Four

We camped late that night with the dark congealing round us and Jones in a temper, short of wood and with no water available save for what still sloshed in the bags on our saddles. Refried beans was heaviest item on the menu.

No sitting around the fire at this place, no grins or pranks. Mouth harps, singing and the usual big windies were conspicuous by their absence. Fern with Flossie went early to bed. Fletcher went up a palo verde with his rifle looking sour enough to curdle fresh milk and Clampas, similarly armed, went off someplace back of the rope holding down our remuda.

Nobody said one word in my direction, not even Jones showed a friendly face. With not the frailest notion what Hatcher might come up with as a suitable reprisal for giving in to Larrimore, I kept Gretchen handy and slept with a pistol under my hull.

We were up before sunrise and on our way within the

hour, some of us half scalded with the heat Jones flung into that java. The sky turned pink and the landscape brightened and the sun shot up in all its glory smack-dab into the horses' faces.

The country looked flat, stretching out long miles in its mildly undulant surface through its haze of brown dust.

Larrimore, despite any change he'd effected yesterday, appeared fidgety with visible worry lines about his stare. "Yes," Fern said when later she dropped back to ride beside me, "he was pretty upset. He had a terrible row with Hatcher when Harry threatened to quit and pull the crew out with him. I think what bothered him more than anything was having his faith in the man undermined. Jeff was banking heavily on Harry's ability to put him onto a real find."

"I expect they'll get over it. Hatcher's lettin' off steam; I don't reckon he'll quit. Not yet anyway."

"That," she said, eyeing me in some concern, "wasn't the impression I got from you yesterday."

"Just wanted you to consider the possibilities is all. I can't tell what he's up to; if it suited whatever's runnin' through his noggin he could leave you in a minute, but I shouldn't think he's anywhere near doin' it yet. And as for pullin' out with all hands, some of these boys might not see it his way. You can bet he won't leave before Jeff gets his dig started."

She looked a little reassured. "How big is this Chaco Canyon?" she asked.

"Pretty big. Some ten miles long and I'd guess about a mile wide between the walls. A heap of ruins in that space. Those old boys certainly built for the centuries. I've poked around in a couple—"

"Is there much there to find?"

"Depends what you're lookin' for. Probably find a few

pots but I doubt they'd be old enough to interest Jeff. He wants to get back to the beginnings of these people. I'm afraid any relics he might come across there, except perhaps the buildings themselves, probably wouldn't be things actually used by those Basketmakers—not the early ones. Best bet," I told her, "is to hunt them side canyons and gulches branchin' off it.

"All the towns—if you can call them that—along the Chaco itself were big places in their time. Most of them had several hundred rooms plus ceremonial chambers. Much like the pueblos bein' lived in today. Most of them—even those that haven't been looked over by folks in Jeff's line of work—have still had a mort of people prowlin' through them."

"Why would those gulches be less likely to be picked over?"

"Some of them ain't so easy to come onto, either deliberately hidden or screened by brush that's grown up through the ages. All the trees within ten miles of the Chaco were cut away and used up at different times by the builders. But get back in some of them tributary canyons and you're dealin' with buildings of sixty rooms and less."

I found her studying me curiously. "You sound as though you know as much about it as Harry."

"Can't speak for Hatcher. About all I personally know comes of observation. Anyone meanderin' over this desert learns to keep his eyes peeled. Same as Flossie," I told her, grinning down at her watchful sheepdog.

She said, "If Harry hasn't taken this job for what we're paying him, what do you suppose he's after?"

"Loot."

She looked considerably surprised. "Well . . . I know—I quite realize the relics Jeff hopes to find and identify would

237

possibly be worth a little something to collectors, but . . .''

"Some people would put up a king's ransom for such things if they went back far enough in reasonably good condition and had nothing broken out of them. And the more rare the object the more they'll fork over. Looting's an enticing and highly profitable occupation for more people than you'd imagine.''

"Now and again,'' she said like she was studying on it, "you use words few persons hereabouts have ever bumped into.''

"Yeah,'' I said. "It's a damn bad habit I've found hard to get shut of.''

That night we camped alongside an arroyo where Hatcher went down into an apparently dry wash with a short-handled shovel he got out of the camp gear. He didn't have to dig for more than five minutes hardly before the hole began filling with water. Jeff allowed we'd be more comfortable camping down in that wash but Hatcher knew better. "A man can mighty quick wake up drowned doing that around here. You get a storm up in the mountains you've got ten-twelve foot of water in this wash.''

While three of the crew and Fletcher was getting the loads off the pack string the other two hands began fetching the saddle mounts down for a drink. I dumped my water bag into my hat and held it while Gretchen cooled her insides, then anchored her to grounded reins and went over and put up the tent for Fern. Jones broke up a couple creosote bushes and got his fire started and Clampas with rifle found him a station on the lip of the arroyo, Hatcher going across to have a few words with him.

I pitched in to help water the pack string while somebody else busied himself setting up the rope corral and pouring oats into nosebags to hang on the horses. I rubbed Gretchen down with my piece of gunnysack and wiped out her nostrils. By that time Turtle Jones had a good bed of coals and was dexterously throwing together our supper which, praise be, tonight featured no refried beans, Alfredo the handyman scouting up wood.

On Hatcher's advice we went early to bed and once more with a pistol stashed ready for use I kept Gretchen by me in case of quick need. No breeze sprang up to whine through the straggle of wind-bent trees along the arroyo's rim where Clampas stood with his rifle. We'd have a late moon tonight and, by the look of things, a hot day tomorrow which most likely was the reason Hatcher aimed to be moving ahead of daylight. Being short on sleep I drifted off almost at once.

Something jolted me awake. Grabbing up my six-shooter I peered through the dregs of the moon's fitful glow to find Gretchen's whiskers not three inches from my cheek. Throwing off my cover I came onto an elbow. There was some kind of hubbub boiling up beyond the penned stock, punctuated by horse sounds and angry voices. Gretchen, sidling closer, softly blew out her breath. Fletcher's furious yell sailed through the racket.

"That goddam mule man! Told you to git rid of him! Prob'ly turned them critters loose a-purpose!"

I got out of my soogans, put a hand out to Gretchen.

Jeff came shoving out of the shadows. "What's the rumpus?" Beyond him Jones was building up his fire. Catching up Gretchen's reins I headed for the corral and the group standing around that motionless huddle on the ground.

"What's happened?" Jeff demanded, singling out Hatcher.

"We're short one man and two of the broncs."

"Who is it?" Larrimore wanted to know.

"Ned Benson."

239

"Is he hurt?"

Fletcher's sarcastic growl said, "Why would he hurt? Hell, he's never been happier!"

"He's dead," Hatcher said. "Been walloped over the head."

I said, "How'd those broncs get loose from the corral?"

"You tell us," Fletcher snarled, starting toward me.

Hatcher thrust him back, hard eyes digging into me. "You got anything to say?"

Two of the boys stepped aside to let Fern through. "Brice had nothing to do with this. You had Clampas on guard—didn't he hear anything?"

Hatcher's stare swiveled to Clampas. "Well?"

"Nary a thing," Clampas told us. "Whoever done this must've moved on bare feet."

"Maybe you fell asleep," Fern said, and Clampas snorted. "Whoever done this was Injun quiet."

Jeff's face looked troubled. Hatcher looked worried, near as I could make out in that uncertain light. I said, "What makes you think two horses are missing?"

"They're missin' all right. Soon's I spotted Benson I slipped in there an' made a count," Fletcher grumbled. Fern and Jeff exchanged a quick look. I said, "If someone was trying to make trouble for us, why stop with two horses? Why not grab all of them?"

Hatcher nodded. "Good point. Couple of Navajos probably snuk up on us someway."

"Come an' git it!" Jones called.

He'd beat up some biscuits and what he gave us to go with them was refried beans.

Harry told off a couple hands to bury Benson, made sure all water bags were filled and hustled us out of that place just as the sky was beginning to turn gray. He and Jones had gone through the supplies and none of the foodstuffs appeared to be missing, but the loss of Benson—not to mention two horses—had put a damper on our spirits. It was a pretty subdued outfit that got under way that morning.

Clampas dropped back to ride alongside me, but had nothing to offer in the way of conversation. After a couple of hours Hatcher came back and motioned Clampas to move on ahead. "This Chaco," he asked me. "How much farther do you reckon it to be?"

"Another couple days, if we push them a mite, ought to fetch us in sight of the south gap, I reckon. Thought you knew all about that canyon."

Harry's face put on a sort of rueful scowl. "Tell you the truth I ain't never been near it. There's red rocks lots of places. I was figuring, long as he wouldn't know the difference, to take him up into them Lukachukai Mountains. Figured he could dig there good as anyplace." He hawked up some phlegm and spat it off to the side. "How do you look at that business last night? Think it was Indians?"

"What about Fletcher? Heard him tryin' to lay it onto me. He wouldn't think no more about killin' a man than he would about findin' worms in his biscuits."

"Keep away from him," Hatcher grunted. "On pretty short notice I had to take what I could get." He kept looking into the swirl of heat haze ahead of where Clampas, lounging in the saddle, was riding point. "Country's changin'," he said. "Bunch grass and grama. Lot of rocks croppin' up—ain't none of them red though. You been through here before?"

"Don't rightly remember."

"Didn't somebody say your old man run a tradin' post?"

"He runs the post at Half Step."

"Doin' pretty good, is he?"

"Gettin' by, I reckon."

"You in that business?"

"Guess I'm too fiddle-footed. Too much settin' around. Too quiet."

"How come," he asked, "you don't ride a horse?"

"I find this mule more dependable. She don't spook so easy, for one thing."

Hatcher's stare wheeled around. "Man could get lost damn easy round here. Mile after mile it all looks alike. Can't see how them Basketmakers stood it. Dry as a brick horn."

"Expect it didn't used to look like this. Don't hardly ever rain here no more."

There was about Harry this morning a suggestion of something stewing in his craw which he wanted to get up but was making rough work of. Two-three times he'd cleared his throat, the gloom in his stare wandering over my face while he chewed on his lip with unaccustomed indecision.

Something hauled my thoughts away from him. Scrinching my eyes, trying to cut through the pack-string dust up ahead, I said, "Company comin'."

It jerked Hatcher's head up. We could both see them now. Jeff coming back with two other horsemen.

"Navajos!" Hatcher grunted, loosening the pistol in its housing on his hip.

When they came up, swinging their horses to ride alongside us, the older Indian, wrinkled of face and gray of hair, was energetically puffing one of Larrimore's thin cigars with every evidence of relish. Jeff with a glance at Hatcher said, "They want to know what we're doing here."

Harry looked them over and with hand on gun butt con-

temptuously spat. The younger Navajo's eyes turned hateful.
I could see pretty quick this could get a little touchy.
"We're huntin' old pots from the time of the Anasazi," I
told the old man.

"I think you better leave," he answered. "This land," he
said with a hand taking in everything in sight, "belongs to
the People."

"Since when?" Hatcher challenged.

"Many years—"

"Soldiers say different."

Both Indians took a long look about. The older man
smiled. "No soldiers here," he announced with satisfaction.
"You go."

Hatcher smiled, too. A nasty thin-lipped grimace; and
there was Clampas with his rifle coming down the line to
join us. "This man," I said, putting a hand out toward Jeff,
"is a friend to the People from a great white man's school
far away. He'd like to take back some things—"

"All white men take. Too much take!" the younger Navajo growled. "All time take!"

We had all come to a stop in the sort of confrontation
that could bode no good for anyone. Something had to be
done before a bad situation piled up a worse hereafter.
Clearing my throat I said to the old one, "This teacher,"
with a nod of the head at Larrimore, "is tryin' to find the
Chaco. He wants to tell the men at his school of all the
wonderful things built there by the people who left this land
for the Navajos."

Those Indian faces didn't offer much encouragement.
Cold sweat came out along the back of my neck. I waved
Clampas back. "So if you'd agree," I said, "to act as scouts
for this outfit and show us the fastest, most direct way to
get there—"

"What you give?" Greedy interest was all over that young buck; and Jeff, catching on, held out his watch to the older one, who gravely accepted it, holding it up to an ear, smiling at the sound it made. The other Indian spurned such baubles. "You give tobacco? Blue stones? You give whiskey?"

I looked at him sternly. "Whiskey bring soldiers. We give tobacco. Frijoles. A tall hat for each of you."

"Give me a chew of tobacco now," the younger one demanded.

I reached into my pocket and handed him my plug, from which he took a great bite and threw the rest in the dust. "You give gun!"

There was naked envy in the way he was staring at the Sharps across Clampas's saddlebow. "No guns," I said, and he glared at me malevolently. "You already have a gun," I told him, pointing to the Henry rifle on his saddle.

"That gun no good." He thrust out a hand toward Clampas. "Give me that one!"

"Where do you want it?" Clampas growled without expression.

"Maybe so," the fellow said, grinning, "some Indian kill you."

"Have at it," Clampas invited, and elevated his Sharps to bear on the man at point-blank range.

Chapter Five

White about the mouth Jeff said, "Put that down. We don't shoot people at a friendly powwow, nor while we're crossing Navajo land."

Clampas for a moment appeared to be of two minds. Before things got out of hand, Harry kneed his own horse sufficiently forward to blank out the threat. The old man, seeming unaware of the danger and smiling sadly at Larrimore, finally spoke. "What you say is good. Since I was no higher than your dog the white man has brought us nothing but trouble. I have not forgotten when blue-coat soldiers took the People away, but your heart is good." Still considering Jeff he sat quietly a moment, then abruptly said, "That we may live at peace I will take you to the Chaco."

The two Indians rode with Larrimore past the stopped pack string and forward to the head of the line. Harry released pent breath and looked at me with a shudder. "A near thing, that." His darkening glance found Clampas.

"Stay away from that fellow." The laden pack string began to move, but in a new direction, still east but more southerly. Clampas rasped a fist across flushed cheeks. "We'll have to watch that buck," he told Hatcher. "We ain't outa this yet by a long shot."

It was obvious Harry agreed. "Have to post more guards at night. Long as they're with us. Old man's all right, but that younger one might be brash enough to try and stampede the whole string."

"Could fix him up with a accident mebbe."

Harry gave him a sharp look. "Don't even think of it. That old duffer looks like to me he might have a bigger than average say hereabouts—in Chaco too for all we know."

"You're probably right," I said. "We sure don't want to fetch the whole tribe down on us. You heard what he said about white men and trouble. He's peaceable now; we ought to do our best to keep him that way."

Clampas slapped the butt of his Sharps disgustedly. "Pamperin' them bastards won't buy you nothin'. Put it into their heads you kin be pushed around an' by Gawd you'll *git* pushed! If you wanta git along with 'em you got to take a firm stand."

That night we made another dry camp.

Wood—even cowflops—was in short supply but Jeff, no doubt as concession to our red friends, ordered Jones to spread himself and we had the best meal we'd been served in six nights. Jerked beef cut up in some kind of white gravy, spuds baked in the ashes with their jackets on, hot buttered biscuits and coffee strong enough to stand without a cup. And canned peaches to round things off.

True to what they'd been offered, Jeff gave each Indian a black uncreased Stetson, a small sack of dried beans, and tobacco. The chewing sort. In addition to this largess the older man was ceremoniously presented with a good round dozen of Larrimore's thin cigars.

Before the rest of us turned in, Harry arranged for three shifts of men armed with rifles to patrol the perimeters and make sure none of the horses managed to get themselves lost. This possibly wasn't necessary but, reminded of the loss we'd already taken and a pair of Indians right in our midst, I couldn't blame Harry for trying to play safe. He had to see that Jeff remembered that a man without a horse in this kind of country was in mighty sorry shape.

It looked like being another hard night. I couldn't rid my head of the many disquieting notions continuing to churn up unwanted activity. Generally I could put such things out of mind but certain faces in this outfit continued to plague me, not the least of which was Fern's.

I recalled how before the start of this jaunt I'd considered her a plain damn nuisance, arrogant and headstrong and like to be a pain in the ass insisting on having a part in this deal. Since then I'd learned she could grow on a man, no fool at all but a girl with real pluck and a heap more sense in a practical way than that dreamy-eyed Jeff with his talk of dead Indians and artifacts nobody else had dug up.

Thoughts of Hatcher and his deadly companions continued to rile and disturb me. For all the airs he put on, his talking talents and confident authority, it appeared to me dubious that if push came to shove he'd be at all able to control that pair.

First thing I'd done when we'd quit for the day was to take care of Gretchen and put up Fern's tent. "Stay away from those Navajos," I told her, but all I'd got out of that was an odd look and laughter. She said, "That old man is no scalp-hunting redskin." A mischievous light danced round in her stare. "He told me his name—Johnny Two-Feathers. Isn't that quaint? The other one's Hosteen Joe—"

"It's that other one we got to watch out for."

"Johnny'll keep him in line. He's pretty well educated by local standards. Brought up by the Jesuits in mission schools, first in Tubac and again at Tucson; even knows a few words in Latin! Don't you hate to think of a man that old having to sleep on the ground?"

"Fern," I said, "he's been doing it all his life."

"You know what he calls you? 'Man-on-a-Mule.' " Her laugh tinkled again like silver bells in the sunset. "He calls Jeff 'Young Man Who Hunts Old Ones.' "

He had certainly made an impression on Fern—a notion I wasn't at all sure I cared for.

Just as I was finally about to drop off, young Jeff came over and squatted down for a chat. "You know," he said, "I believe I've caught up with the bee in Harry's bonnet. I heard him asking old Johnny about beads—"

"May be fixin' to do a little trading on the side," I told him. "Better get some sleep."

Jeff's mention of beads in connection with Harry became one more notion I didn't like the look of. But nothing happened in the night and once again we got off to an extra early start with old Johnny up there at the front of the line and Hosteen Joe and his surly scowls noplace in sight.

Hatcher dropped back and I brought this up. "I dunno," Harry said. "He's out there ahead of us someplace, making sure—according to Johnny—we don't run into trouble. Between you and me and the gatepost he's more like to stir it up and kick the lid off if he can."

Refried beans juned around in my stomach. Dust devils spun across the empty flats and heat waves shimmered and danced in the distance. Noon came and went without rest and no edibles, with the gritty shadow shapes of men and horses drearily toiling in dust-choked silence beside us.

As the afternoon wore on, the gray scarps of clay hills filled with shale began to lift and crawl with interminable monotony across the trackless landscape. There was no sign at all of the missing Joe, nor did he turn up for supper when we stopped at a seep to pitch camp for the night.

Harry growled at me bodingly, "That sonofabitch is up to something!"

But the night was got through without alarm or apparent mishap. For breakfast we had corn bread and another dose of refried beans. Plus some of Jones's Arbuckle. No one had much to say. We got away bright and early, Johnny Two-Feathers riding again with Fern at the front of the outfit, Clampas and Fletch flanking their progress about a hundred yards out.

The morning breeze wafting across that seared and blackened vista ghosted away within the hour and the molten disk of the rising sun began to get in its licks. Hatcher, swinging his mount in alongside Gretchen, gave me a brief unjoyous grin. "Don't blame them basket-makin' aborigines for getting the hell out of this place! Enough to cramp rats!" he growled, sleeving his face.

"Probably better when those cliff towns were buildin'. Expect they had more rain; Chaco was likely runnin' bank to bank. I remember Jeff saying they did quite a bit of farming down on the flats."

"What kind of boodle you reckon he's really after?"

I flipped him a look. "You know what he's here for. No secret about it; he's hopin' to unearth the Anasazi's beginnings and dig up enough evidence to prove—"

"You ain't swallerin' that hogwash, are you?"

"What's your idea?"

"I think he's after turquoise. Why else would his sister rope *you* into this?" Harry peered at me sharply as if to see how I was taking it. "Your old man runs a trading post. Among these redskins, from what I've seen, there's a big demand for them blue stones!" He let the silence stretch out, squirming round for a better look at my face. "Hell, some of them bucks would trade their women off for 'em! I been told," he said, watching, "it's been a prime source of feuding down through the ages—oldest gemstone known."

"Even so," I told him, "what you're thinkin' don't make a heap of sense. Jeff's an academic, a professor of anthropology. His notions in that field look pretty reasonable, I'd say. The man is after kudos, the kind of acceptance and undoubted publicity he could get overnight if he's able to dig up the kind of factual evidence no one has managed to turn up before. He ain't the first of his kind to put a dig on out here, you know. There've been others—the Wetherills, for instance."

Hatcher wasn't convinced. "Maybe. But you take it from me there's something besides old pots drivin' that dude. I've got a hunch he's stumbled onto something. Big an' blue and buried in that canyon!"

Chapter Six

The next day was Sunday.

The night before, while I was putting Fern's tent up, old Johnny had sought me out to say he would soon be released from his obligation, that we should see the red cliffs before another night. This knowledge trickling through the camp had set up a certain amount of excitement, put a new look on the faces of our outfit.

To go with our breakfast coffee Jones gave us nothing but yesterday's biscuits. Harry paid no mind to the grumbling, as anxious to get moving as Jeff was himself. By six o'clock we were well on our way, myself as usual still riding drag with Fletcher and Clampas out several hundred yards ahead of the pack string.

Fern came back to swap a few words with me. I said, "Who had the ordering of grub for this outfit?"

"That was Harry's department. In his behalf I'll have to point out we've a better variety than Jones has dished up.

There's quite a bit of tinned beef but Jones is afraid of it with all this heat. The cans aren't bulged; I believe it's all right." The roan mop of her hair was windblown and tousled. "What were you and Harry so earnest about yesterday?"

"He's got it into his head all this talk about Basketmakers is just so much crap, that your brother's after turquoise—"

"Turquoise!" she cried, eyes locked on mine widely. "Where did he pick up that silly notion?"

"He's been workin' on it. Only thing that makes sense to gents of Hatcher's persuasion is a whopping pile of dollars and the quickest way to get them. He simply can't believe two dudes from Chicago would come all this way just to dig up a bunch of old pots and such."

She bit her lip, looked worried. "That's ridiculous! Exasperating!" The blue-green eyes intently searching my face became anxious. "You don't believe that, do you? I swear it isn't true—for years Jeff has believed these earliest Basketmakers came to this region thousands of years before his colleagues can be brought to admit . . . he's been trying to get back far enough to prove it. This is something he feels very strongly about. If he can only dig up—"

"Yes." I nodded. "I'll go along with that."

She said in a burst of anger, "This idea of Hatcher's is utterly untrue! Oh—I'm afraid this is going to make trouble, Brice. If that notion gets around it could wreck this dig before it even gets started! I'm going to send Jeff back to talk with you."

Jeff looked flushed, and angry too, when some half hour later he swung his horse in beside me. "Fern's told me about Hatcher. I've just been talking to him; wasted breath!" he said bitterly. "The man's impossible! Just sits there and grins at everything I tell him!''

''That figures. Only thing he wants to hear about is profit. Did he threaten you again with taking the crew out of here?''

Jeff shook his head irritably. ''No, he made me a proposition. The fellow's preposterous!''

''What kind of proposition?''

''The man's a mental case! Says he knows of a ready market that will pay big money for any turquoise we come onto, that if we find any gem-grade rough or mounted spiderweb we could make a real killing. He proposes we split, him and me, fifty-fifty. I reminded him again I wasn't looking for turquoise, that what he suggested was completely unethical. 'Who's talking about ethics?' he sneered. 'You better have your head looked at. I'm telling you this could be a goddam bonanza!' ''

The look on his face was furious. ''I tried to tell him it wasn't likely we'd come up with hardly more than a cupful of extremely old and crudely cut beads, and that whatever we found was going back to the university.''

I said, ''How did that strike him?''

''He just laughed. 'All right,' he said, 'you go dig up your pots and *I'll* hunt the turquoise and I'll be claiming every chunk that's found.' I was so mad I could hardly talk. 'Over my dead body!' I told him, and got another of those pitying grins. 'Wouldn't be surprised,' he said, 'if that could be arranged.' ''

We looked at each other through an uncomfortable quiet. Heat writhed above the gray shale-covered ground and shimmered between the distant worn-down bluffs. We set off after the others.

''You'll be knowin', of course, you're not the first to come in here?''

"Yes." Larrimore nodded. "Simpson came here in '49, Jackson in '77. There were Hyde's expeditions of '96 and 1901. Artifacts were found; but what they uncovered, while extremely interesting, didn't even approach the beginnings of these people. What they took out was relatively modern, Basketmaker Three and Pueblo stuff. There's got to be more underneath—that's why I came out here. If there's to be any proof of the dream I've been coddling it's got to be right in this area someplace."

He gave me an anguished, frustrated look. "What are we going to do?"

"Just now, nothing." I shook my head much as he had done. "Right now, if he's got the crew with him, we're crouched between a rock and a hard place. I don't believe more than three of those boys will side with him. I think we'll have Jones and maybe Alfredo. But if it comes to a scrap, that's pretty rough odds. He's going to have Clampas and Fletcher for sure."

Jeff's gone-white face was filled with despair. I peered off across the scraps of those shimmering bluffs and, twisting, swung my glance to where the blue and wavering peak of a mountain thrust above the trembling haze. Jeff abruptly caught hold of my arm. "Look!" he cried, pointing—"isn't that the Chaco?"

I nodded. "The south gap. But it isn't where you're staring. What you're seeing's a mirage. Take a glance at your sister and that old man. You don't see them turning. They're goin' straight on."

Jeff sank back in his saddle. "What if I order—"

"You're not in a position right now to order anything. If Harry's passed the word, and you can bet he has, the greed he's built up in that pair of gunslingers could get you killed

254

at the first sign of trouble. Leave it alone. I want to think about this.''

The broiling hours dragged on. The sun sagged into its downhill slide. A little breeze sprang up, too hot to afford relief. When our shadows began to drop behind us the Navajo, riding with Fern perhaps a quarter of a mile ahead, pulled his piebald pony to a stop with lifted arm. The whole line stopped. A mumble of voices reached us in a faint jumbled sound.

Jeff cried, ''What are they talking about? Why have they stopped?''

''Let's go find out.'' I tightened my legs against Gretchen's ribs and pushed her into a trot, Jeff's mount following. Harry, Fletcher, the old man and Fern had all dismounted, the first pair staring like they couldn't believe it into a huddle of blasted rocks where a seep formed a pool of unexpected water. Fletcher scrubbed a fist across beard-stubbled cheeks. ''Heap good water,'' Johnny Two-Feathers said. And Harry with a jerked-up glance at the sky slammed his hat on the ground. ''We're campin' right here—we've rode far enough!''

No one felt inclined to argue with that. Alfredo got an armful of sticks and Turtle Jones began to build up a fire while a rope was stretched round the pack string and the crew began peeling off loads and saddles. In almost no time at all Jones was treating us to refried beans.

It was crowding six in lengthening shadows by the time tin cups and pans clattered into the washtub and those who cared for it began to light up. We were in a locality of old rocks and outcrops with night closing in and no prospects showing for a better tomorrow. Fletcher and Clampas with instructions from Hatcher went grumblingly away to take up stations with their sour looks and rifles; and it was at this moment, taking a final survey of our unenviable situation, that I saw Fern with Flossie making her way in my direction.

Hatcher's sharp stare had discovered this, too.

The grin fell off his face as the dog with lifted hackles, growling softly, bared her teeth. "You better keep that bitch in hand," he said, ugly, stopping in his tracks to stand and glower in my direction. Fern grabbed the dog's collar and Hatcher straightened up to send a scathing glance across her face before turning the full weight of his inspection on me.

"Things have taken a change in this setup. I can see you've been told," he chucked at me with a laugh. "From here on out, those who ain't with me are in line for bad trouble," and he went stamping off, muttering under his breath.

Gretchen waggled her ears and hee-hawed like a rust-clogged pump rod. Hatcher half turned like he was minded to come back but presently went off without further remark.

Fern sank down, legs folding under her, with an audible sigh. "Jeff's going about with the look of a zombie."

"He's come too far to give it all up now."

"But what can we *do?* He won't deal with Hatcher." There was a tremor in her voice. "He's just about lost all heart for this dig."

I had no doubt Hatcher'd meant what he said. He figured he'd got hold of his life's best chance and was going to stay with it come hell or high water. No use kidding ourselves about that.

"Maybe things'll look better in the morning." I put a hand on her shoulder and gave it a squeeze. She got wearily up with an attempt at a smile that came off so stricken I made an extra effort to promote a cheerful outlook, but what was there to say remembering Hatcher's ultimatum? I could probably get the drop on him, but with Clampas and Fletcher with the camp spread out under the snouts of their rifles, such a move would be worse than not doing anything. To effectively improve this situation at all, those two hard cases had to be near enough to Harry to hold all three at a decided disadvantage.

I watched her move toward the tent, Flossie ambling along beside her.

She'd made it apparent she was neither meek nor biddable. She might not be any beauty but I had learned she was a girl with a good bit of bottom, in the main optimistically good-humored and not one to find relish in a jaundiced view of things. A down-to-earth sort of person . . .

I hauled myself up with a muttered oath. This was not a time for that kind of thinking. My sort of drifting held no place for a woman and nobody knew this with more conviction than myself. If she and Jeff were to have any chance of wresting the whip out of Hatcher's hands, it behooved me to do something pretty damn quick.

Chapter Seven

Daybreak found us mounted and moving. By all the signs and signal smokes the next camp should place us in Chaco Canyon. I'd done a mort of thinking without latching on to the faintest glimmer of how to disabuse Harry of the notion he was boss. The fellow was much too cagey to be taken unawares or let himself be lured beyond reach of those gun-slingers' rifles. Catching him off balance was going to take some doing.

The molten arc of the sky showed not the ghost of a cloud. The sun crashed down with insensate fury and all about us appeared not to have known a touch of moisture since the Anasazi vanished. If other springs existed in this burned black flat, no one but Navajos knew of their location. If this drought-ridden country had any charm we had yet to discover it, a grim and empty place steeped in the stillness of the centuries. Burning sands and swirling dust storms, a hard land to picture as ever having been any different, yet it surely had; no people could have settled and flourished for hundreds of years in such desolation.

I was in better case than most of our outfit for I had crossed this waste before. Had actually encountered a few of these ruins Jeff and his sister had come to investigate and drearily discerned how little could be hoped from digging ground already disturbed. To provide Jeff's theories any chance of proof, he had to have ground untrod through intervening ages. No easy chore, though I reckoned it possible if we could find some solution to Hatcher's threats.

There was little to be gained by openly opposing him. Any such attempt must be a last-ditch risk, for he was obviously prepared for ruthlessly crushing any action we might launch. Any turning of the tables called for guile and much patience.

Needing to make Jeff understand this, I sent Gretchen forward. But Harry, catching this maneuver, came up at a brisk trot, forcing his horse in between Fern and Larrimore with a nasty grin. Ignoring him I went on to pull up beside Fletcher, hoping to start a bit of counterirritation. "Has Hatcher mentioned his latest scheme?"

Fletcher's look crawled over me morosely. "Keep away," he growled. "I got nothin' to say to you," and shifted his rifle.

"The man's told Larrimore he's claiming any turquoise we happen to find. I imagine what he has in mind is beads or nuggets; you can generally find a few around any old ruin. Just wonderin' if he was intending to share with you boys."

Before the fellow had time to digest this or show enough expression to afford me any lead, Hatcher loped up with an oily smile. "Won't do you no good trying your blarney on Fletch. Or anybody else. All my boys are in on this bonanza.

Don't let me catch you suckin' up to 'em again.''

Turning away with a shrug I felt his hard look following. "If you want to start trouble," he called after me, "just stir up them dudes and you'll get yourself a bellyful."

The heat-blasted bluffs got closer and rougher as the morning dragged along. By this time, blue hazed in the distance, you could see where the south gap cut into the canyon and guess at the rubble that lay all around it. I was presently surprised, staring through the lifted dust, to find our old Navajo riding back in my direction. "How!" he hailed, swinging in beside me with a lifted hand. "Pretty soon I go."

"Thought maybe you were figurin' to throw in with us."

A faintly humorous glint briefly touched his glance. "White man's troubles like white man's whiskey. No good for Navajo. I got sheep to look after."

"You on your way?"

"Plenty soon. When you come to Chaco." He eyed me a moment. "You got message?"

"Heap smart Indian," I agreed with a grin. "Tell missy to keep her tongue between teeth. And tell her that goes double for her brother."

Watching his paint horse go loping back to where Jeff and Fern rode at the head of the line, I wasn't at all hopeful he'd be allowed any private conversation. I saw Clampas gesture, saw Hatcher wheel and take a long crusty look. But contrary to my assumption, he sank back in the saddle and continued whatever he was laying on Clampas.

If only those dudes would take my words to heart I might have time enough to cobble together some means of forcing Hatcher to leave them alone, for it had to be Fern they'd level their spite at. It would be me they'd want to be rid of but might figure to keep me in line through the girl.

I kept cudgeling my brain without hitting on a notion that wasn't loaded with dire consequence should I fail to bring it off. That smart dog, Flossie, was sticking close to her mistress. The Navajo had left them to ride out a ways ahead, leaving the rest strung out behind; and Harry, abruptly beckoning Fletcher, turned his mount and swung toward me, the pair of them bracketing Gretchen.

Hatcher said belligerently, "So's you know where you stand in this, mister, I'm telling you now to stay away from my boys. You're not goin' to change 'em, they're all in this with me. You make any trouble you're going to get hurt—*bad* hurt. Savvy?"

I forced a false admiration into my look. "I can see you don't miss much."

"You better believe it! I've got the whip hand and I intend to hang on to it. First wrong move outa you will be your last—just remember it."

With a final hard stare he wheeled away.

Fletcher, bending toward me, thrust out a hand, a jeering derision taking hold of his face. "Fork over that rifle an' don't give me no back chat." Hatcher had stopped and was watching intently. I pulled the Remington from its scabbard and held it toward him, butt forward. "You're learnin'," he chuckled, and galloped off after Harry.

Hatcher ordered camp pitched in the south gap entrance to the canyon. Jeff hadn't toted a rifle, nor had Alfredo or Jeff's sister, but Clampas had lifted Jones's artillery. I was surprised they hadn't taken my pistol. Hatcher probably figured, now that he'd spiked any attempt at sniping, to extract it later.

The Navajo departed with several more of Jeff's skinny

cigars, and the crew got busy unloading the pack string while I tended to Gretchen and put up Fern's tent. "Pin your faith on patience and don't start anything," I muttered as she ducked inside it.

Alfredo with sticks he had fetched from our last camp built up a small fire while the cook, with several tins stacked beside him, began beating up dough to put into his Dutch oven. I'd have hunted up more wood but there obviously wasn't any. What the Anasazi hadn't taken to put into roofs and ceilings the Pueblo builders had completely exhausted.

For supper, in addition to hot biscuits and lick, Jones had provided corned beef in abundance, saying he'd just come onto it and hoped we appreciated the effort. Nobody else said anything but all took copious helpings. When we had finished and dropped our pans and eating tools into Jones's tub, Harry asked Jeff where he was aiming to start his dig.

When Larrimore shrugged without answering, I took it on myself to say, "Not far from where we stand right now, just inside those walls, you'll see what's left of Una Vida. Lots of adders, rattlesnakes and gophers, but without an extensive dig I doubt if you'll be happy with anything you'll get. It's not one of the larger pueblos and there's not much left. I did pick up a handful of beads which," I added with a quick glance at Harry, "my old man managed to sell at considerable profit."

All that got from Hatcher was a grin. But Fletcher and a couple of the crew went off to try their luck. Harry said with curled lip, "Penny-ante stuff. Someplace hereabouts there's a big cache of stones that ain't never turned up—a whole goddam wagonful! That's what I'm aiming to get my hooks on. That or what Geoffrey here is goin' to find for me."

The gloat in his voice got under Fern's skin and the hot

look she gave him would have withered an oak post, but Harry took it in stride with a satisfied chuckle. "Careful there, honey, you'll be poppin' a gasket." He rubbed a look across me. "Your old man trades in turquoise, don't he?"

"Expect he does when there's any call for it."

He dug in a pocket and tossed me a chunk about the size of a walnut. "How's that look to you?"

"I'm no expert."

"You must have seen enough to have some idea. Come on, be a sport. Fair, average, good or gem grade?"

I tossed it back. "About average."

Hatcher snorted. "That assayer at Ajo called it gem grade." His stare winnowed down to bright shining slits. "That's no way to get yourself cherished. Try playing along on my side of the fence an' you'll have a good chance of putting money in the bank."

I put in my glance a rapt admiration that drew a twinkle from Fern when I told him rueful-like, "With your flair and style you ought to own the bank by this time."

He kept the grin on his face but there was nothing to comfort in the cut of that stare. "Always the joker," he threw back at me smoothly. "When I drive that wagonload over to Half Step, your old man better figure to buy gem grade."

The sun was beginning to turn the sky pink all along the east flank of the little still left of Una Vida time we got through with breakfast next morning. Harry appeared bushy tailed and, at least on the surface, his old hearty self when "Well, Jeff," he said, "what's the program today? You aim to clear some of the rubble away from this site or try someplace else?"

"I believe the sensible way to tackle this would be to

have a good look at what's available first of all.''

"You mean explore the whole canyon?"

Jeff nodded. To me he said, "You're the only one of us that's been here before, Brice. How many ruins are there?"

"Hell—I dunno. Ain't too much left of a lot of them. As I understand it these places were towns. Inside the canyon there probably ain't over five or six that look worth botherin' with and I expect every one of them has been pretty well pawed over.''

Jeff said, "The two largest, I believe, are Pueblo Bonito and Chetro Ketl that Simpson examined in forty-nine. Hyde, too, did quite a bit of work at Pueblo Bonito just a few years ago I'm told. I'm not familiar with Wetherill's work or Putnam's, but Wetherill I think had a trading post somewhere in this area. Very likely he went over the best of these sites.

"I realize, of course, there may be more to uncover even in towns like Pueblo Bonito, but my time is limited. I'd probably do better tackling one of these sites like this one right here that appears too negligible to hold any interest.''

"Let's get at it then," Harry grunted, rolling up his sleeves.

"I think I'd rather look at the rest first." Jeff turned to me. "Wouldn't take over five or six days to see the lot, would it?"

"If it's just ridin' through without dawdlin' you can cover the whole canyon by nightfall.''

"Will I see any cliff dwellings?"

"I can't recall any inside the canyon. There's places where the cliff walls are pretty well broken down with gulches leading off. Could be something back in there maybe.''

"The point is," Jeff said in a thoughtful voice, "these

pueblo towns mostly date back not more than seven hundred years. The earliest evidence of Basketmakers we know anything about—and precious little at that—indicate they were in this vicinity at least two thousand years ago. That's the period I'd like to put my dig in.''

Hatcher said, glancing around, ''Let's get the pack string loaded and be on our way.''

During the next couple of hours it became fairly evident he had no intention of allowing private conversation between the Larrimores and me. He had them segregated up at the front with Clampas cozily riding between them, while keeping Fletcher and myself accompanying him behind the pack string and crew as the best way to thwart any trouble we might attempt to kick up.

He mightn't be smart but he could be plenty cunning when he put his mind to it.

We passed quite a number of ruins without pausing. Several textbooks had been published, mainly based on the investigations of earlier expeditions and the work of persons such as Wetherill and Putnam who, whatever they may have found, hardly did much more than scratch the surface. Along the eastern seaboard it seemed there were quite a number of people who wanted to know more about such antiquities and the Indians who created them.

Hatcher said after a while, ''Any fool who'd spend his life in this godforsaken place should have been shut up with a string of spools! Fair gives me the jitters—can't you feel it, Corrigan?''

''It is kind of depressin', sure enough.''

''Depressing! Is that all you notice? By Gawd I don't look forward to spending a night here!''

''Guess someone must've filled you with them stories about the chindi.''

265

"Chindi?" he growled suspiciously. "What's that?"

"Spirits of the ancient dead. Must be a heap of them around. Stands to reason. What the college crowd refers to as original Americans were tramping these localities at least six thousand years before Christ."

Fletcher gasped, goggling, "Jesus! I didn't know he'd ever been around here—"

"Oh, be still," Hatcher said, and brutally kicked his horse into a canter, in a hurry it seemed to catch up with the others. "What's the matter with him?" Fletcher grumbled. "He's been jumpin' around like the seven-year itch."

Chapter Eight

We camped that night at the canyon's far end where he had
two of the crew with the sweat rolling off them go down
into the wash and dig a monstrous great pit, deep enough
pretty near to bury the whole outfit. We didn't know what
Harry was after, but if it was water he sure didn't find any.
By the time each horse had drunk a hatful out of our canvas
sacks there wasn't enough left, putting them all together, to
put out the puny fire Alfredo kindled. "By Gawd, that does
it!" Fletcher snarled, glaring at Harry. "What the hell do
we do now?"

"Guess you'll have to do without."

"I can open some canned pears," Jones offered with a
scathing look at the skimpy fire. "I can open some corned
beef but you'll have to eat it cold. I mean, just the way it
comes from the tin."

I saw the amusement slide through Fern's glance as she
took in the comical look on Hatcher's face. "Go ahead,"

he growled. "Be better than nothing." His stare swiveled irascibly. "In the morning," he told Clampas, "send a couple of the crew out with rifles and see if they can't scare up some fresh meat."

It was a sour-faced outfit that sought their blankets after wolfing down Jones's provender. Jeff's look, no matter the desert's heat, appeared five shades paler than it had that noon. I could understand his stunned expression for, on top of all the other tribulations, to find ourselves without water and no flowing stream nearer than fifty miles in any direction, everything he had planned was on the brink of disaster. These horses couldn't last long without water. He was faced with the ruin of everything he had hoped for.

"Damn it all," Hatcher muttered, "there's got to be water around here someplace. Along the sides of that wash you could see where floods had almost crept up to more than one of those ruins. Jones, you an' Alfredo get down in that hole and do some more digging!"

Nobody yet had gone out to hunt meat. I hadn't seen one rabbit in the last thirty miles but there were coyotes probably if you could manage to stomach them. I'd noticed signs of ancient irrigation at Una Vida and one or two of the larger pueblos we'd passed, and downslope east of where we'd come into the canyon there might be a spring, though it wasn't a heap likely.

. "What about that fork where the canyon branched off in a gulch toward the west?" Jeff asked anxiously. "Perhaps we could find water there . . ."

It was possible of course; anything was possible. I had been intending, if we could shake Harry and his pair of trigger-happy hard cases, to slip Jones and the Larrimores down that arroyo and whatever tinned stuff we could manage to get out with. Branching off of it somewhere along the left side, pretty well hidden last time I'd been through, was another narrow trail with the kind of thing Jeff had been hoping for. Not a large community—perhaps thirty rooms— but in a pretty fair state of preservation and no evidence of vandalism. It even had a small kiva, or ceremonial chamber, I seemed to recollect. And a well you could reach with a long rope and bucket.

I peered around for Flossie. She was not with Fern or anywhere in sight. Jones and Alfredo, armed with shovels and a pick besides, had just reluctantly started for the wash when Fletcher said bitterly, ''I'm goin' to git outa here—''

Hatcher swung round. ''You'll go when the rest go!''

Seeing the way they were glaring at each other I was mightily tempted to make the big push till I saw Clampas with those pale eyes fixed on me and that black-bored Sharps pointed right at my brisket. Clampas's gaunt cheeks twitched in that high flat face and I turned away, cursing under my breath just as Flossie, coming out of the wash, stopped to shake. Jones's yell came up after her. ''Two foot of water in that hole!''

The next hour was spent filling up our water sacks and taking the horses, one by one, down to drink. When the pool cleared a bit I took Gretchen down under Clampas's watchful eye.

''Well,'' Harry said in his old hearty manner, ''what's next on the agenda?''

Jeff still looked unsettled by this change in prospects, like he was finding it hard to pull himself together. ''I don't know,'' he said vaguely, ''most everything we've seen either entails more work than I have time for or has been worked over by somebody else. I'd thought,'' he said, looking north, "to try up there but it doesn't seem very promising . . ."

It certainly didn't: badlands far as the eye could reach, a vast desolation it would take weeks to explore. I couldn't see nothing for it but to take them on back to where that side gulch branched off and try our luck there.

I told him, "That side canyon we passed near that last big pueblo just might have something, or you could try that ruin. I don't think anyone's done a serious study there or done any sort of a scientific dig, though the refuse heaps have been pawed over and vandals—"

"Let's try that side canyon," Jeff said without hope; and Hatcher sent off the crew to pack up the supplies and get the pack string loaded. It was close to ten o'clock before we got out of there.

Every mile—sometimes less—along the canyon's north side there were ruins large or little, and only the most insignificant remains had been bypassed by persons who had been here before us. Since the publications of Lieutenant Simpson's *Journal of a Military Reconnaissance from Santa Fe, New Mexico, to the Navajo Country,* dude pot hunters and others had prowled through here in ever increasing numbers by what you could reckon from the look of these places.

Some of the towns had practically disappeared save what was left among the rubble of centuries, some battered and broken walls with scarce a foot or two showing above scattered rocks turned black from the heat with hardly a tuft of seared grass showing where once there must have been considerable farming. If the Anasazi had left anything from the time of their occupancy not taken away by those who came later, it would probably be in such near-obliterated remnants as these.

Mule Man

It was well past noon when we reached the branch canyon and started along it with skeptical glances sweeping across the bleak cliffs. "I don't think there's much here," Harry told Jeff with a disgruntled snort. "We better go back an' try one of them others."

Fern and Jeff exchanged glances near as hopeless as Hatcher's. Gretchen heaved up a sigh. I wanted to suggest Jeff should look a mite farther but thought better of the notion. Hatcher would send someone with him and not like to be me. I said, "Can't be sure, but around that next bend there's another ruined place I seemed to remember that might not be too torn up."

Harry shrugged and we pushed on.

There *was* such a ruin and of pretty fair size. Jagged holes had been poked through the nearest wall where looters had busted through in their search for anything they figured worth taking. Harry dismounted, jerking his head at Larrimore. "Rest of you stay here, we're going to have a look."

They'd been gone about ten minutes when we saw them coming back. "Place has been ransacked," Jeff told his sister. "By the shards I picked up it's a long way from old enough to waste any time on. Basketmakers hadn't anything to do with it." He put his look on Harry. "You want to go any farther?"

Harry, scowling at me, abruptly made up his mind. "Might as well," he grumbled, and climbed back into his saddle.

It was a twisty trail, half obliterated, the floor at this point not over a hundred yards wide with the walls closing in and no sign at all of travel. Stunted bushes cropped up here and there, prickly pear and cholla, an occasional ocotillo thrusting up its thorny wands.

Some mile or so beyond that demolished ruin we'd

stopped at, the walls opened out again. A lot of rock was strewn about where great sections of the heat-cracked cliff had broken loose to fall among a scraggle of stunted iron-wood. Since leaving the Chaco we'd come four or five miles in what was now little more than a gulch when, greatly astonished, the crew stopped to gape. What we saw was another seep with a ten-foot pool of gleaming water shining under it and tamarisks and salt cedar stretching tall beside it.

Hatcher grunted with a pleased look around. "We'll make camp here an' start back tomorrow."

They got the horses penned after letting them drop their heads for a drink and got busy unloading the pack string. I watered Gretchen and rubbed her down and left her on grounded reins to limp over and help Jeff set up Fern's tent, Flossie watching with her tongue lolling out. Just as Fern ducked through the flap, wiping the sweat off her cheeks, I told her brother as Harry started toward us, "There's a cliff house not two miles from where we're standing."

Hatcher came up with a suspicious stare. "You know this place was here?"

"Figured it was bound to be if it hadn't dried up."

"Why didn't you open your yap about it yesterday?"

"Wasn't too sure we could find it."

"Yeah. I bet." A nastier expression took hold of his mouth. "Don't push your luck, Corrigan. I meant what I told you. If you want to keep healthy, better watch your step." With an angry nod he strode off to join Clampas, who had his back to a rock watching cozily while Alfredo dug out tinned ham from the stores and Jones stirred up dough for the biscuits.

We had a good meal that evening and a medium-sized fire that we could loll around afterward, and the majority of us—except for a guard sent off to stand between us and the way we had come—took a thankful advantage of it. Smoke from hand-rolleds curled and fluttered among the bouquet from Jeff's slim cigar. Flames winked and danced above Jones's bed of ashes. No voice was raised in anger. Talk was sporadic, stretched out and thin until Harry, making a push to get Larrimore started, asked from his place between Fern and me what Jeff thought of the prospects.

"Well, all the ruins we've so far looked at were put up in at least three different time spans. I can't believe even the earliest of these had a great deal to do with the earliest Anasazi, the first influx of Basketmakers. My guess would be they most probably date from Basketmaker Three.

"One has to realize, of course, that all those far-back aborigines didn't come from the same mold—nor fit it. These prehistoric people arrived in this region in successive waves. The first group," Jeff said, warming up to his subject, "are the people I'm most interested in, the original tribe to cross the Bering Strait; primitive, with few skills, who lived in pit houses and built no permanent shelters."

The happy eagerness of Flossie's look as she lay by her mistress and hopefully watched me, occasionally waving the plume of her tail, was the pleasantest view I had seen in some while. Fern's head with its freckled nose and that mop of roan hair was obscured by Hatcher's shoulder between us.

"After them," Jeff went on, "came Basketmaker Two and Three as they're called. Following these at widely separated dates came the Pueblo peoples. The original Basketmakers were nomadic hunters and gatherers who constructed neither pottery nor permanent quarters. Understanding this, it becomes obvious at once that any Basketmaker remains in the Chaco are either deeply buried or the work of Basketmaker Three."

"And so?" said Hatcher.

"So," Jeff replied, "a dig under such considerations and with less than five weeks before I'm expected back in Chicago seems out of the question. An archaeologist of any repute is not one to throw dirt helter-skelter. Much as I hate to, any dig I make here will have to be left to some future date."

"Mean to say," Hatcher growled, "you're throwin' this up and taking off for home?"

"Not precisely. I will do whatever I can to find facts and leave from some point closer than Ajo."

Ears cocked, grinning face on paws and her behind in the air, Flossie was trying to encourage me to play. As Fern had said, the dog evidently liked me. "If that brute," Hatcher said, "tries jumpin' on me it's going to be her last jump!"

Fern took hold of her, pulling the dog back and showing in the scath of her look a bristling indignation as it settled on Harry. "Meantime," Jeff went on, "the most I can hope to pick up in this manner are relics or artifacts from people designated as Basketmaker Three, which really isn't what I came for. And if you're thinking of burial sites," he told Hatcher, "it's been established on pretty good authority these persons also had gone by 1200 A.D., near enough."

There wasn't any of this what Harry wanted to hear and he studied Jeff dourly.

When it occurred to me to take enough stock to find out where the divers personalities of this field trip were placed in relation to the others, I couldn't see Jones and had no idea where Fletcher had got to until I heard him slamming his way through the tamarisks.

Red-faced and panting he came barging up, to gasp out

at Harry, "There's a *cliff house* up this trail! Just a whoop and a holler beyond them trees!"

The whole crowd was galvanized. Hatcher jumped up with every other last thing fallen out of his head to go at an accelerating gait in the direction of that water-fed growth as though determined to be the next to see this marvel, the rest of us strung out in his wake and Flossie barking in a seventh heaven of excitement.

Nobody stopped to rope out any mounts and our exodus from camp soon resembled a rout. Fern, as I went past, caught hold of my arm. "Do you suppose that's true?"

"It's true enough. I was hopin' they wouldn't find out about it till your brother had a chance to go over it private."

"You think it's—?"

"Couldn't tell. I been hoping it would fall into the right age bracket—looks older than Moses, and I don't believe any vandals have got to it. Nine chances out of ten that kind of trash would never have pushed through those woods. Been content," I said, "with the discovery of that water and gone back the way they came."

She peered up at me anxiously. "What do you think will happen now?"

"I don't know. Try, if you can, to keep Flossie away from Harry. And away, particularly, from that prize pair of killers."

The goal that had drawn us all like a magnet was still some distance ahead of where Hatcher and Jeff spearheaded our invasion. Most everyone now had dropped to a kind of shuffling walk though the quiet habitual to this hidden place hung in shuddering tatters in the battering from voice sounds. Jeff's small torch threw monstrous great shadows that continually hopped around us like a band of frightened chindis.

"There!" Fletcher cried. "Right there! Do you *see* it?"

Not even those nearest, pressing forward in the awful grip of ungovernable excitement, managed to conceal this wonder from Fern's riveted gaze. There was a tenseness in her grip, the breath seemed caught in her throat. "It's magnificent!" she whispered. "Just the sort of place Jeff's been praying he could find!"

In the moving light, as the torch was flashed about, the sheer wall built against the cliff's red rock must have reared a full fifty feet above the gulch's passage, unpierced in its lower dimensions. Larrimore, attempting speech through his emotion-blocked throat, was heard to say, "Tomorrow we'll have a good look at it; there's nothing we can reasonably accomplish tonight."

Chapter Nine

No one lay abed or lingered beneath cover once the hours of darkness had passed. They were far too excited, too anxious to get inside that relic of ages and learn what sort of treasure had lain hidden here through uncounted years. Not one of the bunch even thought to complain at the refried beans Jones had hashed up to give body to his java.

Harry, in the first bright shaft of the rising sun, appeared as innocently expansive as a con man in possession of his neighbor's billfold. Even Alfredo was grinning as he piled out used breakfast gear into Jones's wreck pan. And Flossie, dancing about, divided her attention between me and her freckled mistress.

All the world was agleam that morning.

Fletcher's muttered claim that he should be given no less than a finder's fee brought a general laugh. Not even Hatcher spoiled it. "What's the procedure?" he inquired of Jeff. "How do we tackle this?"

"First off," Jeff told us, "I think we'd better find some way to get in. And the most important thing to be borne in mind is for the rest of you not to touch anything till I've had a chance to examine the place. Should we move our camp? I ask because if we don't, someone is certainly going to have to keep an eye on it."

"Not me!" Fletcher growled.

"Me neither," spoke up Clampas.

Harry's roving eye pinned Alfredo. "You'll do. Give him Corrigan's rifle. Fletch—you stay here too. I don't want to come back and find this camp all over hell's kitchen."

Fletcher's cheeks locked into anger. Hatcher, ignoring him, bade me go break out a pick and shovel and step lively.

I passed these tools to one of the crew that I knew was too stupid to open his jaw and limped off to throw my saddle on Gretchen, after which I stepped into it. And heard Flossie growl as Harry brushed past her. But Fern had a hold on her so Hatcher went on, increasing his step to catch up with Jeff. "How," he asked, "do we get into this place?"

I kicked a foot from the stirrup and hauled Fern up behind me. "No sense in you walkin' like the rest of these peons." Felt pretty good having her arms around me, and I thought to myself I'd better try this again. We could see that place a lot plainer with the sun up. Against that red rock it was even more impressive than it had seemed the night before, the whole towering face of it built up from little flat stones. And no openings at all in the lower two thirds of it.

Jeff, standing there with Harry, thoughtfully eyeing it, said, "Looks like we'll have to go in from the top unless we can make out to rig up a ladder—"

"Can't we just knock a hole in it someplace?"

The turn of Jeff's head showed what he thought of that. Fern got off Gretchen's rump and I got out of the saddle, letting go of the reins to stand with the others peering up at that sheer wall.

Trouble was we hadn't any ladder and, as Harry pointed out, no trees tall enough to make one that would be long enough to reach those openings.

Jeff said, "We'll have to send someone up to have a look on top. Bound to be some way of getting inside it. Anyone care to volunteer?"

Nobody clambered over the rest to become the first to get his name remembered.

Hatcher said, "We'll all go then. It's a cinch there won't nobody get in from down here."

"Time's a-wastin'," I mentioned. "Which way do we go?"

"Straight ahead," Jeff answered. "No way up back there."

I left Gretchen hitched to the ground, glad I'd remembered to throw some oats into her, and took off after the rest of them, expecting to have a pretty stiff hike. Without finding some kind of stairway we'd have to keep on till we found a spot where a section of the cliff had broken off to give us handholds.

It took an hour to come onto one.

And a pretty depressing sight it was, with great chunks of rock tumbled hell west and crooked, just about choking off what was left of this gulch. Catclaw and cholla grown up in tangles all through it. Hatcher led off, warily picking his way with Jeff right behind him, the rest of us strung out and myself helping Fern as seemed only natural at the end of the line.

Getting up took the bulk of another half hour with the sun hammering down and sweat rolling freely to mix with the dust raised by those ahead. "And it looks like," I muttered, "we'll come back the same way!" But one good thing, I thought to myself, at least some of these rannies would have had a bellyful.

We now found ourselves on a kind of plateau with a wide sweep of country stretching off a far piece to a haze of blue hills slithering out of the distance. "Wake up," Fern exclaimed. "Let's not get left here!"

On this high scarp we trudged after the others, presently catching up to hear Hatcher wanting to be told how we'd know when we got there. It was a fair question. The serrated lip of this bluff sure as hell wasn't posted. "I guess," Jeff answered, "we'll have to keep looking over."

Harry, snorting, caught hold of one of the crew and with a shove sent him forward. "Get on up ahead an' find that place, Frisco."

Eventually he did. "Right under me now," he called, going abruptly motionless in his crouch above the rim. Hurrying forward I followed his look. Down there beneath us in a scrambling tug of war was a hatless Fletcher on one end of her reins and Gretchen on the other setting back with bared teeth.

"Get away from that mule!"

Fletcher's head spun around, glittery eyes trying to find me. "Up here," I called, and shoved off an egg-sized rock to nudge him. He let out a yell, eyes big as a bull's when he spotted my pistol about to open him up. He let go of those reins in such an explosion of hustle he tripped over his spurs and went down like a tree with all branches crashing.

"D-Don't shoot!" he gasped, a quivering bundle of terror. "Lemme tell—"

Gretchen's raucous complaint sawed the rest of it off just as I felt three-four others crowding back of me, and Hatcher told his henchman, "Never mind the windies!"

Fletcher's weather-roughened features ran together like sloppy dough. "But I come after that mule t' help me find you fellers—"

"A likely tale."

"Like or not," Harry's hard case shouted, "Alfredo's all spraddled out like a bunch of old clothes with a knife buried back of his wishbone. An' I'm tellin' you, by Gawd, there ain't a horse left in camp!"

Chapter Ten

You'd have thought we were figures chopped out of wood.

No telling how long we stood clamped in this paralysis staring at the horrid thing that was now spelled out in front of us. Locked in this catastrophe, it was Hatcher's snarl that broke our shackles. "Stay right there!" he bellowed, and took off pell-mell over the way we'd just come, the whole crew but Jones going hellity larrup after him.

I found my look on Clampas, who gave me back a cynical grin. "If them broncs are gone they're gone, that's all, and the boys'll hev to chase after them. Me, I stick with the main chance, mister. Right here with the professor."

Jeff, turning away, said, "We've got to find that entrance."

"But Jeff . . ." Fern cried. "If the horses are gone?" She appealed to me with her eyes seeming black against the pallor of that freckled skin.

"Like Clampas I'm stringin' along with Jeff." I dropped

a hand on her shoulder. "Buck up. We're like to be here a right smart while before those horses become important."

She eyed me uncertainly. "That poor man . . ."

"Very sad." Clampas nodded without visible grief. "These things happen. A business of this sort is hazardous at best."

She twisted around to have a sharp look at him. He stood there smiling in the best Hatcher fashion but making no attempt to dress it up in fine linen. "One learns to adjust."

Quite true, I thought, but no need to be so blunt about it. Fern moved closer to me. "But how could it happen? Who do you suppose killed him?"

"You want it tied up in pink ribbons?" Clampas shifted his weight. His glance touched mine. "I wouldn't put it past Fletch . . ."

With a look of abhorrence she turned her back on him. But, it came over me, there'd been no one else down there. Still, in a larger view, this *could* have been something handsome Harry dreamed up, using Fletch for the cat's-paw. . . .

Jeff, with no heed for us, was down on one knee picking at the cliff's edge with his silver-handled jackknife. Grunting now he stood up, slipping the knife back into his pocket. "I believe this end has been built up with masonry. Take a look at it, Brice. Built up and smoothed and made to look solid rock with some kind of reddish mud plaster."

Now that I looked closer, I could see what he meant. The top of the bluff where we stood, the end nearest Chaco Canyon that is, for eight or ten feet felt different to the touch. "Let me have that shovel," Jeff said, and proceeded gingerly to scratch at the surface.

He'd guessed right. It was some sort of mud mortar artfully plastered over a cunningly contrived sheet of masonry. Long ago it seemed likely a fairly large chunk had fallen out of the cliff at this point. "This has to be where the entrance was—there's no other place for it," Jeff panted, busily scaling off that whole stretch of plaster to uncover the work of men long gone. "When they quit this building they did their best to conceal the way in. Look there," he pointed. "It's a kind of blind window they've laid up across what used to be the doorway. When everything was ready they simply filled this in."

It seemed plain enough now he'd pointed it out.

"You'll notice," he said, "when they sealed this up they set the rocks in vertically instead of crossways like the rest of this stretch; it proved handier I suppose."

"How you reckon to get in there?" I asked.

"We'll have to be careful. I certainly don't want to break this up. What we need right here is something we can use to poke out the mud between those upright stones. A case knife or bowie—"

"I've got a bowie," Jones said, stepping forward. "Let's have a look at that."

Jeff made room and Jones, kneeling, began to pick at the binder. It appeared to have hardened considerably through uncounted ages, though in some spots it had deteriorated noticeably. After about twenty minutes of steady digging, the rock he was working on let go and fell with an echoing rumble and clatter into whatever lay directly beneath.

Jeff motioned Jones aside to put his face to the hole. "Blacker than pitch," he said. "I can't see a thing. Try the next stone," he muttered, getting out of the way. "You'll have to admit," he remarked as Jones resumed his labors, "those old boys were indefatigable workers. They must have quarried, transported and tediously shaped several million stones in the building of this place. A prodigious task with the primitive tools available to them; at least as difficult, I would imagine, as the construction of the Egyptian pyramids.''

At the end of half an hour Jones had three more stones out, the last pair caught and gruntingly laid to one side. ''Not quite so dark down there now.''

Jeff, taking his place, peered into the hole for a nerve-rasping spell. Fern asked, ''Can you see anything?''

''Not much,'' Jeff muttered, getting up to stretch his back. ''Near as I could tell, there's a five- or six-foot drop. Probably know more about it once we get the rest of these stones lifted out.''

''Let me take a whack at it,'' I said, and Jones passed me the knife.

It soon became evident that, because of the weight and the awkwardness of how we had to go about it, you couldn't remove but one stone at a time without risk of damaging whatever was below. Between us during my stint with the knife, Jones and I managed to get out three more of the stones used to seal up the entrance. This left only four more in place when we moved back to give Jeff another look.

''Well,'' he told us as he got to his feet, ''what we're faced with is a narrow room some four feet high, every wall of which is plastered and without any sign of an opening except for the one we've just made.''

''Oh dear,'' Fern exclaimed. ''You mean it doesn't go anywhere?''

''There'll be a door, I'm sure, or another blind window, but we're going to have to hunt for it.'' He considered it, frowning. ''We're not going to get into that place today.'' He took a squint at the sun. ''We'd better get back to the camp while there's still light.''

*   *   *

We built up the fire while Jones dug a hole in the dwindling pile of our supplies and Flossie quartered the site with her nose to the ground, dashing first one way and then off at a tangent. I led the hee-hawing Gretchen to the pool for a drink, then fetched her back and hung a nosebag on her. Hatcher and his horse hunters weren't anywhere in sight, nor was the corpse of Alfredo, which I reckoned they must have buried.

Jones opened several tins of ham, got out his Dutch oven and started working up dough for his biscuits. Fern peeled potatoes and sliced them into a bowl while Jeff sat figuring on a page of his blue-backed notebook. The sun was gone and it was getting dark fast when a strengthening sound of travel pulled all eyes in the direction of the trail.

Looking pretty well beat, Hatcher and his helpers came up to the fire. No one ventured to prod them with questions for all could see there were no horses with them. Hatcher said finally, "No we didn't find them. I reckon them ponies must've run halfway to the canyon."

You couldn't hardly call Jones's fine supper a hilarious occasion. Hatcher perked up a mite when told we'd uncovered the entrance to our objective. No one sat around the fire once the meal was finished. Off to one side Clampas beckoned Harry for a low-voiced conversation with several frowning looks in the direction of Fletcher, and a short time later—Harry having put two of the crew on guard with Clampas—the rest crawled into their blankets.

Despite the daytime heat, which must have been topping out at close to a hundred, the nights were cool and, toward morning, often rightdown chilly. Though strongly tempted to hitch Gretchen, in the end I did not do so but fetched her under the tamarisks and there made my bed. Not that I expected to get a lot of sleep.

Mule Man

A jumble of thoughts juned around in my noggin, fleeting visions of Fletch in his various attitudes interwoven with sundry pictures of Harry. Having Gretchen, thoughts of the horses did not unduly worry me. For once Jeff made up his mind to depart, we could strike out for Farmington on the Denver & Rio Grande, not over fifty miles away. About two days by shanks' mare. I could put Fern on Gretchen.

I probably dozed, off and on, but in more wakeful moments I kept coming back to the unexplainable raid on our horses. Who but Fletcher could have set that in motion? The man was mercurial enough for just about anything, yet the suspicion kept nagging me that Hatcher might have been back of it, that a couple of those nags might not have left with the rest. Once Harry got his hands on any loot of real importance he would be long gone in one hell of a hurry.

If any off-color business got afoot during the night I certainly wasn't aware of it.

I did not wake at the crack of dawn, but came alive shortly after to the aroma of coffee and the sight of Turtle Jones hunched over his fire-blackened skillet. Jeff and Clampas were already stirring and it looked like being another hot day.

Gretchen was happily browsing on such tufts of grass as she could find about the pool and, looking around with lifted head, gave me a cheerful gate-hinge greeting which could hardly have failed to rouse the whole camp. "Well," Hatcher growsed, untangling himself from his bedroll, "does that godforsaken critter have to wake us every day!"

Flossie slipped out of Fern's tent and with great aplomb came to a squat behind the closest bush. She then cantered round with her nose to the ground taking inventory of any new smells the night had left behind, vigorously flailing her tail when she caught sight of me, further expressing her

287

delight by hustling over to jump about with much enthusiasm, never quite touching me. "Good girl!" I said, and she ran off to find Fern.

Jones yelled, "Come'n get it!"

We wasted no time in putting it away. Returning from dropping our tools into the washtub, Jeff said to Hatcher, "Off to more horse hunting, are you?"

"Not me," Harry declared. "That bunch—if they ain't been stole and spirited out of the country—will probably wind up makin' Navajo stew!" His glance checked Jeff's face. "I been talkin' to Clampas—think you'll get into that place today?"

"The date of our entry," Larrimore told him, "could be anybody's guess. People who put up that apartment house went to some pains to close it up when they left. All of yesterday's work didn't get us any farther than a completely sealed room."

"Don't pay to be too particular. Bust a hole through the wall and you're on your way."

Jeff shook his head. "I wish it were that simple. I think I'll borrow Jones again if you've no objection."

"Good worker, is he?"

"Opening up that house in an acceptable manner," Jeff said, "requires skill and know-how, not just muscle. Far as I can tell, no looters or pot hunters have got inside yet. Which makes it imperative," he went earnestly on, "that I allow nobody in there but authorized personnel." He stopped to give Hatcher a very straight look.

Harry gave it back to him. "Suits me," he said, and grinned. "I authorize Clampas to be your chief helper."

Young Larrimore showed him a wintry smile. He knew as well as Harry there was no getting around it, that whatever Hatcher wanted there was nothing to stand in his way.

He took a deep breath. "Do I get Jones too?"

"Sure. Take anyone you want. I think we understand each other," Harry said smugly.

Fern, coming up, asked, "Couldn't someone manage to construct a ladder? With all those trees . . ."

"Yes, ma'am." Harry trotted out his charm to affably assure her, "I'll see what I can do."

As before, I took Fern up behind me on Gretchen; Clampas, Jeff and Jones took to hoofing it. And once more, as before, I left Gretchen standing below the great wall and limped on with the others to the place of fallen rock. It must have been about nine by the time we stood before the hole we'd made in the entryway yesterday. There were still the four stones we had yet to prize out of it. Jones picked up his bowie and went methodically to work.

"What is Harry," Jeff said to Clampas, "going to do about those horses?"

"What *can* he do?" Clampas shrugged with spread hands. "When you're ready to go we'll just have to walk. We can probably make Farmington in a couple of days. You can catch a train there." He eyed Jeff curiously. "What I can't savvy is why you picked Ajo to take off on this jaunt."

Larrimore said grimly, "I left the arrangements up to Harry."

No more breath was wasted on talk until Jones and me had got those four stones out and carefully laid them outside the hole. At that point Jeff said, "You go first, Corrigan."

Not sure how much of a drop there might be in that uncertain light, I took my time and went in belly down with considerable care, remembering the stones we'd dropped in there yesterday. "How's it look?" Jeff called with his head through the hole.

"Not much room to work in down here. Anybody think to fetch that bar?"

"We've got it right here." He passed it down and I handed up the loose rocks that cluttered the floor. Jeff said, "I'm coming down," and stood a few moments after he had joined me, taking a long look around. "Not much headroom," he grunted.

"No. You'll have to watch out for your head. They did a good job—not a crack in these walls. Where do we start?"

He stood awhile, cogitating, mulling it over. "Let's see ... that left-hand wall will probably open into space. Chances are we'd best tackle this one. And low down, Brice—about two feet up from the floor and close to this end where it connects with the cliff."

I picked up the bar, driving the chisel end into the plaster. Nothing came of the impact other than the merest splatter of dust and the negligible mark the bar had left on the wall. I looked at Jeff. "Go ahead," he said. "Try it again. A little more to the right."

Same story. "Feels like solid rock."

Jeff nodded. "Probably is. Try a bit higher."

I did, but no improvement. I banged the bar into it again, lower this time. It went in about two inches and when I jerked it out about twelve inches of plaster flaked off. No seams showed behind it. "They've set a single rock upright," Jeff said, "to seal off the passage. See if you can scale off some more of that plaster."

Starting at floor level and working upward, I cleared a space some three feet by five and when the dust finally settled we had ourselves a look. What they had done was plain enough now. As Jeff had surmised, they had set in an upright slab of rock measuring two feet by three. "Be just about big enough," I said, "to let us squeeze through. Once we've got that slab pried loose.''

"Hey, down there," Clampas called. "How about givin' me a turn with that bar?''

"You bet!" I said and, with the sweat dripping off my chin, was glad to climb out. "Whew!" I puffed, flipping Jones a wink. "You can have my next turn. Talk about Turkish baths—that's got them all beat!''

"Not much room." Jones grinned.

"Toss down that knife," Clampas grunted. "I've got to loosen this mortar.''

Pretty soon Jeff said, "Try it now." We could see Clampas laying into it with that forty-pound bar, bent over like a gnome to keep his head off the ceiling. He'd got out of his shirt and even in that half light you could see the gleaming roll of huge muscles and the way they jumped every time that bar slogged home. A steel-driving man if ever I saw one.

"Stand back," he grunted some five minutes later. "I think it's moved—couple more whacks and it's goin' to come out of there." He spat on his hands and took a new grip.

"A genuine pleasure," Jones breathed in my ear, "to be up here watchin' that feller at work.''

"You bet," I said, "and it's something you ain't like to see every day. I'd admire to give Fletch a dose of the same!''

"Look out!" Clampas hollered. There was a grating wrench and a resounding crash and through the dust I could just make out that great whopping slab laying flat on the floor.

"Bravo!" Jones cried, and we both clapped hands.

Clampas grinned up at us. Jeff pulled his head back out of the new hole. "Can't see a thing. Pass down that torch.''

Jones put it in Clampas's lifted hand and he and Jeff moved over to the opening, pointing the light on whatever lay beyond. They took a good long look, so long Jones growled impatient, "Hell's fire! Cat got your tongues?"

Jeff shook his head. "Another empty room. Bigger than this but otherwise just like it."

I guessed he was pretty disgusted after all that work and so little to show for it. "Go ahead—take a look," Jeff said. Clampas wiggled his length through the hole he'd just opened, disappearing from sight. Jones lit a smoke. Jeff stepped over to the hole. "Just the same?" he called.

Clampas's voice when it reached us had a faraway sound. "Just the same, except size. Plaster on every wall. Not a crack showing. What the hell time is it?"

I consulted my shadow. "Round about three." Jones looked at his watch. "Three-twenty." I said, "Where's Fern?"

"She went back a couple hours ago. Guess she got hungry—which reminds me," Jones said. "I prob'ly better be gettin' back too."

"Guess we all had," Jeff said as Clampas rejoined him. "Too late to get through another wall today. Anyway this torch needs fresh batteries."

Some things, I thought, can't hardly be mistaken.

We were bound for camp, picking our way through the catclaw and cholla garnishing that fall of tumbled rock, grim of eye and thin of lip, nobody opting for conversation, each of us turning things over in private. Peering at Jeff as we moved along, one could not help noticing the harried expression that in the past several days looked to be becoming habitual. I suspected this sample of life in the real world had descended on him as a pretty rugged jolt.

Mule Man

He must have found Harry a rude disappointment, to have discovered in the man an unscrupulous schemer where he'd looked for a knowledgeable enthusiastic friend. To realize he'd hired a purveyor of illusions must have been a sad shock. Even more than the affront to his self-esteem had been the growing conviction his whole trip had been wasted unless something of value could be dug out of this cliff house.

Clampas, I reckoned, would have been a pleasant surprise. The way the man had pitched in, the prodigious work he had done could have given Jeff assumptions which had no basis in fact. Absorbed in his own concerns, determined on the renown which must so far have eluded him, Larrimore was in no condition to see Clampas as I saw him— hard, twisted, coldly calculating, a man without sentiment who would kill even quicker than that lout of a Fletcher if it suited his purpose.

I was glad I didn't stand in Hatcher's boots.

We were back at camp, pushing through the tamarisks about the pool when Jeff in the lead stopped with such suddenness Jones banged into him. No need to search for the cause of their astonishment. It was there in plain sight.

The horses were back.

Chapter Eleven

Back, too, was the Navajo, Hosteen Joe, the man who had left our hospitality in fury, that brash young buck who had wanted Clampas's rifle.

Hobnobbing with Harry, plump with smiles and self-importance, proudly fastened to my confiscated Remington, Joe had the strut of a visiting chief. Harry, too, looked to be in fine fettle as he beckoned us forward in his heartiest manner.

"Look who's here and see what he's fetched us—every last pony that departed this camp!"

No mention, I noticed, of poor old Alfredo.

"What happened?" Clampas asked. "Couldn't he find a buyer?"

"That's no way to make a man welcome," Harry chided. "Took him three days to get these broncs rounded up."

"Yeah," I said. "What's he doing with my rifle?"

"Not to worry. We gave him that as a very small token

of our appreciation.'' Turning to Jones he said, ''See if you can't dish up something extra special tonight. You know— in honor of the occasion, eh?''

Jones without answering went off toward the fire some jubilant soul had thoughtfully built up for him and began rattling round among his pots and pans.

Fern with Flossie scampering alongside came over to ask her brother what he'd found. ''Well,'' she remarked after his unenthusiastic answer, ''that's encouraging, don't you think? They'd hardly have gone to so much trouble if they'd left nothing behind other persons might value.''

''Perhaps you're right,'' Jeff nodded dourly, and tried then to show a more cheerful countenance. ''It's not the work of the original Basketmakers, but it may well prove to have been constructed by some of the descendants not too far removed. It doesn't have the appearance of Pueblo work.''

I sensed an anxious look of foreboding in her glance as Clampas came up to consider her blandly. ''Not worrying about the chindis, are you? After all these years there shouldn't be much left of them.''

Jones outdid himself with supper that night. Baked potatoes and ham, johnnycake and java hot from the coffeepot with juicy canned Bartlett pears to wind up with. Harry pronounced it a feast fit for kings.

Hosteen Joe was feeling his oats. ''By myself I catch these horses. Not many peoples could do such thing—you know that? Me, I'm one smart Indian, no?''

''You're a wonder.'' Clampas smiled.

''That hat still fit all right?'' Jones asked.

I went off to palaver with Gretchen. Before I got out of earshot Hatcher told Larrimore, ''Tomorrow I'm going up there with you. We'll leave Clampas in camp to keep an eye on our belongin's.'' When Jeff made no comment Harry divulged as though dispensing a favor, "We'll take Fletch along to take care of the rough work.''

Gretchen cocked an ear when I stopped beside her and twisted her head to nuzzle my pocket, pulling back her lip while ogling me with great expectation. "Such a moocher,'' I said as she lipped the sugar lump off my palm.

But I was bothered in my mind, uneasy as Fern, thinking about that Indian fetching back our horses. It seemed a most unlikely action. Why had he done it? What was he up to? I reckoned we'd find out before we got done with this. But, I remembered as I got into my blankets, it was the Sharps Joe had wanted. . . .

Had Joe killed Alfredo? Then stampeded the horses?

It didn't appear to make any great amount of sense to do these things and then fetch them back again. Could he have brought them back to make Hatcher feel beholden? Hatcher was pleased enough to give him my rifle. But it hadn't been mine Joe had taken such a shine to. . . .

Much as I distrusted Clampas, I could think of no way he could have mixed into this. He'd been with us up there on the clifftop when those broncs had left camp and Alfredo at that point had certainly been alive. Now the horses were back and that Navajo with them. And if Harry had sense enough to pound sand down a rat hole, he'd surely be bright enough to watch that Indian.

I was back in my thinking to that notion Clampas had pushed out for our scrutiny, that Fletcher was the one we should have had our sights on. Had Fletch driven off our caballos on orders from Harry? Then again, if Hatcher'd had no part in it what could Fletch have hoped to gain?

It must have been about there that sleep overtook me.

Next morning, after getting outside Jones's refried beans, I took Gretchen along to the pool for a drink. Coming back with a bucketful to leave outside Fern's tent, I stopped to exchange a few words with Jeff and asked if Fern was going with us this morning. Jeff said, "I suppose so," and frowned. "Must get pretty tedious for her up there but she's refused to stay in camp if that hard-eyed gunslinger is going to be staying here—says he makes her skin crawl. You don't think he'd—?"

"Clampas," I said, "has got his sights set on loot. Same as Harry. It's occurred to me, Jeff, we should have been posting a guard up there."

He peered at me wide-eyed and vigorously nodded. "You're absolutely right. We'll do it hereafter." He stood there thinking about it, then said with a grimace, "Here comes Harry. Guess we better get up there."

"You go ahead. We'll come along as soon as Fern's ready."

It didn't take long to put the saddle on Gretchen. I knew she was not real keen on carrying double but reckoned another sugar lump would improve her outlook. When Fern came out of the tent to join us I could see she was troubled. She said, "I've this frightful feeling we're heading into something that had better been left alone. Do you suppose, Brice, it was never intended that we should get into that sealed-up place?"

"It's just the strangeness—"

"I feel so alone," she said, looking out over the sunlit surroundings. "This landscape's so big, so bare, it depresses me."

There didn't seem to be very much I could say to that. Flossie then came gamboling up and we got aboard Gretchen and took off for the cliff house, catching up with the others just short of the rockfall.

"Didn't you mean to leave Gretchen back—"

"I'm going to leave her up here where there's something she can browse on. You go ahead. I'm goin' to take the saddle off. Give her a chance to roll if she wants to."

She went off with Flossie eagerly beside her. Jeff, Harry, Jones and Fletcher were halfway to the rim when Fern with a scream abruptly froze in her tracks. I made a pass at my hip and shot the head off the rattlesnake coiling on the sun-bright rock just ahead of her. "You're not going to faint, are you?" I kicked the wriggling mass off the rock.

"No . . ." She looked kind of peaked. "No—of course not!"

"I'll go ahead," I said. "You step where I've stepped."

Jeff, alarmed by the shot, had stopped and was looking back at us. "Snake?" Harry asked, and I nodded. "He didn't get a chance to strike," I assured Jeff. "Gave her a turn—she'll be all right."

At the site of our labors Jones and Fletch were looking things over, Fletch wanting to know how far we had got. "Then you haven't found anything yet," he sneered. "If," he said, "there's anything to *be* found."

Jeff ignored this. "Jones, I expect you remember how we tackled that first room? I want you and Fletcher to get into that second one and get enough of that plaster off to find us a door."

Jones picked up the shovel and followed Fletcher into the hole, then reached up a hand. "Might's well take that bar along, too. We're sure goin' to need it."

It was not long before we heard the shovel flaking off plaster and Hatcher demanding to know if we aimed to spend the day improving our tan. Jeff gave the fellow a very cool look and suggested if Hatcher wasn't entirely happy to be an onlooker on this important occasion no one would insist that he remain standing about.

A startled, half-furious expression skidded across Harry's widely opened stare. A flush, rapidly darkening, crept above his collar as he backed off a couple steps, mouth opening and shutting but with nothing coming out.

Larrimore turned away. "How's the dust down there?" he called into the excavation.

"Not too bad," Jones called back. "There's room enough here if you want to come down. We've got the baked mud off two of the walls." His voice grew less intelligible. Then, much louder, he informed, "Fletch is clearing the wall to the right of our opening—*I believe we're on to something!*"

Flossie barked and disappeared into the clifftop opening. "I'm going down," Jeff said, and followed the dog. "Oh—I do hope they've found something," Fern declared excitedly.

Harry, bending, tried to discover what was going on below. I said, "You can't see where they're at from up here; the place we pulled that slab from is at right angles to the hole you've got your head in."

Fern's hand gripped my arm. Jeff called up, "They've cleared the third wall and there's a real five-by-two-foot door just waiting for us to get at it. Come down if you want to have a look."

Hatcher wasn't one to step aside for women and children. Thrusting a leg through the hole he lost no time in dropping onto the next level, the four-foot-high room we'd got into a couple days ago. Not wanting her to skin a leg or otherwise collect a hurt, I reached up and brought Fern safely down, observing the excited look on her face. "Watch out for your head in this cubbyhole," I muttered, noticing with pleasure the way her nose wrinkled up beneath that mop of roan hair.

Jeff was in the next room with Jones and big Fletch, with Harry just beyond the hole we'd made yesterday. "Move over," I told him. "We'd like to see, too."

When we'd all got in there Jeff gestured toward the sealed wooden door they had just uncovered. I was surprised to notice that while it showed considerable age, as might have been expected, it was still a sturdy obstacle. Jeff said, "You're probably about as curious as I am, and I'll admit the desire to tear down this door and get beyond it is almost irresistible. But no reputable archaeologist can afford to give in to that kind of action. There's a meticulous discipline to the way we do things."

He gave Jones a nod and our cowpuncher cook unlimbered his bowie knife and with tedious care began chipping away at the ages-old mortar that held the door shut. "When this was set into the wall," Jeff informed us, "hinges as we know them had not been invented, nor had iron been discovered. What we have here is a solid sheet of wood chopped from a tree with some sort of stone implement, set into the opening and held in place by wedging it with a mud-base mortar filled with tiny pebbles. Once that's been removed the door can be lifted out."

You could see the impatience on those watching faces and I could feel it in myself. It put a strain on our tempers, honed our expectations. By the time the door moved and was brought away in Jones's hands every one of us, I guess, was about ready to pop. First through the opening was Flossie, then Harry Hatcher. We were all crowded around the opening, staring with an intensity that must have been laughable to anyone not caught up in our emotions. The frozen expressions on those roundabout faces were as plain as they were comical. There was nothing to be seen in the uncertain light and that tomblike quiet but another empty room with an open doorway off the left wall.

"Jesus!" Hatcher said. "I might's well have stayed in camp!"

Jeff, stepping forward without remark, crossed the room to the open doorway, through which Flossie had just disappeared. And there he stopped.

To the rest of us, watching in that unearthly quiet broken only by the patter of the dog's clawed feet, there was an arrested quality in Jeff's stance that put, I think, a quivering chill into all of us.

Frustration thinned Jeff's voice when he said, "Nothing in there but a pile of loose sand and off in one corner a hole in the floor."

Chapter Twelve

Hatcher crossed the room with Fletch at his heels, roughly shouldering Jeff out of the way. The dog barked somewhere as they passed out of sight. "Here, Flossie!" Jeff called as the rest of us joined him, but the dog didn't come. We could see Fletcher and Harry crouched over the hole, light from below shining bright on their faces, on dropped jaws and bulged eyes. "Oh—what is it?" Fern cried. "What are you staring at?"

In a stunned tone of voice Harry said, "Damned if I know . . . a lot of stuff down there, all piled up in a corner. Bunch of different-size pots . . ."

Jeff looked disgusted. "The Basketmakers weren't potters." Fern pushed past him. "Do you see Flossie?"

Harry said, "Yeah, she's down there."

"Is she all right?"

"Looks all right to me."

"Let me have a look at those pots," Jeff grunted as we

302

all ganged up behind Fletch and Harry. "What color are they?"

"Black on white," Fletch mumbled.

I said, "Looks to me like they're all Anasazi. They weren't made yesterday, that's for sure. I see a couple of storage jars and what seems like a wedding pot. There's a low flat bowl—maybe these people were Mogollons or some of the late Cochise people. That bowl looks to be about half full of corn."

Said Jeff, like he was turning it over, "Might possibly be Cochise. They made pottery after contact with some of the Mexican Indians."

"How," asked Fern, "are we going to get Flossie out of there?"

"That's about a five-foot drop," Jones said. "We can easy make a ladder—"

"We'll probably have to make several ladders," Jeff said, looking around, "if we don't come across some, which we probably will. We'll have to have short ladders to find out what we've got here. Must be at least five floors to this place."

Fern said to me, "Can't you get Flossie and hand her up?"

"You bet," I said, but after I dropped down there Flossie proved elusive. She'd come up to me and sniff in what seemed a friendly fashion, but each time I tried to get a hand on her she'd duck away.

"You go," Fern said to Jeff. "She'll let you pick her up."

"We'll get her tomorrow," said her brother. "Spending the night here isn't going to hurt her. Tomorrow we'll have a ladder."

I said, "What time you got, Jones?"

303

"Pretty close to two, about three minutes till."

Harry, catching on, said, "Fletch, you hike back to camp and fetch us a ladder."

There was very little enthusiasm in the scowl Fletcher showed but muttering under his breath, he went back through the hole we had taken the door from. Yet, oddly enough, his departure did not erase the anxious look from Fern's face.

This room I was in was lighter than the upper ones by reason of the window hole that was in the outside wall. There was an elongated shaft of sunlight on the floor and Flossie with her tongue lolling out was sitting in this watching me. "Come on, Flossie," I said, bending toward her. I held out a sugar lump. Her tail thumped the floor but she showed no intention of coming any nearer.

Jones said, "Reckon I better be gettin' back too. I ought to go over that tinned stuff. All this heat . . . you never know. Maybe I can help put together that ladder."

Jeff gave him rather detailed instructions and some ten minutes later he set out. "Keep a lookout for snakes," Jeff called after him.

Fern, still with that anxious look in her eyes, appeared to be keeping a close watch on Flossie, who had gone back to sniffing around that bunch of old pots. Larrimore heaved a despondent sigh. I said, "This place looks to be in pretty good condition. No sign of them—I mean the folks that built it—having been attacked or driven out. If they'd been hit by a plague—"

"It doesn't seem to have been that," Jeff said, shaking his head. "If it's corn in that bowl it couldn't have been lack of water. Perhaps they had a lemming complex, or just an itch to move. Let me look at that bowl, Brice."

I limped over to where Flossie was still nosing the collection, picked up the bowl and passed it up to him. "It's corn. Hard enough to be petrified."

But it wasn't the corn that concerned Jeff. It was the container he was studying.

"Does the design tell you anything?"

"Not really. It was obviously made a long time ago. It's a lightning design repeated with variations through hundreds of years; you'll still see its use in some of the pueblos. It's Anasazi ware, you were right about that. We might get a relative date from that corn."

"How many rooms do you reckon we've got here?"

"Possibly thirty. I wouldn't guess more than that. Probably less."

Flossie came over, stretched out a yawn and sat down beside me, thumping her tail as we exchanged looks. Then she was up again, moving off a few feet to stand intently staring at the door hole opening out of the west wall. Just above a whisper Fern said, "She's listening to something. You don't suppose there's anyone . . . ?"

"Not unless," Jeff said, "there's another way of getting in that we haven't found."

While he was talking I started toward that across-the-room doorway. This was all the encouragement Flossie needed. At a bound she was off and through the opening, the sound of her flying feet rapidly fading. I passed through after her and through three more, pulling up, gun in hand, before a fourth doorway hung with strung beads.

In the breathless quiet I caught the sound of her again, growing plainer. I heard her shake. And then there she was coming out of the beaded doorway, giving a wag of her tail as she sighted me. "Good girl!" I said as she stood looking up at me. "Guess you must've been chasing a chindi."

Jeff, when we got back, was down in the room below

Fern, looking over that pile of pots with an expression I felt was unduly thoughtful. "Each of those two largest storage jars," he said, pointing, "are filled with white and black beads. And that pitcher is filled with blue ones."

I picked up the pitcher and poured out a handful. "Fossil turquoise, and enough of it here to gladden Harry's heart. Prime grade, I'd say—and, by the way, where *is* Harry?"

"He went up top to watch for the ladder."

I poured the handful of turquoise back where it came from. "What do you want to do? Let Harry and friends get a look at this and we're going to have trouble."

"Yes." Jeff grimaced. "Throw a handful of those white beads on top of them and put that pitcher at the back of the pile. We'll have to figure some way to keep them out of sight."

Hoisting myself up till I got a knee hooked over the hole's edge, I climbed out onto Fern's level. "Poor Flossie," Fern said, looking sorrowfully down at her. "Poor, poor Flossie."

"Yes," Jeff said. "Well, shall we go outside? If we had Clampas here he would say his heart bleeds for her."

"You staying down there?" I said.

"I want to poke around a bit. And if you've no objections I'd like you to count on staying here tonight. If we can keep them from it I'd like to keep the vandals in our party from taking over."

I looked up at the sound of running steps approaching. I could feel the whole length of me tightening up. Was this what Fern felt? This queer foreboding? It was like receiving a telegram just as you're about to tuck into your supper. It was Harry, of course, and one glance at his face told us this was no joke.

The words tumbled out of him. "I sent Jones on to camp. Fletch is down in that rockfall with an arrow in his throat!"

Chapter Thirteen

I left Fern with Hatcher and went hurrying along the cliff-top, grimly wondering if this was a second installment of what had been started with Alfredo's death and the stampede of our horses. I wasn't far into those rocks when I found him, face down in the hollow between two large boulders.

You generally know when you're looking at death. There's something about it that makes itself manifest. I knew at first glance Fletcher'd cashed in his chips. I climbed down there and turned him over, wondering what had given Harry the notion an arrow had done for him. Then I saw it and guessed you could call it an arrow if that suited you.

It was there in his throat just below the Adam's apple, a slender shaft no more than eight inches long, almost certainly propelled from some kind of blowgun. There wasn't much blood.

I took Fletcher's pistol, thrust it into my waistband. No sign of his rifle. If an Indian had done this there wouldn't

be. But what kind of Indian around here used a blowgun?
Clampas would have said, "Must've been one of them chindis."

This wasn't going to help Jeff's hunt for glory. Our three-
man crew was like to cut for the tules when they glommed
on to this. If they'd take that smartass Navajo with them . . .
A small palaver with Hosteen Joe, it occurred to me, would
be at least a possible move in the right direction. Given his
makeup . . . We knew nothing at all about the bugger . . .
Well, I knew in my own mind Joe was a troublemaker, a
rebel and misfit who felt he had been shortchanged in life's
lottery. Joe in a number of ways looked cut from the same
cloth as Harry—out for anything he could get. And not particular how he got it.

If I'd been bossing this deal I'd have run him out—him,
Harry and Clampas—and the sooner the better.

I left Fletch where he was and limped down to see about
Gretchen. She didn't like showing it but I could tell she was
glad to see me. I gave her a sugar lump and threw on my
saddle and, after rummaging my notions, climbed aboard
and headed for camp. And got there just as Jones, toting a
short ladder, came bucking his way through the tamarisks.
"I'll take it," I told him. "Guess the camp's fair buzzin'
with the news of Fletch's passing."

"Ain't too much bein' said but plenty wild looks are
bein' chucked about." Jones grinned. "Clampas allows the
chindis must've got him."

"I thought he'd get around to that. Well, keep your eyes
skinned. I'll be stayin' up top tonight, me an' the mule
here."

"What about grub?"

"Won't be the first time I've missed the wagon." I

hooked an arm through the ladder and gave Gretchen the go sign.

When we reached the rockfall I got down with the ladder and looped the reins around the horn. "You're a smart enough critter to get up there if you've a mind to," I told her. "Just watch your step and follow my lead."

She hee-hawed a couple of times, then took after me. Figuring he'd earned it we bypassed the place where Fletch was resting. I guess she found it rough going but five minutes after I came out on top Gretchen joined me, nuzzling my pocket like she understood her due. Wrapping her lip around a sugar lump beat everything.

She kind of rolled her eyes when she came up to the entrance we had made in that cliff house. You didn't have to spell things out for her; she could read body language and was quick to catch on. I called out to alert the Larrimores, and then told Gretchen, "Browse up here anyplace you've a mind to," and stripped off my gear and cached it just inside that four-foot room that once had served as an entryway.

I found Fern and Jeff in the room above Flossie and set up the ladder. "Be a little careful with this thing, it's not an A-1 job. When the red brothers set out to put a ladder together they lash each joint with a strip of wet hide. Once that dries, you got a real foundation. Well, there you are."

"Jeff," Fern said, "go fetch up Flossie." Then, to me she said, wrinkling up her freckled nose, "I can't stand this place. There's something about it that makes me squirm."

Her brother fetched Flossie up and set the dog down. She went straight to Fern, wriggling all over, tail threshing ecstatically.

"I'm going to leave this torch with you," Jeff said, putting it into my hand. "Who do you suppose killed that fellow? And with a blowgun! I never heard of our kind of Indians—''

''You never heard of Hosteen Joe till you came out here and met him. I'm not sayin' he did it. Jones tells me Clampas has been laying it on the chindis. First thing you know— Well, never mind that.''

''You think he believes it?''

''No. Local tradition tends to back him up, though. You'll find these abos set a great deal of store on that sort of thing. Good excuse for pretty near anything.''

Jeff shook his head. ''Next year,'' he said with a determined glance, ''I'll come back and find out where these people went. And I'll be bringing my own crew with me!''

''They'll be your kind of people and that makes sense. Have a better grasp of what you're tryin' to accomplish.''

He rummaged my face with a sharpened glance. ''You've had an education—''

''Sure. School of Hard Knocks. My old man had his own set of notions, didn't subscribe to such dodderin' thoughts as all work and no play makes Jack a dull boy. I got the hell away from him quick as I was able.''

''Still,'' said Jeff, running a thoughtful tongue across his mouth, ''some of his lore must have rubbed off on you. That turquoise we found . . .''

''Fossil stuff. Formed as a mineral replacement in reeds, pithy sticks and the like. It's tubular—fine stuff for makin' necklaces.''

''Valuable?''

''Rare,'' I said, ''and like most rare things at the changing of hands the price goes up and it's strictly hard cash. How are you figurin' to go over this place? An overall look to see where you're at, or room by room?''

"In the time available I think I'd better see the whole layout first."

"All right then; I'll see you in the morning and we'll get right at it."

Fern's look lingered briefly and then they were gone.

I went out to see how Gretchen was doing, then sat for a while with my legs idly swinging in the entrance hole, staring off at the purpling shape of a distant range showing low against the far horizon. There were bushes enough up here I reckoned to keep a mule happy for most of the night.

It was fortunate Jeff had been stupid enough to give me this chance to have a good look around, even leaving me the bonus of a torch to do it with. I say "stupid" because that's just what it was. He didn't know enough about me to have the least basis for such reckless trust. His own sister when she'd hired me out of desperation had put me in the same class as Fletcher and Clampas, a man who lived with a gun. And she had pegged me right. More right than she knew.

Pushing off my perch I dropped into the house Jeff had claimed for his own. It was hard to picture this place as the seat of a community, filled with the noise of a people going about their everyday affairs. They might not have been the ape-men Jeff hunted, or even very close to the beginning of things, but primitive enough to be an unwelcome sight backed into a corner in the dead of night.

I'd a hunch Fern was right in her distrust of this place. I didn't like it either though I couldn't uncover any practical reason. Just a feeling, that was all, a kind of aura that reached out to curl about one. A sense of watchful, breathless waiting as if the place were about to gobble one whole. Damned silly, of course, and I knew it, but knowing didn't chase the feeling away. I went forward again, pulled along by remembrance of that beaded doorway I had seen hunting Flossie.

A thing like that didn't belong in this place. No Indian I had ever brushed up against would have hung a bunch of beads across any doorway. Someone else must taken over this dwelling after the original inhabitants had departed. And if this was the case it had to have been this later group who had so meticulously sealed the place up. Some of Clampas's chindis?

Such bead-hung doorways were not uncommon in Mexican houses.

Thinking of the way this place had been sealed I felt reasonably certain the ones who had been here after the builders had gone must have come and departed many hundreds of years ago. The stillness of centuries hung over these rooms. As I've said, you could feel it.

I switched on the torch and went down the ladder up which Jeff had fetched Flossie.

The pots and bowls still sat where we'd left them and I moved on through three rooms to stop and stare at the preposterous sight of that bead-hung doorway.

The vastness of this quiet seemed to hover just beyond me in those jet-black shadows retreating before my light, before the sound of each step. I was tense with excitement, with a feverish anticipation and with the prickling dread with which we face the unknown. I kept telling myself there was nothing to be afraid of and, trying to bolster this belief, wouldn't let my hand touch the pistol at my hip.

With the torch aimed dead ahead of me I pushed through the beads with a muttered oath. No one grabbed me. I was faced with nothing but an empty room with a floor hole black before the left-hand wall.

I limped back and got the ladder.

Dropping the heavy end of it through the hole I climbed cautiously down to get off it onto a lower floor which offered little reward for the effort it had taken. A couple of moth-eaten goatskins lay in one corner beside a crude wooden flute. And a handful of pebbles that shone blue in the light.

A few more of these lay scattered this side of the archway giving onto the next room as though dropped in hurried flight or fallen from a burst sack in someone's clumsy fist.

Picking a couple of them up I gave them a closer look. Turquoise nuggets. Good but not gem-grade. All right for beads. I strode on through the arch and stopped with caught breath.

Chapter Fourteen

The sun was close to two hours high before sounds on the trail below warned that someone at last was approaching from the camp. With a frowning impatience I looked down from the cliff to see Jeff, Fern, Harry and Clampas riding toward the rockfall and, strung out behind them, Jones with six laden packhorses.

I collected Gretchen, flung on my saddle and headed in the same direction, busting to know what the hell they were up to.

When I reached the top of the rockfall the cavalcade below was just coming up to the trailside end of it. Harry, spying me, flung up a hand. "Come down here, Corrigan!" he called like he owned me.

If Gretchen hadn't been all night without water I might have ignored him. In the end with clamped jaws I sent the mule into that jumble of rocks and, sitting back like I was Lord of the Mountain, let her pick her way through them.

We came out into the trail and I fastened my stare on a pale-faced Jeff. "What's the idea? You shiftin' camp?"

Jeff looked sick, Hatcher angry, Clampas amused, and Fern about ready to throw in the sponge. "Crew slipped away during the night with that goddam Navajo and better'n half our tinned stuff!" Harry snarled like he eyed it as a personal affront.

"I don't guess he left my Remington, did he?"

Hatcher snorted. "Clampas—who was supposed to be on guard—fell asleep! It's a goddam wonder we didn't all get our throats cut!"

"So we're moving camp," Jeff said tiredly. "I thought if we set up atop that cliff we'd be in a position to keep our eyes on things—"

"And what did you figure to do for water? Pipe it up there?"

Jeff looked embarrassed. "We hadn't thought of that," Fern said.

"You better think of it now." I directed some of my irritation at Clampas. "Why didn't you tell them they'd be killing half the horses trying to get 'em through those rocks?"

Clampas shrugged. "Harry ain't partial to advice from hired hands."

"I can see that," I said. "It's about time someone told Harry where to head in at. Any kid just out of diapers could have made a better job of this than he has." Catching hold of my temper I told Jeff bluntly, "If I was in charge of this I'd damn quick show Harry where he belongs—at the foot of the line, stripped of all authority."

I saw Larrimore wince, but Fern coming to life said approvingly, "You *are* in charge."

"You can't do this to me!" Harry shouted. "I got a contract with you!"

"Not any longer," I said. "It's been canceled. From here on out you're just one of the hands. And if that doesn't suit, you can spin your bronc an' light a shuck out of here."

Spluttering, frothing, Hatcher was so pissed off he couldn't get a word out. He finally slammed a hand at his gun. Then let go of it like it had scorched him when he found himself staring into mine. I said, "You brought Fletch into this. Now get up there and bury him!"

I watched the man fling out of his saddle and go stomping off to the packs for a shovel. "If I were you," Clampas said with his glance gone solemn, "I'd keep a spare set of eyes in the back of my head."

The Larrimore Expedition was now reduced to a party of six. Knowing the risks of trying to get flatland horses onto the clifftop through that jumble of rocks, I'd have sent the whole lot of them back to the pool had Fern not volunteered to see to their water needs. "I'm afraid it will take up most of your time, Fern."

"Oh, I'm used to commuting. One of the primest facts of life in Chicago. Don't look at me that way—I'll be all right. Don't you think you were just a bit rough on Harry?"

"Man's a born schemer; you should never have employed him."

"I didn't employ him!" she came back angrily. "He was Jeff's idea." Then, more quietly, "You have to realize my brother has little experience outside of the classroom. Most of his life has been devoted to archaeology. After trying for years to get a full professorship he hoped, coming here, to uncover new facts of indisputable significance, credit for which no other scientist would be able to minimize or take away from him.'' There was a pleading in the smile she tried so desperately to show me. ''He knows nothing at all about people like Harry.''

''I can understand that.''

''Can you understand what he's been hoping to accomplish? Our earliest ancestor, Mousterian Man, has an accepted existence of approximately sixty thousand years, a nomad cropping up in many and diverse places. Now these Basketmaker people of the Anasazi are generally believed to have come into this region some twenty-five thousands of years ago. What Harry hoped to do—and *will* do if he can come up with sufficient evidence—is to connect these two up. Don't you think that's worth doing?''

''I'm just an ignorant country boy, Fern. I wouldn't know up from down about such things.''

Jeff, coming over to us, said impatiently, ''Hadn't we better get up there, Corrigan?''

I nodded, still choused around in my mind by Fern's pitch. All that kind of guff was so much ancient history, I couldn't see how it could matter today. It was today I'd stuck my neck out to deal with, a time full of danger I could easily recognize. I knew a lot more about what lay ahead of him than Jeff did, and what I knew he wasn't going to like. ''Who do you want up there for a helper?''

''Oh, Clampas, I guess. He was certainly a help getting us into this place.''

You couldn't fault that. ''All right. Take him up with you. I'll be along soon's I've tended to Gretchen.''

I would rather have had Jones. Not so smart but reliable.

When I caught up with them Jeff and his helper had just got as far as the room with the pots he'd had to carry Flossie up from. The pair of them were standing there peering at that collection of relics. I was forced to decide quickly which figured to be the lesser of two tough choices, and said, "Why not start right here?"

"But I told you yesterday," Jeff remarked with surprise, "I'd prefer to go over the whole area before attempting to evaluate anything."

"You're the boss," I nodded, and to Clampas, "Better fetch that ladder along."

"I can see"—Clampas grinned—"you're not one to overlook the natural advantages."

"You look strong enough to carry it," I said, motioning him on after Larrimore.

Each of the empty rooms we went through appeared to deepen the gloom that showed so plain on Jeff's face. "What happened," I said, "to that Mousterian tribe?"

He looked at me in some astonishment; then, catching on, said, "I guess Fern's been talking shop. As a matter of fact there are a number of theories but no substantive evidence."

"Just disappeared like our Basketmakers?"

"That's about the size of it."

The bead curtain now was just ahead of us. Both men stopped to stare, neither liking it. Clampas's eyes jumped at it. "What's that thing doin' here?"

Jeff looked appalled, licked his lips like he couldn't believe it. "Someone's been here. . . ."

"Not since that entrance was sealed," Clampas objected.

"The people who built this never added that touch. Someone's been in here since the builders departed."

"You reckon they cleaned the place out?"

"I don't know," Jeff said bitterly, "but even if I find it the evidence I'm hunting will be open to doubt. Who's going to say now when and how it came to be here? Not with two sets of people running in and out of here."

"Maybe," I said, "we better hunt another site."

"No time for that now," Jeff said miserably. "Might as well get on with it."

He pushed through the dangling strings and stopped, much as I'd done, eyes going to the goatskins and the scattered beads. "Harry"—smiled Clampas—"will be happy to see those."

"Harry," I said, "has pretty well lost whatever edge he was countin' on."

Clampas's glance twinkled amusement. "Time will tell," he said blandly.

"Take this," I told Jeff, handing over Fletch's pistol. "You may find a use for it."

"That's right," Clampas nodded. "Place like this, who can say what might happen?"

"I can tell you what won't," I said. "None of this turquoise is going to wind up with Harry!"

Clampas looked at me and shrugged. Jeff, walking into the next room, swore. Clampas hurried after him and I went in on Clampas's heels. "Jumpin' Jehoshaphat!" Harry's gunfighter cried. "Looks like the hideout of the Forty Thieves!"

It did indeed. A great assemblage of pots and relics—Jeff called them artifacts—was heaped about the walls in astonishing profusion. One two-foot jar of the storage variety was filled with a miscellany of spear points and arrowheads.

Several others of equal dimensions—as I'd already discovered—were filled with rough spiderweb turquoise. Eight others were filled with strung beads, also turquoise. Quivers of arrows. A considerable pile of bows of divers styles and vintage were piled alongside. There were hide shields and wooden spears, scrapers, metates and forty-eleven other items too varied to enumerate.

319

I noticed Jeff staring at something he'd picked up and Clampas, ogling those jars of sky-blue stones, chucked a wink at me with an enchanted grin. "I ain't no authority," he declared with a chuckle, "but what we've got here oughta easily ransom any king those Conquistadores managed to overlook. Congratulations, Larrimore! Looks like you hit the jackpot."

Chapter Fifteen

There was such a petulant, resentful twist to Jeff's features, I could almost have felt sorry for him if he hadn't made such a mishmash of things.

"What's that you're holding?" I said to him brusquely, and he dropped into my hand a small stone lamp—leastways that's what he called it. To me it was nothing but a rock with a hollow worn into it and a more or less flat bottom, maybe two inches thick and three in diameter. "Valuable?"

"Hey!" Clampas said. "That looks older than Moses."

"Quite a bit older," Jeff replied with a sigh. "Not that it matters. After being found here its age, like its value, has little significance. With two sets of tenants calling this place home, nothing I discover will be worth a plugged nickel."

"In that case," Clampas hurried to assure him, "you can give me the blue stuff and forget you ever saw it."

"Well, come on," I said, "we might as well get on with

it. We've still got a couple dozen rooms to get through."

"Sounds like Christmas," Clampas chuckled, giving his hands a promotional dry wash.

Jeff gave him one hard look and thereafter ignored him. He set off for the next room in line, but instead of discarding that "worthless" stone lamp I noticed it went into his brush jacket pocket.

Any freebooter would have found in this trek through the cliff house a quite ample compensation for the time expended. The next eight rooms provided three motheaten goatskins, a discarded wooden flute, a scatter of mixed black and white beads, three broken pots, an elegant pitcher with a broken snout, three bundles of corn shucks and not another thing.

Jeff sent Clampas back for the ladder.

When the gunfighter returned with it we canvassed two additional rooms, both empty. The first of these, however, had a hole in the floor, and into this Jeff had Clampas drop the ladder. When the man stood aside Jeff motioned him onto it. Clampas looked Jeff over with a speculative stare. "You wouldn't be thinkin' of leaving me down there, now, would you?"

Jeff with a grimace motioned him on, stepping onto the ladder as soon as Clampas got off it on the floor below. So there we were, all three of us, in another empty room. As it eventually turned out every room on this level was empty, much to Clampas's disgust. "How much longer am I totin' this thing?" he growled, giving the ladder a slap with his gun hand.

"Till we're through with it," Jeff said. "Now put it down that hole and let's see what's below."

This next level, I'd been thinking, would likely be the last, so after we'd gone down it I told him to leave the ladder where it was. There were more rooms down here than on any of the upper levels. "How many people," Clampas asked Jeff, "do you reckon lived in this place?"

"I'd say about five hundred."

"At one time?"

"Certainly." Jeff produced a wan smile. "To the people using it this place represented a complete community—a town. Each family had a room."

It was plain such an arrangement held little charm for Clampas. The next fourteen rooms we toured held nothing but discarded odds and ends apparently not cherished by those who had abandoned them, except in the fourteenth, where Clampas picked up a rather bleached-looking turquoise ring and two bracelets, all of crude workmanship. Dropping the bangles in his pocket Clampas threw the ring away. Jeff, however, retrieved it, saying, "Keepsake."

The fifteenth and last of the rooms on this, the bottom level, turned out to be an eye-opener, extending into the cliff itself for a distance of possibly some forty feet. "Originally," Jeff told us, "this was probably a cliff shelter, in use sporadically for several hundred years before it was hidden behind this building. One would have to do quite a bit of digging to uncover and date the successive layers of use."

We'd been using the torch on the last couple levels and there wasn't much left in it. I said, "We had better vamoose before we find ourselves stumbling around in the dark."

They'd set up camp just below the rockfall and, time we got down there, Fern was just returning from the pool with the last group of horses she had taken to water. When he saw she was back, Jones beat on his washtub and advised us to come and get it. Advice which no one disregarded.

The main course was beef stew supplemented by cornmeal muffins, java and refried beans. To all of which they did full justice. "Well, how'd it go?" Harry asked, trying for a show of his old hearty charm. "Find anything worth carting home?"

"Been more'n one bunch living there," Clampas told him. "Jeff looks about ready to blow the whistle."

Jeff said nothing, just picked up his eating tools, stepped over and dropped them in the tub. Fern said with obvious concern, "Didn't you find a thing?"

Jeff put the stone lamp into her hands. "Why, this is marvelous!" she cried, turning it over and over. "It must be quite the oldest artifact you've ever found."

"It's old enough, all right," he said glumly, "but how do you prove how it got where and when? I can date it. That's not the point. The problem is provenance. How can I indisputably prove it appeared with the builders, not with those who took over after they left?"

She pushed it around through her head, suddenly smiling in a way that lit up her whole face. "Tree rings," she cried. "We can date the building by the age of the timbers—the roof poles, the wood they put into those ceilings."

"Sure." He nodded. "I thought about that. But what if the age of the stone doesn't match? And it probably won't."

"But if the stone should be older than the timbers—"

"You forget. It's the people, the builders, I'm trying to put dates to. With two different groups having used this place, who's to say which of them first had this lamp?" He thrust it back in his pocket with a lugubrious look. "It may even have been found here, and probably was. In which case, being older than this cliff house, it's of no use at all."

"What do we do now?"

"Tomorrow," Jeff said, "I'm going to have another look at certain features I didn't take the time to study properly.

Also I've got to decide which of the pots we'll want to take back with us, for we certainly can't spend more than another week here.''

''I'll go with you and help,'' Fern said. ''I don't believe we've enough horses to remove very much. We'll have to box any pottery we take . . .''

''Let's have Brice up there with us,'' Jeff surprised me by saying.

''Maybe,'' I said, ''it would be better to take Jones. He's pretty handy.''

I could feel the probe of her swung-around stare. I'd no idea what she felt about me. For my own part I reckoned I'd been seeing a sight too much of her, one reason she was hard for me to talk to. We had nothing in common. She was big-city, long used to things I knew little about, nor wanted to. My sort of life—if she could have had a good look at it—would have appalled her. The men she knew didn't go around strapped to a shooting iron.

''Don't you want to go with us?''

''Not particularly.''

Biting her lip she continued to consider me, almost as though she thought me willfully stupid. Catching hold of my arm she drew me aside. ''What is it with you? Don't you know my brother is counting on you?''

''In a way, perhaps—''

''In every way! You saw how things were. Harry running roughshod—why don't you get rid of him?'' Her glance sharpened angrily. ''I expected when I gave you Harry's job things were going to be different.''

I said, ''They are different. Giving me that job has made a prime target out of me!''

Having seen how upset she was I probably shouldn't have said that. A startled look came over her face. Then, flushed and furious, she lashed back. "If you're afraid of him—"

"Don't talk like a fool! What's left of this outfit's about ready to explode. With this goddam heat and all that guff about chindis it'll take damn little . . . Point is until we know—and I mean *know*—which of those buggers is throwin' the wrenches . . ."

"It's your job to find out!"

I gave her a hard look and turned away. I hadn't figured right now to bring things to a boil, but if she thought—Ah, to hell with her! Finding Hatcher watching with that sly smirk on his puss, I snarled, "Get a horse and a shovel and don't keep me waiting!"

I tossed my saddle on Gretchen, kneed the air from her belly and cinched her tight. She gave me no argument, knowing I was in no mood to be trifled with. I slipped the bit through her teeth and climbed aboard and, picking up my ex-boss, headed for our previous camp.

"What's up?" Harry said and, getting no answer, buttoned his lip.

When we got through the tamarisks I said without beating around no bushes, "If you found it convenient to get rid of a body, what would you do with it?"

Harry's cheeks turned the color of pummeled dough. "I . . . I—"

"Never mind. I reckon I can find it," I said with a curse, and sent Gretchen over to where Jones had had his fires. I got down, kicked the circle of stones aside and put my eye on Hatcher. "Start diggin'."

With a pasty face Harry bent to the task.

I could tell by the ease with which the shovel bit into that fire-blackened dirt we had got the right spot. With the sun not yet down it looked like pretty hot work. He didn't have to go far. I could tell when he straightened, looking sick, he

Mule Man

had put his shovel on something that yielded. "Careful now, I don't want him dug up. All I want is a look at his face."

"Wh—Who d'you think we're going to find?"

"Hosteen Joe."

Squatting down, having motioned him out of the way, with my hands I brushed back enough of the loose sandy soil to see that the cadaver had been planted face down, to make out the dried blood and powder marks on his shirt. "Shot in the back close up. With a pistol. Turn him over."

Harry's sweat-shiny face was a picture of horror. Shaking like a leaf, he drew back in repugnance. "For Chrissake," I said, "he's not goin' to bite you!"

I caught hold of the hair, jerked the head up enough for him to see it was Joe, then let it fall back. "All right. Cover him up."

Chapter Sixteen

We hadn't much more than got through the tamarisks on the way back to camp when, rounding a bend, we found Clampas riding toward us.

"Ah, the Mule Man and stooge," he hailed, combing us over with his sardonic look. "Much as we'll regret the loss of your company, if I was you, Harry, I'd trot right along."

Hatcher, with the look of a frightened rabbit, appeared only too glad to be let off the hook.

Clampas's gaunt face swung back to me. "Where the hell you been? They're all out huntin'—figured the chindis had got you."

I just stared at him, not saying anything. He laughed. "So you found him. Kinda figured you would. Takes one to know one." He looked amused. "That Harry," he chuckled. Then his brows drew down. "You don't believe it?"

"He hasn't the stomach for that kind of thing. You were using that smartass buck all along, right from the time he showed up with old Two-Feathers. What'd you promise him—that Sharps? It was you put him up to makin' off with those horses. You probably used him to get rid of the crew."

"Sure. I had to figure some way of cuttin' down the odds." Clampas grinned. "Hell, Fletch was no loss, an' I won't shed no tears if something happens to that mealy-mouthed Harry. You been around. Quit usin' your head for a hat rack. Comes to that, your friend Harry propositioned me two days ago, wanted us to team up and split that turquoise right down the middle!"

I felt an almost overmastering impulse to go after him right then. "Guess you allowed you didn't need his help."

Clampas smiled. "Not likely. If I'd said anything like that he might of taken the notion I aimed to grab it myself."

"I suppose that never entered your mind."

"Oh, I've thought some about it—of course Hatcher doesn't know about that pile we saw this morning. If I was figurin' to team up with anyone it sure wouldn't be with no chump like Harry."

"Guess you'd want a man you could count on."

"Now you're talkin'."

"Don't look at me. I like this layout just the way it is."

"Here," he said, tossing me a penny. "Flip it—I'm going to show you something."

Almost before the coin left my hand Clampas's gun flashed up. It coughed just once and the penny disappeared. "Kid stuff," I said.

I could see he was graveled. "Corrigan," he said, "you amaze me."

"Just be careful that shooter don't point in my direction or you ain't going to care whether school keeps or not."

He didn't like that either. He looked me over for a while

before he said, "How's Burt Mossman getting along these days?"

"Haven't seen Burt since I quit the Hashknife."

"No accountin' for tastes," he said lightly. Then he fetched out that bullypuss smile once more. "Just do yourself a favor and stay out of my way."

Next morning, with the promise of another hot day, I heard Jeff telling Jones to take over Fern's watering chores, that she'd be going with him to decide what relics they wanted out of the cliff house. When Jones turned away to get this work started I led Jeff off a piece and told him bluntly, "You better take Harry up there and leave me in camp."

"I don't want Harry up there."

"It ain't a question of what you want but what you can afford. I don't think you'd be real smart to leave Hatcher and Clampas here with no one to keep an eye on them."

"Not sure I get your point," Jeff said, frowning.

"All right, I'll spell it out. How do you aim to get whatever artifacts you want back to your headquarters in Chicago?"

"I'm intending to use those horses."

"And when you're ready to go suppose there ain't any horses?"

"You think Harry—"

"Harry," I said, "is under Clampas's thumb. He's scared to death of that bucko."

"Why would Clampas want to tamper with our horses?"

"He's already tampered with them once through Harry. You think Clampas was asleep when your crew took off? Wake up, Larrimore. You're dealin' with the *real* world here! Clampas saw that turquoise yesterday, damn near a

wagonload, and I'm telling you fair and square he has no
intention of seeing it wind up in some university."

"What makes you think—?"

"Hell, he as much as told me. Said Harry had offered to
split with him. Be no problem at all to run off those horses
and cache them out of sight till you and your sister have
started hoofin' it for the railroad."

Jeff stared at me, shaken. "You want me to make them
a present of it?"

"All I want you to do is face the facts and make it no
easier for them than you can help."

I watched him go off and beckon Harry. When I swung
around there was Fern with a tired look to the set of her
shoulders. "So you're not going up with us?"

I shook my head, not wanting to get trapped into another
unprofitable argument. But she wouldn't leave it like that.
She said, coaxing, "I'd feel a lot safer if—"

"Fern, believe me, it won't do to leave Harry and Clampas down here together."

She kept searching my face with that blue-green stare, the
rising sun in her hair like copper. She was not a person
easily put off. "Look," I said, "both Harry and Clampas
are bustin' to get their hooks on that turquoise. Harry's
soft—we can handle him. But Clampas is something else
again. He's got no more scruples than a goddam snake."

"You don't have to convince me; I had a feeling about
him as soon as I saw him. I told you that. It's why I wanted
you to come with us. But I'm just as upset by those rooms
up there. I've a very bad feeling about that place every time
I step into it. It isn't anything I can easily explain; there's
something evil about it, a feeling of menace as though
something horrible had taken place there and was waiting—

just waiting like a spider in its web—to happen all over again."

She put a hand on my arm and I could feel her tremble with the freckles standing out against the pallor of that tipped-back face as she stood there looking up at me with the need so apparent in those searching eyes. "At least come with us—"

"As I've just pointed out to your brother, if you intend to take anything away from this place you can't afford to lose those horses, Fern. Jeff may not have found what he hoped to but the things he *has* found are commercially valuable, enough to pay for more than one extensive dig. He can't want to throw all that away through losing the means of taking it out of here."

I could see these things weren't touching her at all. I'd been throwing my words against a locked mind, a stubborn conviction it seemed nothing would loosen. What she wanted, I thought, and really needed, was a man of her own, and she had fastened on me.

Her next words proved it. In a voice gone husky, her hand tightening its grip, those near-whispered words banged against me like fists: *"If you care at all for me, Brice..."*

I jerked myself free. "It's no good, I tell you! Stay away from me, Fern. I wouldn't fit into your life. Nor you in mine!"

Chapter Seventeen

After Fern, her brother and Harry went into the rockfall on their way to the cliff house entrance I sleeved the sweat off my face and looked around for Clampas. Jones was just coming back from a trip to the pool with the first batch of horses he had taken to water. I hailed him to ask if he'd seen the fellow. "Clampas? Sure. He's down at the old camp."

"Doing what?"

Jones said dryly, "I didn't ask." Something in my expression apparently spurred him to say, "You want I should tell him to get his ass up here?"

"No, let it go. What I've got to say to him can wait a while longer."

I rolled me a smoke while he penned the horses he had just brought back and set off for the pool with the rest of our stock. Which reminded me that Gretchen hadn't been watered yet. "You'll just have to wait a bit," I told her. "I ain't about to go off and leave them critters unguarded till I've had me a little chat with that bugger."

God but it was hot. Seemed like each day was even hotter than the last. And by the looks of that sky there was no relief in sight. I felt mean about Fern but it was one of those things you had to nip in the bud, and I reckoned I'd done the right thing if I could stick to it.

I looked around for Flossie and then remembered she'd gone with Fern. I hoped that ladder Jones had put together for us wouldn't decide to come apart while somebody was on it. Seemed like I was working up a fit of the dismals. I wasn't the kind to set around and do nothing. Aside from keeping an eye on the penned horses, which I got to admit was becoming monotonous, what was there to do?

Jones came back with the last of the watered stock and after he'd penned them came over and hunkered down on his bootheels. He picked up a stick and made doodles in the dirt. "When's the professor pullin' out, do you know?"

"Within the week I guess." I shifted my weight. "Clampas still down there?"

Jones nodded. "What happens to us when they get to the railroad?"

I looked up without interest. "Reckon they'll pay us off."

Even in the shade sweat was all over us and the goddam flies wouldn't let us alone. I finally got up and just about then horse sound swiveled our heads toward the trail.

As expected it was Clampas. He swung off his horse with that sardonic grin, stood looking at us with the reins in his hand. "Still up there, are they?"

Neither one of us bothered to answer. With a shrug he went off to put his mount in the pen. "Wonder," I said, "what he was doing down there."

"Wasn't doin' nothing. Just settin' there under them tamarisks."

"Hatchin' up more devilment probably."

He came back after a while and bit himself off a chew from his Picnic Twist. "I see Harry comin' down but no sign of the others."

When I heard Hatcher's boots coming out of the rocks I turned around for a look at him. He wore the shine of sweat on his troubled face. When he got back his breath he said, "I couldn't take no more of it. That's the scariest place I ever been into."

"See any chindis?" Clampas grinned.

"No, but I sure seen a mort of turquoise." Naked greed gleamed out of his stare. "You reckon he's sure enough aimin' to pack it all back to that fool university?"

"It ain't got there yet," Clampas mentioned, and swiveled his glance for a look at me. I paid him no heed. "Have they made up their minds what stuff they're going to take?" I asked Harry.

"I guess they're takin' six or eight of them pots. And the turquoise." He scowled. "Sure makes me sick to think of it. If we had any gumption we'd take it away from him."

"Watch out," Clampas drawled. "That sort of gab don't set well with Corrigan."

Hatcher eyed me, disgusted.

"When are the Larrimores comin' down?" Jones asked. He slanched a look at the sun. "Mebbe I better wrastle up some grub."

Harry kicked at a horse apple. "Jeff allows he's goin' to spend the night up there."

Clampas chuckled. "Figures to keep his eye on the turquoise, I reckon." He spun the rowel of a spur. "Wouldn't want anything to happen to him. . . . Maybe I ought to go up an' keep him company.''

I reckoned he was trying to get a rise out of me.

A shadow crossed my lap. I looked up and saw Fern coming toward us. ''Hi,'' she said, flushed of face and looking straight at me. ''Hi,'' I said. ''That right about Jeff? He's really fixin' to stay up there?''

''That's what he says. He wants Jones to fetch him some food and a water bag when it's ready.''

Harry said, ''I wouldn't spend a night in that place for all the gold in the Denver mint!'' And Clampas said solemnly, ''Ain't likely, Harry, they'll offer it to you.''

After we'd eaten, Jones with a water bag slung from his shoulder took a pan heaped with grub and set out for the cliff house. Fern said to me with an expressionless face, ''You meant that, didn't you?''

''Yes. Where's the dog?'' I saw the whole shape of her stiffen, but whatever she felt it wasn't being advertised. I thought for a moment the breath had caught in her throat; her eyes never left my face as she replied, ''She's staying up there with Jeff.''

It seemed to be awful quiet for a second. Then she turned, moved away toward her tent, and I found Clampas watching from between the two pens Jones had put the horses into. In an effort to put Fern's look out of mind I walked up to him grimly and stared him in the eye. ''You're not going to get it, Clampas. Make up your mind to it. And if anything should happen again to what's left of our remuda you can look for big trouble.''

Jeff was back in time for breakfast. Flossie, too; and the first thing she did was make a beeline for Fern's tent. When Fern came out with her a few minutes later it was with her usual calmly competent appearance despite the dark smudges I saw under her eyes.

After we'd eaten Jeff drew me aside and speaking under his breath said, "There was something up there—must have been about four o'clock. I'd been dozing I guess and had forgot to turn off my torch. It was pretty weak when I jerked open my eyes and saw this shape slipping out of the room. Just as it seemed about to fade through that arch I yelled. The top part of it turned and I was staring at the most terrifying face I've ever seen in my life. Great ringed eyes beneath fluttering tatters of ropelike hair, and a leering mouth parted over two teeth behind lips that must have been at least an inch thick."

"Sure you weren't dreaming?"

"I wish I could think so, but when I saw that horrible face peering at me I was wide awake. Believe me I was! I can see it now, grinning around those two teeth!" He swallowed convulsively. "You think it was a chindi?"

Some of what he felt must have rubbed off on me. The sweat grew cold on the back of my neck. I stood motionless, not answering, trying to control leaping thoughts, my eyes fastened on Clampas. "No," I said, looking again at Jeff, "I think you saw an illusion—"

"Damn it," he growled. "I *saw* it, I tell you!"

"Of course. I'm sure you did. I'll stay up there tonight and see if I can catch a glimpse. Were you in that room with all those jugs of turquoise at the time this happened?"

Jeff nodded. "I was trying to make up my mind how much of it we could pack."

"All right," I said. "Keep your mouth shut about this," and limped off to saddle Gretchen.

* * *

Riding up through the rockfall I left the mule outside the cliff house entrance, wriggled my way through the hole we had made and set off to find if there was anything I could discover. Like, for instance, if there was some other way of getting into the place. I figured Jeff had been too shaken to make any kind of thorough hunt himself. Of course we'd already canvassed the place but I had an idea I wanted to check out.

Down the ladder I went and into the room where we'd found the first pots. Jeff had separated a few of these and set them to one side, possibly the ones he was figuring on taking. He'd fetched up and put with these that pitcher with the broken snout. I hadn't thought to bring a torch so there wasn't much point in going stumbling about through the dark of those lower rooms scratching matches to see with.

This being the level with the occasional apertures left in the outside wall for windows, I was about to head for that room behind the strings of beads when a swift patter of feet wheeled me around to see Flossie happily wagging her tail in the doorway behind me. "Where's Fern?" I said, and Fern answered for herself, coming to stand beside the dog and holding out a torch. She said, a bit uncertain-like, "I came up to fetch this for you. Didn't think you could do very much without a light."

"Too right," I said. "I tore off in such a hurry I forgot to bring one with me."

I expect I felt more awkward than she did, remembering the things we had said to each other. "If—if you'd like to come along, I want to check on that turquoise . . ."

"If I won't be in the way."

"You carry the torch," I said, watching Flossie scamper eagerly ahead of us.

Still with an occasional window hole lighting the way,

we came to and pushed through that bead-hung doorway and came into the room with the pair of old goatskins where a handful of turquoise had lain scattered on the floor. "We picked that up yesterday," Fern said, and we moved on through the arch, stepping into the room where we'd found what Clampas had termed the "chindis' hoard." There were changes here too.

"We picked out what we thought was the best of it and piled it over there," she said, pointing. "Neither one of us, however, knows hardly anything about turquoise. We'd be obliged if you'd go through it and weed out the ordinary stuff. It's going to be a real weight problem taking very much of it, I'm afraid."

"If we all went on foot you'd have six more horses you could pack," I pointed out. "And if you don't take it out— all of it, I mean—by the time you're able to return somebody else will have scooped it up."

She looked at me tiredly. "I guess you mean Harry and Clampas."

"You bet. One of them anyway. When's Jeff figurin' to leave?"

"He says tomorrow." She sighed. "I don't think we can be ready by tomorrow. Too much to pack up and all that carrying down through the rockfall. I dread to think of it."

"Speaking of dread," I said, taking a look at her, "do you still have that feeling about this place?"

"Yes. More than ever. I'll be glad to see the last of it."

"I remember you thought something terrible must have happened here, that these rooms were waiting for it to happen again."

"Yes." She shivered. "I still feel that way."

"I've had a few uncomfortable thoughts about the place myself. There's a brooding, sinister sort of atmosphere I find

339

it hard to explain away. More than just this tomblike quiet. It's as though the very mud and stones have soaked up the horror and anguish—''

''Don't talk about it, Brice. I'm just about ready to scream right now.''

She looked it, too.

''All right. Let's go—where's Flossie?''

Fern whistled. Away off somewhere down below a dog barked. ''Here, Flossie!'' Fern called, and the dog barked again. ''She's on a lower level,'' I said. ''Stay here. I'll fetch the ladder.''

''I'm coming with you,'' she said, hurrying after me.

I hooked the ladder over my shoulder and we started back. When we got to the hole I dropped the ladder into position. ''Throw some light down there.'' When she did we saw Flossie, tail wagging and looking proud as Punch with a long bone sticking out from both sides of her mouth. I said, ''Good girl, Flossie,'' and to Fern: ''How will we get her up? Can you carry her?''

''I don't think so, not and climb that ladder. She's pretty heavy. I better get Jeff.''

I said irritably, ''You'll have to have the ladder to get onto the next floor.'' With exasperation mounting, I hauled up the ladder and manhandled it back where I'd got it. When it was in position she said, ''You keep this,'' and handed me the switched-off torch.

The sun coming through those window holes made it plain it would soon be dropping out of sight. In this kind of country black night wouldn't be long delayed. It was odd we hadn't found any Indian-made ladders. By the time I'd quit wondering about this I was back in the room above Flossie so I switched on the torch and there she was, still chomping that old bone she'd dug up.

With the torch still on I remembered the notion that had fetched me up here. Squatting down put me under the sun glare coming in from outside and I switched off the torch, juggling that notion around and thinking it had to be sound. Because, unless Jeff's apparition turned out to be a permanent resident, it someway had to get in from outside, and the only feasible way it could do this was through one of these top-level window holes. And that meant a rope with an anchor at one end of it.

Why not, I thought, go and look for it now? There ought to be time before Fern brought Jeff up here. I shoved to my feet and walked into the next room—nothing there, nor in any of the others on this level until I remembered I hadn't thought to check the three rooms on the downtrail side of that bead curtain.

Well, I expect you guessed it. Our chindi had climbed into the turquoise room; there was the rope coming in across the sill of the window hole, held in place by the metal bar it was tied to—only, by grab, it was no metal bar but the dismantled barrel of my given-away Remington!

Chapter Eighteen

Jeff went down and brought up Flossie, bone and all. He did not appear too happy about it; I expect he felt considerable put out, dragooned into playing errand boy to a dog. Flossie fetched her bone over for Fern to admire and was visibly delighted by Fern's lavish praise.

Jeff, looking at me, said, "You want to check this turquoise for me? Seems to be all I'll have to show for this trip."

"You've got that Stone Age lamp in your pocket."

"Well, yes," he nodded, "but I can't tie it in to what I came here for. Offhand, how much of this mineral would you say is worth moving?"

"Offhand, I'd say all of it. And by walking the forty miles between here and the railroad you'll have enough horses to tote it. You've got a king's ransom here if you can manage to get out with it."

"I hope you know what you're talking about," he muttered, perking up a little.

This was my hope, too, but getting it to Chicago was like to take a heap of doing.

It was just about then I saw him suddenly stiffen, startled stare clamped intent on the bone Flossie was gnawing. "Here—let me see that," he grunted, bending over.

Flossie growled, backing off.

"Let me have a look at that," Jeff said warily. And Fern said, "He isn't going to keep it. Here—let me have it."

The dog, distrustfully dancing about, reluctantly surrendered her coveted prize.

Peering over his shoulder I said, "Doesn't much look like it came off a steer."

Looking immensely excited, Jeff looked up to say, "It's a human leg bone, what there is of it. I'll have to get it dated, but near as I can tell it's about the same age as that stone lamp I found."

"Good girl!" Fern told Flossie. "Let's go find another, shall we?"

Flossie, thus encouraged, straightaway leaped to the floor below and was off like a bat out of Carlsbad. "Come on!" Jeff cried, and went hurrying down our makeshift ladder. With a deal more care Fern and I followed. But the dog was no longer on that level. "She's making for that cave shelter," Jeff declared excitedly.

When we reached it Flossie, half out of sight, was making the dirt fly. In less than two minutes she came scrambling out with another aged bone, an arm bone this was, and Jeff looked even more excited than she was.

Peering into the excavation with the aid of the torch, we could see a number of other half-buried bones and the lower two thirds of a badly smashed skull.

Fern, looking sick, backed hastily away. Eyes bright, Jeff said, "I'll have to get a shovel—"

I caught hold of his arm. "We forgot to fetch the ladder."

But there was no holding Jeff. "Wait here," he growled, and took off at a run. Looked like Flossie's find had made a new man of him.

Fern, I could see, did not share his enthusiasm. With waxen cheeks and worried stare she followed me into the part of the room that was not under the fire-blackened overhang. Recalling the look of that smashed skull I couldn't help wondering how many other mangled bodies had been buried here. Fern tried to get Flossie to leave the bone alone but, having been robbed once, the dog had no intention of giving up this newest prize.

My thoughts shifted to the man who had climbed that rope with the aid of my dismantled Remington, a dangerous feat exposed as he must have been against that sheer wall. He could not be seen from our present camp but he risked at the least a very nasty fall in the event the rope broke or any portion of that wall collapsed. Was this the man with the horrible face described by Jeff?

I reckoned Jeff was into the rockfall by this time. Even without the ladder, getting out of this place offered no great problem; I had done it myself without any ladder. Be different of course for Fern and the dog.

In the creeping breathless quiet the sound of approaching steps carried plainly and Clampas came into our cave-shelter room on the heels of Jeff and the shovel he'd gone after. I could see Flossie bristle. Clampas reached for the shovel. "Just show me where and I'll do the digging. Expect you've already seen all we're likely to find."

Mule Man

But he was wrong about that. In little more than half an hour's work he uncovered six skeletons, not counting Flossie's find, and the heads of each had been smashed like the first. "Looks like they been poleaxed," he said. "No jewelry. You want to clear any more?"

"I guess we've seen enough," Jeff allowed. "We better get back to camp. You all right, Fern?"

"I've felt better."

Jeff picked up the shovel. Flossie picked up her bone and hustled after Fern.

"Don't you think," Fern said, catching her brother's arm, "we ought to cover them up?"

"They're not goin' to object," Clampas said. "But here's the shovel if you don't feel right about it."

By the time they'd moved the ladder twice and twice lifted Flossie onto the next level, Jeff's feeling that all was well with his world looked to have dampened down somewhat. The sun was nearing the horizon when we came out on the clifftop and Fern, Flossie and Jeff up ahead were again debating their time of departure. Clampas, several yards behind, showed a mocking smile when I caught up on my faithful steed.

"You're goin' to wear that goddam mule to a frazzle if you ain't careful," he said.

"She paces herself—got more sense than a horse," I told him. "I been wonderin' about the way Fletch was killed—with that dart, I mean. You got any idea where it came from?"

"Hell," Clampas said, "I just retched up an' jabbed the thing into him."

"I wouldn't put it past you."

Clampas looked amused. "Come off it, Corrigan. You must think I'm some kinda one-man exterminator."

345

"Jeff had a bit of excitement last night. While he was up there sleeping with that turquoise some cat-footed jasper in a ceremonial mask slipped into the room trying to give him a fright."

"That so? Was he frightened?"

"Reckon it startled him some. They're not used to chindis in Chicago. I gave him Fletch's six-shooter, told him next time he sees one to salivate the bastard."

Clampas laughed. "By the way," he said, "didn't it strike you as odd there wasn't no jewelry on them guys we dug up?"

"I doubt if them Basketmakers wore any gewgaws. If they did they were probably stripped before they were planted." We went along a few mule lengths without any more chitchat. Then I said to him casual, "I'll be staying up there tonight. Happen you run into that venturesome chindi you can tell him he needn't risk his neck on that rope. I'll leave the door off the latch and he can walk right in like he's one of the family."

We went down through the rockfall and put on the nose-bags.

After we finished feeding our tapeworms, and I got back from getting Gretchen a drink at the pool, Fern waylaid me before I could start once more for the cliff house.

"Do you feel you really have to spend another night up there? Why don't you just forget that turquoise—surely you can't believe it's worth such a risk. Now that Flossie has discovered those bones . . ."

"Those bones," I said, "if they pack the right date, might well put Jeff where he's achin' to be, right up at the top of the archaeological totem pole. And if he can get that turquoise back to Chicago he can be almost certain of coming back here next year; no one could afford to stand in his way.''

"But why should—Brice, why should you care whether he comes back or not? I'm afraid of that place. I don't think you ought to stay up there—it's dangerous!"

"Aren't you forgetting? Danger's my business, my stock in trade. As for carin' whether or not your brother comes back . . . hell, I'm countin' on him hiring me at double my present wages."

I endured a long look, hoping she wouldn't bawl. With the orneriest grin I was able to dredge up I pointed Gretchen into the rockfall, still feeling the drag of her stare on my back.

At the cliff house entrance I pulled my bridle and tack off the mule and turned her loose to forage for herself, pretty sure she'd come running if she heard me call. Then I went inside, picked up Fern's torch, went down the ladder onto the next level and listened to the rasp of my spurless boots stalking through the piled-up silence of centuries. I had the same creepy feel the place had given me the first time, but I was no silly girl to let it build fantastic fancies.

Reaching the turquoise room I limped across to the window hole, pulled up that rope and untied it from the barrel of my stockless Remington. The barrel had some fresh scratches but near as I could tell no further damage. I guessed it would still shoot and made sure that it was loaded, taking out the cartridges and dropping them in my pocket. Then I took the barrel with its still workable mechanism into the next room and laid it down in a corner where I hoped it wouldn't be noticed.

I got the rope then and tossed it down onto the floor below, not caring to give Clampas's chindi the least bit of aid I was able to avoid. With this same thought in mind I went back and removed the ladder from where it had rested against the floor above. Now, I reckoned, chindis or not they could hardly drop in without me hearing them. But just to make sure, I moved back out of sight and sat down on the floor with my back to a wall below the hole I'd just taken the ladder from.

After my recent talk with Harry's gunfighter I was not at all sure I would have any visitors. I didn't think Clampas would intrude on my vigil. Dangerous he was, I'd no doubt about that, but men of his stamp preferred the odds to be with them. They didn't like going up against a pat hand.

I was a long way from making up my mind about Harry. I had him figured for a slick-talking con man and all I had seen of him bore this out. Ruthless enough with things going his way, but when push came to shove he had twice backed off. And he had certainly appeared to be afraid of this place. Had this all been an act? Was he at rock bottom a lot tougher than he looked? Appearances for sure could be almighty deceptive.

It seemed three times as quiet now as it had when I came in here. The same breathless hush that had raised my hackles before, the same sense of unspeakable evil Fern had felt to be cooped up in these ancient walls seemed abruptly less than a hand's grab away.

I advised me not to let myself run away with any such preposterous notion but it did not take the curse from this quiet that seemed to be soaking right into my bones. Outside in the heat of a blazing sun a man could scoff at such nonsense, but as the cold of the night settled into these rooms nothing appeared too outlandish to seem possible. Not even chindis.

I would have liked to have had my pistol in hand but was too keyed up now to risk the least movement. Twice I thought to have heard a stealthy foot; once I'd have sworn I'd caught the slither of cloth brushing unseen against something in passing.

I was fast becoming a bundle of nerves.

With no idea how long I'd been rooted there with muscles cramped and ears about ready to fall off with listening, it took a real effort to get off my behind. Every joint in my body was stiff with cramp, so locked in position I fully expected to hear them creak with the strain. But eventually, by degrees, I got onto my feet, feeling like I had been dragged through a knothole.

The place was as still as the night before Christmas, and if anything was stirring I sure didn't hear it. When I felt I could move without breaking apart I crept into the next room and over to the window hole for a look at the night. The moon had got up, but although not in sight the argent gleam of its presence lay wraithlike along the opposite wall of the gulch.

Pulling off my boots to cut down the racket, I slipped through the bead strings and over to the door hole that let into the room where the king's ransom lay. Someone a long time ago had assembled it there and never come back for it.

Would Jeff's luck be any better? I wondered.

Chapter Nineteen

It must have been pretty well along toward morning when I got to remembering my days on the trading post at Half Step. I didn't think of them often. Growing up as a kid, every day had been an adventure—learning to ride and see-ing new faces, getting to know a lot of interesting Indians, admiring the jewelry they brought in to trade or leave as pawn when they ran short of cash. But when I reached my teens this was all old stuff and hanging around that place bored the hell out of me and going off to school, after the first couple of years, seemed just as bad. I was probably fiddle-footed. What I wanted was excitement and I found it with Burt Mossman. He had the coldest eye I have ever looked into. . . .

Of a sudden I found myself bolt upright, listening into that brooding silence, staring wide-eyed into the dark around. Something, I thought, had shifted its weight. But what? And where?

Mule Man

Motionless, listening, I snapped on my torch, aiming it into the black hole of that doorway, thinking to see a faint blur of motion. I couldn't pick it up; the light was too nearly spent to give any definition. I lunged to my feet and tore into the room where the two goatskins lay and found nothing but shadows that drifted away in the fading dimness of my torch. All I could hear was a wild thudding inside me. Then a sound like a fast freight car passing and something whacked into the wall behind me and I threw the damn torch in a passion of cursing. No grunt or cry came out of the shadows, nothing but the clatter of the rolling torch.

Strangely enough as I crouched there panting I had a vision of that dart in Fletcher's throat and sensed it must have been sped from an ordinary peashooter. And there was nobody near me and I knew for sure that except for myself this room was empty. No one had left by that moonlit window hole.

I pulled in a fresh breath and straightened out of my cramp. I turned back to the doorway I'd come through so reckless and felt along the wall but there was no dart there. What I jerked from the wall was a feathered arrow.

It was getting light fast with the night all but gone when I limped back to cautiously examine the window hole. No rope nor any mark of one. What the lift of my stare discovered outside was a deal more startling. Spread along the rim of the gulch wall opposite were the motionless shapes of a long line of horsemen, black against the brightening sky.

Indians!

I tore out of that room through the dangling beads and through three more and straight up the ladder and squeezed through the holes we had made getting in here and out on the clifftop and, not stopping for breath, flung my saddle on

Gretchen and took off for camp.

Only Jones was afoot, building up his fire, when I went down through the rockfall in a clatter of hoofs with six-shooter lifted, belching out the alarm. "Indians!" I yelled, pulling up by the fire in a splatter of dust. "Not two miles away—must be half a hundred of 'em!"

Clampas and Harry came running with rifles and Fern and Flossie tumbled out of their tent just as Jeff appeared, struggling into his shirt. "Where?" Harry cried with eyes so bulged I thought they'd roll off his cheekbones.

"They were on that wall across from the cliff house—"

"But there's no place to hide! We'll be slaughtered like sheep!" Harry jittered.

"Not if you can get yourselves into the cliff house."

"But the horses!" Jeff wailed. "They'll—"

"Hell with the horses!" To get them moving, knowing better, I snarled, "If you don't want to find yourselves over a fire, for Chrissake get out of here! Pronto!"

"Too late," Jones muttered, throwing out a pointing arm.

I wheeled. He was right. Whatever the outcome, we were trapped here now. Both cliffs were black with jostling horsemen. Spears, bows and a miscellany of rifles were plainly visible as were many of the faces. Navajos, all of them, and not to be trifled with.

Now, on the opposite wall, the ranks opened up and a commanding figure put his pony down the precipitous slope on skidding hind legs to pull to a stop less than twenty feet away. The vicious slam of a shot ripped the sudden silence and I whirled to find Harry staggering backward off balance. Clampas, his face gaunt, had wrenched the rifle from Hatcher's grasp and thrown it into the brush. The Navajo—it was old Johnny Two-Feathers—sat his mount imperturbably, making no move at all.

"I will talk," he said, "with Man-on-a-Mule."

"Go ahead. I'm listening."

"This is bad thing you do. Going into the house of the Anasazi, stirring up the chindis. Taking away things that do not belong to you. Bring very bad trouble."

He studied me awhile. "Where Hosteen Joe?"

A very sticky question.

"Dead," I said finally.

"So," the old man smiled thinly. "You admit it."

"I don't think you'd care for a lie."

"Where?"

I said, "Matter of fact we thought he'd gone off with the boys who deserted our crew one night . . ."

"We talk with crew. Joe not with them."

I could see what was coming, but no way around it.

"You show," he said.

"Joe's at the old camp. By the tamarisks."

Johnny Two-Feathers nodded.

"Come," he said. "You show."

I could feel the sweat trickle down my back. But there was no way around it, not without blood shed, and most of the blood would damn sure be ours.

"All right." I put Gretchen onto the trail and the old man swung his horse in behind. A grim and talkless ride. Some awful thoughts churned through my head, but nothing I could dredge up offered so much as the faintest glimmer of any way out of this.

I put Gretchen through the trees. The old man on his horse came through behind me. "Where?" he said. "Where you put Joe?"

It was plain no explanation I might make could wash

away the fact of that bullet through Joe's back. "I should have fetched a shovel."

He waved that away. I pointed out the place, thinking maybe he wasn't minded to have Joe disturbed, a forlorn hope that didn't last any longer than it took him to walk over there. He shoved away the stones, began scuffing at the soft dirt under them.

When he was down about a foot he got onto his knees and began scooping the dirt out with his hands. It didn't take long before Joe's shirt came into view with the dried blood still showing. The old man stared a long while at that sight without opening his mouth.

When he presently got up he considered me grimly.

"Who shoot Joe?"

So I told him how I'd wondered if after all, as we'd supposed, Joe had really ridden off with our crew, and how I'd come down here on a hunch to have a look. And found him. Not putting any name to the man who'd come with me.

But I could see straightaway it wasn't going to be enough. Still holding me with that bitter bright stare, "Who shoot Joe?" he said again.

"I wasn't there—how could I know?"

That bleak brown stare stayed on my face for an interminable while, then abruptly he said, "Paleface say one eye for an eye. You no tell I pick someone. Navajo have roast brain for breakfast." With a teeth-showing scowl he climbed back on his pony and rode through the trees.

It looked like Larrimore's ill-fated expedition was in for more trouble than it could happily stomach. If I didn't divulge my suspicions of Clampas . . . It just wasn't in me to play that game. I could, without regret or compunction, kill that devil if it came to a showdown, but turn him over to be tortured by these Indians I simply couldn't do, even though I'd Two-Feathers's word somebody was going to have to pay for Joe's murder.

When we came once again into a camp gone silent as that damned cliff house, the old man, staring like a graven image on his piebald pony, held up both arms and wasted few words. "A young Navajo man has been killed at your camp-fire. The People have suffered much and long from the white man's duplicity. You will take nothing from this house of the Anasazi. You have until sunrise tomorrow to give up man who kill Hosteen Joe. I have spoken."

With no more talk he drove his colorful mount up the opposite slope.

You can imagine the result of those remarks once he'd gone. The stupid uproar, the fright and the bluster, everyone trying to shout down the others. When I'd heard enough of it I said sharply, "If we refuse to dredge up a sacrifice for him he'll do the picking. This camp is not defensible. We're sitting ducks."

"Why don't you do something?" Harry demanded of me, and there were nods all around; the only dissensions being Flossie and Fern.

"I intend to," I said. "Soon as it's dark I'm going up to the cliff house and if the rest of you want to stay alive a little longer you'll do the same. Up there, until we run out of ammunition we can probably hold them off."

"And what about our horses?"

"The Navajos have gone," Hatcher cried. "I say let's make a run for it!"

"They haven't gone. They've only dropped out of sight. There's no way they'll be leaving this place till they've got what they came after. They'll be satisfied with that and our empty-handed departure. But you try to slip out of here and you'll be dead before you've gone a half mile."

"We ain't givin' nobody up!" Harry howled.

"They're not after you." Clampas grinned. "I'll lay you forty to one it's the—"

"Shut your damn trap!" I snarled at him, but Fern had already sensed it was her they'd demand. "Put it to a vote," Jones suggested, and I nodded. "All those in favor of letting them have Fern—if that's who they ask for—stick up your hands."

Harry's hand went up like a shot. No one else moved, but the look in their eyes showed what they thought of him. Clampas said, "Corrigan should have told that Injun it was you killed Joe."

Jeff came enough out of his trance to want to be told where the cavalry was, and Clampos laughed. "Settin' around in their friggin' barracks, of course." He threw a look at me. "Sure goes against my grain to pull out of this place without them stones the chindis been hoardin'."

"Surely," Jeff said, trying to pull himself together, "some of us could break through if we made a concerted rush for it?"

"You're welcome to try," I said dryly. "It's going to cost them something to lift my scalp." I looked them over once more. "If the one who killed Joe doesn't give himself up there ain't one of us going to leave here alive."

As soon as it got dark enough to hide our movements we slipped one by one into that jumble of fallen rocks to make our attempt to get into the dubious safety of the cliff house. Each moment of that climb I expected to hear or feel the slap of a bullet and had little doubt the others felt likewise. We were fetching what stores we were able to carry. Way it turned out none of us had thought to bring up any wood.

I had purely hated to leave Gretchen behind, but in the interest of harmony had turned her loose without saddle or bridle to fend for herself.

It was a nerve-racking climb but we got to the top of the cliff without incident. Flossie, eager as always, was the first one in. Lathered with impatience, the rest of us wriggled our way through the entrance Jones and Clampas had opened, though not in some cases without second thoughts.

Fern and I were the last ones in and she said, voice husky, "I'd give a good deal to be somewhere else. Do you think we've any chance of ever getting out of this?"

"Do you know if anyone thought to fetch a torch?"

"I brought one. I think Clampas fetched two. You haven't answered my question."

"The probabilities are self-evident. Even," I said, "if by some sort of miracle we do manage to get clear, it doesn't seem a heap likely we'll get as far as the railroad."

To the others I said, "Let's not show any lights. Longer it takes them to discover we're up here the more chance we'll have of staying alive."

"We can't stumble about this damn place in the dark!" Harry snarled.

"We're going down to the next level—the one with the window holes—and that's where we'll stay. Careful now on that ladder. If you've got a pistol, Jones, I wish you'd stay up here for a bit till we're sure those Indians haven't found out we've come up here—but don't shoot anybody without you have to."

"Okay," Jones said, and edged past me. "It's blacker in here than the gut of a camel; can't see a hand in front of your face!"

"What good would it do you if you could?" Clampas asked from below.

"Can you catch hold of that dog, Jeff?" I called when he'd joined Clampas. "All right, Harry, you're next on the ladder. Now you, Fern," I said when Harry got off.

I left the ladder where it was after climbing down myself. "Have you got hold of Flossie, Jeff?"

"I've got her," Fern said.

"We don't want her running loose down below. Everything we want is on this level so keep a good hold on her till I scout up something to put over that hole."

Trouble was I could not recall seeing anything that would cover a hole three feet wide; the tent, I reckoned, would do very nicely but we hadn't fetched the tent. "Be better," Clampas said, "if we spread out, don't you think? Each of us pick out one of them window holes so we'll know where we're at. I'll take the one beyond the room with the chindis' hoard."

We could hear him moving off. Harry said, cutting through the boot and spur sound, "I'll take the room this side of him," and went tramping off through the dark in the wake of his gunfighter. And this was when the dog slipped her collar and went scampering off in the same direction. "Flossie!" Fern called. "Come back here, Flossie!"

"I'll get her," Jeff growled and, when she refused to heed his whistle, went irascibly after her, muttering under his breath.

"Oh dear," Fern sighed. "She can be an awful nuisance . . ."

"Stay here," I said in the sudden grip of an unwanted thought. "Let me have that torch. Where are you?"

"Here—" she said, and put it into my hand, but before I could move we heard a yell and a thump and pitiful whimpering sounds out of Flossie.

Chapter Twenty

Fern started off but I grabbed her. "Wait!"

"No!" She jerked loose of me. "Flossie's hurt—she needs me!"

I was too impatient, too crammed with the bitter black thoughts whirling through me, to waste time arguing. I switched on the torch, went dashing through rooms, and to hell with the noise, caring only for getting there in the shortest time possible. Through the clattering beads, through the dark doorway, past the chindis' hoard and up to the floor hole where Harry and Clampas crouched peering into the black pit below.

I played the light down there, my worst fears realized, staring aghast at Jeff's crumpled shape and the dog whining beside him. "Looks," Clampas said, "like he's broken his neck."

I grabbed hold of Harry. "How'd it happen? Quick—tell me!"

But the man was too hysterical to get any sense out of him. I put the light onto Clampas. "It was the dog," Clampas said. "He was trying to catch hold of her and missed his footing . . ."

I looked a long while at him, hearing Fern come up and her gasped "Oh, God!"

Clampas said, quietly grim: "He *fell,* I tell you—I didn't push him. I was at the window when Flossie dashed past with Jeff racing after her and me diving after them, too late by ten strides. He was already down there when I got to the hole."

I blew out my breath, put an arm around Fern. She was trembling all over, trying to stifle her sobs against my shoulder. I said, hating the necessity, "We'll have to leave him down there—for right now anyway. I'll bring up the dog." I slid my legs through the hole and let myself drop.

After making certain that Jeff was dead, and not just badly injured, I turned to the dog.

Flossie, still whimpering, must have understood more than you'd normally allow for, making no fuss when I hoisted her into Clampas's reaching hands. Clampas passed her to Fern and reached down for me. I got a knee over the hole and heaved myself up.

I thought later I should have shown Fern more sympathy in the shock of her loss, but at the time, right then, my head was too filled with the consequences and the needs they forced on me. At any moment now, with dawn scarce an hour from bursting over the horizon, that old man would be coming to demand a victim. I had to find some way to get us out of this trap; and I could see no way without a distraction.

I finally came up with a harebrained expedient, a notion so wild I damn near threw it away till I recalled Two-

Feathers's words about the Navajos' sojourn at Bosque Redondo. Latching on to no alternative, I reckoned it was better than nothing; not much but worth a try.

To Clampas I said, "Somewhere in one of the rooms on this level you'll find the barrel of my rifle and a coil of rope. Get them. There's an Anasazi flute, too; fetch me all three of them and don't waste no time."

I saw the speculative look that slid through his stare. He wasted no words but went off at once. Harry, I could see, would be of no use whatever. Fern was still holding Flossie when Clampas came back with the things I had asked for. "Take a look out that window hole," I told him and, while he was doing it, I knotted one end of the rope round the rifle barrel, the way it had been when I found it. "How does it look?"

"Can't see anyone. You goin' down that rope?"

"If we're to get loose of this we've got to have some kind of distraction. Don't any of you try to leave till I come back. If I don't show inside of an hour you'll be on your own."

With the rifle barrel wedged the way I had found it I tossed the rope out the window. "Don't do it, Brice," Fern cried, her voice filled with alarm and her eyes big as saucers. "If you're seen they'll shoot you!"

"They're like to shoot all of us unless I'm able to come up with a diversion."

I thrust the flute in the grip of my waistband and catching hold of the rope thrust my feet through the window. Swinging around with feet keeping me clear of the wall I started down, hand under hand. Forty feet on that rope seemed more like forty miles with the expectation of being shot any moment. The horses in their pens were on my mind likewise but they were two miles away and almost certainly were watched.

Ten feet from the ground I let go of the rope and took off in great strides in the direction of the pool, flute in one hand and my shooting iron in the other. I was anxiously conscious of passing time but didn't dare run until I'd gained more distance. Fern was too right. If I was seen I'd be shot. When I figured I'd covered enough ground for safety I broke into a run.

I went through the trees around the pool without stopping, but slowed to a walk trying to catch me some breath and ease the cramp in my side. Five minutes later I stepped up my pace and, pretty quick then, I started running again. It seemed like when I quit I must have covered about five miles. I stretched out on the ground till I caught up with myself, rummaging my memories, recalling my youthful admiration of the boys in blue.

When I got my wind back I scrambled erect and, grabbing up the flute, blew the cavalry charge. Loud and clear it sailed through the dawn, not quite like a bugle, but near enough for a Navajo. Then at a limping run I started back and ten minutes later with the sun throwing my shadow long ahead of me I sounded the cavalry's get-up call.

At last, within two miles of the cliff house I put the Anasazi flute to my lips and blared out the cavalry charge again.

I moved with a deal more caution now, eyes skinned sharp for the first hint of trouble. I had done what I could but was afraid deep inside it would not fool an old man sharp as Johnny Two-Feathers. I watched every rock, every bush and shadow, eyes strained to catch the least blur of movement. I still had the flute and the sweat creeping cold down the length of my spine when I rounded the last bend and saw the cliff house before me.

Clampas spotted me at once and came sliding down the rope. "Corrigan, you're a wonder—you really are! That flute cleared them out of here, lock, stock an' barrel!"

"How about our horses?"

"They didn't stop to grab 'em. I sent Jones out to look."

"We've got a chance then," I said, "and that's all we've got. No time to fool around. They'll be back just as soon as they discover they've been tricked, and they'll be looking for blood."

He considered me brightly. "What about that turquoise?"

"If it was up to me I'd leave it. After losing her brother I guess Fern will not be wanting to leave any of the stuff that cost him his life. They brought a bunch of sacks, I remember. We'll take whatever they'll hold and no more. When they're packed we'll let them down on that rope, pick 'em up here after we get the horses."

I was right about Fern. She wanted the pots they'd set aside, all the turquoise and several bones. I said, "Be reasonable, Fern. We can't take all that stuff. We oughtn't take any of it. Those Indians will be back, and damn soon probably."

Ignoring this she said, "And I want that stone lamp Jeff's been carrying in his pocket—we'll have to take him, too."

I shook my head, seeing the futility of argument. "We'll put the stuff in those burlap sacks—"

"You can't put Jeff in a sack!" she flared. "Anyway there are no sacks up here."

I reminded myself of her loss and the shock and kept my temper where it belonged. Just the same, with my experience of Indians and time running out, I was just about ready to jump out of my skin.

Jones came down from his lookout. "You want I should fix us some grub?"

"We got no time to be lallygaggin' around. Go fetch me those sacks from the stores we carried up—and I mean right now. Stir your stumps!"

"Where's Flossie?" I said to Fern.

"She's around here somewhere—"

"Damnation!" I swore as my glance lit on Harry. "What the hell have you got in your pockets?"

He backed away from me shaking. His left eye twitched. "I only done what Clampas told me—"

"You turd!" Clampas snarled. "Anything I want I'm big enough to carry!"

Fern, paying no attention to this, was moving jugged turquoise from one place to another. Exasperated I said, "Never noticed before that you were into Jeff's line—"

"Enough of it's rubbed off for me to know what's worth saving . . . I want that flute, too! If we could I'd take back one of those skeletons; never mind how I feel about them. Bound to be a demand for anything that old."

"Most of the horses we're going to have to use aren't pack animals. They'll be the devil to load and there's a limit to how much they'll carry. We'd do a damn sight better to be riding them."

Clampas, I noticed, was eyeing Fern distastefully. I said, "Get over to that aperture and keep your eyes on the prowl for them Indians. You better pull up that rope. . . ."

Jones came in with an armload of sacks. "Fine," I told him. "You can help Fern fill them," and catching up one of those burlaps myself I began dumping jugs of turquoise into it. "You'll have that all mixed up!" Fern cried censoriously.

"We haven't the time to pick and choose—you should have done all that yesterday! Can't you get it through your female head a Navajo's just as human as you are? They'll be back here full of sound an' fury—"

"Company comin'," Clampas called from his aperture. "Good God A'mighty! Come look what's down there!"

I flung over there. Some jasper was sitting down there in a buggy like a syndicate ranch boss, all togged out in his big-city duds. "Who the hell's that?" I snarled at Clampas.

"Hello up there!" this dude chucked at us. "What do you people think you're doing?"

"Fishin'," Clampas told him. "What's it to you?"

"D'you know who I am?" He sounded plumb riled. "Happens I'm the Inspector of Antiquities for the sovereign people of New Mexico. How'd you get into that place? It was sealed up tighter than a boar's ass! Don't you know you're violating the law?"

"Do tell," Clampas said.

"I'm gettin' out of here!" Harry declared through chattering teeth.

"Get down on your hunkers and help fill these sacks!" I gave him a shove. "And you can empty those pockets into one of them too."

"That joker still down there?" I snarled at Clampas.

"Sure is—can't you hear him?"

"Them horses," I told Jones, "must be bustin' for water. Get down there and see to it."

I had so much on my mind I couldn't think straight. That jasper in the buggy called up to say, "All the old ruins in and around Chaco Canyon have been declared off-limits to vandals and all you pot-hunting buggers. By rights I ought to take you people—''

"By rights," I yelled, sticking my head out the aperture, "if you don't get out of there in one tearin' big rush you're like to find your hair on a Navajo lance!"

"New Mexico's at peace with the Navajo Nation. Those redskins have been pacified—''

"Stick around awhile and you'll learn how peaceful and pacified they are." I told Clampas to get that rope tied around a couple sacks and start them on down. "We've got to hustle this up and get out of here''

That old fool in the buggy was still shooting his jaw off. "Breaking into this property will probably get you three to ten with—Here, you! What's on that rope? You can get ten years if you're caught looting a ruin—Haul that back up!"

"Get it down there," I told Clampas, and stuck my head out the aperture. "Be a gent for a change," I told the goggling bureaucrat, "and unloose that rope so we can pull it back up. We got a lot more to go and time's gettin' short."

He peered as if he was staring at a two-headed calf. "Get at it," I said, "before you catch a blue whistler," and thrust the front end of Clampas's Sharps out where he could see it.

He couldn't believe it. I shifted the muzzle till it was looking right at him. Red-faced and spluttering, he got out of his buggy and bent over the sacks.

I hauled up the rope and lashed a couple more onto it.

It was while this second batch were on their way down that Fern clamped a hand on me. "Listen!" she cried, the freckles showing up like splatters of paint. "Don't you *hear* it?"

"I hear it."

In the blazing wrath of that midday sun there was a quality that made the blood run cold in the sound of those throbbing drums.

Chapter Twenty-one

"Navajos?"

"You bet." I yelled at the dude, "Catch hold of that rope and we'll haul you up."

He stood there like something built out of matchsticks. Fern shook my arm. "What are we going to *do*?"

"They're comin' back!" Harry gasped. Way he was shaking it was a wonder he was able to stay in his clothes.

I called down to the dude, "Tie the rope around you under your arms and grab on to it." He was about as stupid as a newborn sheep. "Hurry it up!" I yelled; when he finally got fixed we started reeling him in. He was no featherweight with all that soft living but we got him up with a face like spoiled putty, and Clampas hauled him in through the aperture.

Fern shook my arm again. "If we left right now couldn't we still get away?"

I said with some hope, "We'd have a chance anyway. Grab your hat and—"

"But I've still got some of those things to be packed and somebody will have to fetch that stone lamp and—"

"You can't leave right now and do forty-'leven other things! Make up your mind. It's either one or the other. Forget the rest of it. You'll have enough turquoise—"

"Oh, I couldn't—How could I abandon the result of all Jeff's work! How can you ask me to?" She looked around distractedly. "And I *did* want to take poor Jeff with us. If I can't he'll have to be buried . . . I hate to leave him in this horrible place. . . ."

"All right. Now we know where we're at, I hope. Best chance left is for the jasper who croaked that smartass Indian to own up to it and take his medicine." I looked at them, disgusted when no one rushed forward to take the blame. "Then all that's left if you want to keep breathin'—"

The dude, looking horrified, broke in to say, "Did I hear correctly someone needs to be buried?"

"My brother," Fern said.

"What did he die of?—By the way, my name's Witherspoon."

"I understand he fell through a hole in one of the floors," I told him, impatient.

"Broke his neck," Clampas said.

Jones came through the doorhole this side of the beads. I said, astonished, "Thought you'd gone to the pool with the horses?"

"Well . . ." Jones fetched up a sick-looking grin. "When them drums got to poundin' it didn't seem advisable to get that far from shelter. I used up what we had left in the water

369

bags, lettin' them guzzle it outa my hat.''

"You see any Navajos?"

"Didn't see any, no; but I bet they seen me."

"See Flossie anyplace?"

"Came past her in that room with the sandpile; didn't see no cat but she was diggin' like she figured one was in it."

"Come on, Fern." I gave her a nudge. "We'd better get hold of her."

"I'll go with you," said Witherspoon promptly, and ran a jaundiced look over me. "I gather you're the head of this 'scientific' expedition?"

"Just a hired hand."

"My brother, Professor Larrimore, was head of it," Fern told him. "This dig was—"

"Just where *is* this dig? You been digging in *here?*"

"Jeff never got around to—"

"We've had a heap of hard luck," I butted in to say. "One damn thing after another. Now, with you jumping in—"

"Great Scott!" Witherspoon gasped, staring in astonished dismay at what our Flossie had uncovered in that sandpile. I wouldn't be surprised to learn my own jaw dropped. For there in the midst of that pile of loose sand stood three medium-sized jars of perhaps the finest cut stones of spiderweb turquoise I had ever laid eyes on.

"Get a sack, Brice," Fern said crisply. "The regents will be delighted with the display they can make of this. And these Anasazi jars—"

"I forbid you, madam, to remove one piece of that off these premises!"

That hoity-toity dude was all swelled up like a carbuncle, crammed with the righteous wrath of his office. "I will remind you of the law. The law unequivocally states that any person digging or carrying off relics and/or artifacts of any nature whatsoever from terrain protected by the State of New Mexico—''

I caught his eye, jerked my head toward the door, beckoning him after me into the next room. He came reluctantly and even more reluctantly listened eventually to what I decided to tell him. It was plain he didn't like it and stood there spluttering like a batch of damp firecrackers. ''I don't care at all for your attitude, young man, and if that's a threat . . .''

''Just a promise,'' I said, and went to fetch Fern a sack.

It was astonishing the way that girl had recovered from the loss of ''poor'' Jeff. She appeared to have taken on a whole new character, I thought with just a shade of resentment. Doubtless this was just her real self emerging after years of standing in the shadow of an ambitious brother. Looked like she had made up her mind to step into his shoes and reap any credit she could from this trip.

This didn't come over me all at once, you understand. The notion just sort of grew on me. Right then I wasn't doing much thinking with the sound of those drums steadily banging through my head. I reckoned to have Witherspoon stymied for a spell, but getting around old Johnny and his braves was a horse of a different color.

On the way back to Fern with the sack Jones caught hold of me. ''You set that gasbag down in a hurry.'' Still eyeing me curious, he asked, ''Are we goin' for the broncs? I'd like to get the hell out of here.''

I sighed. ''So would I.''

''That girl got the bit in her teeth?''

''Looks that way. She wants to take all the pots and at least a few bones. Fact is she's honin' to pack one of those

371

dead Basketmakers Clampas dug up down in that cliff shelter—''

''We can't take the time to pack—''

''What I told her. Be lucky to get away with that turquoise, but she's some set on it.''

''Why don't you put your foot down?''

It didn't come easy but I managed a grin. ''Want to try your luck?''

''I'm just the cook. She wouldn't pay me no mind.''

''Me neither,'' I said. ''Grab up a couple more of them sacks.''

When we got back to Fern she said, ''I'm glad you fetched those extra sacks. We'll wrap them around these jars and leave the stones inside them.''

We did just that. I gave the sack to Jones and told him to send it down on the rope. ''Then you and Clampas head for the horses—''

Fern said, ''Don't forget that stone lamp Jeff's got in his pocket.''

''Yes, ma'am. I'm going down right now to pick it up.'' Giving her a servant's look, I inquired, ''Will there be anything else? How about one of those skeletons?''

She gave me a rueful smile. ''I'm reasonably sure those skeletons are the most important finds we've made. I hate not being able to take at least one.''

Clampas, at that moment joining us, said, ''Them Injuns might be downright uncivil if they caught us luggin' off one of their ancestors.''

She appeared a bit startled. ''I hadn't thought of that. Anyway it doesn't seem practical . . . unless Mr. Witherspoon would take it in his buggy.''

''Better ask him.'' Clampas smiled. ''Seems to be a real obligin' sort.''

Mule Man

I limped over to the floor hole and down the ladder, dug through Jeff's pockets and, lifting his wallet in addition to the lamp, fetched them back to Fern with another of the bones Flossie had been playing with. "Let's go."

Out on the clifftop with the sun bearing down and that goddam drumming still banging up a storm, the only movement I could see came from Jones, Clampas and that fatass Witherspoon picking their way down through the rockfall. No sign of a redskin, I was relieved to note. I couldn't set much hope on that since you seldom ever spot one till they're about to lift your hair.

Ten minutes later Fern and I reached the rockfall and, at that precise moment, the drums went silent. A whole flock of wild thoughts fluttered through my head and the sweat turned cold underneath my hat.

"Look!" Fern cried.

I didn't need any coaching. I'd already seen them. The Navajo Nation, it looked like, spread out across opposite bluff.

Chapter Twenty-two

"Never mind," I said. "I'll get you out of this."

She twisted her head about, looking appalled. "Brice—I can't let you *do* this!"

"We'll see. Just remember one thing: when you're free to go, by God you *go*. Understand? No lallygaggin' round. You make one stop. At the tamarisks, and don't let those caballos drink too much. Fill the water bags and get the hell out of there."

She looked rebellious with her chin up that way. But I nudged her along. "Worst thing you can do is let those Navajos think you're afraid. Remember how upset you were to think that old man had to sleep on the ground?" I managed a laugh, and nudged her on ahead of me, wishing I felt as confident as she thought me.

Old Johnny was waiting for me there by the pens.

Before we could speak the fat Inspector of Antiquities came bustling up to him, puffed up with importance and the authority of his office. "My name's Witherspoon. I guess you know I speak for the Government? Yes—yes indeed! Our Great White Father up in Washington has much admiration for our Navajo friends and has appointed me to look after their best interests . . ."

"Lucky Navajos!" Clampas muttered in back of me someplace. Myself, I was trying to think how best I could put what I had to say to this red brother who was a heap less simple than Witherspoon thought him. One thing was sure: this old rascal hadn't forgotten what he had come for or how he'd been balked of his prey once already.

With an expressionless face old Johnny sliced through the rhetoric with a lifted hand. "My business here is with Man-on-a-Mule."

Fern and Flossie, I saw, were with Turtle Jones some thirty or forty feet back of Clampas—far enough off, it was my devout hope, not to latch on to what I aimed to say. I didn't want it spoiled by any words out of her. Two-Feathers faced me with some asperity. "Speak, Man-on-a-Mule!"

"You're here," I said, "for the man responsible for the death of Hosteen Joe. We're prepared to give him up if I have your assurance the rest of our party will then be free to leave this place."

"Where this man?"

"Do I have your assurance?"

I watched his glance passing over our company and settle on me with a long, searching look. And at last, reluctantly, he nodded. "Where this man?"

"He is in the old cliff dwelling."

"Why you not bring?"

I could read the suspicion abruptly staring from his glance.

"Well . . ." I dredged up a sigh with a rueful look. "I

couldn't get him out of there."

"We get. You show."

He looked again at Clampas, at Jones and the girl with her hold on Flossie's collar. Once more he nodded, and to them said, "You go." And then, as an afterthought: "One horse each."

"Two ponies," I said, shaking my head.

Despite what I'd told her, Fern of course had to put in her oar, stubbornly declaring, "I'm not about to go unless you're going too!"

"Be quiet," I growled, scared the whole thing would start to unravel. "I'll catch up with you later." To the old man I said, "Two ponies. They're going home—have to catch iron horse."

Those Navajo eyes never left my face but thin of lip he nodded. "Agreed."

Clampas, Jones, Witherspoon and a whey-faced Hatcher went into the pens and fetched out ten horses, on one of which, under Johnny's watchful eye, they packed a sack of tinned food, our eating tools, and the washtub. Then they all mounted up and with Flossie in the lead started off down the gulch on the trail to Chaco Canyon.

Beckoning several of his warriors down from the bluff, Johnny eyeing me reflectively commanded, "You show. Now."

So I limped off on foot up the climb through the rockfall nervously wondering if this would be the last time. I couldn't hear those redskins but knew they wouldn't be far behind. "Who this man?" grunted Johnny, directly back of me.

I told him it was Larrimore, boss and organizer of this field trip.

"The great scientist friend of the Navajo?"

"Yeah."

"Why he shoot Hosteen Joe?"

"Joe had a rifle one of the others had given him. Larri-more didn't like it."

"For one rifle he kill Joe?"

Pretty weak, I thought, but said, "Looks that way. He's no great hand for explanations."

When we got to the entrance we had made getting in there the old man motioned me into the lead, alertly following my snug passage through the hole. "Bad. Bad," he grumbled. "Chindis not like."

When I mentioned we had no torch, he gobbled out something unintelligible to me and one of his clan disappeared to return with an armful of creosote brush from which several torches were speedily fashioned. Each of these men he'd picked to accompany him had a rifle and three of them wore bandoliers of cartridges. I reckoned he was determined to exact his due, and again the cold chill of this place crept over me, not lessened in the least by the thought of his outrage when he finally confronted the man I had promised him.

I took as long as I could guiding him to this denouement. When we got to the hole through which Jeff had plunged he ordered a torch lit and in its flare stared, it seemed like forever, at the crumpled shape below.

Chapter Twenty-three

At last he looked at me. "White man cheat."

I'd had plenty of time to think about this and, for what it was worth, had my answer ready. "Not at all," I said. "You demanded Joe's killer but nothing was mentioned about him having to be alive."

"Why you kill?"

"I wasn't there when he died. I was told he'd been chasing the dog, lost his footing in the dark and plunged through the hole."

"This is true?"

"I can only say they didn't want the dog in the lower levels. It seems logical to believe it might have happened that way."

He looked at me hard. "What you do with these people? Why you not with Ranger?"

"Ain't Ranger now—leg caught a bullet. Was on my way home when I ran into the Larrimores. They were afraid of the crew hired for them by Hatcher.'' A little edge of bitterness got into my voice when I said, ''They thought I could protect them.''

He told the rest of them what I had said and it was plain by the angry sound of their gobbling they were determined I should pay for my duplicity. Strange as it may seem the old man stood out against them. When they finally buttoned their lips he said to me with an unshakable dignity, ''The Navajo is an honorable man. I not like what you do, Man-on-a-Mule, but my word is good. This time you go. I have spoken.''

The sun was low down above the western rim when I got back to the camp and limped over to the pen and dropped my hull on her, kneed the air from her belly, yanked the girth tight and climbed wearily aboard. There was a saying among Mossman's men that a Ranger was a man who never looked back. I set my jaw and put Gretchen down the trail.

Pausing briefly at the pool by the tamarisks, I let her have a short drink and then sent her along at her rough-gaited trot with little expectation of overtaking Fern's party this side of night.

There had been no sacks below the cliff house when I'd passed; with them so burdened it seemed fairly obvious I'd come up with them at my faster pace before they reached the Chaco.

About an hour after dark I heard the rattle and skreak of Witherspoon's buggy not a great ways ahead of me. When we drew alongside I motioned for him to pull up and, when he had done so, asked if he'd any oats under the seat.

''Well, yes,'' he admitted, ''but not any more than I'll be needing myself.''

''Pass them over. My need,'' I said, ''is greater than yours

379

and Mossman will reimburse you on my note of hand.''

"You're way out of your jurisdiction, Corrigan."

I scribbled him a note and tossed it into his lap. "Reckon that's so." I gave him a look at my pistol. "Let's not waste any time over this."

Grumbling and spluttering dire threats he surrendered the sack. Settling it in front of me I told him I was obliged and left him still fuming.

Fern and company had made better time than I'd ever expected, packing all the weight of that turquoise. Flossie let out a wild series of barks before I caught sight of them in the moon-dappled shadows perhaps two miles short of the canyon. The others pulled up in a bunch when the dog ran to meet us with Fern right behind. And the first thing Fern said was, "Brice! How'd you ever get away from them? Of course! You must have given them Jeff . . .''

"Yes. He was the only one they couldn't reach."

"But wasn't Johnny furious?"

"I expect he was; but with Navajos, Fern, a deal is a deal and the old man was stuck with it. Where's Clampas?"

"Gone," she said. There was a world of bitterness in that bleak voice. "Gone with every last ounce of our turquoise!"

Well, I thought, I should have expected this. "How long?"

"Pretty close to an hour . . .''

"Never mind. I'll catch him. He'll be heading for the railroad at Farmington." And without further words I set out after him.

With any kind of luck I reckoned to overtake him before he was able to get out of Chaco Canyon. That was the first thing that crossed my mind. But before I had gone more than a whoop and a holler other thoughts latched on to me.

Like he might, at this point, have no intention of busting out of the canyon. He was sure to figure I'd be right on his tail.

Given this situation what, I wondered, would I do in his place? He had all the advantage, knowing me as he did. Always big Clampas was a man for the edge. Brave as a lion, audacious but never reckless. Slicker than slobbers. I could see, thinking that way, he was going to hole up. Hole up someplace with that goddam Sharps and let me come to him.

Without hideous risk I'd no way to get near him. Long as he could keep me out of pistol range he could tease me the way a cat does a mouse, and enjoy every minute of it. Even if I waited for the others to come up it wouldn't change the odds enough to matter. Harry, back when he was riding high, had taken the rifles away from us peons; and then, after Fletch had been killed, Clampas had become the he-catawampus and leached all the courage Hatcher'd ever had out of him.

I had known all along Clampas was the deadly one. Even though, for my money, he'd eliminated Alfredo, Fletcher, Hosteen Joe and then Jeff, I'd nothing but my own belief— not so much as a scrap of proof. Which was why he'd been getting so much pleasure out of me. He'd known I was on to him, known I couldn't touch him. And he hadn't made the least effort to conceal from me that no matter the odds, he meant to have every bit of that turquoise. And now he had it!

I found it a mighty humiliating fact.

Nor was I able to work up any great enthusiasm for playing six-shooter tag through some ruin's empty rooms, for there again all the edge lay with Clampas. Ambush was his stock in trade.

As was happening all too frequent of late, a picture of
Fern with her roan hair and freckles came into my mind
with a poignant clarity I could not deny. I thought if things
had been different . . . and dismissed such empty dreams
with an oath.

I kicked my thoughts back where they belonged, centered
squarely on Clampas. A glib, wryly humorous, slippery villain to whom fair play was nothing but a laugh.

Already Gretchen had carried me past several ruins and
a glance at the heavens assured me it would not be long
before daylight would give him, with that Sharps, an additional edge. I began watching for tracks that turned away
from the trail, went the best part of another mile before
locating any that seemed sufficiently fresh. When I did come
on to some they went angling away toward another ruined
pueblo. He'd be holed up inside, squatting like some ob-
scene spider, waiting for me to come into his sights.

I thought there had to be some other way to get at him,
some way to cut down the advantage of that Sharps. If I
could find his horses . . .

I cut away from his tracks, aiming to circle this ruin—it
was one of the larger ones—at a distance hopefully sufficient to ensure my safety. I was thinking also of Gretchen;
I couldn't afford to lose her in so desolate a place.

We got about halfway around those crumbling walls, towering in some spots almost fifty feet high, before in a patch
of still, deep shadow I made out what I took to be the horses
I was hunting. Those were horses all right; a questioning
whinny confirmed this. Before she could answer I clamped
a hand on Gretchen's nostrils.

Now what to do?

It was entirely probable Clampas was as aware of that
whinny as I was. He might not be able to see me yet. Should

I make an attempt—with the attendant risks—of trying to drive those horses away? Leave him afoot and force him to move? But with the size of this place I could see right away such a notion was foolish. Then another occurred to me that seemed a heap better. Grab the horses if I could and light out for the railroad, reverse our positions and force Clampas to be the hunter.

There was, I figured, considerable merit in this notion. For unless he could get himself mounted again I could be at the railroad a good piece ahead of him.

But the thought of that Sharps in this growing light put a cold chill through this jubilant thinking. That sonofabitch would knock Gretchen from under me sure as God made little green apples! Fond as I was of her, it wasn't this that deterred me but the knowledge he could then pick me off at his leisure.

Any jasper who could shoot a flipped penny into oblivion was not to be taken lightly.

Turning Gretchen ever more away from where those whinnying horses stood, I went on with the circling inspection I had started. In about ten minutes the sun would be up. Whatever I decided was going to have to be done quickly. I could picture Clampas crouched in there someplace grinning over the sights of that Sharps, chuckling while he waited with Indian patience for me to move into range.

Some forty yards farther along I saw a whaleback rock with a fringe of greasewood some thirty feet closer to the battered walls than where I sat Gretchen, and the sight of this put a new aspect before me. The rock rose perhaps two feet above the shale-strewn surface of the ground all about it.

The possibilities this opened up were simply too tempting

for me to resist. I got off the mule and considered it some more while I ran a hand across the loops of my belt, finding plenty of cartridges for what I had in mind.

The next step, of course, was how to reach it alive and in reasonable working order.

I didn't want to sacrifice Gretchen. Nor did I want to catch one of that Sharps's blue whistlers. I thought about it some more and moved Gretchen back a bit and sat down cross-legged to study it in depth, hoping these tactics might prod Clampas's temper or maybe stretch his nerves a little.

I gave it another five minutes and without more ado, with the rock between me and where I hoped he might be, I got over on my belly and began to wriggle toward its shelter.

Wham! went the Sharps and a lead plum went skittering off the rock's rounded top. He tried a couple more with no better result and by that time I was snuggled up against it. I blew out a held breath and sleeved the sweat off my forehead.

I had him placed now, but no guarantee he would stay there. Near as I could tell, without seeking a new and even more distant position, there seemed no way he'd be able to flank me. Breaking off four or five of the greasewood shoots, in time-honored fashion I edged the crown of my hat a very tiny way above the rock and Clampas promptly drilled it. He must have guessed the hat was empty; just wanted to show me what he could do. Or perhaps he was getting a little mite edgy. After all, he had to know the others would soon be along and he couldn't watch more than one place at a time. While Clampas was dealing with me, Jones and possibly Harry could slip into that ruin and make his position untenable.

While these thoughts were scampering around I had worked off my shirt and stuffed the top part of it with greasewood branches. Shoving another down through these, I set my hat on it and poked this scarecrow enough above my shelter to entice two rapid reports. Both shots scored and as the dummy collapsed I let out a scream that should have sounded pretty desperate.

With much care I got back into my shirt and composed myself to wait for his footsteps.

But Clampas, too wily to let go of his advantage, put in no appearance.

The sun climbed higher. It began to get hot. My ears ached from listening for sounds that never came. An almost irresistible impulse urged me to move and only the knowledge of what it might cost kept me motionless. Certainly I could show as much patience as Clampas so long as those horses stayed where I could see them.

I could, I supposed, afford a bit more. Bothered by flies, those horses were beginning to get restive and Clampas must know this; he must know too that the companions he'd robbed at gunpoint were bound pretty soon to be coming along.

I wasn't surprised when those fretting horses began to drift off. Now, I thought, he's going to have to make a move. With extreme caution I took a quick look around the end of the rock. Nothing happened, nor did I see him. My exploring hand found a piece of flat shale—the kind we used to skip across ponds—and scaled it, cursing, at the ruin's nearest wall.

Chapter Twenty-four

Everything seemed to happen at once.

A rumble of hoofs came up from the trail. Clampas crashed another shot whining off my rock. The confiscated horses he had lifted from our outfit, filled now with a whinnying excitement, went tearing off to rejoin their companions, turquoise and all. Clampas came over the broken wall of his refuge as though flung from a catapult, making straight for me, triggering that Sharps at every jump. How he missed hitting me I've never been able to understand. Only Burt Mossman's drilled-in discipline kept me rock-steady in the face of that charge. When he got near enough I fanned off one shot which must have caught him head-on. Arms flung out, he spun half around and collapsed in his tracks.

I saw Fern's mop of roan hair driving through milling horses, Jones's rigid face and Harry's frightened one, and then they were around me, all talking at once, and creating such bedlam it made my head swim, and I thought this must be what hell was like.

When finally I began to function once more I began looking for Gretchen and found her trying to lift her head off the ground. As through a fog I stumbled over to where she lay with those great loyal eyes staring up at me. I fumbled a sugar lump out of my pocket and patted her shoulder. "You were a real lady, Gretchen," I told her, and put my pistol against her head.

When my surroundings came into true focus again Jones was putting my saddle on one of the horses. "Guess we're about ready," he said handing me the reins. "I've put the sacks on three of our spares. You want to lead off?"

"I suppose so. Keep your eye on Harry—he doesn't have a gun, does he? Good. You and him better ride drag; we don't want to lose any of those loose mounts between here and Farmington. We've got thirty-odd miles still ahead of us."

I rode more or less like I wasn't all there till Fern came up with some more conversation, none of which registered till she said, looking around at me, "I guess you couldn't have saved her?"

I didn't want to gab about it. "She got one of those slugs in the neck. Another broke a leg."

We rode for a while without further talk, which was one blessing anyway. But she was too full of plans and excitement to have kept her notions to herself for long. She kept twisting her head with her blue-green eyes slanching probing glances in my direction and then, unable longer to remain bottled up, declared, "I haven't yet thanked you for saving that stuff—"

"No thanks necessary," I cut into it brusquely.

"Well, you needn't bite my head off! How long will it

take us to get to the railroad?''

"It's around thirty miles from where we are now. We'll have to camp out tonight. With a good deal of luck we might reach Farmington tomorrow—late.''

"Couldn't we just push right on?''

"These horses,'' I said, "ain't made of iron, Fern. They've got to have rest.''

"But with these spares to switch off on—''

"Unless you're prepared to hoof it and leave all your booty.''

"Oh, I couldn't do that—I mean give up that turquoise, those bones and the lamp.''

"Then we camp out tonight,'' I said with finality.

And that's what we did.

Seemed like we were all more worn out than we'd been ready to admit. The sun was just creeping over those distant hills with Shiprock looming blue-gray against the brightening sky when Jones roused us out to eat our refried beans, sloshed down with java.

We were loading the horses when Jones grabbed my arm, swinging me around to follow the lift of his hand toward where a column of smoke pale gray in the sunlight was rising above a distant mesa. Even as we watched we saw the smoke cut off. Then three quick puffs shot skyward after it. Flossie was looking up at us nervously.

"Signals?'' He looked to be in a state of shock. I met his rounded stare and nodded, telling myself I wasn't filled with the jumps but knowing damn well I was and couldn't help it. I was about to tell him to keep his mouth shut, but Harry's alarmed cry caught Fern's attention and I saw her cheeks turn gray as she took in the last of that disappearing haze.

"You don't suppose that's Navajos, do you?"

"Could be Pueblos," I said with professed indifference.

But she'd spotted another smoke off to the west and conviction showed in the shape of her stare.

I said to Jones, "Let's get this outfit on the road," and we hustled things up and presently were riding into the morning's strengthening heat. No one but Harry felt inclined for gab. With a twitch in his cheek and his eyes looking wild, he yelled at me, "I thought you'd fixed things up with that sonofabitch!"

"We don't know that it's them. Even if it is, those puffadillies may not concern us at all."

And Fern said, hopeful through stiffened lips, "If Johnny's bunch had changed their minds they'd have caught us up hours ago. Before we had even got out of the canyon."

"That's right," I put in, but couldn't help thinking Johnny's mind had been changed for him, remembering those furious faces at the cliff house.

The morning wore along with the sun glaring down with increasing malevolence and me holding the horses down to what they could handle in this increasing heat and given our shortage of water.

Now and again we saw additional smokes in the hazy distance and when Fern's look grew agitated I said, "They're just making sure we get out of the country." But I didn't believe it and she didn't either.

We stopped at noon to shift the loads and Jones broke open two tins of corned beef, the contents of which we choked down in silence while all of us covertly kept tabs on the skyline.

"You know what it is," Harry kept muttering, "they're after the chindis' horde, that's what!"

At last I said, fed up with his whining, "If you reckon

you can do better, cut loose and take off.''

I could see the hate shining bright in his stare. ''I ain't leavin' without my pay.''

''Your performance with this outfit doesn't merit any pay. You've been nothing but a drag ever since you signed, not to mention your sundry treacheries!''

Fern dug out Jeff's wallet. ''I'll pay him—''

''Pay him nothing,'' I growled, and we rode on through the heat and the vast silence of this waste that grew nothing that lived but the gray wands of wolf's candle.

The hours dragged. The heat pulled sweat out of us that was dried by the ovenlike atmosphere before it could drip. By midafternoon with the sentinel peak of Shiprock much plainer, Harry, forever twisting for frightened looks behind, suddenly cried in a panic, ''There's a dust back there!''

Without bothering to look I said disparagingly, ''Nothing but a twister. What you dudes call a dust devil. In this kind of country you get 'em all the time.''

''I don't think so, Corrigan. I been keepin' my eye on it. Them's horses that's stirrin' it.'' He took another look. ''Might be cavalry.''

''Might be jumpin' beans,'' I said, disgusted,

Fern said, ''Can't we go a little faster?''

I licked dry lips. ''Whatever it is we're not going to lose it by killin' these horses. If it's Navajos they know this region a sight better than we do. They ride light. They don't pack forty-pound saddles or half a ton of turquoise—not to mention pots and bones!''

Chapter Twenty-five

Knowing it was useless but under pressure from those hairy looks I did step up the pace a bit and on we went, worried, brooding, our anxiety increasing with each passing mile.

The horses were beginning to show the strain, especially the ones burdened with packs, all of them seeming more gaunt than I liked. We weren't, I figured, above six miles from the rails but it might as well have been sixty when Harry cried out, "It's them Navajos—I *knew* it! I can see them plain!"

Stood to reason, of course. But, I thought, if we could manage to get within sight of the town there was still a thin chance they'd give it up and pull off. I was coddling this notion when Jones growled on an outblown breath, "There's dust up ahead—they've cut us off!"

"It doesn't have to be Indians," Fern said, voice reedy, and slung a look at me. "Couldn't it be cavalry?"

"Not again," I said; and Jones, in no mood for a laugh,

told her, "Ain't no cavalry around these parts."

I said, "We've pretty near run that dog off her legs. We might's well stop and get it over with."

Nobody liked it but only Jones spoke. "Might's well," he said grimly.

We pulled up. "No gunplay," I said.

"I guess," Fern admitted, "this dig of Jeff's was star-crossed from the start," and I nodded. "Sure does seem so, looking back. An exercise in futility, doomed from the time he signed Harry on."

"I wish," Fern said, "I'd thought to keep out that stone lamp, or one of the bones Flossie dug up to play with. If their dating coincided with Jeff's theories the regents might allow me to return next year, even if they put someone else in charge. Those seven skeletons—"

I said, "I guess we can give the poor dog a bone." Dismounting, I limped over to the horse that was carrying the lightest pack, the one she'd put those three jars into, fished out the leg bone and tossed it to Flossie. Though she made no move to catch it, and with her tongue lolling out a foot and forty inches, she did condescend to drop down beside it. Thoughtfully eyeing me, Fern said, "I wonder if I could someway manage to hang on to those jars . . ."

I shook my head, too used up even to grin.

It didn't take the Navajos long to surround us; I'd have been glad right then of a few covered wagons, considering the uproar. They closed in from all sides waving a miscellany of weapons, gobbling up a storm. Old Two-Feathers let them holler, then shut it off with a lifted hand.

Looking over our sorry company, looking especially and longest at the horse I was hunkered by, he said, "Man-Without-Mule, we meet again."

"Ain't that a fact? Thought you told me we were free to go?"

"To go, yes. But not with things that belong to the chindis. I personally, as our white brothers say, will care for these venerated relics," he smiled, "as though they were my own."

I smiled too. "I believe you will."

Johnny Two-Feathers nodded. "Make much jewelry." Then waved a hand and the whole band headed back to the Chaco with our packhorses and packs.

"Well," Fern said, "we've still got each other," and Flossie, bright eyes peering up at us, wriggled and wagged in plainest approval.

Nelson Nye was born in Chicago, Illinois. He was educated in schools in Ohio and Massachusetts and attended the Cincinnati Art Academy. His early journalism experience was writing publicity releases and book reviews for the *Cincinnati Times-Star* and the *Buffalo Evening News*. In 1935 he began working as a ranch hand in Texas and California and became an expert on breeding quarter horses on his own ranch outside Tucson, Arizona. Much of this love for horses can be found in exceptional novels such as *Wild Horse Shorty* and *Blood of Kings*. He published his first Western short story in *Thrilling Western* and his first novel in 1936. He continued from then on to write prolifically, both under his own name and the bylines Drake C. Denver and Clem Colt. During the Second World War, he served with the U. S. Army Field Artillery. From 1949 to 1952, he worked as horse editor for *Texas Livestock Journal*. He was one of the founding members of the Western Writers of America in 1953 and served twice as its president. His first Golden Spur Award from the Western Writers of America came to him for best Western reviewer and critic in 1954. From 1958 to 1962, he was frontier fiction reviewer for the *New York Times Book Review*. His second Golden Spur came for his novel *Long Run*. His virtues as an author of Western fiction include a tremendous sense of authenticity, an ability to keep the pace of a story from ever lagging, and a fecund inventiveness for plot twists and situations. Some of his finest novels have had off-trail protagonists such as *The Barber Of Tubac*, and both *Not Grass Alone* and *Strawberry Roan* are notable for their outstanding female characters. His books have sold over 50,000,000 copies worldwide and have been translated into the principal European languages. The *Los Angeles Times* once praised him for his "marvelous lingo, salty humor, and real characters." Above all, a Nye Western possesses a vital energy that is both propulsive and persuasive.

WAYNE D. OVERHOLSER

Don't miss these double shots of classic Western action by the winner of the Western Writers of America Lifetime Achievement Award!

Hearn's Valley. Vic Hearn rules his Oregon valley with a tyrant's iron grip, and only Hugh Moberly has the guts to try to destroy the greedy rancher. Allied with defiant Ellie Dunn, Moberly vows to turn his enemy's domain into a cemetery or die trying.

And in the same action-packed volume...

Tough Hand. Jim Sullivan never expects to land in the middle of a range war when he falls for beautiful Troy Manders. But while helping her reclaim her stolen land, he has to cast his lot with some dangerous desperadoes and risk his life in a bloody battle to the death.

_3831-5   **(two Westerns in one volume)** $4.99 US/$6.99 CAN

The Violent Land. Big Jim Perrin is the richest cattle boss Oregon has ever known, thanks to hard cases like Dan Nathan. But when nesters start losing their spreads to Nathan's land-hungry boss, Dan has to choose between joining in the bloodshed and turning his six-shooter on the man he once called friend.

And in the same exciting volume...

The Judas Gun. When Ben Fargo escapes from Carson City Prison, the thirteen men who sent him there fear for their lives. Fargo has sworn to get even with them, and with hate in his gut, and a six-gun in his hand, he returns to San Lorenzo for revenge.

_3802-1   **(two Westerns in one volume)** $4.99 US/$5.99 CAN

Dorchester Publishing Co., Inc.
65 Commerce Road
Stamford, CT 06902

Please add $1.75 for shipping and handling for the first book and $.50 for each book thereafter. NY, NYC, PA and CT residents, please add appropriate sales tax. No cash, stamps, or C.O.D.s. All orders shipped within 6 weeks via postal service book rate. Canadian orders require $2.00 extra postage and must be paid in U.S. dollars through a U.S. banking facility.

Name _____

Address _____

City _____ State _____ Zip _____

I have enclosed $_____ in payment for the checked book(s).

Payment <u>must</u> accompany all orders.☐ Please send a free catalog.

ARROW IN THE SUN
T. V. OLSEN

Bestselling Author Of *Red Is The River*

The wagon train has only two survivors, the young soldier Honus Gant and beautiful, willful Cresta Lee. And they both know that the legendary Cheyenne chieftain Spotted Wolf will not rest until he catches them.

Gant is no one's idea of a hero—he is the first to admit that. He made a mistake joining the cavalry, and he's counting the days until he is a civilian and back east where he belongs. He doesn't want to protect Cresta Lee. He doesn't even like her. In fact, he's come to hate her guts.

The trouble is, Cresta is no ordinary girl. Once she was an Indian captive. Once she was Spotted Wolf's wife. Gant knows what will happen to Cresta if the bloodthirsty warrior captures her again, and he can't let that happen—even if it means risking his life to save her.

_3948-6 $4.50 US/$5.50 CAN

Dorchester Publishing Co., Inc.
65 Commerce Road
Stamford, CT 06902

Please add $1.75 for shipping and handling for the first book and $.50 for each book thereafter. NY, NYC, PA and CT residents, please add appropriate sales tax. No cash, stamps, or C.O.D.s. All orders shipped within 6 weeks via postal service book rate. Canadian orders require $2.00 extra postage and must be paid in U.S. dollars through a U.S. banking facility.

Name_____

Address_____

City _____ State _____ Zip _____

I have enclosed $_____in payment for the checked book(s). Payment <u>must</u> accompany all orders.☐ Please send a free catalog.

WILL HENRY

JESSE JAMES
DEATH OF A LEGEND

Beneath the bandanna, underneath the legend, Jesse James was a wild and wicked man: a sinister and brutal outlaw who blazed a trail of crime and violence through the lawless West. Ripping the mask off the mysterious Jesse James, Will Henry's *Death Of A Legend* is a novel as tough and savage as the man himself. Only a great Western writer like Henry could tell the real story of the infamous bandit Jesse James.

_3990-7 $4.99 US/$6.99 CAN

Dorchester Publishing Co., Inc.
65 Commerce Road
Stamford, CT 06902

Please add $1.75 for shipping and handling for the first book and $.50 for each book thereafter. NY, NYC, PA and CT residents, please add appropriate sales tax. No cash, stamps, or C.O.D.s. All orders shipped within 6 weeks via postal service book rate. Canadian orders require $2.00 extra postage and must be paid in U.S. dollars through a U.S. banking facility.

Name _____
Address _____
City _____ State _____ Zip _____
I have enclosed $_____ in payment for the checked book(s).
Payment <u>must</u> accompany all orders.☐ Please send a free catalog.

T.V. OLSEN

Don't Miss These Double Shots Of Classic Western Action! $7.98 Values For Only $4.99! "Plenty of crunching fights and shootings! Don't pass T.V. Olsen up!" —*The Roundup*

Gunswift. Owen Rutledge refuses to rest until he finds the crazed killers who reduced his home to ashes and murdered his family. All he wants is to track them down and send them to hell on a trail marked in blood.
And in the same action-packed volume...
Ramrod Rider. Desperate to put his life back on the straight and narrow, Wes Trevannon is prepared to fight a little war that will help him live peacefully or die quickly.
__3939-7   **(two Westerns in one volume)** $4.99 US/$6.99 CAN

McGivern. Out to avenge his woman's death, McGivern has to take on the deadliest gunrunners ever to strap on six-shooters, and whoever survives the bloody showdown will be the law of the West.
And in the same exciting volume...
The Hard Men. Loftus Buckmaster owns half the valley and aims to own the rest. But Krag Soderstrom has other ideas, and he puts together a violent crew to stop Buckmaster. Soon the valley will ring with bullets in a battle as deadly and bitter as the hate that spawned it.
__3612-6   **(two Westerns in one volume)** $4.99

**Dorchester Publishing Co., Inc.
65 Commerce Road
Stamford, CT 06902**

Please add $1.75 for shipping and handling for the first book and $.50 for each book thereafter. NY, NYC, PA and CT residents, please add appropriate sales tax. No cash, stamps, or C.O.D.s. All orders shipped within 6 weeks via postal service book rate. Canadian orders require $2.00 extra postage and must be paid in U.S. dollars through a U.S. banking facility.

Name _____
Address _____
City _____ State _____ Zip _____
I have enclosed $_____ in payment for the checked book(s).
Payment <u>must</u> accompany all orders.☐ Please send a free catalog.

THERE WAS A SEASON

T.V. OLSEN

Winner Of The Golden Spur Award

A sprawling and magnificent novel, full of the sweeping grandeur and unforgettable beauty of the unconquered American continent—a remarkable story of glorious victories and tragic defeats, of perilous adventures and bloody battles to win the land.

Lt. Jefferson Davis has visions of greatness, but between him and a brilliant future lies the brutal Black Hawk War. In an incredible journey across the frontier, the young officer faces off against enemies known and unknown...tracking a cunning war chief who is making a merciless grab for power...fighting vicious diseases that decimate his troops before Indian arrows can cut them down...and struggling against incredible odds to return to the valiant woman he left behind. Guts, sweat, and grit are all Davis and his soldiers have in their favor. If that isn't enough, they'll wind up little more than dead legends.

_3652-5 $4.99 US/$5.99 CAN

Dorchester Publishing Co., Inc.
65 Commerce Road
Stamford, CT 06902

Please add $1.75 for shipping and handling for the first book and $.50 for each book thereafter. NY, NYC, PA and CT residents, please add appropriate sales tax. No cash, stamps, or C.O.D.s. All orders shipped within 6 weeks via postal service book rate. Canadian orders require $2.00 extra postage and must be paid in U.S. dollars through a U.S. banking facility.

Name_____
Address_____
City _____ State_____Zip_____
I have enclosed $_____in payment for the checked book(s).
Payment <u>must</u> accompany all orders.☐ Please send a free catalog.

ATTENTION PREFERRED CUSTOMERS!

SPECIAL
TOLL-FREE NUMBER
1-800-481-9191

Call Monday through Friday
12 noon to 10 p.m.
Eastern Time
*Get a free catalogue
and order books using your
Visa, MasterCard,
or Discover®*

Leisure
Books